MOONSHINE

IN THE FLOURISHING METROPOLIS OF SOOT CITY – IMAGINE A fantastical version of 1920s Chicago – progressive ideals reign and the old ways of magic and liquid mana are forbidden. Miss Daisy Dell is a Modern Girl – stylish, educated and independent – keen to establish herself in the city but reluctant to give up the taboo magic inherited from her grandmother.

Her new job takes her to unexpected places, and she gets more attention than she had hoped for. When bounty hunters start combing the city for magicians, Daisy must decide whether to stay with her new employer – even if it means revealing the grim source of her dazzling powers!

"A highly addictive book full of lush descriptions, and wonderful and intriguing characters, all soaked in magic."
A C WISE

"MOONSHINE is a quirky, often surprising take on the Prohibition Era of the USA, drenched in fresh fantasy elements and strong characterization. It deserves a place on every fantasy lover's bookshelf."
J S FIELDS, author of the
Ardulum novels

JASMINE GOWER

MOONSHINE

ANGRY
ROBOT

ANGRY ROBOT
An imprint of Watkins Media Ltd

20 Fletcher Gate,
Nottingham,
NG1 2FZ • UK

angryrobotbooks.com
twitter.com/angryrobotbooks
Let it glow

An Angry Robot paperback original 2018

Cover by John Coulthart
Set in Meridien and Gallia by Argh! Nottingham

Distributed in the United States by Penguin Random House, Inc., New York.

ISBN 978 0 85766 734 2
Ebook ISBN 978 0 85766 735 9

Printed in the United States of America

9 8 7 6 5 4 3 2 1

In memory of Aunt Cookie

CHAPTER 1

Skyline lights hovered in the hazy city night, glowing motes that lit the horizon. In another town, the glow of street lamps and apartment windows would have shone like stars, but here in Ashland's Soot City, they fragmented and blurred, filtered through a volcanic smog. It was a new frontier, Ashland – old enough for paved roads and brick towers, but still a land of young ideals. A land of immigrants and their vagabond descendants, settled in a terrain of lava beds and dusty woods that had only just become habitable again within the past two centuries. The volcanoes were quieter now, expected not to spew their fury again for another couple hundred thousand years or so, and people needed a place to start fresh.

She was second-generation, which is about as old as blood comes in Ashland. Her grandparents – both sets – arrived on boats from an older world, one of warm farmlands and vineyards. She and her parents had been born in the dust, into this place that was supposed to be different from the rigid traditions of her grandparents' homeland, but some things couldn't be changed with anything so simple as building an entirely new society up from clay.

She watched the skyline from the club's balcony, a glass of wine in hand and two enamored couples either side. She came alone to celebrate, and although it wasn't traditional for girls such as herself to wander about fancy clubs alone, she wasn't a girl of tradition. Not in that sense, at least. The Modern Girl phenomenon had completely swept up the young ladies of Soot City, and she embraced the archetype tighter than anyone she knew. Her classes at the women's college had been full of young women in narrow dresses and short haircuts, but even most of them wouldn't walk the streets alone at night. She did, but it wasn't all brazenness and sociopolitical statement. She simply didn't have a single friend to her name with whom she could celebrate, and she wasn't about to sit on her good news while she read magazines in her apartment in the rickety southwest district.

So, she went to a club, alone. At least there was wine, and patrons to stare at her bright yellow, low-waist dress. She was the very picture of a Modern Girl – slender of frame; her short, tight curls coifed with a shiny pomade; heeled dance shoes dressing either foot; and her dark skin complemented by the contrast of daisy yellow, so vibrant as though it was part of her identity. Which she supposed it was.

Daisy Dell. She didn't choose her name, but it helped with the image – people found the alliteration peppy yet commanding. Not that she needed it. Strangers stared at her like she walked right off a magazine cover, including at least one member of each devoted, adoring couple to her either side. She might have had the makings to be a model, but that's not what she had gone to college for. Granted, she hadn't gone to college to become a typist, either, yet there she was, drinking alone to celebrate the obtainment of an entry level desk job.

She supposed it was a mixed victory.

"Lovely night." She rolled her eyes at the line as a man tried to sidle up next to her, having to nudge one of the couples aside a bit. He was an older man, a salt-and-pepper type, and even just in conversation their age difference was almost scandalous. Handsome, but overdressed for the venue in a black tuxedo, and bespectacled, which was very much *not* in the fashion those days – undoubtedly something of an issue for the vision-impaired. She had to admire his nonchalance in approaching someone so significantly younger, dressed bright as the sun and drinking alone like she was contemplating revenge. They both knew the odds that she would go home with him, so she didn't worry that politely engaging him would confuse him on her intentions.

"Indeed, it is."

"A shame about the smog, though. I hate how it covers up all those glittering lights."

She shrugged. "I like it. The way the lights blur against the shadows of the skyscrapers, it looks like a watercolor painting. And seeing the whole city filtered through ash – it strikes a sense of national pride, don't you think?"

The man laughed – the same sort of belly laugh that her father had, and it was only then that she began to feel personally uncomfortable with the combination of their age difference and any flirtatious undertones to their mild conversation. "Yes, I suppose it does." Their brief talk faltered after that, and just as the silence had nearly stretched into that awkward zone, some of the man's friends called at him from behind, and he politely excused himself to rejoin them. That was about the extent of sharing her celebration that night.

But it didn't matter. Part of being a Modern Girl meant being self-sufficient. Thanks to Daisy's mother and the woman's three childless brothers saving up the girl's whole life to pay for her education, she had gotten through college without having to break her back like other young women, Modern and Old-Fashioned alike. But Daisy was her own, grown self now, and she had rent to pay.

• • •

Shifting against the annoying grate of any kind of cloth against velvet, Daisy struggled to keep herself from rising from the chair and peeking into the parlor from where she could hear raised voices. The maid had told her to wait in the plush front foyer, that Mr Sparrick would be with her in a moment. She heard someone shouting Sparrick's name in the parlor and a gravelly voice shouting back, and she politely busied herself with rearranging her legs, trying not to kick the parcel tucked under the chair.

She had only been on her new job a few days before Mr Swarz assigned her this task. Daisy had been hired as a typist, someone to keep Mr Swarz's business records and transcripts and write letters on his behalf, what with his injured right hand. She had expected that her position would involve some other miscellaneous secretarial tasks, but that day Mr Swarz had asked her to make three direct deliveries to his clients.

Mr Sparrick was the first on that list, who would be receiving the heavy envelope labeled "STRIPES MANAGEMENT, INC." on the front and a small wooden box full of unknown goods, both of which sat in Daisy's lap. The envelope and accompanying bottle of wine for Miss Cadwell sat under the chair, along with a much smaller envelope that just had "Pasternack" scrawled in Mr Swarz's handwriting on its exterior. It was all very confidential, or so Mr Swarz had insisted, and he had told Daisy to not allow his clients to so much as know about the existence of the others' packages. Everything was sealed in boxes or paper and clearly labeled, so his demand seemed unnecessary, but Daisy did her best to follow orders, hoping that Mr Sparrick wouldn't notice the other envelopes and the wine bottle tucked behind her legs.

The parlor door slammed open, striking the wall of the foyer with a smack loud and sudden enough that Daisy hopped to her feet. In stormed a pretty, round-faced woman in a white dress – a little older than Daisy, but with a similar Modern Girl fashion sensibility. She charged into the room with reddened cheeks, appearing not to notice the young woman waiting there with a stack of papers and small crate awkwardly clutched in her arms.

"Don't you even talk to me, Robby. *Don't you even.*"

"Linda!" A disheveled man with light skin and sandy hair stumbled out after her. He wore a wrinkled, white suit that emphasized the purple bags under his eyes. Sparrick, Daisy assumed.

Linda whirled on him. "Robby! *Robby.* Will you listen – *will you listen to me right now, Robby?* Can you do that, can you listen to me for a moment?" Despite her demands to be heard, she didn't seem to be saying much.

Robby Sparrick showed appropriate remorse, regardless. "Linda, darling, I'll fix it, I promise. I–" But he noticed Daisy standing there, alert and startled as a puppy playing guard dog. "Oh, you, ah, you're with them, aren't you? The Stripes?"

"*Robby!*" But Sparrick wasn't quick enough to return his attention to the lady, and she stomped off and out the front door in a great show of infantilism. Daisy might have been more embarrassed for her if not for the fact that Mr Sparrick's own apparent maturity level seemed to call for a tantrum of that variety. He watched Linda go, gaping mutely after her, before hastily trying to pat his hair into place and turning back to Daisy.

"My apologies. You have my delivery?" But Linda wasn't the only one upset with Sparrick, it seemed.

"You even paying attention to me, you rat?" A burly, bearded man wearing a suit as fine as Sparrick's and much better kept charged out of the parlor as well, clubbing Sparrick on the back of the skull with a fist. Daisy quick-stepped back, sliding one of her hands over the other where it gripped the envelope to rub nervously at the silver ring on her left middle finger.

She didn't want to get involved – she certainly didn't want to unleash the power within the little ring, not while she was on the job – but she'd prefer not to get her bones broken in the crossfires. Had Mr Swarz known what kind of shady character Mr Sparrick was? Had he expected that his new assistant would be placed in such danger? Daisy could imagine that some cruel men might find sport in tormenting their new employees in such a way, but such a cruel man would also have to possess a sense of humor, which she was certain Mr Swarz did *not.*

She didn't need to use that secret weapon resting unsuspecting on her finger, as it turned out. Sparrick regained his balance quickly after the stagger and spun to face the larger man. His upright posture and smarmy drawl betrayed the fakery in his pretend calm and good-naturedness when he answered. "Whitcomb, yes! Of course. As I told Linda, I'll take care of it." Whitcomb scowled – "I don't trust your lying weasel smile," the expression said – but Sparrick gestured to Daisy. "But, please, let's not fuss over business in front of a guest."

Whitcomb took a look at Daisy – spindly, wide-eyed, and sportily dressed, she was the classic, pretty image of a free-spirited but otherwise harmless young woman. He huffed, disarmed by her carefully crafted self-presentation, but shot a brief glare back at Sparrick. "*Business* is something we'll be doing less of if these problems persist." Heading toward the door with a tip of his hat to Daisy, he stormed out as mutely as he could manage after such an altercation. Sparrick, for his part, huffed a heavy sigh, his posture wilting as the air escaped him.

"Blazing embers, what a relief that you showed up." He

straightened, repeating that phony cheer that he tried to wield against Whitcomb, eyeing the envelope in Daisy's hands. The intensity of his stare highlighted the red veins streaking through the whites of his eyes. All in all, it was quite a hungry look for some simple papers.

Daisy did her own part to wear a happy face for the exchange, smiling and holding out the envelope and box. "Yes, sir. Straight from Mr Swarz himself."

Sparrick snatched the delivery from her, but paused and squinted at something beyond her. Worried that he might be trying to peek at the other deliveries stored under the chair, she dropped her hands to hang in front of her, lightly touching the silver bracelet on one wrist with the other hand. That ring wasn't the only secret weapon she possessed, or even the only one she had worn for the outing. Daisy didn't often go out without at least a few of her grandmother's old trinkets, tacked on like jewelry. Most of it *was* jewelry, though outdated or gaudy, but the eclectic nature of the look only reinforced her aesthetic – fashionable, but sentimental enough to cling to family heirlooms, and maybe even too new into money to afford better. Not that she was even as into money as her lavender sun dress, sheer neck scarf, and polished white shoes suggested.

Daisy focused less on the look of the bracelet in that moment, though, and more on the power within it. She knew where that power had come from, and she sometimes shuddered to think about it, but Grandma Sparrow's shady dealings from long before Daisy's birth were the old woman's own burden, not her granddaughter's.

She felt a flare of heat – just a little thing, no warmer than walking by a sunbeam sneaking through a curtained window – and Sparrick blinked. She hoped that whatever made his eyes so bloodshot was affecting the quality of his vision, too, and that he would dismiss whatever he had seen as his imagination. There was nothing more embarrassing than getting caught in the middle of doing magic.

Sparrick shrugged, trying to adjust the way his jacket settled on his shoulders, seeming content to ignore the thing that had a moment ago so caught his eye. "Well, Mr Swarz is a lifesaver. As are you." He then squinted at her. "*You're* not the regular boy," he said, as though just realizing this.

She widened her smile. "No, sir. I'm new to the office."

"Ah, well." And he glanced down at his delivery, apparently grown bored with their exchange. It was just as well, because Daisy had two more deliveries to make. Once he returned to his parlor (no goodbye offered to her), she squatted by the chair and touched her bracelet. There was a shimmer, and the awkwardly distorted shadows that had formed there cleared, exposing the remaining packages where she had left them. She did not understand Mr Swarz's insistence on secrecy at all – did he expect that Sparrick would have tried to steal the other packages if he'd seen them, even with Daisy just right there? – but she was determined to impress at her new job.

She was determined to impress, in general.

Hurrying back from Sparrick's fancy house to the street, Daisy strolled through a mild haze of silver ashfall on her way to her next destination. This time she did use the ring and its repellent spell – not to fend off possible attackers, of course, but to keep the soot off her shiny shoes. Magic was more practical as a utility than a weapon, she had always thought. She never understood why the mundanes feared it and its wielders as much as they did. In a place called Soot City, in the nation of Ashland, it was a wonder that they didn't practically worship magicians for their potential to manage the volcanic weather. Granted, the volcanoes had been tame for centuries now, and the ashfall was no longer uninhabitable – that would rather complicate the presence of a city there, of course – or even unbearable. Some days it was just worse off than others, same as weather anywhere else.

She nearly skipped down the quiet streets of the northwest quadrant. This was the old money of Soot City, and they did a decent job of keeping undesirables out, except those like Daisy who hid behind pretty faces and middle class educations so as not to seem entirely unappealing. There was no sign of the homeless or ill or non-human – no one who could be recognized immediately as Not Belonging. It created an eerie emptiness in the neighborhood, and she was the only one walking outside past all the fancy, compact houses and under all the finely manicured trees lining the sidewalk. It was shameful that the city paid people to trim those young, narrow trees while entire streets in Daisy's neighborhood were nonfunctional for how many potholes spotted them, but she enjoyed the illusion of serenity while she was there. If the rich went to so much trouble to maintain such facades, she might as well revel in the prettiness of their falsehoods before the day was done and she returned to the bleaker, grimy southwest quadrant.

Her next stop was about seven blocks over. The house was much like the last. Clean, whitewashed walls (only slightly smudged by the ashfall) tucked between matching residencies on either side, all with imposing bay windows. Daisy suspected it had a similar foyer, too – velvet-cushioned chairs, gaudy curtains that didn't match the wallpaper, and polished hardwood floors – but she never did get to see the inside. When she knocked, a frazzled middle-aged woman answered. She could have been Mr Sparrick's twin for mannerisms, half leaning against the doorframe as she squinted at Daisy.

"You. I know what *you're* about." She smiled even as her words accused. Miss Cadwell. The woman reached

out toward Daisy's face, snaking her finger like she was
going to poke Daisy on the nose, though her arm couldn't
quite extend that far without removing herself from the
doorframe that supported her. "You're not the usual girl,
though."

"No, ma'am, but I was sent by Mr Swarz. Your package."
She handed forward the second envelope and the bottle of
wine. It was easier to hide what remained of her deliveries
this time – the little note was tucked between her dress
and shift. If Cadwell noticed any odd angles in the folds of
Daisy's clothes, she didn't say anything about it. She seemed
fairly intent on the wine, seeming to have recently come
off a completely different bottle. Daisy wasn't sure why a
document management office would bother sending wine
to one of their clients, especially not if it exacerbated an
already apparent problem, so she decided to politely assume
that it was only Miss Cadwell's birthday.

Lucky for Daisy, Cadwell appeared happy enough with
her packages to make no further comment on Daisy filling
in for whoever usually made the deliveries, nor did she
invite her in to see the disaster of a debauched, upper-
middle class life that she led. She simply bid Daisy a good
day, still beaming like a drunken fool, and shut the door to
keep wafts of ashfall from griming up her entryway.

Only one delivery left, then, and this one took her out of
the northwest district.

Northeast wasn't as fancy, but there were efforts to get it
there. Most of its class came from new money – the children
and grandchildren of immigrants who came to Ashland with
only pennies, people who were ambitious and innovative
and lucky enough to build their own fortunes in this
newborn society. Lucrative nightclubs and restaurants set up
in the slums to save a buck on property costs, and wealthy
patrons flocked to these locations to enjoy that rustic feeling

of downtrodden neighborhoods. There were still shambling shacks out in those reaches, in the neighborhoods around where Daisy had grown up. Oddly, the address she had for her final delivery was in one such area, and not for some luxury loft above a new theater, as she expected – quite the variation from Mr Swarz's other clients.

She took the streetcar most of the way there, but needed to make her way on foot for about ten blocks into the residential area. Hopping off at the station, she was distracted by a demonstration taking place in one of the new, gentrified parks that had been built where probably little more than a pile of worn tires had previously occupied.

Soapboxers.

It was a clever location, right off the streetcar stop in a neighborhood where the high class with too much to lose collided with the poor with too much to fear. Hardly a surprise that the topic du jour was people just like Daisy. Magicians were all that the huffy, so-called moderates of Ashland quaked in fear over for the past few decades. It didn't always used to be like that. Magic, alongside ogre technology and industrialism, had probably built half the city less than a hundred years ago. She wasn't sure what had happened to cause the general population to demonize magicians as a collective, but general populations did love to have enemies, she supposed.

A flicker of masochism hit her, and she decided to stop and listen to the sheltered, middle class homebodies preach about the evil of her secret ways. Not that there wasn't a price to be paid for magic, but she was fairly certain these fearmongers didn't even know about that bit. They mostly pulled nonsense out of their own asses, as bigots tended to do. And while they imagined silly things like frantic dances and songs played on flutes made of human bones and magic powered by sex (because *of course* these puritans

were fixated on the notion of sex), they never considered
the laws of conservation or the traditions of their ancestors
or even the reality that humans were not the only creatures
with a command of magic. But Daisy supposed none of that
was quite scandalous enough to scream about on a street
corner.

She stood amongst the crowd next to a short woman in
a tan men's trench coat, listening to the screeching of the
seven soapboxers, one whose voice rose above the rest. A
tall, pale man shouted over his companions and the crowd
of gawkers that hovered around them. "These wizards are
corruptors! They brew their poison and infect our neighbors
– good, innocent people – and turn them raving and
wild, with the minds of beasts! They have taken over our
businesses and temples and universities to drain us of our
hard-earned money and hoard it for their nefarious ends!"

Unimpressive, as far as fearmongering went. Basic, bland.
No rhythm to his frantic shouting. People loved rhythm –
that's the way to go when looking to captivate an audience.
He could have at least waved his arms around a little, give
the performance a bit of urgency.

Daisy glanced at the woman next to her. "Ash and embers!
Maybe if they shout a little louder they can be heard up
in the high heavens. What do you suppose? Think these
magicians are as bad as they say?"

The woman – short, a little stocky, probably of Gao or
Pheje descent with dark ochre skin and shiny black hair
cut to her chin – shrugged with one shoulder, too apathetic
to bother with two. "Mana's already outlawed. Not sure
what these protesters think magicians are gonna do. They
probably have to go to enough trouble to get their own
that they won't waste any poisoning their 'good, innocent'
neighbors."

Mana was the blue fluid magicians typically used to

fuel their powers, drinking dosages after casting spells to replenish energy. "The brew of the gods," it was called by some less conservative than the soapboxers before them. While magic itself was not technically illegal by Ashland or city law, the production, sale, and possession of mana was. The stuff apparently kicked the metabolism into overdrive, and so long as practicing magicians kept themselves well-fed, the thick potion allowed them to keep their bodies balanced. But it was addictive, from what Daisy understood, and non-mages could get manic highs off it, having no lost energies to be replaced. Daisy didn't need it for her own style of magic, but she had heard even a small dosage of mana ran for a hefty fee, and this woman was probably right that Ashlanders did not need to be concerned about magicians or addicts sharing too much of it with innocent mundanes.

Daisy was tickled with an urge for mischief. "What about their magic, though? I've heard that some of those spells require blood sacrifice."

"And *I've* heard that magicians are trying to create a spell that allows them to eat the sun. Most things that one hears about magic are more shit than what goes in my toilet."

Daisy laughed, but the woman beside her was quiet and dour. The stranger ignored the soapboxers to watch the light, smoky specks of ash drift downward and back up on the city's gentle but flustered every-which-way breeze. "It must be handy, I assume," the other woman said. "Magic. And some people, you know, they just need a little more. The game of survival doesn't start everyone out with the same resources, after all. Everyone does what they do to get by. It's not that magicians are so bad – we're just all animals." She tore her dark gaze away from the atmosphere to lock eyes with Daisy. "That's how I see it, anyhow."

"Very philosophical." Daisy didn't mean for it to sound

sarcastic, although the other woman turned away from her again. She wondered if the stranger had, like Daisy herself, more than just a passing interest in magic. But that was too dangerous a question to ask, for the both of them and for too many reasons. Instead, Daisy left the stranger to her lofty musings, returning to her task for Mr Swarz. The woman would understand – Daisy only did what she did to get by, abrupt and impolite goodbyes included.

Moving away from the intersection of posh and drab to the out-and-out slums of northeast, Daisy located the rickety townhouse that her final delivery was destined for. It was a sizable building – bigger than an apartment, certainly – but the paint was peeling down the outside walls, and only one of the four front single-paned windows was without a massive, spiderwebbed crack in it. Packed all along down either side were other townhouses of matching quality, stretching in a line both directions until either corner of the street. She knocked on a door that had "307" nailed in wooden letters at eye level, pulling out the envelope labeled "Pasternack" as she heard heavy, uneven footfalls approach. When the door flung open, she took an instinctive step back while the home's occupant staggered to lean against the frame.

Much like Sparrick and Cadwell, he was pasty and apparently inebriated to some degree. To match the condition of his residence, he was not nearly as fancy – smudged pants and an oversized stained shirt hung from his medium frame. He squinted at her, his pose and expression almost identical to Cadwell's earlier. Were all of Mr Swarz's clients drunken slobs half-blinded by brandy? It seemed so contrary to Mr Swarz's own prim, prickly manner.

"What d'ya want?" the man asked. He mumbled a bit, which Daisy might have mistaken for a side effect of his condition if not for the way he pronounced his vowels, all as a half-formed "uh" sound. It was apparently his accent, some holdover from whatever northern country his parents or grandparents had hailed.

Daisy held forth the letter, putting on a smile she was too weary for. It was nice to stretch her legs on the job, but if she had to run around dealing with this sort to accomplish a light exercise, she wasn't sure it was worth it. "I was sent by Mr Andre Swarz to deliver this to you, sir."

The man – Pasternack, she assumed – relaxed, his scowl melting into something not only more neutral but also lucid-seeming. There was a vividness to his eyes that had been hidden under all the squinting. "Swarz? What's this about?" He pushed himself off the doorframe to take the envelope and open it. Pulling out a note and discarding its shell on the doorstep, he unfolded it and scanned its contents twice before bursting out in rough laughter.

"Oh, hell and brimstone, can you believe this? Look at this!" He waved Daisy closer to read the note, and she resigned herself to humoring him. Stepping closer and glancing over his shoulder, she read:

> Pasternack,
>   It is imperative you return to work by tomorrow. Any further truancy, barring medical emergency, will result in termination.
>   I'm not kidding.
>   Swarz

The man laughed again as Daisy pulled away, looking him over. This wasn't a client – he was one of her coworkers. He smirked at her as he crumpled up the note in his calloused hands. "Listen to that! 'Imperative.' Ha! Thinks he can scare me with his big dictionary words." He gave the note a firm squeeze, and she could hear the light crinkle of paper under his rough laborer's grip. "He had you running errands today, didn't he? Got you hauling documents and secret gifts up to the fancy-pantses out in northwest?"

Daisy felt inclined to smile back, sincerely this time, finally feeling that she no longer had to put up a polite front. Clients were one thing, but she could be casual around a coworker, so long as Mr Swarz wasn't there to be a crotchety raincloud about it. "How did you know?"

Pasternack dropped the note and hooked a thumb proudly toward himself. "That's my job, most days. Course, I've been playing hooky the past week. Guess not no more, huh?" His smile shrunk – not disappearing, just mellowing – and he held out a friendly hand. "Vicks Pasternack. I work in the warehouse. You must be the new desk lady. That cranky bastard Swarz got you down yet?"

Vicks might have been the very picture of a ne'er-do-well, the kind of caricature on posters put up by groups like those uppity protesters she had seen by the streetcar stop, but his easy attitude was charming in its own right, and he was upfront and friendly with her. Daisy saw no reason not to be candid as she took his hand.

"Of course not. Mr Swarz might be a bit stiff, but he's been polite and friendly with me. A better boss than I'm likely to get bussing tables or tending bars, I'm sure."

Vicks threw back his head and laughed. "Damned if that isn't the nicest thing I did hear anyone ever say about that snarling housecat. He's just a hotheaded piece of work with me." Vicks rolled his shoulders, and that light in his eyes took on a mischievous glint. "But if you got such nice things to say 'bout working for Swarz, then I guess I'm feeling pretty inspired to haul my ass back there, too. You can tell him I said that – he'll be real impressed. Not a lot that can convince me to go to work on my own accord." Of course, Daisy had just seen that Mr Swarz had threatened to fire

Vicks for his extended absence, but she only smiled again in response.

Vicks chuckled and clapped her on the shoulder. Being a stylish Modern Girl had its advantages, but physical strength wasn't one of them, and she staggered under the friendly but rough pat. "Well, then. I guess I'll see you at work tomorrow. What's your name, again?"

Daisy righted herself and adjusted her dress so the folds fell straight and clean. Prim and sporty, just like on the magazines. "I'm Daisy. Daisy Dell."

Vicks smirked. "Well, welcome to the crew, Daze." She was sure the grin was supposed to be friendly, and perhaps it was only that the ordeals of her day had set her on edge, but she couldn't help the thought that there was something wolfish about his smile.

CHAPTER 2

When Daisy returned to the offices of Stripes Management to report on her task, Mr Swarz was not there. Rudolph LaChapelle, their bookkeeper and the flighty young beau to Miss Agatha in the office across the lobby from Mr Swarz's, was at the table in the corner of the front room, pouring himself a cup of coffee from the carafe there. "He went to check on something down at the warehouse," Mr LaChapelle said when she inquired about Mr Swarz's whereabouts, though he frowned to himself as he answered, as though just remembering something. Shaking off his uncertainty, he added, "He'll be back within the hour, I'm sure." Daisy didn't think further on it and returned to her post at the lobby desk to finish out her work day. Mr Swarz did, indeed, return little less than an hour after that.

He was almost silent coming in the front door, somehow able to open it without aggravating the squeaking hinges, a feat unmanageable by anyone else in the office. He was an uptight sort, with his black clothes, his tidy little bowler hat, and plain, thin-rimmed glasses. Curiously, though, he also wore his straight black hair long, down to his shoulders, in a womanly style. Not that most women wore their hair that long, anymore. He carried a cane with him, too, though he did not always necessarily need it. It was his hand that bothered him more, most days.

That's why Daisy's typist position existed, when a competent desk clerk such as Mr Swarz would otherwise be perfectly capable of dealing with his own paperwork. The contents of the envelopes she had delivered to Mr Sparrick and Miss Cadwell had likely been typed by someone else in the company, and the note to Vicks was short enough that Mr Swarz could have pecked it out on his own, given enough time. His right hand had been mangled in a childhood accident, along with most of the right side of his body down to his hip, and although the wounds had healed as much as they could years ago, his hand was still not flexible enough to handle a task so delicate and precise as typing. Daisy could see sometimes, when Mr Swarz clenched his fists in irritation or while trying to grab small objects, that his right fingers just didn't close as tight as his left ones.

Mr Swarz didn't look Daisy's way as he leaned his cane against the wall and took off his hat and coat to settle them on the rack by the door, and she waited for him to slip into his office before rising from her desk to follow him.

"Mr Swarz." She hovered in the doorway of his office, glancing around at the cluttered mess. His desk was impeccable – a cumbersome old piece of furniture with chipped dark blue paint, neatly organized with pen holders, and cleared in the middle with a plain black address book and a strange little figurine of a phoenix chicken, with a round little body painted flame-red, set neatly in the corner. It was the row of shelves behind him, stocked with overstuffed binders and uneven stacks of loose paper banded together, that made the room appear untidy. Daisy assumed those were his clients' records. When she had first met Mr Swarz in this room for her job interview, the frantic disorganization of those shelves hadn't made sense, but after meeting some of his clients, she was beginning to understand.

He settled behind the desk and pushed his glasses up his nose. Daisy wasn't sure how old he was – his angular, pale face was without wrinkles, his black hair without any streak of silver, but he had a gruffness that reminded Daisy of her eldest uncle Basil who had been working as a quarry foreman for the past twenty years. As she told Vicks, though, Mr Swarz had been nothing but cool and polite in all their interactions together so far.

"Yes, Miss Dell?" He flinched just slightly, his left eye twitching in remembrance of something unpleasant. "Ah, you must have finished with those deliveries. Did it go well?"

Daisy considered mentioning the near-brawl that had broken out in Mr Sparrick's parlor, but she thought better than to besmirch his clients like that. She had no idea how much he respected the wealthy socialites that paid him. "Yes, sir. Mr Sparrick and Miss Cadwell received their packages without complication."

"Good, good." He nodded absently for a moment before his brow dropped to a stern, flat line above his eyes. "And did Pasternack receive his note?"

"Yes, sir. He said that he was so inspired by my dedication to my job that he would return to his own tomorrow."

Mr Swarz scoffed. "What an ass." Daisy choked down a laugh. "I'm glad to hear it, though. We've been needing more hands in the warehouse, which is why Amelia was moved from your current position to one better suited to her talents there, and it doesn't do to have the workers we already pay refuse to–"

He cut off as a momentous tap to Daisy's backside sent her staggering further into the room with a startled yelp. She straightened herself to find Mr Swarz frowning at a lovely woman who had hip-bumped Daisy out of the doorway to take her place.

Miss Angel Agatha was the Senior Accounts Manager for the company – a tall, fat woman with shiny platinum blonde hair and pink cheeks. She was the very antithesis of Mr Swarz in her persona and energy, all throaty laughter and conspiratorial winks, dressed almost always in white or pale blue. In the few days that Daisy had been working there, Miss Agatha frequently tried to chat her up at her desk in the lobby, only to be chased away by Mr Swarz, complaining how she was distracting his typist from her duties, and she would laugh at him but comply. They had the rapport of old friends or close siblings – loving but snide. Mr Swarz didn't care for Mr LaChapelle, though, and only his insults toward the bookkeeper ever coerced a sincere frown from Miss Agatha.

"Good afternoon, Daisy," Miss Agatha said, ignoring Mr Swarz's pouting from his desk. "I saw Andre had you out and about this morning. Must have been nice, getting to stretch your legs at work."

"Yes, Miss Agatha, it was lovely." Daisy shifted her hips, wondering if the dull sting she was feeling in her backside foreshadowed a bruise. Miss Agatha was solid as a mountain, and she could probably swing her hips into a slender girl like Daisy hard enough to break her in half.

Miss Agatha smiled. She always smiled with her eyelids half lowered. "Well, I hope you aren't too tuckered out. I've a proposition for you."

Mr Swarz sighed. "Angel, no."

"Oh, hush. It's all in good fun, and I don't hardly know a thing about our new typist. She's got to meet the girls from the warehouse, too. Besides, Daisy, you've been working here long enough that you should be expecting your first paycheck soon. Got to have something to spend that money on, right?"

"What's going on, now?"

Miss Agatha placed a hand on Daisy's shoulder. "Maybe Andre has told you already, but us around the office like to go out every now and again after work to blow off some steam. Do you care for dance halls? Rudolph and I are meeting the girls from the warehouse at one tonight, if you're interested in coming along."

Daisy glanced Mr Swarz's way, noticing that he still wore a scowl. She didn't know if she should take that as a warning or if he was just like that. Regardless, she thought back to her lonely night of celebration several days ago. Every fiber of her being aspired to be the epitomical Modern Girl, to live free and on the edge of society's rules, and she couldn't do that without a throng of equally stylish and independent friends. She didn't know if the warehouse girls were like that, but if Miss Agatha was any indication, they would be just the sort of spunky but elegant working girls that traditionalists on the radio wailed in horror over. Perhaps she would even genuinely enjoy their company, too.

"Of course, Miss Agatha–"

"Oh, darling," the older woman interrupted, patting Daisy gently on the cheek. "Angel, please. I'm not some stuck-up grouch like Andre. If we're to dance together, we can't be on a last name basis."

Mr Swarz steepled his fingers. "Angel, what are you up to?"

She removed her hand from Daisy to place it delicately upon her own collarbone. "Me? Andre, my intentions are perfectly amicable, I assure you." Daisy noticed the little phoenix chicken figurine on Mr Swarz's desk wobble where it stood on its twiggy legs. She had noticed it doing that during her interview, too, whenever a draft swept through Mr Swarz's office. It was a distracting little trinket, and entirely out of place with Mr Swarz's personality in its colorful whimsy.

"I suspect you intend to take my assistant out partying and drinking so that she'll drag herself in tomorrow morning hungover."

The idea of taking a night off to relax was appealing, she had to admit. Mr Swarz paid her enough that she could afford her dim studio apartment in the rundown southwest district with enough left to put away for savings and buy a new dress or a ritzy meal out every now and again. Ambitions for her new job were well and good, but the whole point of earning that money was to eventually spend it.

"Don't worry, Mr Swarz. I can hold my drink. Angel, I'd love to go along with you."

Angel smirked, showing off the pretty curves of her round cheeks. "Excellent. We'll come pick you up after dinner, then." Daisy smiled back, ignoring the irritated hiss from her boss. She respected her employer, but she wouldn't allow his misgivings to deny her a bit of harmless fun on her own time.

But for now, she was on his time. Once Angel strode out of the office, Mr Swarz pushed back his chair and stood. "While I have you here, there is another task I need to train you on. I would like to include in your duties checking the company post office box for deliveries. Come, I will show you where it is."

Another foray into the city? Daisy's toes and heels ached in protest, but she supposed she couldn't complain to her boss, especially given the condition of *his* legs. Instead, she drew on her reserves of energy to muster up a smile. "Of course, sir. Lead the way."

Andre brought his cane and a face mask for the outing, though when they stepped outside it seemed the latter wouldn't do him much good. The ashfall in the morning had been raining larger particles, but humidity had rolled in during the afternoon, and the flecks of soot dissolved in the moist air. It was so much worse than the heavy ashfall, he thought. A face mask could shield one from solid flecks of ash, but when it was hazy it was fine enough to sneak into throats and nostrils and eyes. And the smudging on his glasses' lenses – a nightmare.

Miss Dell hadn't brought along anything for their excursion. That left her hands free for Andre to hand her a folder with details on the post office box.

"Everything you'll need," he said as they headed out the front office door.

Miss Dell flipped the folder open and scanned through the few documents within as they walked, looking too miserably bored to convince Andre that she was actually reading any of it. "Is it far from here?"

"It's the nearest postal office there is. I would consider it something of a trek, though, yes." Miss Dell's eyes flickered toward his cane, holding her gaze just long enough for Andre to notice but not long enough to be rude. She was clever enough to understand his insinuation – on her own, she would likely be able to make the trip much more quickly. But perhaps she would appreciate the more leisurely pace, having run about covering Vicks' ass earlier that morning.

"Who's... J R Elroy?" Miss Dell asked.

"Who?"

"The PO box is under their name. Do they work at Stripes?"

Apparently she was reading the documents, after all. "Oh, Mr Elroy, yes. He doesn't work with us, but some of our accounts are listed under his name for tax reasons."

"Would that tax reason be the evasion thereof?" Miss Dell cast Andre a sideways look that left him unsure if she meant the question as a joke.

Regardless, he answered casually, "Of course not." It was.

"Mr Elroy was an early investor in our company and still retains a number of financial and institutional ties to us." Mr Elroy was fictional, named after a dog Angel had owned as a child.

Andre didn't take any pleasure in lying to his new assistant, of course, but this was all quite above her head so early on in her career. In time – and perhaps after a few promotions – she would be prepared to hear about the grittier business details of their company. Until then, Andre needed to be sure she could at least survive a week in her position before he shared any legally-dubious trade secrets with her.

His lies seemed to satisfy Miss Dell, at least. "Uh-huh. And how often do I need to make runs to the PO box?"

"Twice a week, typically. More frequently if we are expecting packages." Miss Dell made a humming noise that expertly walked the line between a neutral acknowledgement and a whining groan. It was less complaint than he ever received from Amelia or the Pasternack twins, Andre supposed, so he didn't comment on it. Instead, he focused on leading her to their destination, turning north down Ivy Street. The neighborhood surrounding their office, just off the edge of the industrial district, was laid out in a neat if tight grid, so there were a number of routes to the post office six blocks down, but Ivy was the largest and safest of these streets. He didn't care for the thought of Miss Dell trying to cut through back alleys.

"It's not a strenuous walk," he continued as they made their way down the street. It wasn't the ritziest of Soot City's neighborhoods, but the little shops packed together along the road gave the area a sense of community. They passed by bakeries and pottery stores and little urban temples and shrines occupying the relatively cheap spaces available in this district's narrow brick and sandstone buildings. Across

the street was a dress shop, and Miss Dell watched with
rapt interest as a seamstress set up a short blue dress on the
mannequin in the front window.

Turning down two more streets, they soon arrived at the
post office, a squat little building occupying a good half of
the block on its own. A bank of iron grated lifts – distinctly
of ogre design with their aesthetically-exposed gears and
wheels – lined the outside of one wall, where postal workers
went up and down between the ground level and the post
office basement with carts filled with bundles of letters. The
postal workers scurrying into and out of the lifts had a busy
rhythm to their hurrying, like worker bees in a hive.

Miss Dell appeared unimpressed with the efficiency of
her local public service employees, again peeking into the
folder that listed the PO box's information. "So, I just give
them the number and they'll bring me whatever's there?"

"Yes, and then you'll sign off for it. They may call me
to verify the first few times, since you're a new face, but
eventually they'll recognize you as someone responsible for
this box."

Miss Dell made that not-quite-whining hum again and
snapped the folder shut. Andre led her inside to the front
desk to walk her through the process, which was as simple
as he had just explained – Daisy provided the desk attendant
the company's PO box number, the attendant went into the
back room and returned with a small box of stationery that
Angel had recently ordered from a catalog, and Daisy signed
a form verifying her authority to retrieve items from the
Stripes' box. They were soon on their way back to the office.

Their route back was the same as the one there, and again
Andre noticed Miss Dell staring at the dress in the boutique
window. It seemed a frivolous thing to fixate on, but he
supposed she was young and just coming into her own, and
material objects were easy to become distracted by at such

a time in one's life. It did remind him of something that he wanted to buy, as well.

"Excuse me while I stop by the newsstand," he said, as they neared the general store on Ivy Street. A small stand was set up outside of it, tended by a young, pasty man trying to flirt with two young women who appeared to have just emerged from the shrine next door. The newsstand boy didn't notice Andre and Miss Dell approach, struggling too much trying to form coherent sentences. Most Ashlanders spoke the Iongathi Trade Language – not because there were many Iongathi immigrants in Ashland, but simply because it was so common in international trade – but this young man kept stumbling into some kind of Algretau-Glynland pidgin. The bronze-skinned women in beaded Awros-style veils snickered at his patchwork language, whispering between themselves about his stilted efforts to communicate. Given what the man was saying to them in his mother-languages – Andre's family had come from the Ridgelands of Algretau, and he had picked up a fair amount of Algretau-Glynland pidgin from his mother – he thought it was for the best that the young ladies did not fathom the content of the young man's babbling.

Andre turned his attention away from that exchange, browsing through the print selection while the newsboy was distracted. Ogre technology had lent itself well to the print industry, and Soot City was already building for itself a reputation as a hub of communication. No fewer than three dozen different publications were laid out on the stand before them. Some were even in color, but Andre wasn't about to pay the extra nickels – it was the same news, no matter what flourishes bordered the page.

"Do you read the newspaper, Miss Dell?" he asked as he picked out one. The *Chapton University Times*. A student-run press, but much more reliably progressive than many private papers.

"Not particularly, sir."

"Where do you get your news from, then?"

"Franklin Blaine's radio program."

Andre's blood chilled, and he turned to stare wide-eyed at her. Franklin Blaine was some blustering radio pundit enamored with the traditionalist ideals of his ancestors from Berngi, complaining about refugees and forward-thinking women and magicians. Although Mr Blaine's family fled to Ashland presumably to escape the fascist regime in Berngi, it seemed he was quite content to embrace their talking points. Could Miss Dell really listen to that pompous, reactionary dreck? When she saw the look on Andre's face, and with the folder and parcel from the post office tucked under one arm, she threw up her free hand. "No, I'm kidding! My apartment walls just do nothing to block it when my neighbor has it blasting from their radio. Absolutely loathe the man." She stepped closer to the newsstand and plucked from it a magazine printed with a color cover. "I'm more fond of the quarterlies, myself."

"It's not quite news, though," Andre said. The magazine she held was titled *Vim* and decorated with a drawing of a young woman with dark golden skin wearing a silk wrap over a short dress. The long legs extending from her meager skirt were disproportionate to any actual human – Andre was sure it was supposed to be abstract, but it just looked absurd to him. She was framed by headlines written in Iongathi and Elvertan that exclaimed about the cinema and fashionable new jacket cuts. There was only one headline that referred to current events – an exposé on a bank robber that had been arrested after a string of hold-ups. Sensationalist garbage.

Miss Dell set the magazine back on the stand but made an effort to defend the publication, regardless. "Magazines aren't for breaking news, no, but they provide social commentary on the current cultural climate. Essays and interviews... even advertisements can be a valuable lens into the values of a society."

Andre considered and took another magazine off the rack, this one featuring a drawing of a young model dressed in a skin-tight pink and green costume fringed with fake feathers. "Interesting hypothesis. What insight does *this* give about our society?"

Miss Dell looked carefully over the cover before raising her eyes to glare at Andre. "This woman is dressed to look like a faerie, so I would think this speaks primarily to how our society sees faeries."

Her answer was clipped and measured. Andre could tell he was annoying her, but it was better than listening to more of her bored sighs. "And how would you qualify that viewpoint?"

"Disconnected. If a human model were to dress like an ogre or faun in this regard, it would be seen as demeaning and tasteless, but no one expects any faerie to ever see this image. Sexual – she's near naked and posed to give an almost complete view of her backside. Intertwined with nature and magic, what with all these flowers and watercolor flourishes in the background."

"And what is the value of these observations?"

Miss Dell looked at him again, holding his gaze for a long, silent moment before answering. "It tells me that Ashlanders don't quite understand non-humans or magic – that they see such things as alien and exotic – and that faeries in particular are unknown to them. That if I wanted to talk to my countrypeople about these topics, it's a conversation that would be prone to misinformation and misunderstanding." She leaned over and pointed to the newspaper that Andre had picked up. "What does this article on stagnating stock values tell you about Ashland?"

Impressive. Even if Andre still found these magazines to be silly things, Miss Dell was certainly an analytical thinker. It would be unwise to underestimate her like that again, and Andre tucked that thought into the back of his mind.

"You buying?" Before Andre could respond to Miss Dell's coy turning of his own challenge against him, the newsboy barked over at them, as the young women of Awros-descent had grown bored of his antics and walked off.

"Yes, yes," Andre said, setting the magazine aside and digging around in his pockets for change to purchase the newspaper. The newsboy muttered something unpleasant in his pidgin as he waited for Andre to conjure up the coin – which Andre politely pretended not to understand – and took his money without any gesture of thanks, though he did spare a moment to look Miss Dell over. Worthless lout. Tired of the young man's presence and eager to return to work, Andre said to Miss Dell, "Let's get back to the office. I've already had you out and about over half the day, and I won't keep you longer from your desk duties."

After a quick dinner of rice and cauliflower, Daisy fussed over her reflection in the bathroom mirror, preparing for her night out before Angel and Rudolph arrived to pick her up. She had already changed into a slim, knee-length amber dress and white thigh-high socks and was fast at work applying her makeup. She heard through her apartment's thin walls a radio switch on, and the raving and frothing of her neighbors' favorite talking head carried in muffled waves into her living space.

"What do you hate today, Franklin Blaine?" Daisy mumbled as she examined her reflection under the single, yellow bathroom light. Sunken eyes, tired from a day at work, and her hair in a frizzy, springy mess after picking loose the day's ashfall. A bit of eyeliner would be enough for her face, but it always took a healthy dosage of pomade to smooth her hair down. With a few weeks between her and her last trip to the salon, her hair was beginning to curl just past her ears, and she nearly emptied her current bottle slicking those curls back into place. As she worked on that, Franklin Blaine answered her question from her neighbors' radio.

"–and these *magician* folk. All this higgledy-piggledy jabber about energy flows and… and quantum what-have-you–"

"It ought to be illegal," Franklin Blaine's guest complainer interrupted.

"It's unnatural, it's twisted, my *family* doesn't need to hear that! And these *magicians* treat it like… like a *fashion statement*."

"Well, they… they try to get people in on it. The kids, especially. Kids are too… they aren't developed enough, mentally, to understand why it's so… it's–"

"It's *unnatural*."

"Aw, Franklin," Daisy said, running the shiny goop through her curls. "You're hurting my feelings." When her fingers snagged on a tangle, it at least provided a distraction while Franklin Blaine and his equally huffy, indignant guest went on ranting, probably blaming new immigrants and women's agency for the increase in magicians and illegal mana production and the decline of morality. It was more or less the same every evening. Perhaps unsurprisingly, Franklin Blaine's disapproval never stopped her from being or doing much of anything. There was a bit of a power trip in knowing that this man that the radio paid to try to control people could not, in fact, control her.

She could use that sort of self-confidence that night. As if going out with coworkers off-hours for the first time wasn't nerve-racking enough, Angel was an intimidating figure. Daisy wanted the older woman to like her – not just for the workplace favor, but on a simple, human level. Angel drove a car and dated a younger man and had a job with the word "Senior" in the title. She was the kind of woman that even the bankers in their nights off at the bars bowed to and called "ma'am," and when she said no, the matter was considered settled. Daisy respected her for all that and, even more so, for the fact that Angel seemed happy with her life and herself as a person. Maybe it was selfish, but Daisy recognized that a part of her desire to know Angel better was a flicker of hope that her commanding presence and attitude could rub off on Daisy herself.

She heard a staccato of light car horn beeps from outside just as she finished slicking down the last of her curls. Hurrying to the kitchen window, she peeked outside at the street running behind the back of her building. A dark jalopy with its headlights on waited below. From the glare of the light, she couldn't tell for sure if it was Angel and Rudolph sitting inside. It was about time for them to arrive, though, and she stumbled back across the room to the box of her grandmother's trinkets she had sitting on her dresser.

Her hand hovered above the open box as she considered what she wanted to bring, if anything. The hardest part of living up to the expectations of a Modern Girl, in her experience, was reconciling ideals of progress with the traditions left to her by Grandma Sparrow Dell. Back when Sparrow first began teaching Daisy of the Old Ways – that was literally what she had called it – it had been no big matter. Ashland was still a young land, and its citizens were expected to cling to some of their immigrant ancestors' ways. And the backlash against magic had only begun a decade or two ago, just starting up when Daisy was first learning. Of course, while the "mainstream" magic in Ashland wasn't as horrifying as the propaganda always made it seem, the traditions that her grandmother had passed on would certainly draw alarm if they were better known.

The Dell lineage had never practiced methodical magic – they were ritual magicians. What separated magic into types was largely each magic's mode and source. Methodical magic was all math and algorithms and code phrases powered by the magician's own internal energies, or at least that's how Daisy understood it. Ritual magic stored power in the physical world around the magician – in baubles and trinkets that could be easily carried and disguised as ordinary objects – but that power came from... elsewhere. It was not an efficient transfer of energy, and a magician could never survive putting their own power into a trinket. It was a practice that, in some ways, was better left behind.

But Daisy was not her grandmother, and abandoning magic completely would not undo the twisted horrors of the past. Even knowing what her grandmother had done, Daisy had loved her, and Grandma Sparrow was gone now. Sparrow had fled to Ashland in a time of war, and she was hardly the only one who had to disregard the lives of others in order to survive. Tossing her handiwork now would hardly bring any of those souls back, and as long as Daisy never recreated the process to fashion new trinkets, there was no reason she could see not to make use of the ones that already existed.

All that left, then, was the matter of whether she would need any of those trinkets that night. She didn't expect anything to go disastrously wrong while she was out on the town with friends in tow, but she preferred to play it safe.

She plucked a white headband from the tangled trove. When triggered, it could create a smokescreen, one that was hardly noticeable as anything unnatural outside on hazy days. Perfect for when creeps followed her around on the sidewalks. She slipped the headband on and considered a moment longer, eyeballing a solid bronze bracelet. The headband was a little outdated in its style, but it was white and simple in its make – entirely inoffensive even if it went noticed. The bracelet was bulky and drab and clashed with everything in her closet, and it didn't even fit right on her narrow wrists. Still, she picked it up and slipped it on. A single questionable accessory was worth the energy-boosting properties locked within the trinket. Just the thing in case she needed help keeping up with her coworkers.

With that, she rushed to slip on her dancing shoes and grab the keys hanging from a plain nail near the front door. She could hear a few more toots of the horn even out in the hallway as she locked the door and skipped down the stained, carpeted stairs two at a time until she was out of the building.

By the time she had circled around the apartment complex, Angel and Rudolph had stepped out of the car, with the latter slipping into the backseat. Angel waited by the driver's side door and waved at Daisy when she approached.

"Evening, dear. My, terrible weather it's been lately." More ash clouds had rolled in just around dusk, but Angel stood before her in a long white dress, cream overcoat, and matching hat, all completely unmarred by soot. Daisy wasn't given any time to wonder over this before Angel began shooing her toward the passenger seat. "Well, come on. We're supposed to meet the girls in five minutes, and it'll take half an hour to get there."

"Oh, my," Daisy said, settling into the clean leather seat and allowing Angel to shut the door behind her before returning to the driver's side. "Will they be upset?"

Angel laughed – a warm, bellowing sound. "I don't doubt they're just as behind as we are. I've never had a single one of those women show up on time for anything. If we leave now, we might just time our arrival perfectly with theirs." Daisy laughed along as Angel started up the car again and began down the road toward the gentrified northeast district – the very opposite side of town.

"I do hope you don't mind a bit of chatter. You've been such a lovely employee since you've started, but I feel I haven't had a proper chance to make your acquaintance," Angel said as she sped through the streets. Daisy herself didn't know how to drive – she had been too anxious the first time her father tried to teach her, and she had always lived in walking distance from her schools and places of employment, so she had never bothered to try again. "Andre mentioned you graduated from the Catherine Eleanor Ruthell Women's College. A lovely institute. I have an old beau who's a professor of physics there. What did you study?"

Daisy was relieved that Angel didn't make any remark on the fact that college, theoretically, was supposed to educate students for a life in the workforce beyond the kind of menial labor she was now employed for. She cringed at the idea of being seen as some airheaded girl who got an education just to pass the time, but the academic scene in Ashland was modeled largely after Berngi and Algretau academia, including their backwards ideas about women. Judging from her name and looks, Angel's family had probably come from Berngi, and although she was a learned woman herself, Daisy worried she would think of her field of study as flippant and useless.

"Modern Ashland history."

"History? Splendid. I've always loved to read about history. Sadly, I devoted my college education toward a path that would lead to easier job security." She shrugged, hardly seeming sad at all, though her interest in Daisy's education sounded sincere.

"You went to college, as well? What did you study?"

"Chemistry."

Rudolph leaned forward from where he hunkered in the backseat. "That must be why your chemistry with everyone is so phenomenal, dear."

Angel made a show of rolling her eyes even as a thin smile crossed her face. "He makes that joke *every time* I mention it. Thinks he's so damn funny." Rudolph only smirked at her chiding and leaned back again.

They talked more as they neared their destination, discussing families and hobbies and favorite foods without getting too personal or detailed on any one topic. It was a pleasant chat, comfortably superficial, and Daisy got to watch the towering buildings speed by, their bright lights blurring from the movement of the car and the volcanic dust drifting in the night air. They soon arrived in a glitzy neighborhood surprisingly close to Vicks' area. She hated all these club and restaurant owners for chasing out the poor to take up cheap neighborhoods, she hated the city that it only bothered with upkeep of these neighborhoods once the rich rolled in, and she hated herself for playing along as a patron. Glamour and money were lovely, but the alluring sheen of it all smudged when she thought about what others had to lose for it.

Daisy wasn't the rich, though, and she had her own needs, and so long as she could justify the partying aspect of her persona and increasing social networks with coworkers as a "need," she was able to choke down the guilt and disgust.

Angel parked her car in a well-lit lot, and the three of them made their way to a dance hall two blocks over. As the ashfall continued, Angel's pristine outfit remained untouched, even while grey flecks clung to Daisy and Rudolph. It would be easy enough to brush the ash off without too much smudging, but Daisy did wonder how the older woman managed to keep her clothes so clean. It must have been the type of fabric, Daisy ultimately decided. Daisy herself could have used a spell to accomplish a similar effect, but she had left her repellant ring at home, and it would have been too obvious. Outing herself as a magician – as a *ritual* magician, no less – was not how she wanted to make her first impression with her coworkers.

"I do hope they're here," Angel said, strolling into an old (well, as old as building got in Soot City) two-storied brick structure crammed between two slightly taller buildings, decorated with white plaster molding around the windows and doors. Dull chatter and the soft melody of a piano and trumpet singing to each other drifted out from the white front doors. It was calm and elegant while also appearing rundown and pedestrian. Daisy and Rudolph followed her in, and while Rudolph went immediately to the front cashier to pay for their cover charges, Angel paused on the club's plush red and gold carpet, swiveling her head as she examined the round tables set up around the edge of the dance floor and stage. Her eyes landed on one occupied by four young women as trim and sporty as Daisy, all with bare arms and tall heels.

"Ah, that'd be them." Angel hooked her arm into Daisy's and headed toward the table without waiting for Rudolph to catch up. "Evening, dears."

The four women, who had been laughing raucously over some joke one of them had told, stopped abruptly and stared at them. Daisy could tell they were unlike Angel and her beau, as the group gave the larger woman a collective sharp look when they approached. They were glares that were both admiring but also wary and exasperated – these were menial labor working women, like Daisy, mistrustful of Angel even as they considered her a friend and colleague.

Some things did not transcend social class.

"New meat, Angel?" one with a jawline bob cut and a glittering red sequined dress asked. The angles of her white face were severe, and that combined with her dark eyes glancing Daisy up and down gave her the impression of an alley cat or a sadistic school teacher.

"Ladies, this is Daisy Dell, Andre's new typist."

The woman sitting – very closely – to the left of the first stiffened her back. "Oh-ho! Replaced already? I've hardly been in the 'house for a month."

"Andre always needs someone to type for him, Lia. You know that."

Lia – *Amelia*, Daisy assumed, whom she recalled Mr Swarz mentioning on occasion as his previous typist – smirked and leaned on the shoulder of the woman sitting beside her, regardless of either of their bony skeletal shoulders. "He doesn't miss me at all, does he?"

The woman she leaned into laughed, while a third woman stared off into space, appearing completely detached from the entire conversation. The fourth woman, strikingly familiar to Daisy, only grinned along. "Nah, Lia, you're too fun for a crotchety snake like that," the first woman said. She scooted away from Amelia and stood, offering a hand to Daisy. "Frisk Pasternack. I work in the, uh–" Daisy had taken her hand, but Frisk pulled away and turned to Angel. "You got a second?" The two stepped aside, putting their heads together to whisper in hushed tones. Daisy glanced at Amelia and the third woman while this went on, but they only examined her with silent, curious stares. Daisy looked again to the familiar girl, and she wondered if it wasn't because she looked so similar to Frisk with her sharp facial features. A moment longer of looking, and she realized the true reason behind her *déjà vu*.

"Vicks?"

Vicks' wolfish grin widened, and Daisy remembered the complaints she had from Mr Sparrick and Miss Cadwell while she had been covering Vicks' errands. Mr Sparrick had noted that Daisy wasn't the usual delivery boy, whereas Miss Cadwell had said something about a delivery *girl*. She hadn't noticed the discrepancy at the time.

She tried to politely hide her surprise, averting her eyes from the narrow-cut black dress or the bobbed wig Vicks was wearing. "Fancy seeing you here. One last shebang before you get back to work tomorrow?"

Vicks snickered. "You seem a bit shocked, Daze."

"I just... took you for more of a suit and tie sort of man, is all."

"Well, sure, when I *am* a man. I'm not now." Daisy took Vicks at her word and resolved herself not to bother her with any more questions or observations on the matter.

When Frisk and Angel pulled apart and rejoined them, the former returned her attention to Daisy. "Sorry 'bout that. Anyway, I work in the warehouse, 'long with Amelia, Regina, and some of the boys. And my twin, here, Vicks. You met Vinnie and Jonas yet?"

"I haven't had the pleasure yet, no." Rudolph rejoined them at that point, asking Daisy and Angel if they wanted drinks from the bar. He ignored the warehouse girls, who each already had at least one glass in front of them. While Daisy and Angel settled at the table to wait for his return, the band on stage started up a light, hopping beat, and Amelia bounced in her chair.

"Babe," she said, whacking Frisk on the arm. "Come on, let's dance."

Frisk waved her off, leaning forward with elbows on the table. "Later. I wanna get to know our new girl better, first." Amelia's bouncing halted as she pouted and shot a glowering stare toward Daisy. It wasn't any of Daisy's business, but the brief glare made her gut turn a bit cooler. Amelia then turned to the woman sitting on the other side of Frisk.

"How 'bout it, Regina?" Regina's eyes were still a bit glassy and unfocused, but she nodded to Amelia's request without looking directly at the woman and stood. While they went together to the dance floor, Vicks scooted her chair closer to her sister's, and the Pasternack twins watched Daisy with intent and wild stares.

"So, how'd you get pulled on as Andre's right-hand?" Frisk asked.

Angel cleared her throat, but Daisy could barely hear it over the blaring of horns and the twanging thrum of the piano. "I saw the job posting in a newspaper." Daisy shrugged, unsure of how exciting Frisk expected her answer to be. "It seemed decent enough work."

Vicks threw back her head and laughed while Frisk grabbed a glass of scotch in front of her, muttering with a chuckle, "*Decent*," before taking a long sip. Angel cleared her throat again, and when Frisk waved her hand dismissively at the other woman, Daisy realized that Angel wasn't suffering the beginnings of a mild cold.

Frisk leaned forward again, so far this time that her bony ribs pressed against the edge of the table. "And is, uh, our line of work very interesting to you?"

Daisy tried not to frown. What did Frisk expect her to say? Even Mr Swarz hadn't bothered with the usual question of "Why are you interested in this job?" at her interview, knowing full well that there were only so many things about document management that a person could find appealing. "Well, work is work," she answered, her voice wavering slightly. She feared she wasn't making much of a first impression, and the Pasternacks with their hyena-like stares were starting to make her jumpy. What kind of Modern Girl allowed herself to appear bland and skittish?

A pulse of relief flooded through her chest when Rudolph sauntered back, awkwardly balancing three flutes of white wine between his two hands. Just as he set them down before Angel and Daisy, the older woman stood and tapped Daisy on the shoulder. "I *love* this song. Care for a dance?"

Daisy hesitated. The song had already been going for half a minute, and Angel's enthusiasm felt forced. The wolfish smiles had faded from the Pasternack twins, and now they only watched Daisy with blank expressions. Still, she would be happy to have a moment to collect herself away from them. Maybe she could appear more sure of herself doing something that didn't involve running her mouth.

"Of course."

She stood as well, allowing Angel to take her arm and hurry her over to the dance floor. Rudolph watched them scurry off without him with his mouth just slightly agape before calling out, "All right. I'll just be right here. Enjoy yourselves!"

Daisy began to relax more with the firm feeling of polished wood under her shoes. Angel guided her to near where Amelia and Regina danced together, kicking up their heels and flinging their bony arms wildly to the rhythm of the trumpet flares. Angel was a gorgeous woman, and Daisy admired her for every bit of that womanhood, but she wasn't a fit for the Modern Girl image like the dancing girls in skinny dresses. She was too old, fat, and wealthy for that. Daisy wasn't sure that the magazines had a pithy phrase for women like her – she wasn't sure she wanted them to. Regardless, she expected that Angel wasn't going to be doing any dance that involved kicking up her heels.

Whatever spell of frantic alarm had taken hold of Angel at the table disappeared on the dance floor, and she smiled her warm, rosy-cheeked smile. "How about something a little calmer to start with?" she asked, nodding toward

Amelia and Regina. "Warm up with a waltz? I'll lead." Daisy agreed and stepped up to place one hand in Angel's and the other upon her shoulder. When the older woman's hand went to her hip, she drew Daisy closer than expected, and with Angel's ample bust, it left no room between them. Heat flushed through Daisy as Angel's breasts pressed against her own, and she counted herself lucky that she didn't have the same pale pink skin of her dance partner to betray her flustering. Angel was merciful enough to keep the dance itself tame, spinning about in a quick-footed modification of a classic waltz. Confident in each step, Angel was a sturdy leader, and Daisy found herself genuinely enjoying the way they glided about across the wood, guided by the drummer's beat.

Once Daisy began to grow dizzy and thirsty, Angel stopped them to return to the table. Rather than hold Daisy by the arm, Angel kept a hand on her hip with her arm hooked behind Daisy's waist. "I do hope Frisk and Vicks weren't bothering you too much. They can certainly be... aggressive."

Daisy barely heard her, distracted by the heat of the arm wrapped around her waist. "Oh, it's no bother." When they reached the table again – Vicks now gone to dance with some other patron of the hall and Amelia and Regina returned to gossip with Frisk – Daisy tried her best to slip out of Angel's embrace without being too obviously bashful. She hurried to plop herself in her chair and reach to take a drink from her glass. However, she had misremembered where she sat – Amelia had shifted to where Vicks had earlier sat, and Daisy had mistakenly taken Amelia's previous seat – and she didn't examine the glass before raising it to her lips and swallowing.

It was not wine.

She slammed the glass down, nearly choking on raspberry

vodka as it raced down her throat and up her nose in a fiery blur. While Frisk cackled at the sight, Amelia scowled. "Hey, that's mine!" Daisy blinked furiously, trying to regain her composure as she pushed the glass across the table toward Amelia. Rudolph reached over to give her an assuring but awkward pat on the back. She didn't bother trying to locate her own glass and just slumped quietly where she sat. Perhaps she *was* better off living her nightlife solo.

She committed to keeping her head down as much as she could the rest of the evening. Angel clearly noticed her distress and occasionally tried to engage her in mild conversation underneath the blaring of the band onstage, but eventually Rudolph insisted that they dance together, and Daisy was left on her own with the warehouse girls. Vicks, when she was at the table long enough to sit and drink for a moment, flashed her a few friendly grins, but something about her toothy mouth and the sharp facial features framing it made it feel somehow predatory. Regina was content to ignore Daisy entirely, and Frisk and Amelia sometimes looked her way with either curiosity or disdain – she wasn't sure which. Maybe they weren't sure, either. There was a moment where she wistfully considered activating the smokescreen ability enchanted into her headband and slipping away entirely, though of course for the smokescreen to go off indoors would be too obvious and cause a panic. For a while, she tried to just focus on the music, humming along to the strings so softly that even she couldn't hear herself.

When Angel and Rudolph returned, Frisk and Amelia began whispering to each other in hurried tones. While Angel and Rudolph still looked radiant, and even Daisy was only beginning to feel tired, the warehouse girls were starting to look exhausted. Frisk glanced over at Regina and turned back to Angel, and Daisy was surprised that instead of suggesting that they turn in for the night, she said, "We're thinking of taking this to a different scene." When Angel frowned, Frisk rolled a shoulder, adding, "You know," as though that were supposed to mean anything.

Angel crossed her arms and sighed. "Well, go if you want. I should probably take my team home. Andre already let me know that he'd skin me if I brought Daisy back unfit to work tomorrow, and Rudolph is already in his cups." Indeed, Rudolph had to lean to his girlfriend to keep himself standing upright, and his eyes were merrily glazed. He had ordered a few more drinks since that first glass of white wine. Daisy hadn't seen Angel drink anything since that introductory glass, which she hadn't even finished, and she assumed that Angel would still be in the driver's seat on the way home.

Frisk's lips pulled into an expression that was not exactly a sneer. It gave the impression of being both disappointed and unsurprised. "Right, right. Want me to, uh, pick you up anything while we're out?"

Daisy noticed Angel's eyes dart quickly toward her before settling back on Frisk with a darkened expression. "That won't be necessary." A chill went up Daisy's back, and she suppressed a shudder. What was that about? Angel and Frisk talked like friends, but it seemed as though the latter had hardly said a thing all night that didn't get Angel all prickly. It felt at odds with the calm and charismatic woman Daisy had seen Angel as in the office or on the dance floor.

With a brief and tense exchange of goodbyes, Angel was soon escorting her dates back to the lot where she'd parked the jalopy. She had to help Rudolph clamber into the back seat, struggling to get his feet pushed all the way into the body of the car rather than left to dangle out the door. Daisy settled in the passenger seat, stewing quietly in her own embarrassment over how dull and foolish she had made herself out to be that night. When Angel had successfully stuffed her half-cognitive boyfriend in the back, she nearly flopped into the driver's seat, heaving a grating sigh. Her frustration and exhaustion appeared to vanish a moment later as she turned to Daisy and beamed a sunny grin.

"Well, that was a lovely evening, wasn't it?" Daisy wanted to be polite and charming – she wanted Angel to know that the misery she was feeling was not the older woman's fault – but she couldn't summon the same reserves of cheer as Angel could. The wan smile she offered felt listless and lopsided on her face. Angel pouted when she saw it, and that expression quickly burned into a scowl. "Oh, that brat Frisk!"

"No, truly, I had an excellent time," Daisy hurried to say, but Angel ignored her, turning in her seat to face Daisy fully.

"Now, you listen. Those girls can be rough, and although they should and do know better, sometimes they let their worser natures get the better of them. I don't want you worrying about what they think. Frisk and Amelia are territorial, and Regina is a ditz who goes along with whatever they say. Vicks can be sweet, but she's a wild one, and when he's one of the boys, he *is* one of the boys. They'll all be crass and reckless till it kills them, but I don't want you thinking that it has anything to do with you or what they think of you as a person." She sighed again, turning to face the steering wheel and start the car, and the exhale carried off her anger. "They're a bunch of silly punks who are nervous about newcomers, is all. Trust me, when Amelia was first hired, Frisk was the same way about her, and now they're dating." She turned the key in the ignition and paused, glancing again at Daisy. "Don't date Frisk."

Angel's outburst surprised Daisy, and although it didn't do much to make her feel better about Frisk and the others, it did make her more at ease with Angel herself. She had never had friends growing up who were close enough to care about her emotional distress, and her parents had always been avoidant types to skirt around firm heart-to-hearts. It was an intimate compassion that Angel offered to her, one that she wasn't used to, and she felt the tension under her shoulders loosen.

She smiled at Angel, even though the other woman had her eyes on the road as she pulled out of the parking lot. "Thank you for saying that. I needed to hear it."

The drive home was peaceful, and in the quiet darkness of the car Daisy's fatigue began to catch up with her. She wondered, as her eyelids drooped and the spots of light from the city blurred through her lashes, how long Frisk and her friends intended to stay out, and what kind of condition they could expect to return to work tomorrow. Rudolph, at least, would probably sleep off the night's entertainment – he was already snoring in the backseat. Daisy was about ready to follow suit when she heard Angel cry out, *"Damn!"*

Daisy blinked once, and it was far easier to keep her eyes open once she spotted the large trailer truck swerving into their lane from the opposite direction. There was a warning blare of a horn as the truck tried to correct its course, and Daisy's breath caught, her heart nearly stopping. Angel slammed on the brakes, and all three occupants of her vehicle cried out as they were flung forward from the momentum. Head whipping while her body remained strapped in tight by the seatbelt, Daisy caught a view of her own knees and lap, and a taunting devil in her mind whispered that this would be her last sight. She heard a booming thud and the screech of friction on metal, and then a hush of silence. Wondering for a brief moment if she were dead, that taunting voice in her head changed its tune, politely reminding her that she could still see her knees and smell burnt rubber. She looked up to see Angel gripping the steering wheel with knuckles lined with bulging blue veins, staring unblinking ahead while she panted wildly. Daisy peered out through the windshield, too.

The truck, in its desperation to realign itself in the correct lane, had flipped on its side, and the passengers of Angel's car stared at its steely underbelly. The thankful silence of survival stretched on for a long moment while Angel and Daisy gawked at the enormous vehicle that had nearly run them down, breaking only when Angel gasped and clutched at her chest.

Rudolph, shaken from his drunken slumber by the momentous event, scrambled to unbuckle himself and lean into the front half of the car. "Angel, darling!"

"Are you all right?" Daisy asked, unable to keep herself from pawing helplessly at Angel's arm.

Angel took two more shaky breaths before waving them both off. "I'm f- fine. Go, check the other driver." She was nearly wheezing, and Daisy worried that she was suffering some heart issue in response to the stress of the situation, but she did as she was told, no less alarmed over the possible fate of the trucker. She hurried out of the car, her legs shaking hard enough to send her staggering her first step onto the road – empty but for the accident – but she hobbled as quickly as she could to the cabin of the truck. The driver's side door was pinned to the asphalt, so Daisy had to climb up the sideways cabin to get to the passenger's side, smudging her dress with dust, ash, and oil from the truck's exterior. Pulling the passenger's side door up and open, she peered down to see a heavy-bodied individual struggling to untangle himself from his seatbelt.

"Are you all right?"

The driver paused and looked up at her. He was an ogre, one of the non-human races native to the continent who had come to Ashland about two hundred years before humans began returning. Much taller and broader than the average human, with longer arms and thick, greyish skin, most ogres still lived in the mountains in towns like Oleylo, out where the ash and gas was still too severe for most humans. Some, however, chose to live in the company of humans in the greener lowlands. While other intelligent beings like faeries, fauns, and doppelgangers lived on the distant margins of human society, sometimes so far disconnected that history had nearly forgotten them entirely, ogres integrated in sizable – though still minority – populations, at least in Ashland. The human's word "ogre" was a derogatory term, Daisy knew, but so widely in use that she didn't know what they called themselves, and thus she had no other name for such beings.

The ogre pushed his hair up from his forehead, shaking off shards of glass from the shattered driver's window. If he had been human, the impact of the turnover or cuts from the glass might have killed him. Thick skin and heavy bones appeared to leave the ogre largely unharmed, or so Daisy hoped. He waved up to her.

"Battered a bit, but fine. Just give me a–" He gave up on trying to unbuckle himself and gripped the strap across his chest, jerking it aside until it tore. Free from its constraint, he struggled to stand in the sideways compartment, but once he was on his feet, it was easy for him to reach up and pull himself out. When his head and shoulders emerged from the open doorway, he glanced at Daisy before trying to peer around the body of his truck. "Are *you* all right? Were you in that car?"

"I'm fine," Daisy said, only just then realizing that she hadn't even thought to check herself for any sort of injury. "I think the others with me are, as well, although maybe I should…" She paused, uncertain of *what* she should do.

She didn't know the neighborhood they were in and wasn't sure where she might find a payphone to call for help. And although Angel and Rudolph had both been conscious and speaking, she worried about Angel's frantic breathing. "I need to make sure they're OK. Are you sure you're all right?"

The ogre finished pulling himself up, clambering out of the cabin to settle on its upturned side. "Yes, just need to catch my breath. Go see to your friends." Daisy climbed back down to the road, slipping on the last step down and tumbling to her knees as she landed, but she ignored the scrapes to her legs and the tear in her skirt to hurry back to the car.

She circled around to the driver's window, which Angel lowered for her. "Angel, how are you feeling?"

"A bit in shock, dear. I'm not hurt, though." She seemed calmer, but her breathing hadn't evened out much, and she flinched as though she had a migraine. "How is the driver?"

"Alive and unhurt, or mostly unhurt."

Angel sighed, slumping her shoulders. Daisy began to feel her own heartbeat stabilize seeing Angel relax.

"We should call the police," Angel said, staring absently ahead, again in the direction of the truck's underside. Daisy didn't like the sound of that – ogres and other non-humans weren't high society in Soot City, and the police had a history of giving them trouble when they could, and it didn't help that the trucker appeared to be at fault for the accident – but there wasn't much help for it. The truck couldn't drive away, and the road would have to be cleared sooner or later. The flat delivery of Angel's suggestion made it clear that she didn't much like the circumstances, either, although she couldn't have known that the driver was an ogre.

Rudolph, still in the backseat, reached up to place a hand on Angel's arm. "Darling, do you need to stay here and rest?"

Angel didn't blink as she nodded. "I think that may be for the best. Will you be able to assist Daisy in helping the other driver?"

Her beau patted her hand. "Of course, my sweet." Daisy helped him out of the car – panic and concern appeared to help him through the haze of alcohol, and he climbed out with less stumbling than Daisy had suffered – and together they returned to the trucker, where they found a pair of nearby residents already gathered to examine the scene and assist. The pair, a couple who lived close enough to hear the crash, offered to phone the police for them before fussing over the safety and well-being of all the parties involved. Once sure that the trucker would find assistance with his vehicle and after assuring everyone that their own car and everyone in it was safe, Daisy and Rudolph excused themselves to make their way home.

As they returned to the car, Daisy could see Angel in the driver's seat drinking from what appeared to be a flask. That didn't make sense to Daisy – Angel was a responsible woman, from everything Daisy had seen, and she hadn't allowed herself to drink too much while they were out, knowing that she'd be accountable for driving them home. Daisy shook her head, telling herself that it was probably medicine. Maybe Angel had some sort of chronic condition that had been aggravated by the crash. Whatever it was, she had it tucked away by the time Daisy and Rudolph climbed back in.

"Are you well enough to drive?" Rudolph asked, and Daisy understood the hesitant lilt of his question. He was drunk, and Daisy didn't know how to drive. If Angel was too out of sorts to continue, they would have to call a cab.

Angel nodded. Breathing now even, she looked alert. She still appeared shaken, but under control. "Yes. Let's get ourselves home, shall we?" As she reached for the steering

wheel, Daisy noticed a smudge on Angel's thumb. In the
dimness of night, it looked almost like blood, but there was
just enough light from the city around them to make out a
blue glint. Not dark blue, like ink, but something brighter
and more vibrant than a clear summer sky. Daisy wasn't
sure what it was, but she thought to the flask she had seen
Angel drinking from. That certainly wasn't alcohol she saw
daubed on her friend's hand.

CHAPTER 3

Sleep came uneasily to Daisy after that ordeal, but she had enough of her senses about her when she arrived at the office the next morning. She was about five minutes late, hurrying in with her hair left unslicked and tucked under a maroon felt hat. Mr Swarz, already in his own office, appeared not to notice her tardiness. At least she could expect work to be uncomplicated after the previous night's excitement.

Mr Swarz had no special tasks for her that morning, and the phone on her lobby desk was silent, so she took to menial cleaning to pass the time. She tidied the refreshment table in the back of the lobby, washed out the coffee carafe and scrubbed Angel's lipstick off of one of the white mugs sitting next to it. She had decided to slip on her bronze pendant that morning – one of her grandmother's more useful trinkets that could levitate objects lighter than about a dozen pounds, as she had woken up with the feeling that she'd be more butterfingered than usual. Her prediction proved accurate when, while moving aside the sugar bowl to wipe down the table, the little ceramic dish slipped from her hold. It didn't flip as it fell, leaving most of its contents inside its belly, and she was able to activate the spell fast enough to keep it from slamming into the hardwood and exploding white grains and shards all over the room. It hovered intact little more than an inch off the floor.

Once she wiped down the table and returned the sugar bowl to its place, she noticed flakes of dirt that had gathered around the front door. Mr Swarz's cane had toppled over from where he had rested it against the wall, too, and was now also smudged with filth. There must have been a broom somewhere in the office, she reasoned. There were three narrow doors in the back corner beyond the refreshment counter, one which led to a toilet and at least one of the others presumably connected to a supply closet. She went to the furthest one and tried it.

Locked.

She stepped back, examining the door. Why lock a supply closet? She tried again, wondering if perhaps the door was jammed, but the handle resisted with the definite feel of a lock. She turned to the other unknown door, which opened to reveal what she wanted – a broom and bucket and smaller cleaning tools stacked upon clustered and grimy shelves. The first door must have contained overflow from Mr Swarz's shelves of client paperwork, she decided, when she grabbed the broom and went to clear up the office entrance.

She swept the most obvious of the mess out the front door and off the steps before leaning the broom against the wall to see to Mr Swarz's cane. As she knelt to pick it up, though, she noticed something too shiny to be dirt on its shaft near the head. The head itself was polished copper, but what she saw was a narrow strip of silver just below that. Taking hold of the cane and lifting it, the exposed silver expanded as the head of the cane slipped further away from the shaft she clutched. Grabbing the head and pulling it further, she realized what she was looking at.

A narrow steel blade was hidden within the cylindrical body of the cane.

She slammed the head back into place. It was nothing to be alarmed about, she assured herself. Soot City had crime just like any other, and honest residents might feel the need to prepare defenses against muggers. Daisy herself had her trinkets, and it wasn't uncommon for others to hide small blades in their purses or pockets. That Mr Swarz had a slightly more dramatic means of self-defense did not detract from how ordinary and reasonable it was for him to keep a weapon. He needed the cane, regardless, so why not stash a mode of defense within it?

She twisted the head, and she could feel it lock into place along some grooves on the inner top lip of the shaft. Ordinary and reasonable, she told herself again as she gingerly set it back against the wall.

"Miss Dell?"

Daisy nearly knocked the cane over again as she hopped to her feet and hurried over to Mr Swarz's office. "Yes, sir?"

He was at his desk, scrawling something into a notebook with his good hand. "I've a letter I need you to transcribe into type – I hope my handwriting is clear enough for you. If not, I can–" He broke off as he glanced up at her, his nose wrinkling with such a furious consternation that it nudged the bridge of his glasses up. "Are you quite all right?"

Daisy heard the front door open behind her as he asked this, Angel and Rudolph's muttering voices echoing across the lobby walls. "Yes, sir, I'm fine."

Mr Swarz made a soft *hmph* noise. "You seem a bit jittery this morning. I hope Angel didn't keep you out too late?"

"Not at all, sir. It was a lovely time, and Angel was wonderful to me."

Mr Swarz scowled, but it wasn't quite aimed at Daisy. Angel, who had appeared just behind her in the doorway, stepped into the room and stood at Daisy's side. "I'm hardly surprised. Angel, don't tell me you and Rudolph are trying to seduce my new typist?"

Daisy flushed, but Angel, even under weary eyes from last night's accident, managed to put on a sly grin. "Oh, darling, are you getting jealous?"

Daisy was no longer concerned with the implications of Mr Swarz's accusation toward Angel when he smirked back at her. "I had enough the first time, thanks."

A laugh escaped Daisy before she could think better of it. "*What?*"

Mr Swarz shrugged as though it were no matter. "Angel and her beaus have a history of occasionally taking on a third. She had one a few years back who took a fancy to me. And he was… persuasive." Angel glanced over at Daisy and winked. "I liked him much better than LaChapelle, certainly. You should have kept him."

"*You* could have kept him, if you were so inclined." Mr Swarz only shrugged again, and they both ignored Daisy's grin of delighted scandal as Angel shifted her attention to the typist. "Anyway, I wanted to check in on you, after the accident and all. How are you feeling this morning?"

The humor and nostalgia faded from Mr Swarz, taking his uncharacteristically playful smirk with it. "Accident? Miss Dell, you didn't mention an accident. What happened?"

"On the drive home from the dance hall we were nearly hit by an oncoming truck. I was able to brake fast enough while the truck swerved, and it flipped over before our vehicles could collide."

"It flipped?" His words were clipped with incredulity.

"Yes. It turned very sharply in trying to avoid us and fell onto its side."

"Were you hurt?" His question seemed to be directed towards Angel, but he looked to Daisy as soon as he voiced it, so she decided to answer.

"No, I wasn't. It's just that sleep was a little unsteady once

I got home, but I'll be fine."

Mr Swarz stood, bowing his head. "I apologize, Miss Dell. I shouldn't have made those comments about your night out, earlier. Do you need any accommodation to get you through the day?"

A voice in the back of her head – one that hadn't quite woken up when she pulled herself out of bed that morning – whispered to her to ask for a half-day, but she shook her head. Work would be uncomplicated enough, she promised herself again. "No, sir, I'm fine."

"Very well." He handed her the notebook he had been writing in. "If you would please transcribe this, then, I need to have a word with Miss Agatha about business matters."

Daisy did as she was told, leaving them to work on typing out the vaguely-worded letter Mr Swarz had drafted for one of his clients. Her employer's handwriting was, indeed, difficult to decipher at times, but it did not require any complex thinking, and she was through it quickly. That left the rest of the day to tend to the silent lobby phone. She spent the empty time doodling on pads of paper and daydreaming about a new pair of shoes that she'd like to buy with her next paycheck, and occasionally she would glance up only to have her gaze fall upon Mr Swarz's cane. It was difficult not to dwell on that with little else to occupy her until afternoon came to a close and she made her way home.

The next few days passed slowly as well, and Daisy started bringing a book to work with her. She still came with one or two of her grandmother's trinkets, mixing them up from day to day. When she woke up one morning to a chilly apartment, she wore the garter that could produce a gentle heat, keeping her legs warm while she sat at her desk. Another day, it was the jade lizard brooch that could consolidate moisture in the air, which she used to water the potted ficus by the front door without moving from her chair. Three days later, she wore her pendant again, expecting that she could levitate pencils and paperclips across the room to amuse herself if she didn't have enough work.

That was the same morning that, shortly after she arrived and settled in at her desk, the front door slammed open and a dark, broad-shouldered man wearing spectacles stormed in, baring his teeth like he was ready to start a fight. He ignored Daisy entirely as he raged into the lobby, even when she stood to insist he calm down or leave or… something. He made a beeline to Mr Swarz's office, shouting in a heavily accented snarl, "*Swarz!* My money!"

Just as an impulse nearly pushed Daisy to chase after the man and try to drag him out of Mr Swarz's office, another man appeared at the door, ducking and turning sidewise to fit through it. He was an ogre, like the trucker Daisy had met the night of the accident, and he dressed in plain overalls and had a floppy newsboy hat covering his course yellow mane. Wispy bangs almost concealed the nubby horns on the ridge of his brow. While indiscernible shouting rose from Mr Swarz's office, the ogre turned to Daisy and bowed his head in the most gentlemanly fashion. "Good morning, miss." His voice was low but had a sort of musicality to it that reminded Daisy of a small and tender child. His demeanor didn't do much to ease her alarm over the angrier man, though.

"Um, good morning. Is that–?"

The ogre took off his hat and kneaded it between his heavy hands. "Ah, sorry about Vinnie. There was a mix-up with the checks, and he's got a little brother and a grandma to take care of. He doesn't take money matters lightly. I'm Jonas, by the way. Bauer." He offered one of his giant hands, large enough to wrap entirely around one of Daisy's thighs.

She stepped forward to shake it, even though her own hand couldn't so much grip his as just sort of settle in the center of his palm.

"I'm Daisy; nice to meet you." She remembered Frisk mentioning both these men the night at the dance hall. "You work in the warehouse?"

"The ware–?" He jolted, struck with a bolt of either recollection or realization. "Ah, yes, that's right. You're Mr Swarz's new assistant, right?"

The voices raised in Andre's office interrupted her chance to provide a response. "This matter is for LaChapelle. I don't know why you keep bringing it to me."

"That worthless fop is never here at a reasonable hour. By the time he drags his sorry ass in every day, I am already at work in the 'house! I cannot come here to argue over my rightful payment when I am on shift."

"You could, actually. Have you spoken to Grey about this?" The raging man, Vinnie, appeared in the doorway with Mr Swarz gently steering him out of his office with a hand placed on the small of Vinnie's back. "I'll speak to LaChapelle. He'll straighten the matter out, and you'll both get accurate paychecks returned to you before the week is done."

Vinnie didn't resist Mr Swarz's dismissal, but he did glance back with a sneer. "This is the third time this has happened. I have a family to feed, and my landlord does not care what clerical issues are occurring at my workplace. You need to fire that damn useless piece of shit." When he turned away, he noticed Daisy standing there for the first time since initially storming in. "Oh. Pardon my language, miss."

Daisy smiled politely, but she wasn't going to let his apology go without comment. "Oh, sir, I couldn't give a fuck about any of that." Jonas chuckled as Vinnie grinned back bashfully, but Mr Swarz didn't react at all to the joke. He kept his eyes on Daisy with a blank expression, as though he were watching for something. His gaze flickered down to her bronze pendant before he turned again to Vinnie.

"You'll get your due soon enough. I'll speak to Grey about the possibility of a small bonus for you both to compensate for the hassle."

Vinnie shook his head. "I do not want money I did not earn. I want you to hire an accountant that knows how to count." Jonas, however, did not protest the offer of a potential bonus. "I will be back to hound you again if I do not receive that check by the end of the week."

"Please do so," Mr Swarz said, and the warehouse workers left without another word, although Jonas did offer Daisy a goodbye wave. Once they were out the door, Mr Swarz turned his attention to her. "Miss Dell, would you please come into my office for a moment?"

"Of course." She hoped that he had another transcription project for her to work on – anything to keep her from being bored.

There was no notebook out on his desk when he circled around to sit in it, though. It just had its normal, neatly organized supplies, an empty coffee mug, and that odd little phoenix chicken figurine. Daisy stood before his desk and waited for him to assign her whatever task he had.

But he sat there in silence, examining her still with that watchful look. The way his eyes narrowed was almost accusatory, and she began to feel nervous. Had she done something wrong?

Mr Swarz kept his eyes locked on her as he reached out to the coffee mug and smacked it off the desk.

Instinct took control of Daisy. She had so been proud of herself in activating her pendant's inlaid powers to catch that sugar bowl a few days before, but forethought in her actions might have served her better in that moment. Her fingers flew up to the necklace, sending a pulse of her own will into it to unlock its power, and she caught the mug with its magic to levitate just an inch off the ground.

Mr Swarz leaned over his desk to examine the results, and in a rush of panic, Daisy let go of the spell, and the mug tumbled the rest of the distance harmlessly. Mr Swarz hummed and leaned back.

"As I suspected."

Daisy swallowed, creating an echo between her own ears. What did this mean for her? Mr Swarz had known about her magic? While the practice of magic itself wasn't illegal in Ashland – only mana was – the stigma of it was no minor thing, and she could very well lose her job over it. Or worse, if Mr Swarz saw fit to spread this revelation.

But he only tilted his head, his expression still blank except for the slight crease in his brow, as though this were all some theoretical matter under academic debate. "Angel kept telling me that she couldn't feel anything, but I suppose I have always been more keen to sensing it. It's like static, or… or a smell, in its way. No matter." He pulled a key from his pocket and unlocked one of the drawers of his desk, removing from it a small glass vial. At first, Daisy thought it was filled with ink – a layer of thick, congealed blue substance clung to its inside walls, and within that swam liquid of a somewhat fresher color. Mr Swarz held out the bottle to Daisy. "Here. I know it was a little thing, but it can still strain the mind to leave it unreplenished even with the smaller spells."

"I don't need…" Daisy stared down at the vial. *Mana*. Where had Mr Swarz obtained such a thing? And why was he so generous with it? She took a step back, wondering if there was still a chance to weasel out of the situation. "I'm sure I don't know what you're talking about."

The phoenix chicken bobbed as it did when a draft blew through the office, but Daisy was certain the air in the room was still as silence. Mr Swarz glanced over at its movement, too, and reached out to grab it. It continued to wobble in his grip, and he frowned at it before glancing up at Daisy's pendant.

"I believe I understand." He slipped the vial of mana back into the drawer and set the bobbing bird in the dead center of his desk. "I was given this as a gift by a colleague with... common interests. As you can imagine, this particular type of kitsch doesn't really fit my aesthetic tastes. My friend thought I might be more interested in its other properties, though." The bird had stilled, its painted-on eyes with their crooked pupils staring up at Daisy.

"Enchanted objects are rare enough, so I decided not to pass on it due to its questionable appearance." He tapped it on the head, and it bobbed once before settling back into motionlessness. "It detects deception." Daisy recalled it moving about during her interview with Mr Swarz for the job, which had inevitably included a few half-truths on her part. "Useful, to a degree, but I've always been more interested in how such a creation came to be. Artifacts like this do not drain mental energies the way methodic spells do – it would be quite the discovery for the field of magic study."

Daisy swallowed, glancing over her shoulder as she wondered how he could be so open about such things.

He noticed her discomfort. "You don't need to fret, Miss Dell. I am not the only magician employed here."

She turned back to him, eyeing the phoenix chicken. It didn't move. "How did you know? About me?"

"As I said, I could feel the shifts in reality when you used your spells. Your artifacts' spells, I suppose. How many of those do you possess?"

She wasn't interested in explaining herself to him, not with what he had just revealed to her. "Did you know when you hired me? Is this...?" She glanced at the shelves of binders and paperwork behind him. What was the purpose of filling a company with magicians as employees? And what did "document management" even *mean?*

She was going into a panic over this information her boss was imparting to her, but Mr Swarz remained calm where he sat, spreading his hands casually as he answered. "I did not know, no. Some part of me hoped, considering what you told me of your education. A women's college is far more likely to teach a less sanitized version of history, I feel, and you did a successful job of making a first impression as a clever and inquisitive individual. I assumed you would, if nothing else, be the sort of person who did not pass moral judgments on magic and acknowledged its uses and past contributions to society. I'm pleased to find to what degree that proved to be true."

Through all her worry about having herself found out – and her alarm at finding out about Mr Swarz's own dealings with magic – she was struck with indignation. "All due respect, sir, you don't know me or my relationship with magic."

He sat back, looking surprised for the first time all morning. "But you *do* practice magic. And that's really what I was looking for – someone with familiarity of the product and culture aside from mana addicts. I can't tell you what a relief it is to have an actual magician in my employ."

"Mana addicts? Why would...?" Daisy stopped, glancing down at the drawer where Mr Swarz had tucked away the vial. "What does this company *do?*"

Her employer folded his hands on the desk, his shoulders slumping. His calm shifted abruptly to weariness. "I do apologize, Miss Dell. In the past, we've hired trusted acquaintances of those already within the company. You are the first untested hire we've had in my entire time here, and my own boss was reluctant to allow me to try it. The secrecy was necessary until we were sure you could be trusted–"

"And what makes you sure that I can be?" A flicker of rage tore through her. She expected a certain amount of being pushed around as an entry-level employee, but not so much that her employers would lie to her about the very nature of the company she worked for. "What makes you think I won't tell someone about what you're keeping in your desk?"

The threat didn't faze him. "Because I know your secret, too. Furthermore, this entire company is a valued establishment in an industry that has methods for dealing with... breaches to confidentiality. I might go to prison if you tattled, but *your* fate would be worse." He stood, and that rage flashing through her blood turned to a chill. "But, please – I have no desire to ruin our amicable business relationship. I understand that this is all perhaps shocking to you, but I am willing to be open about whatever inquiries you may have."

"Why share your secrets with me?"

Mr Swarz blinked as though the question confused him. "Because I *do* trust you. As menial as the tasks you've been given are, you show an admirable work ethic, and Angel tells me that you handled yourself with a level head and compassion the night of your auto accident. And I should like to learn more of what you know of magic." He pointed to the pendant. "I've studied methodical magic for years, as has Angel and my supervisor, Grey. Jonas is more of a novice, and Vinnie really only knows aural magic. Our company could stand to expand our understanding of the whole spectrum of the art, and your practice is nearly unknown to us. It was my understanding that few, if any, ritual magicians were able to flee to Ashland during or after the war in Noeyen."

His final comment was posed like a question, but she wasn't going to let him derail the conversation into a discussion on recent history. Daisy covered the pendant with her hand in half-aware self-consciousness. "What is this company? What do you really do?" she asked again.

Mr Swarz folded his hands in front of himself, glancing toward the window. The blinds were half-closed and no one could be seen walking in front of the office, but it was clear that Daisy was pushing him to the limits of his comfort zone. He seemed equally aware that Daisy was nearing her own breaking point.

"I understand that this information has put us both in precarious positions. Here is what I propose: if what I've told you here makes you so inclined, you are free to walk away from the company. I am the only one who knows definitely of your practice, to the best of my knowledge, and I will keep what I have learned to myself. I will also never again bother you over the matter of sharing knowledge of our craft between each other. You may wash your hands entirely of this conversation we have just had.

"However, if any of what I have said in regards to your participation in this company interests you, understand that I cannot say more here. Any questions you have will be answered, but it will have to occur elsewhere. Should you be willing to follow me to another location, I will tell you whatever else you wish to know."

Daisy narrowed her eyes at him. "Where?"

"The warehouse."

She recalled the blade hidden in his cane and his purposefully unsubtle threats about "breaches to confidentiality." Alarmed as she was to discover that her place of employment was some kind of front for one of

Ashland society's most despised groups – even if she herself belonged to such a category – a part of her trusted Mr Swarz, too. Enough that she believed him when he promised that she could walk away from the situation unharmed.

But the thing was, she wasn't sure that she wanted to walk away. It wasn't just that she didn't want to lose her job – there was something to gain in all this, too. And it wasn't like a Modern Girl to flee from an opportunity just because it came with a shadow of danger.

"All right, Mr Swarz. Let's go to the warehouse and talk."

He blew a soft huff from his nose and surprised her with a tiny smile. "Very well. Please follow me." She expected him to lead her outside, but instead he went to that locked door in the back corner of the lobby. He removed another key from his pocket and unlocked and opened the narrow portal, revealing a solid darkness beyond. Daisy could only see far enough into the space to spy two steps leading downward, and beyond that it was pure blackness.

"Could you please step inside?" Mr Swarz asked, moving aside to give her room to enter. "Just on the top landing. I will tell you when it's safe to move." Daisy did as she was told, realizing that while Mr Swarz promised her safety if she didn't choose to prod further into the matter of the company's business, he did not make the same guarantee if she *did*. Once she was settled in the spot where he told her to stand, Mr Swarz followed, awkwardly crowding himself onto that same landing. He closed the door behind them, leaving them at the top of the stairs in complete dark.

She heard a series of smacks against a hard, flat surface, and soon a glimmer of light appeared to her left. The snaking strokes of a glowing glyph appeared on the wall, tracing into a geometric pattern of pointed peaks and straight, descending lines. It was about the size of her palm, and the white light it emitted was enough to reveal the next few steps downward. Other glyphs began forming further down the stairway, filling the entire passage with glowing light all the way to another door at the base of the long descent.

"All right, it's safe now." Mr Swarz gestured for Daisy to continue down the stairs. She did so, finding no additional surprises as she walked down. She did glance back at Mr Swarz once to find him rubbing at one of his temples with a gloved hand, his other hand steadied against the wall as he descended, moving slow and deliberate without his cane. He had left his vial of mana in his office, and it seemed that even a spell so simple as turning on a few lights was enough to disorient him a bit. Daisy didn't remark on it – Mr Swarz was a grown man who could take care of himself.

Stopping at the second door, Daisy waited as her employer unlocked it. "This is the warehouse," he said, as he pushed the door open. "Of course, that's mostly a euphemistic misnomer that we use in public."

"So then the 'warehouse' is…?" But Daisy didn't need to finish the question once she stepped into the space.

Mr Swarz hit a button that switched on the room's electric lights along the ceiling. Dark, lacquered floorboards were under her feet, but throughout the wide room were imported carpets laid out under billiard and card tables. There was a low stage just to her left, occupied by a rickety piano and some large string instruments. Along the wall to her right was a polished oak bar lined with empty stools, with a doorway into a dark room beyond. On the far wall was a closed door inlaid with stained glass, but no light emitted from within. The whole place was vacant and silent – a subterranean bar, closed for the morning.

"This way," Mr Swarz said, moving past the stage and to yet another door on the far side of the room. "I want to show you something." She followed, eyeing velvet drapes hung over the wall behind the stage as she passed. Beyond this new door, Mr Swarz led her down a short stone hallway to a dark room, illuminated only by...

She choked down a gasp. Shelves along the wall were filled with glass bottles or in some cases entire gallon jars of faintly glowing blue liquid. From the luminescence, she could see a set of giant, cylindrical vats in the center of the room. Other implements covered tables pushed against the walls of the mysterious chamber.

She stepped into the room, the blue glow bouncing off the folds of her dress and gleaming off the oil and little hairs on her arms. Mr Swarz activated more glyphs in here, brightening the room until every clinical tool and questionable container in the space was clear as crystal. She turned to him, understanding at last what sort of job she had landed for herself.

"You brew mana. Stripes Management is just a front for... *this*."

Mr Swarz nodded. "Yes. We call ourselves a document management firm to explain our expenses for taxes and to third party partners. In actuality, Stripes is a collective operation of magic supplemental productions, including our 'house' here, Pinstripes. We are speakeasy operators, bootleggers, and moonshiners."

"But that's *illegal*." Daisy nearly slapped her hands over her own mouth after blurting out such an obvious observation.

Mr Swarz's brow wrinkled at the pointless accusation. "Correct. That's why the secrecy is so necessary." He turned away from her. "I suppose it is still not too late for you to turn away, if you wished. Of course you understand that were you ever to breathe a word of this to anyone, we would have to take measures to deal with that matter."

Daisy didn't intend to tattle on Stripes regardless of his threats. She had her own hide to keep from getting skinned, which is why she considered – for a just a moment – taking Mr Swarz up on his offer and just walking out on the operation entirely. It would be safer, certainly, to go back to browsing newspaper ads for job listings.

But a Modern Girl was daring, and she wasn't entirely without curiosity to go chasing down some of these rabbit holes.

"You said you wanted to know more about my magic?" She took off the pendant as Mr Swarz turned back to her, holding it out for him to see. "If your little chicken trinket upstairs is anything like this, it doesn't require mana. You should already understand that what I do has nothing to do with your moonshining."

Mr Swarz stepped closer to examine the bronze necklace, reaching out to feel its surface under his gloved fingertips. "It does, though. You must be aware that methodical magic is one of the more widely practiced forms in Ashland – what the fearmongers refer to when they speak of magic in general, as though it were all the same. Our methods come with a price, and our society has learned to recognize this and hamstring us by outlawing the currency we use to pay that price. Your way bypasses all of that. It would be of great interest to the magic community to have not only a loophole in the issue of mana, but one that our society's legal system would not immediately notice given its focus on methodical magic, and therefore would be unable to regulate."

Daisy withdrew her hand, pulling the pendant away from him, awed by his short-sightedness. "You think my magic doesn't have a price, too?"

Mr Swarz recoiled at her quiet admonition, but he quickly collected himself, settling back into his mask of steely professionalism. "Discussions like this are exactly what I would most like to see in a continuing work relationship with you. I believe you and I have much we could teach each other. I will not retaliate if you choose to leave, provided you keep reasonably quiet about what I've revealed to you today, but I must know soon: will you stay on?"

Daisy stalled, meeting his stare as she considered. In school, she had never had many friends, not even in the early years. A part of it was the magic – it was just about then that the mundanes were starting to get up in arms about magicians, and her grandmother warned her to be careful with who she trusted. Aside from Grandma Sparrow, this was the first occasion that Daisy was able to look another in the eye and find a common interest in magic. Money was a worthwhile reward to be gained from a career, but she was young and still carving out her place in the world. An ally she could trust with her secrets might be more valuable than all the dollar bills in Soot City.

She slipped the necklace back on and held out her hand. "Mr Swarz, you have my continued service." The corners of his lips turned up at just the slightest angle, and he took her hand in his.

CHAPTER 4

Northeast Soot City was known sometimes as the Grime District and sometimes the Crime District. Ming Wei, born and raised there, never thought of it as much more than just another neighborhood, but neither description was wholly wrong, either. Built into a corner of the city founded on craggy volcanic outcrops, the dramatic cliff faces and steep hills tended to gather ashfall in a manner that flatter portions of Soot City did not. The city dismissed upkeep of the northeast as a futile and costly effort, so the place was a sooty mess and housing was cheap as a result. That drew in the desperate, and the desperate tended to cultivate less-than-legal habits. Ming had grown up in that life, but it wasn't as though the bigwigs in downtown and northwest were so above it all.

The prim figure of Councilwoman Daphne Linden stood stark in the lamplight of Ming's crowded, dim office in a dilapidated building next door to an abandoned corner market. Linden wore an ironed royal blue suit piece, including a shin-length pencil skirt over dark brown tights. Her dark blonde hair was lightly curled and hung to her shoulders, framing a face of makeup carefully painted to hide the wrinkles of natural age and stress around her eyes and lips. A proper city official, laughably out of place in the slums of the as of yet untouched neighborhoods of the northeast quadrant. Perhaps the bigger joke, though, was that she was far from the first to come through Ming's door. It was quite the regular thing to see politicians with enemies who needed to be dealt with, and Ming had been doing that sort of dealing for years.

It had never been something she intended, not in the beginning. As a teenaged kid, short and stout without being properly muscular, she had been present to witness her brother fall into some trouble with money. He owed to the wrong people, and they sent a debt collector to come calling one day. As far as toughs went, he wasn't much. Ming had taken him down with a cleaver from their kitchen. Her brother, fool that he was, bragged to his friends about his baby sister's ruthless ability, and soon other foolish young men in the neighborhood came to her when they needed help out of money problems or when they wanted to cause those problems to someone else. More powerful clients began noticing her accomplishments, and many recognized the advantages she had over the big, bulky musclemen that most ne'er-do-wells bothered to hire.

She was small, plain, and tomboyish. She didn't dress or conduct herself as women were expected to, which gave everyone around her the sense that they were right to ignore her existence as a fellow human. Insulting, but it was to her benefit when she needed to drive a blade or a bullet into someone.

It was a useful persona, and she cultivated it into what it was now – a woman nearing thirty in a dusty trench coat hiding away in a poorly-lit shack on the Bad End of Town. Just another face in the crowd – hard to see coming, harder to trace once her task was done.

The woman standing before her was a bit less subtle. Ming recognized her name from the newspapers. Councilwoman

Linden had won her seat on a vicious anti-magician platform. Now, re-elections were merely weeks away, and the biggest threat to her seat was some bureaucrat from the city's Office of Education, previously a professor of the hard sciences. While most were not *openly* pro-magic, scientists and engineers were known to have something of a soft spot for the magicians, and this challenging candidate was expected, at the very least, to cater indirectly to magicians by taking a stance of leniency and focusing on "progress," a buzzword magician sympathizers responded well to. It might have been enough to tip the votes in his direction where it would otherwise be rather evenly split between himself and Linden on economy and infrastructure.

Ming would have never expected that Linden's counter-strategy would involve a hired hit, but then Ming never did quite understand the politicians that came crawling through her door. Even more shocking was Linden's requested target, though.

"It doesn't matter who," the councilwoman said. "Just find one, and take them down. Make a show of it. Remind my constituents what they voted me into office to protect them from."

Ming kept silent following the demand. She had built something of a network of fellow slum crawlers over the years, but she didn't know any magicians – none who were open about it with her, at least – or have any idea who to go to if she needed to hunt one down. There was reason to hesitate at the thought of going toe-to-toe with someone who could produce fire and lightning from their mind, however.

"If you're asking for a hit on a magician, that's going to run you a steep fee. I won't put myself at that much risk for pebbles."

"I have the cash, but I can sweeten the pot with

something more valuable." Linden paused, and Ming could see her running mental calculations about how best to pose herself for this apparently delicious reveal. In the end, she decided to just keep standing aloofly, spine erect. "I have a dear friend who works for the Springwell Trust Bank. He's been sharing with me details on properties that the bank has marked as places of interest for commercial development."

It took a second of mental translation for Ming to get what she meant. Her buddy at the bank was trying to cash in on gentrification. "So?"

Linden reached into the pocket of her blazer and removed a folded piece of paper. "Correct me if I'm wrong – is your homestead not in this zoning area?"

Ming sat up straighter as Linden unfolded the paper on her desk. On Springwell Trust Bank letterhead, it listed a number of addresses, though no names of their occupants. Had Linden somehow figured out Ming's home address? Ming was too careful for that, unless Linden had somehow tracked down her brother, Yun. But how could she have even managed that? Maybe she was just bluffing, taking a guess that a hitwoman would live in the Crime District.

Even if Linden were bluffing, Ming did indeed see her address on that bank memo. She did her best to hide any concern. "All due respect, Councilwoman, I'm not telling you a damn thing about my homestead. Especially if you don't intend to get to the point about how this relates to this magician hunt that you want."

Linden took back the memo and folded it up. "Just an observation: anyone living in those addresses who doesn't own their property is likely to soon receive a notice from Springwell Trust that they are buying them out of their leases. A clever renter who wants to preserve their residence would be sure to pay off whatever is left of their lease before the bank finds a corporation willing to pay them more for the land."

Ming's house had been in her family since her grandmother had "bought" it over fifty years ago, when Ashland was only a few years into being a codified nation and banks were buying up land to lend out as rent-to-own deals. Neither Grandma An nor her daughter nor Ming could afford to make big payments on the lease every month, so the property was still not entirely paid off even three generations in, but Ming was close. She had been thinking she could get it all paid up by the time she was in her mid-thirties, but if corporations began waving their cash at the bank before then, Ming wouldn't have that time. She would still receive compensation from the bank for whatever was left on the lease, of course, but that was little enough now, and she would lose the house she had lived in her entire life.

Still, she couldn't show Linden that she had successfully stoked fear in her. "I'm sure they would. But we were talking about how much *you* would be willing to pay for a magician's head."

Linden offered a number, and Ming scrambled to remember how much was left on her lease. Even before she could recall, she asked for more. By the time Linden came up with a second offer, Ming remembered how much she needed and rounded up to account for the cost of the job itself. She asked for more again. They went back and forth with negotiations until Ming agreed to a price, not bothering with her usual shtick in such conversations of pretending like she was giving the client a great deal – Linden was too slimy to fall for that.

"Very well, Councilwoman, you got it. I'll need half payment upfront."

Linden nodded stiffly. "Of course. My assistant will deliver it tomorrow. And I expect your discretion in this matter, Roxana."

Linden was probably clever enough to understand that the name Ming operated under was nothing more than a *nom de plume*. If she didn't have Ming's real name, Ming could probably expect that she didn't have her exact address, either, but the possibility still left Ming feeling like ants crawled under her skin. "I wouldn't still be alive if I was in the habit of tattling on my clients, never mind still in business. Silence comes part and parcel with my services."

Linden grinned, and it was a chilling sight to behold. It was one thing for people like Ming, doing what they had to in order to get by. A crow sometimes has to steal a bit of meat from another animal's kill, but people like Linden – like most of Ming's clientele these days – were more like eagles up in their aeries, killing not to eat but to keep the other birds too weak and starved to try crowding into the nest. If Ming had the luxury of a moral code, she would have exposed every politician that had ever come through her door. As it was, like most people in the slums, her primary concern was putting food in her pantry and keeping a roof over her head, and these were the people with the money.

"I'm glad to hear it. Don't bother to contact me once the job is complete – if you did it right, I'll be seeing it all over the papers." Ming nodded, and with that, their meeting was over. Councilwoman Linden was out the door, leaving Ming in her shadows to plan how, exactly, to catch a magician.

"I am just absolutely *thrilled*."

Daisy shifted in the back seat of Frisk's car, squeezed between Angel and Rudolph as the former heaped compliments and exclamations of excitement onto her. Driving was Frisk, who kept glancing in the rearview mirror at her, and Amelia ignored her entirely from the passenger's seat.

"Bet Swarz is stoked, too," Frisk said as she steered them toward their destination, a sister establishment to their own speakeasy on the southwest side of town called Walter's. "Seems awfully sick of trash like me and Vicks hanging around. I know he hates mana freaks – thinks we waste the stuff."

They were, of course, talking about Daisy's magic, which had become common knowledge around the office since her talk with Mr Swarz a few days ago. She hadn't seen any of the warehouse folks since then, so she had decided to take Angel up on her offer for another night out. It was somewhere more daring this time, and Daisy hoped that without all her guards up to hide her magic, she might make a better impression on Frisk and her friends.

As excited as Angel and even Frisk were, Rudolph and Amelia both sulked while their girlfriends chattered with – or at – Daisy. She was fairly certain that neither of them did magic, and they both seemed a bit put-out by conversation. Maybe it made them feel that they owed some of their favorable standing at the company to their lovers' good graces. Not a comfortable mindset to be in, Daisy was sure, but she didn't know how to help either of them. She could barely even keep up with Angel's questions.

"Now, you said that your grandmother gave you these artifacts. How many did you say you have?"

"Twenty altogether. Some more useful than others."

"And to activate them, you – and do correct me if I'm getting this wrong – you apply your will to *pull* the innate magic out of them, rather than apply will to push the magic out of yourself as it is with methodical magic? That's why you don't need to replenish your mental energies with mana, yes?"

Daisy shrugged, hoping it came off more as ignorant than uncomfortable. "Maybe. You might be better off asking Mr Swarz that."

Amelia glanced back at them. Her eyes narrowed into a glare for just a moment, clearly irritated with all the talk of magic, but it faded as she looked to Angel. "Hey, Angel, how come Mr Swarz doesn't ever come party with us?"

Angel waved a hand, covered in a pristine white glove. "Oh, you know him. He's just a grouch." Even joking about Mr Swarz wasn't enough to distract Angel from her interest in Daisy's abilities, though. "So, tell me more about these artifacts. Can you explain to me what some of them do?" Angel didn't notice it, but Amelia huffed and faced forward again when the older woman reverted her attention.

Before Frisk had come by Daisy's apartment to pick her up, Daisy had decked herself in a short, pale gold dress decorated on the breast with white beads; white flats; and a charm bracelet. Five of the twenty trinkets she had mentioned to Angel were attached to that bracelet. She held out her wrist to Angel and poked at one charm, shaped like the silhouette of a dove in flight. "All right, so this one creates a nexus of silence – it muffles sound down to nothing for about a seven-yard radius. This one–" She tapped a simple, round nickel dangling near the bird. "–creates a pressure blast. It's one of my more powerful ones; it can move a bit over a ton."

Angel's blue eyes glimmered with a hungry sheen as she examined the trinkets. "Astonishing! And where did your grandmother *get* these? Did she make them?"

Daisy refrained from pulling her arm away on instinct as her blood chilled at the question. Before she could make any reply, every passenger in the car was flung forward, straining against their seatbelts, as Frisk put her foot a bit too heavy on the brake. "Here we are: Walter's." She put the car into park and glanced over her shoulder at Angel. "We won't be here long. Just gotta pick up Gina, then we'll head to the Gin Fountain."

"We aren't staying here?" Daisy asked as they began piling out of the car.

"Nah. Walter's is a drag. We just got some business relations here, is all. Gina's friends with their cellist. They used to play together at the temple they went to as kids. She wanted to visit him before the night got going, not that Walter's ever *gets* going."

"Plenty of time to stop in and say hi to our friends across town," Angel said, linking her arm with Rudolph's as their group followed Frisk from the curbside where she parked down a poorly-lit street in a neighborhood filled mostly with cafes closed for the night. Daisy knew the area – it was several blocks from her apartment, between that and the Catherine Eleanor Ruthell Women's College where she had studied. It was a bit of walk from home, so she didn't frequent it often, but they passed by a deli that was shuttered up for the evening where she had eaten before. Walter's was a run-down bar snugly fit between a second-hand book store and a vacant brick building. "The Gin Fountain is only two streets over, too. We won't need to cram all six of us into the car."

"Not until the drive home," Rudolph joked, looking a bit merrier already without Daisy between him and his lady. Daisy thought back to Mr Swarz's warnings about the two of them, but she didn't take it seriously. Angel was flirtatious, certainly, but there was a particular delicacy she applied to it, as though she were afraid of chasing Daisy off. For her own part, Daisy wasn't much interested in any entanglements with Angel and definitely not Rudolph, who likewise seemed uninterested in her. She suspected that unless she actively responded to Angel's attentions, the older woman wouldn't press the matter.

The interior of Walter's was nearly as shabby as its façade, but there was a sort of pleasantness to the dim lights and smoky air. It was cozier than Pinstripes, but, as Frisk and Angel predicted, it was a sort of quiet affair. A burly bouncer nodded them in when he recognized Frisk and Angel, and he otherwise paid them no mind. A band was set up on a small stage, but rather than playing, they chatted with a woman standing up there with them. The woman faced away from the front door, but judging from her bushy black hair, Daisy assumed that was Regina. A few other patrons milled about or lounged at tables with drinks, some of which glowed with a faint blue hint of mana. At the bar, a lanky woman wiped down the oak surface while lazily watching her customers. A short, dark-haired woman in a long coat sat before her, drinking in silence while staring into the pages of a battered paperback novel.

"I've got to give the bartender my greetings – professional courtesy and all," Angel said to Daisy. "Why don't you go with the girls to chatter with the band? I'm sure they'll be more sociable."

Daisy agreed, and together with Frisk and Amelia, she went to the base of the stage. Regina turned away from the three men sitting with their instruments as her coworkers approached. "Hey, Frisk. Lia." She squinted at Daisy, apparently unable to remember her name, but she made an effort to appear polite. "It's good to see you again. How have things been upstairs?"

"Fine, Regina. How are you?" There was a brief exchange of pleasantries – a few hellos and introductions to Regina's musician friends, whose names Daisy forgot almost immediately. They then spent a while joking about Regina leaving the Stripes to play the piano at Walter's, or for the Walter's boys to quit to join the Stripes, before Angel and Rudolph came back over.

"It would be rude to leave so soon," Angel said, "so would anyone like to join us for a few rounds of cards?"

Frisk pursed her lips and leaned against Amelia, clearly bored of Walter's atmosphere already. "All right, but nothing too long. If I don't get to a more electric scene soon, I'm gonna fall asleep."

"We can play War," Amelia said, running the back of a finger along Frisk's cheek. "That'll keep you alert."

Daisy laughed. "That's one of those slapping games, isn't it? I haven't played that sort of thing since elementary school."

"Yeah, not the kind of game for proper ladies," Frisk said with a wink. "Exactly my favorite kind." Angel looked less enthused, but she agreed to their proposal of a more physically aggressive sort of card game. While Regina settled at the piano to play a few sets with her friends in the band, the others found a table to play with a pack of cards Frisk withdrew from her purse.

The game started out a bit slow, with Daisy and Rudolph needing a few rounds to remember how to play and Angel being too delicate to stand any chance at winning. Frisk and Amelia weren't afraid to smack everyone else's hands each time a tie was laid, and as Daisy and Rudolph began to hold their own, the game got more noisily under way, earning them an annoyed glance from the woman drinking at the bar. Daisy thought that the woman was familiar – she had seen a woman in a trench coat just like that recently, she was sure – but her attention was drawn back to the game as Rudolph and Amelia both threw down threes. She slapped her hand down on the cards as quick as she could, beating Frisk by a millisecond and earning the scrape of nails on the back of her wrist in exchange for her victory. Daisy hissed as she pulled her hand back, taking the cards with it.

"Sorry 'bout that," Frisk said, sounding more amused than apologetic. Daisy slipped her charm bracelet down her forearm a bit to examine the scratches. The skin wasn't broken, and her dark arm was now decorated with three thin, white lines.

"It should be fine," she said, shaking her arm until the bracelet fell back to hang naturally against the bones of her wrist, and they continued with their game. After about an hour, Frisk wound up with the biggest stack of cards – and Angel having her stack nearly depleted – just as Regina and her friends finished up a set. By then, Frisk was nearly bouncing in her seat to move on to a more exciting venue, and Daisy was inclined to agree. Thrilling as their game was, she would have preferred entertainment that was less likely to leave her with scars.

After Angel went to bid the bartender farewell, promising to give her regards to Mr Swarz, their group shuffled out together into the night, Regina in tow. Frisk again led the way, nearly skipping as she guided them to their next destination. The cool evening air made Daisy want to take her time with the walk, though. It was a clearer night than it had been in weeks, and she wanted to enjoy how well the outing was going, lest she make a disaster of it again.

Ming waited for nearly half an hour before getting up from her stool and wandering over to the table where a loud group had played their cards. One of her bruisers had been useful in suggesting where she might at least begin sniffing out magicians, pointing her to this low-key speakeasy, unlikely to attract the attention of law enforcement for how quiet it was. Unfortunately, aside from a few half-present mana addicts and a handful of people who appeared to treat the establishment just like a normal bar, few people appeared to be drawn to such an atmosphere.

Ming had also discovered that she had no notion of what a magician looked like short of images forwarded by Soot City's population of pearl-clutchers. Those straw-magicians were foppish while still dressed in battered rags, wearing crooked and sinister grins and typically gaudy hats, but Ming wasn't going to trust conservative propaganda on that matter. She assumed real magicians looked just like anyone else. How could she identify one from a distance? That noisy group from earlier had drawn her attention, but they appeared little more than a gaggle of ditzy young people. The boys in the band or the bartender herself were just as likely candidates.

She paused at the table, noticing a glint on the floor. She almost dismissed it as loose change, but when she knelt she could see through the shadows that it wasn't round. Reaching out, she traced its outline with a single fingertip before picking it up and standing to get better light. It was a small, metal – maybe silver – silhouette of a bird with a steel ring looped through a hole punched through the top of its body. The point where the two ends of the little ring connected had gaped a bit too wide, allowing the bauble to drop from wherever it had previously hung. Just some lost piece of jewelry, but she was desperate for a lead.

Ming would have initially dismissed those fops as mana addicts. Most of those women, and even the man, were fairly scrawny in the manner that was symptomatic of emaciating mana addiction. The pale one with curly dark hair had certainly had the gaunt face of a body ravaged by the effects of the liquid. Ming herself had never tried mana, but she knew how it worked – bodies that didn't need to replenish energies wasted by magic were overwhelmed by the effect of mana, creating an over-energetic high that put the metabolism into overdrive. Addicts tended to be skinny and twitchy after long-term use of the drug, but a magician would not be so affected.

Any member of that group could have been an addict, with the probable exception of the big woman in white.

Further, she had been rather overdressed for a casual hole-in-the-wall type establishment such as Walter's. She had overheard them talking about some gin place – there was a bar called the Gin Fountain in that neighborhood, wasn't there? Some place too ritzy for Ming to patronize and exactly suited for a gaggle of pretty dames in flashy dresses. Could that be another mana speakeasy?

It might have been nothing, but...

Ming found a dark-stained glass left unattended by some lone patron who had stumbled off to the bathroom. Still pooled at the base of the glass was a bit of luminescent blue liquid, already beginning to congeal, as mana did when left exposed to open air for too long. She set the bird charm on the tabletop where the glass rested, taking the cup and tilting it until a drop of cerulean rolled from the bottom to the lip, dripping out and landing on the charm. Ming wasn't sure what she expected to happen, but the mana sizzled as it settled onto the silver, bubbling as it was absorbed into the charm.

That appeared to indicate *something*, certainly.

She snatched up the charm and pocketed it before any of the sleepy patrons of Walter's noticed the odd reaction. The night was still young, and the group might not have been so far ahead of her that she couldn't still track them. She didn't know which of its members had dropped the charm, assuming it hadn't been left there by an earlier visitor, or how many among them might be magicians. It could be nothing, but it was worth checking into, and she would want backup.

Returning to the counter, she waved down the bartender. "Might I be able to use your phone?"

Not long after, Ming waited three alleys up from the Gin Fountain, lurking just beyond the circumference of a pool of lamplight above the intersection of Wight and Kellerton. Ming didn't know the west side of town well, but she must have been near the universities if the city had installed electric lamps here. She saw Jase's car wheel on by, and she followed at an easy pace to where he parked one more block down. He was already opening the back trunk when she joined him.

"Clubbing, eh Roxy?" He didn't need to turn to face her as she approached.

"Not tonight, Jase."

"Not ever." He glanced over his shoulder. He didn't smile or cock an eyebrow like some dandy – his mug was too ugly for that kind of casual charm, all pores and pink blemishes. His voice was too gravelly and flat to carry any kind of joviality, either. He just didn't have much going for him by way of likeability, but he was one of Ming's favorite cohorts. "When's the last time you took a day off?"

"Stayed home from school once when I was nine. Had the flu."

"Ah. So, this isn't a date?"

Ming didn't smile, either. She and Jase had that kind of dynamic – playful, but rigidly hidden under steely sullenness. That was how she liked to think of it, at least. Maybe Jase really didn't enjoy her company, but that wouldn't explain his dependability any time she came calling on him.

She joined him at the open trunk. The street where he parked was full of cafes and delis closed for the night, but even if the dead neighborhood did have a spare drunk or two staggering by, she and Jase together blocked any outsider's view of the car's contents.

"I think I got the scent on a decent target for this business for Daphne." She had clued him in to the fact that they were on a headhunt when they spoke on the phone, but now she gave him a quick rundown of her deal with the councilwoman, keeping to bare details. Ming tried not to use last names or titles on the field for the sake of her clients' privacy, lest anyone overhear that she was running hits for council members.

Jase was the sort to read the morning paper, though. He knew which Daphne would be involving herself in this ugliness. "Right – brought a middling stash. What I could grab from the shed on short notice." He flipped up the corner of a felt blanket covering his gear. In the dark street, Ming could only see vague glints off of silver and black metal.

"Any reverb canons?"

"You gave me an hour, Roxana, and not a lot of info on *who* this target is. The hell kind of riot you trying to start, anyway?"

Ming wasn't entirely sure. She needed to keep track of the group that had dropped the charm, and she had little idea of how to safely capture a magician. She had acted quickly – and, she now realized, rashly – in calling for backup. Of all things, Jase's incredulity cleared her mind.

"You're right – that's overkill. I'm trailing a pack of girls and some fop with them, the ones who dropped the odd charm I mentioned on the phone. I suspect at least a few in this group might be mages. It might be best to try to lure one of this group away. The one who mostly likely dropped the charm, if we can."

"You'll have to be the one applying your seductive powers, then. Mine are on the fritz." Again, no smile. "I brought stingers, though. A bit more *precise* than a reverb canon, you know?"

"What kind of stingers?"

Jase shrugged, glancing over his shoulder before tugging back the blanket further to better reveal the mid-length black barrels. "Got a couple different types – mostly non-lethal, except a few poisoned ones. Bit slow-acting, though."

Ming shook her head. "No, it needs to be quick. If we can't make a scene out of it, we need to remove our target from the area and dump their body somewhere noticeable when we're done with it. It has to be a spectacle – no tottering off to die in a hospital bed seven hours after the fact."

"You always were artistic." Ming wondered if Jase's gut felt as twisted as hers in this conversation. Of course, Ming had been doing this work for years, and, yes, sometimes it came down to some cold tasks. Usually it was blackmailers, though – or abusive husbands, rival drug lords, the seedling members of fascist cells, that sort of thing. Ming didn't really believe that some people deserved to die, but damn if she was going to cry at any of their funerals.

But a pack of pretty young women minding their own business on a bar hop? Seemed innocuous, no matter what Franklin Blain acolytes might say about the bareness of their arms or the harshness of their language. And all for some slimy council member's personal gain.

Still, Ming was glad she'd never had to work as a waitress or a factory grunt.

"Can we snipe the person we need with one of these stingers?"

"That's what they're for. Those little darts don't fly well, though, so you need a steady aim and a clear shot." Jase frowned at her. "Who is this person?"

Ming shrugged, wishing she had a real answer. "I just need any magician. You know that's not my usual crowd, and this little bauble that eats mana is the only clue I have to go on."

Jase grimaced. "This is some fire you're playing with, Roxy."

"Not any worse than some of the drug runners I've dealt with before," she said, but she wasn't sure if that was true. This was all new territory for her.

"Well," Jase said, grabbing the stinger rifle and handing it to Ming, "you got me for backup. It ain't nothing, right?" Ming only nodded at him. She wouldn't have entrusted any other person to watch her back in this, but she couldn't bring herself to tell Jase how much she appreciated his help. He politely accepted her nod as thanks enough. "So, lethal stingers, or what?"

Ming pretended to consider for a moment. "Non-lethal. That way, if I hit a mundane by accident, the aftermath will be cleaner." If he could tell that her reasoning was bullshit, he didn't indicate so. He only wordlessly handed her a box of stingers.

"That'll paralyze them quick. We can drag off the target once it takes effect and you can do... whatever it is you need to do." For himself, he grabbed a long-barreled handgun. "For safety."

"I need you to be particularly trigger *unhappy* tonight," Ming reminded him all the same, and he rolled his eyes as he shut the trunk door.

"Right, right. Can't go off too quickly on my lady. I've heard that one before." He nodded in the direction of the Gin Fountain, as though he hadn't made a joke at all. "Let's get going before we lose 'em."

The Gin Fountain was a bit closer to the universities, hopping with life from students and working class locals. The atmosphere was livelier than Walter's in both company and decorum. Polished floorboards had been stained nearly white, and crystal chandeliers dangled from the ceiling, spreading light that covered every surface of the soft yellow walls. A brass band played in the far corner, and well-dressed young folks crowded the bars and the card tables. Daisy noticed that, unlike the Stripes' establishment, there was no billiards table.

"Is it all right that we're visiting competitors?" Daisy nearly had to holler at Angel over the noise.

Angel chuckled and waved her hand. "There's no competition in the speakeasy business. We watch out for each others' interests. Otherwise, we'd all go down. Most establishments have their own strength that appeals to certain interests. Walter's is a more cozy venue, and the Gin Fountain is more ecstatic. Our own Pinstripes is designed for a more intellectual and academic crowd – people like myself and Andre, who go to meet like-minded magicians. Besides, very few speakeasies do more than operate the venue. Stripes is relatively unique in managing both a club and brewery. And where do you suppose places like this get their own?" She gestured toward the bar, where a bartender was making a show of mixing mana with whiskey for a gaggle of college-aged girls dressed much like Daisy.

"It's other suppliers that are more likely to give us trouble, though with all the legislation in recent years many in-city moonshiners without the right connections got busted down. We've got enough friends in the magic community to keep ourselves covered, and that only leaves a few other suppliers within city limits and the rubes out in the country to contend against."

Although Daisy had been mostly joking, it was reassuring to hear. Once Angel finished her explanation, she steered the group toward a large table to settle into, but Frisk and Amelia were soon gone dancing, and Regina pulled Daisy after them.

The night passed much better than her first outing with her coworkers. Regina wasn't talkative, but she was polite to Daisy and thoughtful enough to include her when Frisk and Amelia were too excited or too absorbed in each other. The four of them moved from the dance floor to the bar to the card tables. While they drank and played cards – a gentle game of blackjack this time, joined by a trio of handsome young men from one of the local colleges – Frisk started chatting with Daisy, asking many of the same questions that Angel had on their first night out. As Daisy talked about her education and her family and a bit more about her magic, even Amelia began to warm up to her, laughing along with Daisy's funny stories about growing up or awkward dates she had gone on during college. Angel and Rudolph joined them after a while, and after another hour of blackjack, their group divided again to dance some more.

The second time on the dance floor, she and Regina split from each other to seek out new dance partners. Daisy hadn't brought her bronze wristband and had not touched any mana – unlike Frisk and Regina, who were as energized as children after several spoonfuls of sugar – but the vibrancy of the club kept her feeling awake even after nearly two hours of shifting from partner to partner. She was serendipitously near Frisk when she felt exhaustion begin to settle into her muscles and spread an ache down her legs and to her feet. "There a place to rest my feet for a bit?"

Frisk turned away from her current dance partner, a slightly older man in a gaudy powder blue suit. "You mean like a footstool? Yeah, I'll show you." She gracelessly disengaged from the man she had been dancing with to take Daisy's arm and pull her off the dance floor to an opening on the back wall. Beyond it was a staircase leading into a dim hallway above. Daisy groaned as Frisk dragged her up the steps, but the sound of the band drowned out her wordless complaints.

Frisk led her to a half-circle balcony that looked out over the dance floor. People already occupied the couple of plush armchairs set out in the balcony, and several more leaned against the rail to peer below. Everyone here was dressed in nicely tailored suits or longer, shimmering dresses – wealthy students attending local colleges on their families' fortunes, Daisy figured. Or maybe young-looking businesspeople hoping to awe impressionable young night owls. Either way, not her crowd.

Daisy scanned the dance hall from her vantage, spying similar balconies lining the north and west walls. She nodded to one that was less densely occupied. "There, maybe?" Frisk nodded and they moved to the next balcony over, which was occupied by quiet drunks who all looked like they were waiting for sober friends to come pick them up. There was one armchair available, and Daisy settled in its wide seat while Frisk perched on the arm.

"Having fun?"

"And how." Daisy tried to keep the wheeze out of her voice, but she had been going full-speed on that floor. "I just need to catch my breath."

"You're gonna be useless tomorrow. And not even drunk like these sorry bastards."

"Don't let me keep you," Daisy said. No one around her was talkative or even glancing in her direction – she didn't expect anyone to give her trouble. "I can catch up once I've been off my feet for a bit."

"If you say so. Rest easy, Old Lady Dell," Frisk said, giving Daisy a gentle shove on the arm before standing and heading off. Once she had gone, Daisy closed her eyes and took a moment to enjoy the music dancing up from the band just below the balcony.

The bouncer watching the door of the Gin Fountain gave Ming and Jase crooked looks as they entered, perhaps suspicious of their large coats. Ming had wanted to try to enter through a back way, but Jase had insisted that would draw more attention than wearing unsightly clothing and literally just packing in weapons. "They never actually check for that kind of thing," he assured her, and apparently they did not. Still, Ming could already feel herself sweating down her back as they stepped into the dance hall.

Jase scanned the scene as they walked a circuit around the edge of the floor, eyeing perhaps a bit too obviously across the crowd. Of course, he had only Ming's descriptions of the group she had seen. Ming was more careful not to move her head too much as she shifted her gaze from dancer to dancer. She had not yet seen anyone she recognized when she felt Jase tap her on the shoulder.

"Those balconies can give us a better view," he said, leaving unsaid the fact that they needed a position from which to shoot, as well. She led them to the far side of the cavernous dance hall where a stairwell led up to a hallway connecting the numerous second floor balconies. The nearest ones to the stairs were busiest, so she led them to the very furthest one along the west wall, which was occupied by only one amorous couple passionately kissing in one of the chairs.

Ming interrupted them by delivering a swift kick to the chair's leg, sliding the entire thing a half-foot forward. "Hey!" the young woman in the couple said, as they both scrambled to their feet.

"Beat it," Ming said, and the young woman's beau sneered at her.

"We're not just going to move out for you. We were here first!"

Ming ignored his whining, looking instead to the woman. "You noticed those pocks on his chin? Your fella's got something sickly. That stuff spreads skin-to-skin, you know."

The woman glanced at her partner, jumping a bit as though she had never seen the marks on his face before. The man lifted his hand subconsciously to cover his chin.

"Those are acne scars," he said, too embarrassed to put any conviction in his voice.

The woman glanced back at Ming and then again to her man before saying limply, "I gotta hit the ladies room, actually. I'll catch up with you." She didn't sound like she meant it, and strode off without her partner. He glared at Ming once before following behind.

"Good thinking," Jase said when they were gone, and he and Ming got to work setting up. Jase closed the curtains of the balcony entry while Ming arranged the chairs and the single end table to block herself from view from below or the other balconies as much as possible.

"Hey, that one of your targets?" Ming looked up from her task to follow Jase's line of sight to another balcony on the north wall. The dark-skinned girl from that group sat alone in a chair there, seemingly resting. Everyone around her appeared to be blackout drunk or teetering on the verge of such a state.

"Yes." It was a damn fine shot – none of the surrounding people were in the way or moving about, meaning Ming could take her time with the aim and not worry about hitting some random mana addict – assuming this woman was not one herself, but although she was small, her cheeks and limbs still had a gentle roundness that was an absent characteristic on mana addicts. And if she was neither an addict nor a mage, why else would she be here?

Ming still couldn't be completely certain who in that group was a magician, but she wasn't going to get a better shot than this.

She pulled the large stinger gun from under her coat, fishing around in her pockets for the darts. "Cover me. Once I get a hit on her, be ready to go grab her. Everyone else there looks too besotted to care if someone just comes and sweeps a young woman away."

"People are more inclined to care when it happens to pretty young women," Jase warned.

"I suppose I wouldn't know."

"Ming." She glanced back at his uncommon use of her actual name. He was frowning again, but it looked strangely sincere for him. "You know I hate it when you get down on yourself like that." His eyes shifted back toward their target. "Uh-oh."

Ming looked back, too. One of the woman's friends had come to join her, the bony pale woman with straight hair who had been with her at Walter's. She came around the chair to speak with her resting friend, not blocking Ming's shot but creating a severe obstacle.

"Shit."

"She's not in your line of sight," Jase said.

"The drunks are one thing, but how I am supposed to take out a magician if one of their friends is hovering nearby to notice?" Ming realized as she spoke that it was a question she should have asked herself to start with. She had known they were travelling in a group.

"Still better than if she was in the crowd, right?"

Ming took a deep breath and loaded up a dart. He was right. It was as good as shot as she was going to get. When she readied her gun, a glint of light reflected off the crystal chandeliers hanging above bounced off the dark, polished barrel. None of the dancers or drunks noticed it, but Ming's target caught the flicker of light.

The young woman stood abruptly, speaking frantically to her friend and pointing directly at Ming. Although Ming was crouched behind a makeshift wall of furniture, her weapon and unusual posture would still be visible. The furniture blockade was undoubtedly suspicious, as well.

"Shit," Ming said again. She should have known she was too out in the open to pull this off. Just as she lowered the gun and tried to hide it under her coat again, readying herself to flee, there was a thunderous crack from a pistol.

Ming looked up at Jase, catching a whiff of gunpowder off him like it was his cologne. "What did I tell you?" she snapped, not sure if he could even hear her over the shouts that broke out in the balcony and down below.

Jase grimaced and pocketed his gun, bending to grab Ming by the elbow and haul her up. "She was pointing at us, some kind of... You said she was a magician!"

"I said *maybe*." Ming didn't fight as Jase pulled her away from the balcony and back into the hallway. If that woman was a magician, she did not send any magic after them as they proceeded to flee. "We need to hide."

"We need to *run*."

"Then shed your coat."

"We need to keep the guns hidden." Jase's legs were long and powered him (and Ming in tow) quickly down the hall as panic began worming its way through the establishment, as evidenced by increasingly high-pitched murmurs that Ming could hear all around. One brazen young man stepped out from a nearby balcony, hailing them as they ran by.

"What's going on?" he asked, as though they were any other normal night owls.

Ming's wits finally caught up with her. "Hooligans. Some kind of fight."

"Duel got outta hand," Jase added, even slowing as they neared the questioning man. "Better stay back." The man nodded along appreciatively, turning to his friends on the balcony.

"Some kind of fight broke out. We'd better relocate."

One of his even more brazen friends stepped forward, his chest stuck out boastfully. "I can go break them up. Where were–" But another gunshot fired, and rambunctious shouting erupted from the dance floor. Jase resumed his flight at that point, and he hardly needed to pull Ming along.

The lie had been enough to get them back onto the ground floor, where new chaos had overtaken the crowd. The panic from the first shot seemed to have started a number of conflicts on the ground, and Ming saw several dancers now trying to wrestle away a pistol from a young man while onlookers either fled, jeered, or began jostling those around them to start new conflicts. That would be enough to cover Ming and Jase as they fled the scene, she assumed, but they were out one magician.

She would have to think of something else, but nothing came to mind as she and Jase slunk toward the nearest exit, unnoticed by the brawlers on the dance floor.

Daisy clung to Frisk, trying to keep her upright.

"What was... Are you hurt?"

Frisk hissed and clutched at her side. "Ah, fuck..." Daisy shook in her efforts to keep Frisk on her feet, and not just from the weight of another human body. Blood smeared all over Frisk's bone-white fingers. Someone – one of those lurkers in the balcony across the way – had shot her.

"We need... we need to get downstairs. We need to find the others!" Daisy had to shout to be heard over the growing panic that swept up the club. Was there another gunshot? Were there other gunners? Or was everyone getting worked up into a frenzy over a single attacker? But why would anyone shoot Frisk?

Daisy had seen the one shooter crouched behind a wall of furniture, though. She had been aiming at Daisy. That made as little sense, but somehow she was sure of it.

Frisk's expression twisted in agony. "You... you got a trinket that might–?" She broke off with another hiss, trying to fold in double on herself. Daisy pried her as upright as she could manage before slipping her arm free of Frisk to look at her charm bracelet, wondering if any might have a useful effect. She noticed that one, the dove charm, was gone. Caught in a moment of confusion – it must have been torn loose when Frisk scratched her arm during War – she abandoned the notion of trinkets entirely and grabbed Frisk around the shoulders. "Can you make it downstairs?"

Frisk scowled. "Fuck, Dell." It wasn't a no, Daisy supposed.

To the best of their abilities, Daisy and Frisk hobbled to the stairs, pushing past frantic club-goers who were frenzied either in search of a fight or from being jolted out of a drunken stupor. No one stopped long enough to even ask after Frisk's condition or to assist. Frisk managed the journey to the ground floor with much wincing and few complaints, though.

On the edge of the dance floor, Daisy could see Angel facing down an aggravated youth with Rudolph and Regina hiding an arm's reach behind her. Amelia was closer to Angel, just behind her and shouting something at the man facing them. All around, the entire place had devolved into a tavern brawl, except the magic scene seemed a bit more skittish than typical barflies. Daisy could hear people bandying about accusations of being plants or spies for the cops – the man shouting down Daisy's friends was making a similar claim, and the insinuations of his claims must have been nasty indeed to get Amelia so worked up.

It might have been amusing if Daisy weren't so keenly aware of a number of armed club-goers, many now brandishing their weapons to defend against the mysterious shooter who had hit Frisk. The man facing Angel was one such individual, although he was not so reckless as to actually fire at anyone. Not yet.

They didn't have time to wait around for things to get even hairier. Daisy called out to them. "Angel! Amelia!"

Amelia whipped her head toward them at the sound

of her name, and the man took poorly to their shouting match being interrupted. Wild in the eyes – maybe from mana, maybe only adrenaline – he hollered a rapid string of further accusations of espionage and ratting to the coppers before lifting his gun. Regina screamed in terror, and before Daisy could think to do the same, Frisk gathered up what little strength she had to yank Daisy away toward the stage, closer to the armed man but out of his range of vision.

When Daisy gathered her wits, she saw there was a shimmer in the air around her friends, and the bullet fired at them hung suspended in the air in front of Angel's outstretched hand.

Daisy's breath caught – as much magic as she did herself, she had never actually *seen* methodical magic utilized in such a defensive manner. As the bullet floated in place, it began breaking into pieces, little shards and slivers of lead splitting and drifting to form a metal cloud. The man who had fired watched with a stricken, slack-mouthed expression. While he was distracted, Angel pushed Amelia back toward Rudolph and turned to lead them in flight toward the Gin Fountain's back exit. Daisy was about to take ahold of Frisk to chase after the four of them, but there was another bang of a gun, and Frisk cried out and stumbled into her.

"Frisk!"

"I wasn't... I'm fine. Just spooked me." She gasped against her pain, and the sound came out like a bark. "Bunch of dummies with guns getting worked up into a panic. Nothing worse."

"You've already been shot enough. Let's get you out of here before this gets any more chaotic."

With the crowd rushing toward the back of the club, Daisy didn't think there was any hope of them sneaking out that way. Looking toward the front door, she couldn't see anyone with weapons near it.

"Come on!" Daisy kept one arm firm around Frisk's shoulders and hurried her forward. There were shouts as they scurried toward the front door, but Daisy couldn't tell what they were saying or if they were directed at her.

"The others," Frisk wheezed, hand still on her wound and wincing with every step. "They went–"

"I know, I know. We'll have to catch up to them later." They reached the door, along with a few other straggling club-goers who had also been too late to beat the crowd rushing any possible back exits. Outside, a few of such escapees gathered to check each other and ramble in a panic about whether or not to call the police.

"We'll get busted – all of us!" Daisy overheard one young woman say.

"There were gunshots and spells being fired – someone might have died in there," one of her companions argued, but Daisy didn't linger to listen in. She kept running with Frisk limping quickly at her side. The only destination she could think to reach was the car.

"Do you have your keys?" Daisy asked. Frisk's purse had been with Amelia's, but she nodded.

"Yeah, in my pocket." She gasped as she staggered onward, but Daisy pushed them to keep going until they reached the car. While Frisk leaned against the door, Daisy dug in the pocket of her skirt to fish out the key, but she hesitated once she pulled it out. Frisk was bleeding more than just a trickle, and her already pasty face was growing ashen, her eyes unfocused. She was in no condition to drive.

"There's an oil rag in the glove compartment," Frisk said, shifting aside and curling in on herself in an effort to curb the blood flow. "It's mostly clean. Grab it." Daisy did as she was told, but just as she pressed the rag to Frisk's wound, there was another bang at the nearest corner, and a flush of green smoke flooded from the connecting street. A magician acting in self-defense, she assumed, or another pugnacious one instigating more trouble for everyone. Regardless, she didn't much like the sight of the conflict creeping near them.

"We should book it," Frisk said, shoving herself roughly from the side of the car to scramble into the passenger's seat before Daisy could protest. Frisk didn't know she couldn't drive, but once Frisk was settled inside and leaned her head back, Daisy could see her beginning to fade. She had lost too much blood, and she couldn't hold consciousness for much longer. Daisy hurried to the driver's seat, determined to figure out how to drive passably enough to get them away from the scene, if nothing else.

Looking down at the dashboard and stick shift, though, she questioned her ability to wing it. She shoved the key in the ignition and turned it to wake up the vehicle, since she knew at least to do that much. "All right, Frisk, the thing is, I don't really know how to…" She cut off as she glanced over, finding Frisk slumped against the door with her eyes closed. She was still breathing, but when Daisy reached over to shake her, she didn't react. Daisy bit her lip and gripped the steering wheel with both hands, glancing between the stick shift and all the dials on the dash as she tried to figure out what to do, when her eyes passed over her charm bracelet.

She had lost the dove charm, but the nickel charm – which could propel over a ton of weight – might be just the thing she needed. Shifting her arm to adjust the bracelet until the charm brushed against the heel of her palm, she channeled her energy into it, trying to keep focused on the flow of magic rather than the nearing shouts she could hear in the background.

The car shot forward with a screeching jolt. "*Shit!*" Daisy lost her focus on the trinket, and the vehicle pulled to a halt just as abruptly as it had moved. They had gone forward several feet, one tire now lodged over the precipice of the sidewalk, and she could smell burnt rubber. Daisy cursed herself as she grabbed the stick, jerking it from its forward-most position to one notch back. She knew about putting a car in park, too – she had just forgotten.

With the vehicle now in what she hoped was neutral, she tried the spell again, and this time they were launched forward more smoothly, but that left Daisy the task of steering while they moved. Gripping the wheel until she thought her knucklebones were going to poke right out of her skin, she kept her eyes on the road and her mind on her magic. Her spell had them going a bit below freeway speed, and the steering wheel was more sensitive than Daisy expected. Just a hair too far left or right had them rolling back onto sidewalks or brushing by other cars parked along the nighttime streets.

Her heart hammered each time they almost – or did – run into something, but she never hit anything solid enough to stop them or severely batter the car, until she hit an aluminum trash can head-on, which bounced off the windshield and left a tiny crack before rolling over the top of the vehicle. Choking down alarm, she tried to focus on the names on the street signs and steer herself home. Her goal was to go as generally south as she could, toward the direction of her neighborhood, but she tried to avoid other drivers or nightly pedestrians. When an oncoming taxi turned onto her current road, she jerked the steering wheel left to swerve out of its way and onto a side street, and from there she had to swing three more left turns down what felt like ever narrowing backways before her careening trajectory was aimed again toward home. Frisk flopped limply between the car door and Daisy's shoulder, but Daisy couldn't pull her attention from the road long enough to check on her.

In about ten minutes, she was two blocks away from her apartment, and she decided to let go of the spell there.

She figured it was worth it to carry Frisk inside if she had to, so long as it meant spending less time careening through the streets like a drunken racehorse. This time she remembered to put the car in park and turn the ignition off before scurrying out and over to Frisk's side to pull her out. Frisk was still unconscious, and none of Daisy's charms had abilities that would help much in getting her to the apartment – not gently or in one piece, at least – so she had no choice but to hook one of Frisk's arms over her shoulder and half-drag her two blocks.

Getting her up the stairs was the hard part, and when Daisy didn't have the strength to carry Frisk up, she laid the other woman down on her back and, gripping her under the arms, pulled her up the stairs to the second story. Once inside her apartment, Daisy didn't have the energy to lift her up onto the bed, but she went to the box of trinkets to remove her bronze amulet and slip it on. It wasn't powerful enough to lift Frisk entirely, but it was able to levitate her a bit, easing the weight enough for Daisy to haul her up.

Once she was settled, Daisy found herself a glass of water and the armlet to replenish her energy. Feeling a little steadier, she removed all her trinkets and piled them back into the box before going to the bedside to examine Frisk's wound.

It had stopped bleeding, and even after all that jostling around, it hadn't opened up again. Daisy picked at the tear in Frisk's dress, caked with dried blood, to try to get a look at the wound itself and determine how serious it was. She hoped that the bullet had only grazed Frisk rather than lodged itself inside her, but Daisy was no medical professional and she couldn't tell. All she could see were dark brown flakes clinging to Frisk's skin and clothes.

Daisy's heart was startled nearly to a stop when her phone rang. When her head jerked instinctively up at the sound, a searing streak of pain raced across her neck and right shoulder. How long had she been crouched over Frisk, trying to get a peek at the gunshot wound? She pushed herself up and staggered over to the phone.

"Hello?"

"Miss Dell, is that you?" It was Mr Swarz. But of course. Who else would call at that hour?

"Yes, sir. How did you–?"

"Angel brought the others to my home and told me what happened. Is Frisk with you? Are you hurt?" She couldn't quite tell with the sound scratched over the wire, but she thought there was a frantic twinge to his voice.

"No, Mr Swarz, I'm not hurt but Frisk got shot. She's here with me, but she's unconscious, and I don't know if the bullet's in her or–"

"Frisk was injured," she could hear him say to someone on his end of the phone. Angel's voice answered back, but Daisy didn't catch the words. "Yes, good idea. Miss Dell? I'm going to contact Jonas and send him over to treat Frisk. His magic is not quite up to mine or Angel's levels, but he knows quite a bit more about first-aid healing than either of us. Could you remind me of your address?" Daisy told him, and she could hear the light scritch of pen on paper as he recorded it. "Thank you. I'll call you back once I've talked to him."

"All right, Mr Swarz. I'll be here." She waited until she heard the click, and it sent a pang like reverberating metal through her core. It had helped to hear his voice – to hear any voice – but now she was left alone again with Frisk passed out on her bed, unconscious, maybe dying. Daisy did what she could to hold Frisk over until help came, covering her with a blanket and trying to dribble a bit of water into her mouth. Even preoccupied with fussing, time drawled too slow before the phone rang again.

"Jonas is on his way," Mr Swarz said when she answered. His voice was a bit smoother now, and she could feel her heart begin to settle again upon hearing it. "He has to walk, but he has long legs, so he shouldn't be long. Miss Dell, do you know what happened at the club? Angel was not able to tell me much, except that there was a gunshot and people fell into a panic."

She shook her head, as though he could see it over the phone. "I don't know. There were two folks with guns – one shot Frisk, I don't know why – and by the time we tried to get away, everyone else was so afraid that it sent them all into a mad fury. Frisk and I escaped through the front door while everyone crowded the back ways, and we ran to the car a few blocks away. There was a big boom sound when we were out there, and some green smoke, but I didn't see much more than that."

"Are you sure you're unhurt?"

Her arm felt nearly dislodged from hauling Frisk's limp body around, but she didn't mention that. "I'm fine. How are the others?"

"Well enough. Angel nearly drained herself into a stupor portalling herself and three others to my house, but I've got plenty of mana here for her. The others are untouched, but Miss Estévez won't stop wailing about Frisk." Amelia shouted something at Mr Swarz, earning a scoff from him. "Yes, yes, I'll ask. She wants to know how Frisk is faring now."

"Unconscious, but she's not bleeding anymore. I shouldn't..." She hesitated, knowing it was a stupid question. "I shouldn't take her to the hospital, should I?"

"Ideally, that is something we'd like to avoid. It will be too difficult to explain, and if any traces of mana are found on her she could be arrested. Miss Estévez, do you know if she drank any mana tonight?" There was a pause as Amelia answered. "Yes, it'd be best if you simply allowed Jonas to do what he can. At least with mana in her system, Frisk's body will be working in overtime, allowing it to repair itself faster. Which is probably why she's not bleeding now, though that will prove to be a problem if the bullet is lodged inside her." Daisy's stomach churned, stirring bile until she felt it rising in her chest. "If it comes to the matter of life, you may take her to a hospital. I'll let Jonas make the ultimate call on that."

"Thank you, Mr Swarz. I..." She paused, swallowing down an abrupt sob that rose in her throat. It felt silly to cry, but it had been a stressful turn of events. "Mr Swarz, do you know why someone would do this? Attack folks at the Gin Fountain?"

A soft huff of air blurred through the speaker. "I'm sure there are many who have their reasons. A rival establishment, a personal or political enemy of the owner, morality crusaders, fascists chased from their homelands trying to stir up trouble here, general anti-magician trash. It's hard to say. Did they target Frisk specifically, or just someone at random?"

"I think... I think it was me they were targeting, actually. I don't know if it was random."

A stretch of silence. "Did anyone see you using magic?"

She had only used her magic on the car, but she recalled the dove charm. It had fallen loose sometime in the night, probably back at Walter's. "I lost one of my trinkets," she admitted. "Earlier in the night. Maybe someone found it, but I'm not sure how they would have figured out it was magic or that it belonged to me. I didn't use it all night."

"You lost an artifact?" His question was soft, and there was another long stretch of silence following it. "Well, I am glad to hear you are well, if nothing else. I will give you a while to rest and help Jonas tend to Frisk, and I'll call back in a few hours to check on her progress. Is there anything more you need that I can provide?"

"No, sir." There probably was, but even with the boost of energy from her bronze bracelet, she was too tired to commit to that much active thinking.

"Very well." There was another pause, but he didn't hang up. "Thank you for protecting Frisk. She may be a pain, but she is an invaluable member to our organization and… just, thank you. It sounds like you've been very brave this night." Daisy had to swallow back another sob. She was too exhausted to be receiving heartfelt praise from her steely, hard-ass boss. "You don't have to worry about coming in to work tomorrow. Tell Jonas the same, and Frisk, once she wakes up. Just focus on taking care of her, then take the day to see to yourself."

"Thank you, Mr Swarz," she said, hoping he didn't notice where her voice cracked.

"Goodnight, Miss Dell."

After hanging up the phone, she checked on Frisk – her breathing was even but weak – before grabbing a nightgown from her dresser and changing in the bathroom. Frisk's blood had smeared on her dress. Her shoes had left bruises on her feet from all the scurrying about, too, and she supposed she should count herself lucky that she didn't sprain an ankle hauling Frisk around as she did. Licks of coiling hair came loose from the slicked mass framing her head, but she was too tired either to try to tame them or to wash out the pomade. She returned to the main room to grab a scarf to wrap around her hair until she had the energy to deal with it in the morning. Settling on the edge of the bed, she allowed her mind to empty while she stared at the hazy night sky through the kitchenette window.

She didn't know how long she was lost in absent reverie before she heard a knock at the door. The front of her building was never locked – few of its residents had anything worth stealing, anyway – so Jonas would have been able to walk right up. She went to let him in, having to press herself nearly flat against the wall once she opened the door and gestured him inside. Human apartments weren't made for ogre bodies, but he didn't complain about having to duck his head under the low ceiling.

"Hi, Miss Dell. How is Frisk?"

"Alive. She's on the bed." Jonas went to see to her, and Daisy trailed behind, hovering like a nervous mother with a feverish child. She hated feeling helpless, and a part of her blamed herself for Frisk's condition, unreasonable though it was. Perhaps if she hadn't dragged Frisk up a flight of stairs, she would have at least regained consciousness. Thoughts of her lost trinket flared through her haze of concern, too.

Jonas set a knapsack by the bed as he knelt – or rather, sat – on the floor to lean over his patient. He flipped open the top flap, revealing a collection of mana vials, some bandages, and a metal tool (tweezers, perhaps) that looked like it would be too small for his meaty hands. "She seems to be resting easy, at least. What happened?"

"She was shot. I don't know if the bullet went inside or just clipped her."

After pulling the blanket off Frisk, Jonas hummed and poked about the site of wound, as Daisy had, before frowning and turning to her. "I'll have to, uh… lift her dress, I think. Not to be improper, of course, but the cloth is in the way."

Daisy hardly expected puritanical bashfulness from any of her coworkers at that point. "Oh, of course. Here, I'll help." She reach over to grab the hem of Frisk's dress and pulled it up until it was bunched around her waist, revealing veiny, bone-white thighs and red undergarments that contained a telling lump. Daisy groaned. "Oh, ash and embers, of course she had to lose all that blood when she's on her monthly."

"I'll see what's up with the wound, and then I'll try to get her awake again," Jonas said, pointedly focusing on the bloody mark just above her right hip rather than anything below it. "She'll need some help recovering. Do you have any food you could make? She'll need it once she's up."

Aside from the injury and her period, there was the fact that Frisk had been drinking mana and alcohol earlier that night, too. Food would probably do more for her than magic or medicine. "Sure. I'll get on it." Off to her kitchenette to dig around for anything that could be thrown together as a passable meal, Daisy soon found herself scrambling eggs and grilling thick cuts of salted ham. Just the thing for breakfast, since it was nearly morning, anyway. Jonas worked while she did, and just as Daisy was dishing up plates she heard Frisk shout out in pain.

"*Gah!* Bauer, what the hell?"

On hearing Frisk's cry, Daisy hurried over with a plate in each hand, shoving one at Frisk as she struggled to push herself into a half-sitting position. Her dark hair whipped around her face in oily strands, and her dress was still pulled up to her waist, but Jonas had cleaned the wound at her side, and the dark red mark left behind didn't look so bad. Her eyes were bloodshot, though, and her face more skeletal and gaunt than usual.

"Here, Frisk. You need to build your strength back up."

"Dell, what's going on?" Frisk glanced down at her bare legs, but she only grunted in irritation. Lifting her head, she focused on the plate of steaming food before her, grunting again before sitting up straighter to take it.

"You were shot."

Frisk shoveled a forkful of eggs into her mouth, muttering through it, "Dammit, again?"

"It just brushed you," Jonas said. "Nothing to worry too much about. It looks like you bled an awful lot, though. You should eat up while you have your wits about you. I cast a spell to get your eyes open, and once it fades you'll probably drop like a sack of rocks." Frisk mumbled something back that sounded vaguely like an agreement. "If you hold still, I can just bandage up the wound, and then you should be good to start sleeping this off." He didn't wait for an answer before reaching for the bandage and unrolling a length of it to wrap several times around her torso, reaching around and under her arms while she tore into the breakfast Daisy had made for her. Once he was done with his task, and she with her meal, Daisy gave the other plate to Jonas and got the last for herself while Frisk began asking questions.

"Where the hell am I, even?"

"My apartment." Daisy settled on the floor next to Jonas, feeling a bit like a child when she noticed that her head didn't even reach his shoulder at that position. She wasn't even a short woman. "The Gin Fountain was shot up by some… well, I don't know who they were. I took you to the car and drove us here. Do you remember any of that?"

Frisk frowned and blinked several times. Her eyes were a bit unfocused, but Daisy couldn't be sure if it was from magic, mana, or blood loss. "Some. I remember going back to the balcony to check on you, and being hurt, I think." She shook her head. "Where's my car? Where's Lia?"

"I parked the car a few blocks away. All the others went with Angel to Mr Swarz's house." Frisk huffed a sigh of relief, but the movement in her torso earned her a miserable wince. "He called me earlier to check on us, and he's the one who sent Jonas. He said all three of us could take tomorrow off."

Jonas glanced sideways at her. "Who's gonna be the bouncer, then?"

Daisy shrugged. "I don't know. Weren't you off today, too?"

"Yeah. Pinstripes is closed the sixth day of the week. Everyone in the house gets the day off." Daisy supposed that explained how they could all go out dancing together without having to worry about their speakeasy being left unattended.

Frisk waved aside his concerns. "Vicks will take care of it, I'm sure. Swarz probably doesn't want us running any liquid tomorrow, anyway, not after another speakeasy got attacked the day before." That was about the point when she began nodding off, and Daisy took her plate and covered her with the blanket again.

While she began to doze off, Jonas drank two vials of mana before handing Daisy the bandage roll, suggesting that she dress Frisk's injury again when she woke back up. He was gone soon after that, and Daisy decided not to wait for Mr Swarz to phone her again. She called him to let him know that Frisk was faring better, and his responses barely registered with her. After finishing the call, she slunk to the bed, unsure of where she was going to rest with Frisk stretched out on the mattress. There wasn't much option except to grab her bathrobe and curl up under that on the floor. She hadn't thought much of it earlier, but she was relieved that Mr Swarz was giving her the whole next day to sleep off the night's events.

CHAPTER 5

Ming sat in her kitchen, the bird charm pinched between her fingers as she examined it. Just a tacky piece of metal. Morning light reflected through sheer curtains caused it to sparkle faintly, but other than that, nothing seemed particularly magical about it.

She was exhausted, but she tried to convince herself that she had accomplished something. That conviction was easier to find in the comfort of her family's meager estate.

It was only her estate now, really. Both her parents were gone, and Grandmother An had had to move up north to the countryside when her lungs got too bad. Yun had gotten out of prison a while back, but he was staying with friends on the opposite side of town, trying to stay out of his sister's hair. Maybe he even felt ashamed for all the trouble he had ever brought Ming's way.

It was strange to remember a time when they had all lived together. Ming could even remember when Grandmother An had been excited for her son-in-law's promising new job as a clerk at the county office, before he had been arrested for selling government secrets to fascist cells. Ming remembered being young and fascinated with the painted details on An's porcelain dishes and the embroidery on her blouses. Details – Ming had always had an eye for them.

Maybe that was what made her good at her job, now. Dad had been good at collecting them, but not good enough to cover his tracks. Ming was smarter than he had been.

But she and Jase had still botched it last night.

Ming sighed and slapped the charm on the table. Notches scarred the table's legs from some game she and Yun had played as kids. She didn't remember the rules of it, only that it had involved knives, and both An and Mom had scolded them for it. On the far wall of the kitchen was another table, or more of a cabinet with a cracked glass door, and on it was Ming's radio. She hadn't bought it until An moved out, partly because An hated ogre technology but mostly because Ming had to save up for months to afford it.

She flipped it on.

"...a lair of debauchery and occult practices," the scratchy voice on the radio was saying. Ming pulled up a chair from the table and settled in front of this miraculous information-box. Grandma An didn't know what she was missing out on. "Officers report no deaths on the scene, but a number of individuals involved in the riot were found inebriated, showing symptoms of mana consumption."

Ming and Jase's handiwork, unless Linden had hired an entirely separate set of hands to carry out a similar hunt elsewhere in the city.

"The mayor is praising the Soot City police for their efforts in securing the scene and stopping any magicians involved in the fighting from spreading their terror into the surrounding neighborhoods. More information as details unfold."

The newscaster was followed up by a man reading an advertisement for lightbulbs, and Ming went into her own head as he babbled. An airiness came over her, easing all that tension in her shoulders and jaw. She and Jase had left with no magician corpses in tow, but the police – who

Linden built her career supporting – were garnering praise. Although it was not technically what Linden had asked of Ming, it would achieve the same effect.

That morning, Soot City would wake up fearing magicians and hearing reminders of who would protect them from the mystical threat.

Ming felt easier as she returned to her bedroom, which had once been Grandma An's. A series of carved and painted Gao-style figurines decorated the shelf over the bed, but An had been fond of middle-continent lace, and a stranger would be forgiven for thinking that the room belonged to a Glynlander immigrant, not that a stranger would have ever seen An's bedroom. Ming hadn't changed much about it since she overtook it – couldn't be assed for the effort – and although the old lace-trimmed sheets had had to go for the sake of hygiene, the frilly curtains and tablecloth draped over the wardrobe remained. The contents of the wardrobe were far less fanciful than the drapery or the tiny polished quartz knobs on the drawers. Ming dug out a pair of loose brown pants and one of her nicer shirts – simple, but well-tailored. An's sensibilities were far removed from her granddaughter's, but the familiarity of this place soothed Ming's anxieties, even if she no longer had family around to give it that lived-in sensation from her childhood.

For as backwards as the Gin Fountain fiasco had gone, she felt abruptly glad for Councilwoman Linden's patronage. It was bad enough that she had to watch over her shoulder for cops and competitors, but the bank trying to sell her own home out from under her? She couldn't wait to rid herself of that looming specter, and how much worse it would have been without Linden's warning.

When she was dressed, Ming retrieved the charm from her kitchen table and set out to her bleak, shadowy office. As she arrived and settled at her desk, once more twisting the charm between her fingers as she awaited Linden, she quietly glowed again at her pride in serving Linden's need without actually dragging home a corpse.

When the councilwoman arrived for the meeting, though, she had an odd way of showing her gratitude for all of Ming's hard work.

"No deaths reported," Linden said, barely a foot into the room.

"No deaths occurred," Ming admitted. She could hear the confidence in her own voice. "Quite the spectacle, though, right? The media's even blaming the magicians for attacking their own kind. The police – those who are working under *your* budget measures – are being lauded as heroes for digging up that snake hole." It felt ridiculous explaining all this to her. In big-picture terms, it was so obviously what Linden had wanted. Could she not see that?

She could, Ming soon realized, but she pretended otherwise. "Our agreement was that you would kill a magician. That's not what occurred."

Ming fought a scowl, but judging from the tightness in her jaw, she wasn't sure if she was succeeding in keeping her expression neutral. "Will this not have the same effect? Magicians are vilified, the police are celebrated as heroes. You can take some credit for the latter, and anything your opponent does in reaction to this will risk alienating some group of his supporters or another, depending on how magic-sympathetic they are. This was never about blood."

Linden narrowed her eyes at Ming. "You make poignant observations, Roxana, but we had a formal agreement, and you did not stick to the letter of it. It is not your place to claim that I should be grateful that you failed to live up to your end of the bargain. You will not be receiving the second half of your payment, considering this fumble."

Ming tightened her hand over the charm, feeling its metal

edges jab into the flesh of her palm and allowing the gentle sting of it to distract her from her fury. She was lucky that she and Jase had made it out unscathed and undetected by the police. Of course, she had to compensate him all for his efforts. That would eat up a good portion of the half Linden had already paid Ming, but even without that – even if Jase agreed to a raincheck – it wasn't enough to buy out the lease.

The bank would sell her house. And if Linden was this steamed, she might even push her friend at the bank to move faster on finding a bidder, just to get under Ming's skin.

Linden was still a clown for not seeing how the events at the Gin Fountain worked in her campaign's favor, but maybe Ming had been just as much a fool for not expecting a tight-ass politician to be an exacting control freak. Ming's knack for detail had failed her in that regard, but not again. If Linden wanted to play it like that, it was too late for Ming to salvage their deal and she needed to alter trajectory – quickly – to find another source of income.

"We have nothing more to discuss, then." She stood, and despite her small stature, Linden flinched and took half a step back. "Get out. I don't do business with sneaks who use pedantic literalism to weasel out of agreements."

Linden sneered. "Not so different than every meathead mercenary after all, then, are you? This catastrophe was *your* error, and if you had half a brain, you'd be begging me for an opportunity to make it up–"

"Awfully full of yourself if you think you can wield guilt against a hired assassin. You're damn lucky I did even this much for you – it's clear you're going to need all the help you can get with this re-election. But it's not going to do you any good if you get shot dead in here because you didn't *get out*."

Linden's expression went blank – at least she had enough political savvy to hide her fear – and spun to stride out the door without another word. Ming almost regretted demanding she leave, as she thought of more angry tirades to fire at Linden just as she slammed the door shut behind her. Well, it was done now.

And now Ming couldn't afford to buy out her lease before her bank would try to sell her house to some corporation.

Alone, Ming sat back down and tried to steady her breath as she let the fury run its course through her veins. When it settled, leaving her feeling hollow and rattled, she went to the table in the back of the shady room, reaching for the phone there. She dialed for Jase.

He answered with only a raspy, "Hello?"

"Jase, you follow politics better than I. What's the name of that man running for Daphne Linden's council seat this election?"

On the day that Daisy returned to work, Mr Swarz offered her a late start, requesting that she come straight to the speakeasy rather than the office sometime around noon. Since she didn't have a key to that narrow door in the corner of the lobby, she had to go through Pinstripes' main door.

The front entrance to Pinstripes was located several blocks away from the actual office, indicated by a plain sign posted above an archway between a pawn shop and a barber. Beyond the archway, a set of stone steps led down to what appeared to be the basement of one of the buildings to either side. When she descended, she found it actually led to a brick-lined tunnel lit with oil lamps hanging at intervals from the walls. "All right, terrifying," she muttered to herself as she followed the tunnel, clutching her purse to her chest. Knowing how far this stairway was from the speakeasy's backdoor in the office, she wasn't surprised that the tunnel went on for quite a while. She was alone down there, and she couldn't tell if that made her more or less jittery in the eerie, empty underground. She was similarly conflicted when she finally reached a heavy wooden door at the end of the tunnel. There was a bronze knocker, which she used to rap three times on the door. An eye slit in the wood slid open, and pale beige eyes framed by thick, ashen skin peered out at her.

"Hey, Miss Dell," Jonas said. "Hold on just a second." He shut the eye slit and muffled sounds of clicks and swipes came through the wood. A moment later, the door opened, and he allowed her inside.

"Jonas, you can just call me Daisy," she said as she stepped inside, and she patted him on the arm. "How are you feeling?"

Jonas was a sweet thing, she was coming to find, and she had appreciated his presence two nights ago. He offered her a crooked smile as he shut and locked the door behind her. "Better than Frisk." He nodded toward the bar, where Frisk was slumped on a stool, half-laying across the countertop while Vinnie restocked bottles on the shelf. The stout, bespectacled man ignored Frisk as she whined at him, though Daisy couldn't catch her specific complaints from the distance she was at.

"Mr Swarz is in the brewery lab," Jonas said.

"Thanks, Jonas. I'll talk with him in a minute." She went over to Frisk first, gingerly reaching out to touch her on the shoulder to get her attention. Rather than jump at the contact, Frisk only jerked her head to face Daisy and glared with bloodshot eyes.

"Dell, you gotta help me."

"She already helped you," Vinnie snapped. With Daisy there, he finally acknowledged that anyone was at the bar. "Miss Dell, I heard you saved Frisk's life. Very courageous."

Daisy didn't know why that kind of praise embarrassed her, but she tried not to duck her head like some bashful little girl. "Well, I certainly couldn't have abandoned my friend."

She was still jittery around the warehouse girls – so much so that she wasn't sure how Frisk would react to her casual claim of friendship or its implications. Frisk didn't give any outward reaction to that particular phrase, though, instead sitting up to clutch at the front of Daisy's dress.

"And you gotta help me again now. You didn't save my life just to have me waste away, right?"

Vinnie grunted. "Her mana addiction, she means. Mr Swarz said no juice until she recovers – mana *or* alcohol. Too bad, because she whines like an infant when she is sober."

Frisk flopped back down onto the countertop. "Vinnie, that's *so* hurtful!"

"You see? She proves my point even now."

"How long until she *is* recovered?" Daisy asked.

The barkeep shrugged. "I will keep an eye on her aura. When it returns to its full glow, I will let Mr Swarz know." He leaned over Frisk, saying a little too loudly, "You see? I take care of my kind, even when they whimper like children."

Frisk flashed her teeth at him, mimicking the expression of a hissing cat. "No. You're cruel and heartless, and when I die from this headache, they're gonna put 'Vinnie's Fault' on my tombstone." Vinnie shook his head with a groan and returned to his task. Daisy also left Frisk to bask in her misery, heading toward the brewery room.

Inside, the glyphs were lit and Mr Swarz and Angel were there, both leaning over a vat of the blue liquid while dressed in ridiculous getups. Daisy was sure it was for safety reasons, but both wore bulky white coats that covered only the front of their bodies, blue face masks, matching rubber gloves, and oversized glass visors to protect their eyes. They both looked up as she entered.

"Good afternoon, Miss Dell," Mr Swarz said. His voice was muffled under the mask, but the precise enunciation of his speech mannerisms made his words clear as a song. "If you'll please wait at the entrance there, I'll be with you in a moment."

He turned to grab a pair of metal tongs from the worktable behind him and used them to grasp a small glass vial also resting there. Returning to the vat, he lowered the vial in and removed it once it was filled nearly to the lip with shimmering mana. Angel leaned forward and held out a hand. Even through the rubber gloves, a swirling line of color drifted from her fingertips, dancing and twisting as it made its way toward the vial like a wisp of snow on the wind. When it reached the vial, it sunk into the glass and permeated the liquid contents. The mana glowed a sort of lime green for a moment, then faded to its normal cerulean blue. After a moment of silent examination, both Angel and Mr Swarz nodded toward each other, and he dumped the contents of the vial back into the vat.

"Perfect." Setting aside his tools and pulling off the goggles and the mask, Mr Swarz joined Daisy by the entryway. Angel, meanwhile, lifted a heavy lid to seal the vat. "Apologies for the wait. How are you faring today?"

"Well enough. I slept past lunch yesterday, which was apparently all I needed. After I walked Frisk home, I spent most of the day on laundry. My dress got, uh, a bit messy from that night."

"But you are uninjured?"

Daisy wasn't sure why he kept asking that. "Yes, sir. I'm fine."

There was a tension around his eyes that faded just a bit as she said that. "Good. I'm glad. But we have matters to discuss. I have learned some more about the chaos that ensued two nights ago. It's important that you hear of it." He shed the rest of his safety gear, laying it out neatly on one of the tables and grabbing his cane, which had been set against the wall. To her surprise, he appeared to actually need it that morning. He must have noticed her staring, shifting as he leaned on it. "Stress tends to aggravate my physical condition. Nerves, you know. Please, let's find somewhere to sit and speak."

Back in the main room of the bar, Vicks had appeared – presenting as a man again – and hovered over his twin sister, rubbing her back while she continued to moan through her withdrawals. Mr Swarz ignored them and led Daisy to the nearest table.

"I inquired with Ann-Marie, the bartender at Walter's, about the night of your incident. You said you lost one of your charms that night, correct?"

Daisy felt a squirm in her gut. That couldn't have had anything to do with what happened, surely. "Yes."

"At Walter's?"

"I'm not sure, but probably."

Mr Swarz glanced down where he folded his hands on the table. "I see. It may be nothing, but Ann-Marie reports that after you all left, there was another patron poking around the area where you had been sitting – a short woman with dark hair and skin, perhaps of Gao or Pheje descent. Apparently, she picked some tiny object up off the floor and fussed with it for a little while before asking to use a phone. She left shortly after that. Ann-Marie says she had never seen the woman before, and she didn't display the symptoms of mana addiction. In fact, Ann-Marie said the woman didn't even order alcohol, just coffee."

Daisy kept quiet, feeling guilty but unsure if Mr Swarz was accusing her of anything – or what he was getting at in general, really.

"One of Regina's friends from Walter's also said he saw this woman. Shortly after you left, he went outside to smoke and take a stroll, and he saw her meet up with a lanky man a few streets down. Both were wearing long coats and plain brown hats. He says they stood by a car's open trunk and whispered to each other for a while before leaving, but he couldn't say where they were headed. Do any of these descriptions seem familiar to you?"

Daisy recalled a lone woman matching Mr Swarz's description sitting at the bar at Walter's. She told him this, but the feeling in her gut grew sour to the point of sickening. Was this her fault?

"Mage-hunters, almost certainly," Mr Swarz said, nodding to himself after she confirmed having seen one of these people. He looked Daisy in the eye, studying her. "But were they merely opportunistic, or after something in particular?"

"Does it matter?" Daisy asked, feeling ashamed of herself for her carelessness and – much to her own surprise – protective of her coworkers. In her lap, her hands curled instinctively into claws that were at once defensive and self-eviscerating. "Their motives don't make the Gin Fountain any less trashed."

"It might matter." His gaze scanned her face, neck, and arms, and just as she was about to ask why, he frowned. "No artifacts today?"

"Not necessarily." It hadn't been the warmest of afternoons, and Daisy had her enchanted garter on under her skirt. "What about them?"

Mr Swarz sat up straighter, flexing his right hand as though it pained him, an absent attention to a lingering agony. "If your artifact is what was used to trace you, it is possible that these mage-hunters are interested in your brand of magic in particular. Maybe even you as an individual."

Daisy's blood chilled. She had had professors and classmates at the women's college who had been standoffish with her, but that was about as close as she had ever come to having an enemy.

"Who would want to hunt me?"

"Someone who wants to know the secrets of your magic, I suspect. I told you what that kind of information would mean to magicians in Ashland. Other factions, including those who seek to destroy our kind, can gain leverage from learning those same secrets. Conservative pearl-clutchers can be quite a bit more dangerous than their neat little cardigans would suggest." His hand stilled, and he leaned forward. "I hate to push the matter – I know we are still coming to trust each other – but if mage-hunters are out to unpuzzle your type of magic, it may put our company at too high a risk. I must know what is at stake, here. Please, I need you to explain to me how your artifacts function. How does one use them, and how are they created?"

Daisy flinched. She would have rather been personally blamed for all that had happened than to have him request such a thing. "Mr Swarz, I can't replicate the creation of these trinkets. My grandmother knew how, but I... I never learned." He scowled, needing no chicken phoenix trinket to tell that she was lying. "I've never done it before myself, at least. I can't." That much was true.

"Miss Dell, I want you to understand that you are a part of this company now, and as such I will see to it that no harm comes to you. But if these mage-hunters are after you, or your grandmother's secrets, I will need to know all I can in order to keep ahead of them and adequately protect you."

"Are you sure *you're* not just after those secrets?"

Mr Swarz recoiled, his mouth pressing into a thin line. She expected him to look outraged by the question, but instead he seemed... hurt. "You said you would be willing to share with me. Again, I do not wish to press the matter so early in our partnership, as I understand that we both still have reason to distrust each other, but it seemed clear to me that you intended to be forthright with this information eventually. I am not seeking to obtain anything that either of us did not expect that I would be given at some point or another. And I hope you don't think so little of me that you believe I would use the violence wielded against you and the others as an opportunity to trick you."

Daisy was panged with shame again, and she glanced away from his dark eyes. It was true that she had reasons not to entirely trust him – she was not used to trusting anyone outside of her family, and his line of business plus his personality in general did not inspire great faith in his intentions – but her jibing question had been motivated more by panic than logical caution. It had been crueler than necessary.

"I'm sorry, Mr Swarz. This whole situation is just... alarming. I..." She swallowed, trying to clear her thoughts and feelings. She didn't want to hurt Mr Swarz, but she certainly wasn't going to allow him to emotionally manipulate her into doing anything, either. She needed clarity to ensure that the decision she made was the best she could make.

Mr Swarz had already shown concern for her in light of all this. She still did not understand the reason why, but it was clear that he desired to keep her safe. And, as she had also learned from the night of the attack, he could be a level-headed and competent man in the face of disaster. She was sure she could place her physical protection, if nothing else, in his care.

"I'll tell you whatever it is you need to know."

He let out a slow breath. His eyes were distant, staring at the table top like he had been waiting for bad news from the doctor. "Thank you. Now, please." He lifted his gaze to meet hers. "I know that your artifacts don't require mana to operate, but you said that there was a price to the magic. What price would that be, exactly?"

CHAPTER 6

Mr Swarz showed a remarkable amount of trust in Daisy as he drove through the woods in the hills to the west of the city's limit, passing under bare branches on a narrow road. It had been long enough since the volcanoes' last chain of eruptions that the land was habitable again, but it would be a couple more centuries before these trees could grow as large and lush as nature would otherwise have them. Until then, they stood as lanky, leafless sentinels in the wilderness of Ashland. Trees in lower lands, closer to the city, tended to be better recovered, without clouds of ash hanging so low and thick over them and blocking their access to the sun. There was a deathly eeriness to the bare trees of the hills, Daisy thought, or maybe it was only her association with the region.

Her grandmother had taken her up only twice before to the location that she now directed Mr Swarz toward. After learning the truth of Sparrow's powers, Daisy wished never to see the place again. She had thought she would have no reason to. As Mr Swarz's car rolled across the packed dirt roads, she tried to tell herself over and over that the visit did not have to result in any sin. She knew what to do, and she knew that Mr Swarz would press her to show as much as she could. There was a threshold she would not cross, but she had to steel herself for everything that stood before that point.

In her lap was a bag of supplies, and she clutched at it as she tried to steady the frantic beat of her heart. Mr Swarz occasionally glanced over when she did this. She had not told him what the bag held. She only told him where to drive.

As they rolled through the grey, framed on either side of the road by dry and colorless forest, muffled music from the radio cut through the uncomfortable silence. It was a mournful trumpet song with piano and drums in the background giving it a jazzy beat, a musical expression of the composer's anxiety. Mr Swarz kept the volume down, but the gentle fuzz and scratch of sound waves was better than the wordless void they would be otherwise left with. It was an even greater relief to finally reach their destination. At the end of an ill-kept dirt road in the wooded foothills was a rickety farmhouse, two stories tall and long since abandoned.

"This is the place?" Mr Swarz asked. Daisy nodded, and he put the car in park.

When they stepped out, Daisy didn't waste time explaining anything to her employer. Instead, she made her way directly around the side of the house, stopping at the edge of what she sought. Mr Swarz followed, coming to stand by Daisy's side and frowning at the sight.

"What is this?" In the dusty, dry grass was a ring of mushrooms, their caps showcasing a range of dark blue to an almost silvery grey. The circle was wide enough that either Daisy or Mr Swarz could have laid out flat inside its circumference.

"A faerie ring." Daisy set down the bag and began digging around in it for her supplies. Mr Swarz took a step closer to her as she did.

"I think it's time you begin explaining." It was clear from the edge in his voice that he didn't care for being left in the dark, and Daisy imagined he had more reason to fear than she did in that moment.

"You know much about faeries, Mr Swarz?" From her bag, she removed two fistfuls of cheap, shiny objects she had picked up from a flea market that morning – a fake-gold bracelet, a thin length of chain, several spoons, and about a dozen glittering glass buttons. She stepped into the ring and dropped them in the center.

"Not much. They are reclusive, but I've read that prior to the volcanic eruptions, they used to visit the mortal plane more frequently. It was my understanding that they've only been seen since then in Boltivic." That country, across the ocean to the west, was where Vinnie had been born, judging from his accent. Daisy didn't know much about his family, but presumably his grandmother and little brother that Jonas had once mentioned to her had also emigrated from there with him.

"Not quite. I know only about this ring, but there are bound to be others in Ashland. These formations are the only way they can cross into our world, as far as I know, though of course you've got to give them a reason." She returned to the bag and grabbed more of her supplies – several bars of chocolate wrapped in wax paper and a bright purple scrap of cloth. Laying out the cloth and peeling back the wax paper, she broke off squares of the candy and laid them out on the fabric. There were a few more bars remaining in the bag, in case she needed them.

"Are you summoning an otherworldly entity or a child?" Mr Swarz asked. She knew he meant it as a dry joke, but his voice wavered with the slightest vibrato.

"Faeries have a different appreciation of existence. Makes sense, considering that they live in another dimension. In some ways they are more complicated than humans, and in other ways they are simpler. Plus, everyone loves chocolate, right?"

Andre didn't laugh or so much as smirk, instead watching the offering she left there. "And this all has to do with your ritual magic?"

Daisy didn't reply, both because the answer was too obvious and because he was getting closer to a truth that she would have rather let decay with her grandmother in her grave. But he was right that they would be able to better prepare against anyone coming after Daisy or her trinkets if he knew the full scope of what she dealt with.

"Will it just appear, then?"

Daisy settled on the ground before her offering, reaching up to touch her bronze pendant. She hoped that wouldn't be so shiny as to draw the faerie's notice. "No. The treats will keep its attention, but I need magic to catch it." Focusing her will through the trinket, she used it to grab and levitate one of the spoons, allowing it to drift lazily upward. Mr Swarz was wise enough to stand outside the edge of the faerie ring and watch in silence.

They waited as the spoon floated in the air, about level with Daisy's forehead. After several minutes, Daisy began to wonder if she had done something wrong. She had barely been twelve years old the last time Sparrow brought her to that spot, so perhaps she misremembered. Just as disappointment began to pull on her heart, her little trick of magic was met with a pulse like a beat of deep bass, and a shimmer appeared before her beyond the spoon.

It was just a crack at first, thin and white, almost invisible against the backdrop of sparse, colorless woods. The crack grew, as cracks are apt to do, and began to separate, opening up a portal of swirling blue and green and other colors that Daisy did not recognize from the mortal world's simple rainbows. She heard a quiet gasp from Mr Swarz behind her, but she kept her eyes locked on the portal. A limb reached out from it – slender and almost human, if one ignored the feathery fringes along the elbow or the shining cyan skin – and snatched the spoon. The portal grew larger, and a torso attached to the other end of the arm leaned out. Daisy could feel a tension in the air that had nothing to do with magic, but she didn't look back to see what Mr Swarz was doing. He could pull the blade from his cane, or any knives or guns he might have had tucked under his coat, but so long as he did not yet step inside the ring, it didn't matter. The faerie would ignore him while there were treats to take.

The being stepped further out of its portal, settling both feet on the mortal side. The faerie was a lanky thing – surprisingly similar in its anatomy to a human, which Daisy had always found odd – and was covered in that pale blue-green skin. Fluffed down lined his elbows, ankles, hips, and jaws, and something between that and human hair hung from his skull down to the small of his back. His face was almost human, too – the nose was less defined, more just a shallow bump down the center, and his eyes were too wide and all black, but his cheekbones were no sharper than Frisk's and his chin no more pointed than Mr Swarz's. The cyan-skinned creature lifted the spoon to examine it with those dark eyes, and his near lipless mouth pulled into a razor-toothed grin.

"Daisy," Mr Swarz whispered, but despite his panicked use of her first name, she ignored him, opting to focus on Cyan as he knelt to pick up the other spoons and dig around amongst the various shiny objects. He ran long fingers across the buttons, seeming to delight in the tiny clinking sound of his nails against their surfaces, before spying the chocolate. He dropped the spoons with abrupt disinterest and grabbed a square of candy, sniffing at it before delicately testing it with his tongue. Finding it to his liking, he stuffed it in his mouth and grabbed two more pieces.

Daisy leaned forward. "Hello, dear." Cyan looked her in the eyes, blinking slowly as he examined her face. He didn't say anything. To the best of Daisy's knowledge, faeries couldn't speak, at least not in any language a human could understand. After taking a moment to acknowledge her, he returned to picking at the chocolate, placing piece-after-piece into his mouth.

"I appreciate you showing me this, Miss Dell," Mr Swarz said, "but I am afraid I don't understand how this correlates to your magic."

Content that the faerie wouldn't harm her, she stood and waved Mr Swarz into the ring. "Bring my bag here, and I will explain." He did so, and she dug another candy bar out to hold in her hand, in case Cyan should need some more bribing once he finished his current haul of chocolate.

"*They* are the ones who create the artifacts. Anyone who can convince one to commune with them might be able to talk them into enchanting a trinket. It takes only the most basic grasp of magic to trigger the trinket once it's made, and unlike your methodical magic, it involves using willpower to pull the magic out of the trinket, rather than pushing the magic out of one's own body."

"And that's why it does not require mana?"

"No." Daisy looked away, glancing at the chipped paint peeling off the grimy sides of the abandoned farmhouse. She didn't know how long the place had stood empty, nor how her grandmother had originally found it or when. "The power of the magic is inlaid in the trinket upon its creation, like it has its own pool of mana. That's why it takes none of the body's energies."

Mr Swarz cocked his head, nearly tipping off his tidy

bowler hat. "Then these trinkets have a limited amount of uses?"

Daisy shrugged. "In a theoretical sense, I suppose that's true. They can only hold a finite amount of energy, I'm sure. But that amount must be enormous – I've never heard of casting a trinket dry. My grandmother never mentioned such a thing, and I've certainly never experienced it myself." She glanced down at Cyan, who had finished his initial offering and remained crouched as he leaned toward her, sniffing suggestively toward the hand that held the spare chocolate bar. He appeared to be no threat, but she began unwrapping it and breaking off pieces to toss toward him, anyway. He snatched bit by bit out of the air as she lobbed them in his direction.

"That energy comes from the faeries, then? They simply imbue their own power?"

She shook her head. Feeding candy to the creature gave her something of an illusion of innocence, but she was finding it too bittersweet. "No. They are not that generous. Even if they were, creating trinkets takes more power than they can willfully give." Mr Swarz kept silent, even as she was sure her answer didn't clarify. She sighed and braced herself for the truth she had ultimately agreed to share when she chose to stay on with the Stripes days ago. "The faeries' magic only determines the type of ability the trinket has. The power to use that ability comes from human life, and it requires... more energy than a human can survive being taken from their body."

Mr Swarz was silent, but he took a cautious step around Daisy – nearing the faerie – to face her when she refused to look at him. When she glanced up, his expression was set in a steely glare framed by furrowed lines in his brow and around his eyes.

"You speak of human sacrifice."

Daisy willed herself not to look away. "I do."

Mr Swarz took an abrupt step back, and it startled Cyan to his feet. Standing upright, the faerie glanced once toward Daisy before shifting his attention to Mr Swarz, looking him up and down with a curious glint to his eyes. Swarz was focused on Daisy, however.

Even as he glared, his voice was less accusatory than Daisy expected, and that in itself worried her. "You said you couldn't make these artifacts. Is this what you meant? That you will not take part in the sacrifice required to accomplish it?"

"Yes. My grandmother created all the trinkets I own, and she explained how to me, showed me this faerie ring, but..." Daisy shook her head. "My grandmother, she came to Ashland from Noeyen when it was shattered by war and invasion. She was one of the first here, when it was a wild frontier filled with refugees from different lands, all strangers and willing to destroy each other to ensure their own continued existence. She did what she thought she had to in order to survive, and I don't blame her for it, but the blood she spilled to accomplish that is on her hands alone." She shook her head again. "This is why I didn't want to tell. I thought I might be able to let her methods be a secret that die with me. I won't be responsible for her crimes being repeated."

Mr Swarz's frown eased, but it didn't calm Daisy any. Her other concern about sharing the secret of her magic with him, although she did not say it, was that he himself might not have the same reservations that she did. She glanced toward Cyan, who stood still and upright, watching Mr Swarz. Daisy had summoned him for more than mere show, and she waited to see if she would be in need of her otherworldly acquaintance's protection.

After a stretch of silence, Mr Swarz nodded. "As well

those methods should die. I apologize, Miss Dell. Had I known what kind of position this put you in, I would not have asked..." He trailed off as his eyes drifted toward the faerie, examining the creature as it examined him. He didn't ask why Daisy bothered to call Cyan to the scene if she did not intend to have him craft any new trinkets. "I can understand how mage-hunters would take interest in this. Did your grandmother have any enemies that might have known any of this, or wished to know? If so, I think it for the best that we help you keep this secret from them, whether or not they are related to what happened at the Gin Fountain."

Daisy let out a long breath. She wasn't sure how far to trust Mr Swarz, but every time he proved himself a little more worthy of her faith it was a weight off her heart. "I don't know, but I'm not keen on this getting out to much of anyone, if I can help it. Aside from you, of course."

"I will keep this to myself," he said, "for now. If there comes a time when Angel or Grey needs to know to help ensure your safety or stop these hunters, then I will consult you before imparting anything to them."

"Grey?" She had heard him mention the name before, but she didn't know who this individual was.

"My boss, the founder of the Stripes. I doubt I will have reason to speak of this to anyone else in the company, though. I will keep your secret as close to my heart as it is safe for me to do." With his attention back fully on Daisy, he wasn't looking when Cyan – perhaps noticing the easing tension – took a careful step forward, sniffing experimentally. "This is disconcerting, though. Do you know anything of the identities of the people who were sacrificed? Perhaps one or another has some descendant out for revenge."

"No, my grandmother never told me much in detail. Just that the faerie would draw the life from her sacrifice and imbue it in the trinket. I don't know where she found the sacrifices, or what she did with their bodies afterward. Maybe a few are buried around the property here, but I just don't know."

Mr Swarz bowed his head. "It's fine. The attack on the Gin Fountain will provide us with a fresher trail regardless, so it would a better use of our efforts to–" He broke off with a start as Cyan slunk right up to him, curiously sniffing at his collar. Daisy had to hold back a laugh as she watched her boss' pupils expand in terror. "Miss Dell," he begged in a frantic whisper. Cyan did not appear to notice Mr Swarz's nervousness and leaned closer.

"I think he's looking for more candy." She had another bar still tucked in her bag that Cyan apparently couldn't detect, but she didn't reach for it. She preferred to hang on to one, in case things got a little too strained with their transdimensional friend. Mr Swarz, to his credit, did not make any sudden movements or loud noises as Cyan began plucking at his coat, trying to shake loose any possible treats that might have been hidden there. "He'll be no danger so long as we don't antagonize him, I think."

"But he will accept human sacrifices? More of this difference in appreciation of existence that you spoke of earlier?" Cyan pulled away from Mr Swarz for a quick moment to look him in the face, studying his eyes, nose, and lips before leaning in again, sniffing so close to the crook of the man's neck that he was very nearly nuzzling him. Mr Swarz's back straightened and he shifted his feet with an awkward jerkiness. "Your friend is quite affectionate." There was a soft blush across his pale face, but she thought better than to tease him about it.

"I call him Cyan. He's the same one I saw the two times my grandmother brought me here when I was a child. She only introduced me to him – no sacrifices. I think she was done making trinkets at that point, but wanted me to know in case I should ever need it." The thought of ever needing to murder another human for a magical weapon, or even so little as a utility, sent a shudder through her. Mr Swarz shivered, too, as Cyan sniffed along his jawline.

"So, he's no threat to us?" he asked.

"Not unless I asked him to hurt you, but even then, I'm not sure I've offered enough chocolate to successfully bribe him into that. I have no reason to believe that he would attack us unprovoked. He's rather a sweetheart, don't you think?"

The feathery fringes on Cyan's jaw twitched as he took in Mr Swarz's scent. "Can he leave this ring?"

"Yes, but I don't think he will. The portals between our realms can only be opened inside the ring, and if he steps out, he will not be able to zap himself back home until he steps back in. Or if he found a different faerie ring, I suppose."

"Interesting." Cyan pulled away but kept staring into Mr Swarz's face. The faerie wore nothing that would read as a human expression, but his blank visage only made his examination seem more intense. "Perhaps we should return to Pinstripes, then. Even if there are any clues in your grandmother's past about why you were attacked, the others may have picked up on some more relevant leads. I asked Angel and LaChapelle to investigate more about the woman that Ann-Marie reported seeing. We should check in with them."

Daisy agreed and ushered him outside the faerie ring. Cyan tried to follow but stopped at the threshold created by the mushrooms. He whimpered at them as they began walking toward the car, almost like a forlorn puppy. Daisy pulled the last chocolate bar from her bag and tossed it to him. "Thank you, Cyan. It was good to see you again."

The faerie caught the bar but made no move to eat it, only holding it in his long fingers.

As Daisy and Mr Swarz returned to the car, Cyan turned and knelt to gather up the shiny objects she had left for him before standing before the white crack in the air. It expanded once more, leading into Cyan's native world of color and light, and he stepped back through. Once he was gone, Daisy went to open the passenger-side door, and as she did, she saw Mr Swarz staring at the space where the portal had opened and was now closing again. There was a faint crease to his brow as his eyes focused on the point where Cyan had crossed back into his own dimension, now just a faint white crack, but Mr Swarz shook his head and got into the car.

Daisy liked to think she understood some of what he was feeling.

The first time Grandma Sparrow had brought her out to that farmhouse, she had been just a little child, still wearing shapeless cotton dresses and her hair in twists. Grandma Sparrow wore her hair in twists, too, but it didn't look so girlish on her, hanging in long twirls down to the base of her shoulder blades. Sparrow had been a slender woman of middling height, just like Daisy had grown into, though in her age she walked with a stiffness not unlike Mr Swarz's on his bad days. Her frail form had eventually been her downfall, when she died a few years back from bone cancer. But in Daisy's childhood, she had still been strong enough to take the trek up the hills with her young granddaughter.

They had to walk that whole way both times – an all-day trip – because Sparrow, like Daisy, had never been able to drive, and anyway, cars back then weren't sturdy enough to make the distance. Daisy remembered how her legs had ached from the second trip, but she possessed no such recollection for the first. She had been so young, and all she remembered was the searing image of meeting Cyan for the first time.

He had looked no different then. His otherworldly face didn't age. But he had been snarling the first time she had seen him, standing beside Sparrow inside the faerie ring with an offering – Daisy did not remember of what – laid out before them. His inky eyes had glanced briefly over Daisy before turning to Sparrow, and his thin lips pulled back to flash his razor teeth at the old woman. Little Daisy's stomach had felt like a solid block of ice staring at that deadly expression. That sensation was stained into Daisy's memory, along with the overwhelming scents of afternoon ashfall and crushed, dry pine needles.

Sparrow had held out her hands, shaking her head, but Cyan had not responded to this gesture. Seeing that she wasn't communicating, Sparrow reached out to Daisy, pulling the small girl up to her hip, while keeping her eyes locked on the faerie and stating in a cold, clear voice, "Not this time."

Cyan must have understood this better – though, at the time, Daisy had not – and he dropped the snarl, taking a careful step away from the human pair. Daisy wasn't sure how Cyan or any other faerie felt about the matter of human sacrifice, but he had apparently been angered that day, thinking for a moment that Sparrow meant for him to kill a child.

He had seemed more pleased on their second visit, offering no snarling when he was summoned by Sparrow. Rather, he appeared to remember Daisy, and he marveled at how she had grown while plucking at the grassy green dress she wore, more mature than her last visit but still girlish and modest. Daisy had watched him in return while Sparrow intoned to her about magic and the Old Ways. It had only been on that second visit that Sparrow explained the element of ritual sacrifice. Perhaps she had meant to that first trip, and thought against it after Cyan had misinterpreted Daisy's presence as an offering.

"All power must come from somewhere," Daisy remembered Grandma Sparrow telling her. "Most of the power that humans are capable of utilizing must come from other humans. Exploitation, manipulation. This. It is a cruel thing, but it is the way of the world. If I had not made those sacrifices, I would be trapped – still stuck in Noeyen under the rule of conquerors, or starving in this new place."

Sparrow had been living in Ashland for more than thirty years by that point, and she was fluent in the Iongathi trade language that most Ashlanders had adopted, though her accent was still heavy on the liquids and vowels with Noeyen influence. What Daisy heard the most in those words, though, was defensiveness. "Why did you leave Noeyen?" Daisy asked. They did not teach her about such faraway places in public schools, regardless that a third of her class was of direct Noeyen descent. Most Ashlanders wanted to forget the rest of the world.

"War with the north." Daisy had not learned which northern country it was – the Yen Highlands – until her sophomore college studies, the same year that Sparrow died. "They had taken half our country's land by the time I fled, moving soldiers in to establish permanent homes in the houses we had been chased out of. I would have been forced into marriage or servitude with one of them had I stayed, so I stowed away on a ship delivering wine to Ashland, back when Soot City was just a cluster of stone shacks."

Daisy had never asked much more than that. Not how Sparrow used her trinkets to survive, not whose lives had been sacrificed for them, not who her father's father had been, not even who had taught Sparrow such things in her homeland, or anything about the faerie she must have communed with there.

She had still been a child then, but she understood that her grandmother was defensive because she had learned to live with her defenses never lowered. She had come from a world where she was constantly assailed, where it was better to be constantly on-guard than caught vulnerable.

Glad to have never lived in such a world herself, or at least not to the same extent, Daisy still took to heart Grandma Sparrow's ideals of preparedness, even at the cost of personal morals and basic human ethics. But there were lines that Daisy would never cross herself, and she did not care if it was privilege – the kind never afforded to Sparrow – that allowed her to make such choices.

Things were less tense on the drive back, now that Daisy's secret was out in the open and she and Mr Swarz had not attempted to kill each other in any capacity during the outing. He had more questions for her, but not of the nature she expected.

"You always call those enchanted items 'trinkets.' Why is that?"

Daisy stretched out her legs as far as she could inside the car, glad to be rid of the earlier tension and a mite proud of herself for spooking her boss with that faerie. "That's what my grandmother always called them. And that's what they are, aren't they? Just… trinkets. Little do-dads."

"I wouldn't call anything made from the life energy of another human a 'do-dad.' Your terminology seems self-deprecating, is all."

His observation ripped away her pride and moment of ease, leaving behind a scar of indignant anger. "And what do you call them? 'Artifacts'? What, that particular combination of syllables is more dignified? And this is something that *deserves* dignity? You yourself just pointed out that it's blood sacrifice. It's hard not to be self-deprecating, in that context."

His eyes shifted to look at her for a fleeting moment before returning to the dusty road before them. "Is that what this persona of yours is, too, then? Go to college only to take a secretary job; study magic only to waste your time slinking around clubs with mana freaks; spend all your money on pretty dresses rather than saving for a better future, just because it's stylish? Is this part of your supposedly inevitable self-deprecation?"

Daisy pulled her legs in and sat up straight, suddenly sorry that she had ever shared any information with him at all. She was almost too stunned by his abrupt and hypocritical judgments – Angel did those things, too, and Mr Swarz appeared to respect her well enough – to give a reply. After a brief moment of stammering half-formed words, however, she managed to collect herself.

"I've said before, Mr Swarz – whatever I've shown you here today, you still don't know me or my magic. I understand that you're upset that I'm not orchestrating my life in order to make it how you think it should be, but I will not apologize merely for having different sensibilities than you. I do the things I do because they are the best choice for me. The calculations I run to determine what is best for me are not really any of your damned business, so I'm not going to bother trying to justify those algorithms to you."

"The entire course of your life is no small thing to consider. It's not a matter of a difference of sensibilities, Miss Dell," he replied. The edge to his voice betrayed how emotionally he was responding to the discussion, which she found odd since *she* was the one being insulted.

"Isn't it? Didn't this conversation start as a linguistic

debate about 'trinkets' versus 'artifacts'?" Mr Swarz opened his mouth to argue but wisely snapped it shut before any sound could come out. She found herself calming down in light of his restraint – or maybe it was delight over his embarrassment. "You can pretend that your objections to my every life choice are about wanting what's best for me, but when it boils down to it, what are you claiming about the things in my life that are supposedly such a waste of my potential? That I make reasonable compromises in my work life in order to survive?"

"No, of course n–"

"So, what, you're upset with me for being poor? You don't like the partying, either – are you mad that I'm having fun and making friends?" Neither of them mentioned the obvious, recent hang-up in that particular aspect of her life. "You think that I'm selling myself short by working below my education level and doing frivolous, girly things and using folksy terminology, but that begs the question as to why you think any of that is so terrible to begin with." She paused, wondering if that question was going to receive an answer.

Mr Swarz huffed out a sigh, one of those ones that men tended to make when they decided that a woman had been talking too long or disagreeing too loudly. She was surprised, then, when he said after a moment of thought, "I suppose I *don't* know you. You have your reasons for doing what you do, as does anyone, and it is not my place to scold you on your choices. I apologize for my presumptions."

The anger began to ebb, but there was enough left for a triumphant smirk as she said, "You know, you've been saying that to me *a lot* lately."

"I have a tendency to put my foot in my mouth, it's true. Angel says it's because I have the social graces of a houseplant, though I like to think I'm at least to the level of a goldfish." His own self-deprecation put her more at ease again, but his gentle chiding of himself wasn't enough for her to forgive him, and that tense silence from the drive up returned for the rest of the ride home.

CHAPTER 7

They arrived back at the office to find a dark-haired woman in a red cardigan bent over Daisy's desk, scribbling something onto a notepad. Daisy didn't recognize Vicks until she lifted her head and beamed. Her wig was different than the one Daisy had seen her wear before, dark auburn and a little longer than her black bob wig.

"Hey, look. Now I'm covering *your* job!"

Mr Swarz frowned at the sight of Vicks as he hung up his hat. "Well, I suppose I'd rather have you answering the phones than your half-wit sister. Speaking of, how is she faring?"

"Jonas still hasn't given her the A-OK on hitting the juice again, so she went out gambling to distract from the withdrawals." Vicks rose from the desk and went over to the table in the back corner, lifting the coffee carafe with a showy gesture toward it. "Refreshments?"

Daisy probably wouldn't have minded Vicks' playing around if Mr Swarz hadn't earlier scolded her for supposedly belittling herself as a mere secretary, which was an especially unfair criticism considering what she had shared with him that day. Both she and Mr Swarz ignored Vicks' ill-timed joke. "She left work in the middle of the day?" Daisy asked.

Vicks set down the carafe and gave her a flat stare. "Ever

had mana withdrawals, friend? I'm amazed she got outta bed, even."

"Perhaps someday we'll have a solid week where both of the Pasternack twins show up for their duties," Mr Swarz said with a dry wistfulness, heading toward Angel's office. "Vicks, if you wouldn't mind maintaining Miss Dell's position for a bit longer. Miss Dell?" He gestured for her to step into Angel's office before him.

The room that Angel and Rudolph shared was a bit larger and brighter than Mr Swarz's, with Angel's desk near the side wall and Rudolph's in a corner by the window. In addition to blinds, such as Mr Swarz's window's had, Angel had set up white drapes to frame the windows, too.

She was at her desk, browsing through documents when they arrived. Daisy still wasn't sure how much of the paperwork she and Mr Swarz managed was pretend. Surely all the clients they delivered mana to still needed invoices? Considering that Angel didn't glance up from her work when they entered, that might have been exactly what it was.

"How was the outing, dears?" she asked.

"Informative, which is about as much as I'll say about it. It does seem likely that someone may be after Miss Dell, though, either as an individual or for the general brand of her magic. Have you learned anything about the attackers?"

Rudolph, who had been at his desk busying himself with the task of rearranging pen holders and paperclips, stood up and hurried across the room, clearly waiting for his moment to spring into action. "We have, as a matter of fact. One of the young magicians that was at the scene recognized – if not the exact organization responsible – the type that the attackers most likely belonged to. He reported to us that gangs dressed in similar types of nondescript coats and carrying similar sorts of weapons prowl about in the dingier sections of the Grime District. Apparently, muscle like this hire themselves out for hits regularly."

"We followed that lead and began sniffing around northeast," Angel said. "It took quite a few conversations with the right people and a load of doublespeak, but we managed to get a name." She set aside the documents she was perusing to open her desk and pull out a single slip of paper, handing it to Mr Swarz. "There's a hitwoman who operates under the alias of 'Roxana' up in that neighborhood, though her real name is Ming Wei. According to a young woman who claims to have previously worked for her, Wei was out of her office the night of the attack."

Mr Swarz glanced over the paper Angel had handed him. "This Wei is just a mercenary, then. In that case, it's easy enough to assume why she's doing this. Do you know who might be paying her for her efforts?"

Angel spread her hands. "Sorry, love. No specifics, though we were told that she had a *type* of clientele. Politicians and bigwigs. She's got a high price tag but pays out in silence."

"She can't be that hush about things," Daisy said, "if her friend was willing to tell you so much."

Angel leaned back in her chair, glancing back at her dry paperwork. "Well, it's not as though we asked nicely." Rudolph adjusted the collar of his shirt, looking toward the wall in a more obvious attempt to avoid eye contact with anyone. Daisy was a tad alarmed to hear this, and she might have made a comment about them mussing up their pretty white clothes if it weren't for all the shame and fury from her field trip with Mr Swarz earlier that she still packed around. She already felt like she needed another day to sleep off this whole mess.

Mr Swarz folded the slip of paper and set it back on Angel's desk. "It could be anyone, then, couldn't it? Some bitter bureaucrat trying to run down a magician ex-lover, or a potential mayoral candidate looking to stir up a panic for the political capital." He shook his head. "This could very well be just a random act of violence against our people."

"Our people," as though they were a nation. Daisy had not quite realized Mr Swarz's peculiar devotion to his identity as a magician.

Angel frowned, looking almost sorry. "I'm afraid so. There's not much we can do to protect our own, in that case, other than what we already do every day to survive."

That was hardly a satisfying conclusion, if everything Mr Swarz feared about the mage-hunters searching for Daisy was true. She supposed there was some relief in the possibility that those hunters were not after her individually, but as Angel pointed out, that gave them fewer leads to prepare against future onslaughts.

"I'll report to Grey about this Wei person," Mr Swarz said to Angel, before turning to Daisy. "We will remain vigilant, but I fear there is little else we can do at this point. If politicians are paying mercenaries to harass our kind, we can probably expect more attacks like that one in future."

"City council elections are coming up in a handful of weeks," Angel added.

"We have little choice but to return to our normal work until then. Miss Dell, please do let me know if you run into any more trouble or anything suspicious. And, please–" he looked between her and Angel "–no more clubs for a while. I do not wish to stay up another night managing crisis control for my coworkers." He left it at that, returning to his office, but Angel smirked as he went.

"He means that he doesn't want to worry about his friends, I'm sure." Daisy didn't respond to Angel's optimism. She had thought she was growing to warm up to her steely employer and earning his respect as an equal until his outburst at her that afternoon. He was a difficult man to care for, and he was certainly not her friend.

Jacobus Johnston sat in a plush chair in his office, watching Ming with an inquisitive gaze that appeared natural to his academic background. He had seemed alarmed to get a call from her, and although she could find no sign among her colleagues that he had a history of dealing with their sort, he had not hesitated at her offer.

Daphne Linden had shortchanged her, and Ming would do whatever she had to in order to secure her home from the bank's fickle interests. Ming didn't know how long she had – Linden hadn't deigned to tell her that much, probably hoping to dangle that information over Ming's head to bait her into other work – but she didn't intend to wait around until it was too late. She had to gather enough cash to buy out her lease before anyone else could. A bit of payback against that viper Linden didn't hurt, either.

Johnston was in his middle ages, heavyset with neatly combed salt-and-pepper hair and a short, black beard. His corduroy suit was clean and expensive-looking, but just kitschy enough to give him a sort of jolly old uncle sensibility – approachable, but wise enough to be trusted with authority. A stereotypical look for a politician, and it probably helped him garner votes. He sat with his legs crossed but otherwise appeared relaxed in Ming's presence.

"I must say, it's hardly surprising that Linden is building an anti-magic platform again. I had banked on as much." Nothing in his voice betrayed concern for the lives of the magicians that may have been hurt in the aftermath of Ming's bungled assassination. "But I'm hoping to draw in the votes of those who see her as a tyrant – anyone even vaguely sympathetic to the magicians, and of course the magicians themselves. Why would I wish to hire your services? If anything, these publicized riots could make the general population more sympathetic to them, if it ever comes to light that the instigators were hired thugs."

There was something of a threat to his words, which Ming had expected when she came forward to him about her broken deal with Linden. "Precisely. Which is why you may be interested in seeing to it that I and my people continue these attacks. Turn the narrative into one where magicians are innocents – underdogs being harangued by systematic hatred. Those who are on the fence about voting for you now will surely be won over, and those who are losing faith in Linden may begin to look in your direction."

Johnston waved a hand. "*If* they are sympathetic." But he had once been a professor, and most of his connections were still with academics and scientists. He was counting on the vote of the studious and progressive-minded already, and the circles he ran in might have even given him the impression that most people pitied magicians to some degree.

"Yes. And this will be an opportunity to make more people sympathetic."

He pressed his palms together and leaned forward, apparently convinced. "Mm-hm. Then I suppose this narrative needs a protagonist? The public never rallies around underdogs when they are merely faceless victims – then it's only someone else's problem."

Johnston certainly had a better head for this game than Linden did, and he even seemed a few steps ahead of Ming herself. "Perhaps a martyr?"

He smirked. "Yes, I suppose it would be better to have that than a hero who slays the villain, at least from your perspective." His grin faded. "Speaking of which – if I may be so forward – what *is* our villain's motivation, hm?"

Ming didn't care for Johnston's smarm, but she cared

less for Linden's treachery. If she had to play along with Johnston's quasi-poetic rambling, so be it. "I will expect payment, obviously."

Johnston tilted his head, a gesture he was entirely too old to pull off with any amount of charm. "That's it? Money? What do you need money for?"

She could tell him the truth. Even aside the matter with the lease, there were bills, groceries, medicine, a brother with a gambling problem, a grandmother with bad lungs up in a small town in the northern reaches of Ashland, munitions to keep her current in her line of work, people to bribe into silence, other costs that allowed her to keep her business alive, which in turn kept her alive. It was all too mundane to bother listing.

"A girl's got to eat," she said instead.

Johnston chuckled and uncrossed his legs to stand. He was a tall man with a big belly, but if he meant to intimidate Ming, well, she had been up against taller and bigger. "I suspect your asking price is well above the cost of a meal, though." He turned to the wall behind him, where there were several bookshelves filled with orderly rows of tomes. He paced along the wall, looking at the books he passed with only casual interest. His attention was still focused on trying to intimidate Ming. "Well, if you don't want to tell, it's not my business. Perhaps that particular narrative thread will unravel itself. Tell me, Miss Roxana, do you drink bourbon?"

"Yes." Ming didn't move from where she stood in the center of his office, while Johnston continued his current course along the wall to the far corner where a liquor cabinet was tucked away. As he obtained two glasses and poured an inch of dark gold bourbon into each, he began rambling again.

"You know, I've heard a rumor that Linden is interested in

courting the temperance vote this time around. Not content enough to criminalize mana, oh, no. Alcohol, tobacco, marijuana. Anything that alters the 'natural human state,' as teetotalers like to say. Some say their extremists even condemn *sugar*."

"If Linden were advocating the criminalization of sugar, you wouldn't need to entertain conversations with mercenaries to win this election."

Johnston laughed as he came toward her and handed her a glass. "No, indeed not. And even if it were true, it's absurd enough that the moderates could content themselves with muttering, 'Oh, she would never follow through on that. Not something that would impact *me*.'" He took a sip and squinted thoughtfully before taking another and returning to his chair.

"Very well, Miss Roxana, I see the advantages in this underdog story you propose. You've won me over. Paint my opponent as a tyrant, turn these magicians into victims. Lay a martyr's corpse at my feet so the public can see me weep in all my empathy over so cruel a fate."

Ming would readily kill whoever she had to in order to maintain her livelihood, now more than ever. What sent a shiver up her spine was that to Johnston and Linden, these lives that they asked her to reap were nothing but a joke.

She tried not to think about it, not to think about the poor sap she would turn into a victim. It was business to her, and considering what she had already started with this task – the bird charm she had found, and where that had led her – she at least had the assurance of knowing where she could start trying to locate such a martyr.

CHAPTER 8

Daisy was on-edge returning to work the next day. She was still upset at Mr Swarz for his comments toward her on the ride home from the faerie ring, and the thought of what Angel and Rudolph might have done to obtain the information they had found on Ming Wei haunted her. Much to her relief, neither Mr Swarz nor Angel were in the office that morning. "They're in the brewery," Rudolph said when he arrived several hours after Daisy had begun her shift.

Free to work without having her head clogged with suspicion and anger toward either of them, Daisy spent most of the morning tidying her desk and trying to fix a jammed key on her typewriter. Shortly after lunch, she got a phone call for Mr Swarz from one of his clients who only identified as "Sanders." When she asked if she could take a message, Sanders insisted that it was an urgent matter, and that it was vital that she had Mr Swarz call him back as soon as possible. Daisy didn't want to look Swarz in the eye for a while, but damned if she was just not going to do her job to accomplish that.

Informing Rudolph that she was going to find Mr Swarz in the brewery, she stepped out the front door and around several blocks to the speakeasy front, unable to use the back door in the office without Mr Swarz's key. Fortunately, Jonas was already at his post, having arrived early that day to unpack a recent shipment of liquor.

Exchanging only a brief greeting with her ogre friend, Daisy went directly to the brewery, hanging by the entrance as she watched Mr Swarz and Angel work. They were in their silly aprons and masks again, though they were not working over one of the giant vats this time. Instead, they both leaned over a worktable pushed against the nearest wall, with Angel working some small grinder machine and Mr Swarz measuring out small jars of what appeared to be honey from a clay pot. Over the clanking and screeching of Angel's little machine, neither heard Daisy's soft footfalls. She had to half-shout over the monstrous noise.

"Mr Swarz?"

Angel paused and they both looked up at her. "Yes, Miss Dell? Is there a problem?" Mr Swarz asked.

"No, sir, just a phone call from Mr Sanders. He didn't tell me the nature of his inquiry, but he wants you to call him right back. He says it's urgent."

Daisy expected this information to spark concern, maybe even panic, from her boss, but he only offered a scoff muffled by the mask covering his mouth. "Sanders' shoes would come untied and he'd call it urgent. I'll contact him later. Thank you, Miss Dell."

Daisy was ready to turn away and head back to her workstation, but Mr Swarz caught her eye before she could. "You taught me something of your magic yesterday. Would you care to better know how mana works?"

She hesitated, torn between a desire to spend some time away from the boss who had only the day before told her outright that she was wasting her life and a genuine curiosity about her company's primary product. Most of what she knew about mana, after all, was the same kind of propaganda that Franklin Blaine fed to his listeners, and though she might acknowledge that it was propaganda, it still left her ignorant.

Swallowing her wounded pride, she stepped into the room. "All right, sure." Mr Swarz gestured her closer to the worktable, and she obliged.

"Part of why so many methodical magicians have flocked to Ashland is because one of the primary ingredients to mana is the dust of a gemstone that is relatively common in the area." He nodded toward the hand grinder, and Daisy was close enough to catch a glimpse in the dish at the bottom of the machine, filled with slivers of sparkling blue gemstone dust. "Likely the volcanic activity from centuries past shifted the geological contents of the region, bringing the stone up closer to the surface where it might not normally be. It is called thaumaturcite."

"And it's edible?"

"In small doses, not unlike salt." He took a small pinch from Angel's collection and displayed it in his palm for Daisy. The light from the glyphs on the walls played against the reflective dust specks, sparkling them like glitter. "It's the source of mana's distinctive color, as well as the glow. When paired with sugar beet fructose, raw honey, and gymnopilus mushroom spores, its chemical components can restore the energy pushed from the body by magic." That then explained the pot of honey sitting next to the grinding machine.

"Where do you find thaumaturcite?"

Mr Swarz returned the gem dust to the dish under the machine. "Oh, it turns up in rivers, occasionally, or out in the wetlands to the south. Our company works alongside several, um... independent contractors in rural areas–" which Daisy took to mean hapless rubes living too far outside of civilization for law enforcement to bother with "–

and the Pasternacks are generally responsible for picking up the materials from those sources and delivering them here, in addition to running finished products out to our clients."

Daisy shook her head. "How do people even discover that you can create something like this?" It was rhetorical, just meant to express mild amazement, but Mr Swarz actually laughed.

"Oh, I'm sure Angel or I could go into the history of that, if you're truly curious, but I'm afraid either of us would lecture about it endlessly." His mouth was obscured, so she couldn't tell if he was smiling, but there was a passion in his eyes when he spoke. Daisy was astounded enough to forget her recent frustrations with him. This was something that made Mr Swarz genuinely fulfilled – maybe even happy.

"How did you come into magic, anyway? Either of you?" she asked. Some of the delight faded from Mr Swarz's eyes, replaced with reflexive wariness, but Daisy didn't take it personally. She had been just as mistrustful when he had asked her similar questions.

Angel did not, apparently, hold the same reservations. "As a bored teenager," she answered as she removed the dish from below the grinder to dump the thaumaturcite dust into a glass jar set to her right, "I was one of those bright children whose education was never challenging enough, and my parents' friends were all wealthy elites. I found myself dragged to snooty galas more than I could stand, but at one of them I was introduced to a young woman whom I found considerably more interesting than anyone else in my parents' social circle.

"We became close, though never quite lovers – not from a lack of effort on my part. I was rather smitten with her, but she thought I was too young. Regardless, she was a good friend to me, and she could see that I was not living up to my potential, so she introduced me to her small library of methodical theory texts. From there, I was able to search out more on my own, as well as locating mana suppliers. When I was in college, I studied chemistry so that I might learn how to make my own."

She spoke so casually of it, like it was no big thing that she had learned a rare skill frowned upon by her society as a teenager and then taught herself to keep her practice of it sustainable as a college student.

"And you, Mr Swarz?" Daisy asked.

He pulled down the mask covering the lower half of his face, revealing a mouth drawn taut in a pensive line. His nostalgia for his beginnings with magic, it seemed, was not as sweet as Angel's. "Well, you know of my injuries. As an adolescent, I was frustrated to be physically limited in such a way. It still impacts me now, but it was much worse then. I could not walk at all without a crutch, and even then not always, and my right hand was fully unusable. When I came into my teenage years, I wanted to help provide for my mother, but I had no options for work that could accommodate my needs."

It was only then that he smiled even faintly at the memories, one corner of his lip turning up in a sort of mechanical imitation of mischief. It looked bitter, even cruel, on his sharp-featured face.

"We had these neighbors, an older couple from Glynland who went to church services twice a week. They hated magicians, even back then – they thought magicians were responsible for the famine in Glynland seventy years previously. These two would always catch my mother when she was coming back from the grocery store, standing on their porch and asking her in these frantic, wheezing voices if she had heard about 'what the magic devils were up to now.'" Daisy hoped for a hair of a second that Mr Swarz would actually imitate their voices, but of course he didn't give in to such silliness, regardless of the faint smirk he wore. "If they had any clue that they'd be giving me ideas to help cope with my condition, perhaps they would have kept their bitter judgments to themselves."

"How did you learn it, though?"

Mr Swarz shrugged, removing his work gloves and setting them on the table. "Oh, I was always a bookish boy, and I could stagger as far as the nearest library well enough. Again, this was before the big anti-magician scares were in full-swing, so the libraries still had a few obscure books on the topic tucked away."

"You taught yourself entirely, then?"

"No. I didn't understand a word of it, at first. What I did was find the books I could on the topic, particularly the newer materials, then I sought out their authors. One of the methodical theorists whose texts I had found happened to be giving a lecture at one of the universities. I traveled there, sneaked in, listening to the lecture, and cornered the man afterward."

"And he took you under his wing?"

"No. He ignored me." Daisy frowned. Mr Swarz's story didn't have an engaging flow to it at all. "I was just a crippled boy from the poor part of town. Methodical magic has always had something of a reputation for belonging to the elites of Ashland, even as it was pushed underground in recent years.

"He had an apprentice, though – a young woman born to fortune but disabled like myself. He would have never, certainly, taken anything less than the offspring of one of his wealthy friends under his tutelage, but his apprentice was not so narrow-minded. Grey was moved by my passion and dedication, and she established a correspondence with me to school me in the craft. I soon became skilled enough to focus on spells that would help mend my body. Although some of my injuries are too severe for even the most advanced magicians I have ever met, I was able to repair myself enough that I could become a functioning member of society, as I had intended. But by then, Grey and I were both quite tired of society. Grey established the Stripes and brought me on to assist."

"And you just kept going with it? Because it's your job?" Even as she asked it, she knew it couldn't be true. She had seen the way his eyes lit up.

"I found something fulfilling in magic. Maybe it was the childhood crippled by injury, but to have power, some semblance of control in my life and upon the world – it meant everything to me. I was healed enough during my tutelage under Grey to work normal jobs like all the other children in my neighborhood, and I was paid exceedingly well for the position I have now, back when the Stripes were first formed. Magic kept my mother and I from starving, but even more than that, the mystery of it all, the inquiry... it resonated with me."

He shrugged, trying so laughably hard to appear nonchalant. "I suppose because of my disability, I never felt I could focus on my education. But I've always had a mind for academia, and magic was my first proper outlet into that." He took a glance at the jar Angel had filled with ground thaumaturcite, but Daisy couldn't read his steely expression.

"Well," she said, taking a step back, "I should probably return to my desk, huh? In case Mr Sanders calls again."

Mr Swarz looked up at her, a startled gleam to his eye like he had forgotten she was there. "Oh, I suppose so. But if Sanders continues to harass you, just tell him I'm already investigating the matter." When Daisy opened her mouth to protest, Mr Swarz waved a hand. "He's not clever enough to figure it out."

"Of course, Mr Swarz." Daisy left them to clean up their workspace. Back upstairs, she didn't see Mr Swarz and Angel return to the office until toward the end of the work day. She was pleased for it, happy to have a quiet day at her desk occupied primarily by busywork and reading. It made her feel, for the first time in a number of days, that she was an ordinary Modern Girl working an ordinary day job.

Amelia surprised Daisy the next afternoon with a visit to the office. The front door slammed open as she staggered in overburdened with a cardboard box cradled in her arms. Daisy was at her desk, trying to locate a hole in it that might have matched the loose screw she found on the floor that morning, but she sat up straight as Amelia approached. After Vinnie's raging visit to complain about his paycheck, Daisy was a little nervous about the warehouse folks coming up to the main office, but Amelia only stepped up to drop the box on Daisy's desk and paused to inhale several labored breaths.

"What's all this?" Daisy asked.

Amelia lifted the lid off the box, exposing several thick stacks of paper slips bundled together. "Patron accounts – settled tabs and all that. Help me file them in Swarz's office?"

"Shouldn't they go to Rudolph?"

"Nope. Vinnie already ran the numbers. Here, help me lift this beast." Amelia grabbed one end and Daisy stood to take the other, and together they awkwardly hobbled into Mr Swarz's office. He and Angel had gone out together for a late lunch, but Daisy trusted Amelia that they were allowed in there to file the accounts. Plopping the box down in front of the wall of disorderly client files, Amelia got right to work grabbing a stack and pulling out sheets. "Here, you find the folder that matches the client number." Daisy glanced at the files along the wall, and when Amelia saw her grimace, she added, "They aren't in alphabetical order or anything, so good luck."

Daisy did her best hunting down the files that Amelia called for, glad to be up from her desk even as she felt a little swept away by Amelia's sudden appearance. It was easy but boring work, and as they made progress Daisy tried striking up a conversation. "So, Vinnie does accounting, too?"

"Only because he doesn't trust Rudolph with it."

"But isn't he a bartender?"

Amelia shrugged. She handed Daisy the last sheet in her current stack and reached down to fish out another. "I mean, downstairs we split the work however we have to. The basic breakdown is Vinnie at the bar, me at the tables, Jonas at the door, and Regina on the stage, and we all play a part in guarding the supply down there, but honestly? Stripes is starting to outgrow its unders. We're a bit understaffed, even since you came on board."

Outgrow its unders. Daisy liked that saying – it sounded like something Amelia had picked up from Frisk, which reminded Daisy: "Is Frisk feeling any better?"

Amelia kept her eyes focused on the papers in her hand. "Oh, yeah. She's doing a lot better. Um." She pulled loose the next account to be filed, but she paused before she read the client number to Daisy. "Thanks, actually. I probably should have said it sooner–"

"Thanks for what?"

Amelia looked up to wrinkle her nose at Daisy. "Oh, don't try to be coy with me. You saved my girl's skin at the Gin Fountain. If you hadn't helped her get out of there, she could have been found by cops, or–" She didn't finish the thought out loud, shaking her head like she was trying to shoo the very notion away. "I mean, it's not the first time she's been shot *at*, but no matter how tough she thinks she is, she can't get out of every scrape on her own. So, thanks."

Daisy couldn't have just left a friend in the middle of all that, but it would be rude to brush off the compliment by pointing that out. Instead, she said, "Of course, Amelia. I'd do it for any of you."

Amelia smiled, her lovely brown eyes sparkling with genuine warmth until she seemed to think better of it, and that smile shifted just so to became a sardonic grin. "You did kind of put her car through hell, though. What did you even *do* to it?"

Heat rushed up to Daisy's cheeks even though she knew that Amelia was just joshing her. "I don't know how to drive! If Frisk didn't want me to beat up her car, she shouldn't have fainted on me!" Amelia laughed, but she was quick to get back to work listing off client files for Daisy to dig up. They kept diligently at it until they reached the final stack, around which point Angel and Mr Swarz returned from lunch and stepped into his office.

"Miss Estévez," Mr Swarz said with a nod. "How goes the filing?"

"Not so bad this month. Shutting down for a few days means less paperwork." She gestured at the wall as Daisy searched around for the current client file she needed. "Wouldn't take so long if you bothered to get this in any semblance of order, though."

"Sounds like a job for Daisy," Angel suggested. Daisy's heart nearly stopped at the suggestion, and she turned in wide-eyed horror to Amelia.

Amelia offered her a subtle wink before saying to Angel, "Actually, if you can budget it out, I could use some overtime on an off day."

Angel and Mr Swarz both nodded. "I think we can make that work," Angel said. "But why don't you leave the rest of this filing to Daisy today? The others will need help getting ready to open downstairs."

Amelia handed Daisy the remaining half of the final stack and picked the box up off the floor. "Right. Just don't schedule me for this weekend. The girls and I are going for a day trip." She looked to Daisy. "You should come, too. We're meeting at Market Street Deli in the morning."

Between the mundane office tasks and an invitation to dally about with the other Stripes' girls, Daisy could almost forget about everything that had happened with the Gin Fountain. "I'd love to, thank you." Amelia offered her another smile before leaving, and Angel also departed to return to her own office. Only Mr Swarz remained.

"Have you got much left?" he asked, glancing at the files she held.

She cocked her head. "Well, no, but it's going to take me the rest of the day finding what I need in this disaster. So." She pulled a sheet loose from the bundle. "Why don't I let you know the number, and *you* find the file?"

CHAPTER 9

At the end of that week, Daisy met the other girls at the Market Deli on Brand Street, about three blocks around the corner from the Stripes front office and four blocks from the backway to the speakeasy. Frisk was parked along the side of the road, leaning against the hood of her car with Amelia beside her, their arms wrapped around each other's waists. They kept their eyes on the deli's outdoor counter, waiting for Regina to order a milkshake.

"Is Vicks joining us?" Daisy asked as she approached Amelia and Frisk.

Frisk shook her head. "Nah, she went out with other friends last night and is still hung over." It struck Daisy how alien it was to meet her coworkers in the light of the afternoon like this, during hours when most of them likely worked or slept. Amelia wore a sort of old-fashioned navy blue dress and an embroidered face mask, and Frisk was dressed in what appeared to be some of Vicks' boy clothes – a loose white button-up and brown, high-waisted slacks. Daisy's neighbor's radio had said that morning that ash clouds were expected to sweep into the lowlands, and Amelia and Frisk must have heard a similar report and dressed down for the event. Daisy herself had donned a somewhat tattered steel grey dress – so worn that she didn't mind if it got smudged

167

by smoke and soot, but still nice enough.

When Regina returned with a milkshake in a round paper cup, Frisk rounded them all up into the car, and they set off.

Daisy took the back seat with Regina. A large paper bag filled with snacks and bottled water sat between them. The ride was quiet – a sort of sleepy silence, casual and easy. Frisk didn't even turn on the radio, but there was no tension in the void that filled the car. Daisy began to forget her self-consciousness, relaxing in that space protected by metal walls and stained leather seats from the judgements of the world. Regina handed Daisy her cup to offer a sip of the milkshake.

"Where are we going?" Regina asked as Daisy drank. Frisk was taking a road south out of town, but it was not the one that Daisy had pointed Andre down when going to meet Cyan.

"I dunno," Frisk answered. "Ash fields. Somewhere quiet. You know, *nature*." Daisy's parents had always taken her to the beach as a child. The land lining Ashland's eastern coast was the most recovered from the volcanic destruction that had ravaged the continent ages ago. There were farms and even orchards out there – Ashland's meager agricultural industry, what little they didn't have to import from the Odhero Islands or Elverta to the south. Daisy's mother, Reina, always wanted to go apple picking when they were out there, filling the car with baskets of the fruit. Daisy thought of the contrast to the apples portrayed in a famous Noeyen portrait of a legendary princess being offered gold platters full of shining red fruit, and the Ashland apples in Reina's baskets always found themselves lacking in the comparison. Daisy had never traveled abroad, but from what little she knew, Ashland's idea of "nature" was something frail and withered compared to the rest of the world.

Indeed, on the outskirts of town, Daisy watched industry

and civilization meld into craggy badlands. In the flat plains south of the city proper were housing developments, some with yards, though if those yards had grass it was dry and colorless. Nothing was green out here, only silver and black and charcoal and ebony. Even the blue of the sky drained of color as dark grey clouds of ash came rolling in. It reminded Daisy of a photograph, all shape and shadow. Soon, even houses on withered plots of land gave way to dry, weedy fields, and beyond that, flat plains of dirt and ash.

Frisk continued south upon a road that wound not because it had any hills to circumvent but seemingly for no other reason than to keep the drive entertaining. Shafts of afternoon light broke through the clouds and struck against the fields around them, reflecting off the salt deposits in the soil whenever a gust of wind brushed the loose ash away. All around them, the earth sparkled like dark silk interwoven with glittering threads.

By the time Frisk pulled to a spot on the side of the highway, Daisy's legs were cramped from sitting still in the back seat. She sighed as she stepped out with the others on a short vista point that overlooked a lower slope of field. Frisk again took her position leaning against the front hood of the car and pulled from her pocket a small brown vial that looked like it could have been any old medicine. Of course, when she pulled the cork and dipped a fingertip in, it was a thick, bright blue liquid that she lifted to her lips. It seemed that she was allowed to drink again, now. Or so Daisy hoped.

Frisk noticed Daisy looking and tilted the flask toward her. "Want any?"

Daisy averted her gaze to stare out at the glittering plains below them. "No, thanks."

"Right, right. Gotta keep teetotaling to impress the Boss Man."

"What?"

Regina, who had settled down to sit cross-legged in the dirt, looked up at Frisk plaintively the second she recognized Daisy's tone. "I'll take some."

Frisk ignored Regina's obvious attempt at distraction. "I'm just pulling your leg, Dell. I know you don't need it, and why risk getting addicted if that's just another thing to spend your paycheck on? That's what Lia always tells me, anyway."

"I'm not sober to impress Mr Swarz," Daisy said, and Frisk rolled her eyes.

"Blazin' embers, Dell, I *just said* I know that. Swarz is heavy sweet on you, anyway. You could do fuck-all and he'd still be over the moon for you." She took another dab of mana and licked it off her finger.

"I thought Mr Swarz didn't get like that," Regina said.

"What, with women?"

"With romance. I hear Miss Agatha talking sometimes. He'll fancy sex and all, but not all that affectionate, mushy stuff like in the picture shows. Doesn't even want to get married, except for maybe tax reasons."

"Didn't say he wanted to marry Dell. Just, you know, she's the favorite." Frisk brought the vial to her lips and drank directly from it, and Regina wilted a bit at the sight. When Frisk lowered the vial, her eyes locked onto Daisy, although she didn't turn her head to face her. "Sorry. Didn't mean to make a big thing of it. I'm just bitter, is all."

"At me?" Daisy asked.

"At Swarz. You know, Vicks and I've been at Stripes for years now, doing runs through gang territories and out here with the rednecks, risking our asses daily. We get the product to Swarz's clients, and look how much thanks he gives us for it. Then you saunter on in with your fancy shoes and college degree, and in a week he decides you're the best person he's ever met."

Daisy thought again about the ride home from introducing Mr Swarz to Cyan. "Doesn't seem that way from where I'm standing," she said.

"Yeah, well, Swarz emotes on a bit of a different frequency. You learn to read it after a while." Frisk recorked the vial and stuffed it in the pocket of her slacks. The gleam in her eyes was verging on manic. "Damn, didn't mean to bring this whole outing down. Come on, let's stroll."

Frisk pushed off the car and led the way in a simple walk across the ash plain with the others following. Soot clung to their clothes and skin as every step stirred up a loose layer of dust. Whether the clouds also dropped fresh ash onto them hardly mattered for how smudged they were. They spent their walk chatting about the recent Orion Hevera film and the new dress that had gone up in the boutique window three blocks down from the office. Regina pointed out stray lizards that skittered out of the girls' pathway to duck under porous rocks that littered the landscape. Sitting watch in the distance was one long-legged heron, standing ankle-deep in what was likely a small spring sprouting up precious clean water in the otherwise barren landscape. It looked up at them once when Frisk began hooting and waving her arms at it, trying and failing to see if she could spook it into flight.

Their trek was short, or it felt like it was, before Frisk proposed returning to the car and finding some kind of eatery. "Rubes have all the best food," she said. Daisy had never spent much time out of the city and couldn't recall that she had ever eaten at some backwater diner, so despite her reservations about Frisk's claim, she didn't feel she had the authority to argue it.

They drove further down the road, stopping at a small settlement that seemed to extend its borders no further than the four corners of an intersection between the highway and a smaller back road – two houses on the southern-most corners, a gas station at another, and in the final corner a squat little building marked by a sandwich-board sign reading: "OPEN – TORTILLAS, COFFEE" and a third menu item that was too smudged to read.

Inside the restaurant, they took a seat at a table near the window, though the glass was so smudged it was nearly blacked out. Little candles on the tables provided most of the interior lighting. Each chair at their table was mismatched, all rescues from various neighbors, most likely. Baubles of similarly eclectic aesthetic – stone idols from Iongath, baskets woven in Yen Highlander style, things of that sort – decorated the shelves along the walls. The staff of the joint was quiet and reclusive, all probably family members from one of the two houses across the street. The menu offered mostly Elvertan dishes, and Daisy ended up just copying Amelia's order.

No one else was present in the establishment except a young woman who appeared to be a waitress on break, sitting at a table alone and reading a magazine. The entire restaurant was dim and eerily quiet – most of the noise coming from the clatter in the kitchen – and no one at Daisy's table spoke until the on-duty waitress returned with their food. The plates stacked high with rice and bean dishes were twice the amount that they could get in the city for the same price. Daisy stared at her plate in dismay, knowing already how much of it would go to waste, but Frisk and Regina began devouring their meals with abandon. Amelia, who readily took up a fork but ate at a slower pace than the other two, noticed Daisy's staring.

"It's the drug," she said. The girl at the other table didn't even glance up, although Amelia didn't bother to lower her voice. "Kicks the metabolism in the pants. That's how Angel described it to me."

"That would explain how they stay so trim, certainly," Daisy said.

Regina nodded as she finished swallowing her current mouthful. "That's why I got on it to begin with. I don't get much out of the high – it doesn't last long for me, and then I'm just burnt out. But I had dysphoria real bad as a kid, and the... you know, the stuff helped me control my shape a bit."

Daisy tried picking at her food. The chicken was sautéed in something spicy and greasy, and she wasn't sure if it was good or just abundantly flavorful. "Can't doctors treat that sort of thing these days?" she asked, hoping medical talk wasn't over the line.

Regina shrugged, indifferent to the question. She seemed to quietly revel in being the focus of the conversation, even. "Oh, sure. My mom even got the folks at our temple to put together a little fund to pay for it, but then a drunk driver crashed into our temple – took out a whole wall. My family wanted to use the fund to help repair the temple first, so my surgeries got postponed until we could save up some more again, but I couldn't wait that long. By then, flat girls were all the rage, anyway, so I started dosing to cut down the muscle and fat I didn't want. Once I started losing weight, I looked the same as any other girl who dosed. If you take enough, it just kind of reduces you down to your skin and bones."

"Vicks likes that side-effect, too," Frisk said through a mouthful of rice. "Keeps people from guessing on his, you know, *morphology*. I kinda miss having a little muscle, personally – I feel like I'm made of glass some days." Regina bobbed her head in agreement to that last point, and Amelia kept quiet, going at the plate in front of her at an even pace.

"I guess I never considered that it might have other practical uses," Daisy said.

"It's alternative medicine," Regina agreed, her tone laced with only a hint of sarcasm.

"I mean, people do what they do for a reason," Amelia said. "It's not so different than drinking, really. Probably safer, even. Benefits and risks, either way."

"Then why don't you take it?" Frisk asked, and Amelia sneered.

"I intend to keep my tits, thanks." Frisk cast her a lopsided grin before returning to her task of devouring the mountain of cheap roadside food before her.

Daisy could only make it halfway through her dish before it was time to head back on the road, and the food was too greasy to bag up. Still, the portion she had was more than enough, and with a full stomach, she napped on the drive back to town.

Johnston turned out to be a much more active participant in Ming's operation than Linden had been. He had called her to his office just as she was trying to piece together a plan to locate a target. Her intention had been to track down that group that had dropped the bird charm – the girl in the gold dress or her friend that Jase had shot – but when Ming's efforts to relocate either of them didn't show results within a few days, Johnston intervened and called Ming in for a meeting.

Ming had half-expected that he would backtrack on their deal just as Linden had, but instead he was ready with, of all things, helpful feedback.

"We need to be mindful of this approach, of course," Johnston muttered as he paced along his bookshelf, speaking as much to himself as Ming. "Someone too important – a professor or corporate executive... no, no, that would just breed panic. Fearmongering is Linden's game, so we must take the compassionate angle. Our target must be harmless, pitiful. Someone dainty and pretty."

Ming thought against about the girl in the gold dress. She had never been one to ogle any random beauty walking by on the street, but she could recognize conventional attractiveness as well as anyone. That girl had looked like she could have been on an advertisement for soap.

The bird charm was settled in Ming's breast pocket. She had sort of taken to carrying it around like a lucky token, though little good it had done so far. But when it occurred to her that Johnston might know more about it, she pulled it out and held it forward in her palm. "Could you track this back to its owner?"

Johnston paused in his pacing to squint at what she held before rushing over. If he meant to alarm Ming with his charging, well, he *did*, but she didn't flinch or back away. "What is this?"

"I'm not entirely sure. I found it in a speakeasy. Some kind of magic..." She paused to search for the word... "trinket."

"An artifact, perhaps?" Johnston stepped back, seemingly for the purpose of puffing out his chest a bit, but Ming wasn't sure if he was even aware of his own posturing. "A magic that originates on the Yen continent. Methodical magicians in Ashland have tried to recreate the enchantment process but have found little success."

"I don't suppose you could point me to the kind of magician who could make something like this?"

Johnston rocked on his heels. "Not anyone in my circles, I wouldn't expect. This is... folk magic, I suppose you might say."

"The hell does that mean?" Ming asked. Johnston spread his hands dismissively, but Ming suspected she knew what he was getting at. Unassimilated. Did even magicians in their underworld care so much about establishing and policing norms?

"My best guess would be out near the industrial district. If you found this in a speakeasy, then we can guess its owner is not some loner entirely disconnected from other magicians, and if they don't run in academic circles, either, they're likely working-class. The industrial district is something of a hub for this type – cheap rent, but a 'respectable' enough district that law enforcement largely ignores it."

"Can you narrow it down any further than that?"

Some of Johnston's posturing deflated as he hummed in contemplation before striding over to his desk and procuring a sheet of paper and a pen. "I have only passing knowledge of that neighborhood and its magician culture, so to speak, but these points of interest may be able to lead you to a more solid find." When he finished scribbling his notes – names and addresses of businesses in that area, from the look of it – he held it out for Ming to take, but when she grabbed ahold of it, he wouldn't let go.

"Do you know why I advocate for these magicians, Miss Roxana?" His question was soft and solemn. Ming knew he was keenly aware of the irony in calling what he was doing now "advocacy," so she didn't point it out. "It's the consolation of power. The most moneyed people to first reclaim Ashland feared competition, so they began drawing lines around who and what was considered proper. They draw lines around magic, around gender, around generations, when they could have just as easily drawn them around the pitch of one's voice or the color of their eyes. Maybe they have the wrong kind of sex, eat the wrong kind of food, take the wrong kind of shits."

Again, Ming didn't point out the obvious. Somewhere in the world, any of those exact lines separated people into either places of power or the margins. And even in Ashland, if one didn't fit the right mold, then, yes, all of those things became the subject of scrutiny and suspicion, as well.

"It's dangerous thinking, Miss Roxana, devaluing one's fellow man."

"Person." She wasn't going to let *that* one slide. He had just mentioned gender, himself.

Her correction didn't shake him. "Magicians and ogres laid the groundwork for this nation – all its infrastructure and technology. People were happy to accept their innovation until it became inconvenient or there were opportunities to gain. People with power and a chance to gain more could just as easily turn against any other group at any other time."

"And you're afraid that you'll be next?"

"No." He finally released the list of locations. "I am afraid that this nation will not survive many decades of that nonsense. A society is maintained by its social residents, and all this sneering about magicians and presumptions about what they're like, what they do – that's all quite anti-social. You have guessed that my personal circles run... magician-adjacent." It hadn't occurred to Ming before that comment that Johnston himself might secretly be a magician, but she supposed it didn't matter. She couldn't exactly make *him* the target. "Magicians are no more dangerous than anyone with a knife or gun, and they are not some unified violent ideology. They know they do not deserve what our society gives them. I can tell you that they will not lurk in the shadows enduring this treatment forever. No one would, no one could. If our society continues to abuse this group or that, it will incite backlash, which will turn into – to borrow a phrase from Franklin Blaine – a culture war. And from there Ashland is on a trajectory to become the very fascist state that our ancestors from Algretau or Berngi fled."

So that was it. Johnston's family had been terrorized or killed in one of the fascist regimes across the ocean that had formed a century ago. Some of those regimes were still active or scrambling for a resurgence; the Ashlander children and grandchildren of those who fled from the north continent could sometimes be sensitive to the notion of fascism following them to their young homeland. Ming's family had left Gao to escape plague, not any human machinations, so she supposed she never thought about fascism much.

That explained, too, why Johnston was willing to see one of his dear magicians murdered to further his own ends. A sacrifice to preserve the security of his nation. But it wasn't really a sacrifice when it was someone else's life, was it?

Ming folded the note and placed both it and the bird charm back in her breast pocket. Johnston's grandiose philosophizing was beginning to rub off on her, but it wouldn't help her do her job any better to wonder about consolidation of power and culture wars. She just needed to track down one magician, pitiful and pretty.

"I'll let you know what I'm able to find," she said to Johnston, and she turned to leave before he could ramble on about anything else.

CHAPTER 10

About a week after Daisy had revealed the secret of her grandmother's magic to Mr Swarz, there was a morning when her boss did not arrive on time. She was busy with a newspaper crossword and didn't notice until he stumbled into the office sometime just before noon. Out of habit, she nearly said good morning to him, but when she realized that he was nearly four hours late, she looked up to find him a tattered mess.

"Gracious!" She stood and rushed over to him. "Mr Swarz, what happened?"

His coat was torn – ripped along one side and scarred with what appeared to be shreds from claws on the lapels – his white shirt was stained with streaks of dirt and blots of something dark and congealed, and his hair was dusty and askew. More dirt covered his face, half-hiding bruises along his left cheekbone and jawline. His bowler hat, dented at the crown, sat crooked on his head. Clearly, he had not come directly from home.

He swallowed before answering. "Miss Dell, I am terribly sorry. I– I fear I've made a mistake."

"Andre!" Angel appeared in the doorway of her office, likely drawn by Daisy's loud exclamation over his condition. She began to step forward but he held up a hand.

"Please, don't trouble yourself. I'm fine." He winced, placing that hand gingerly over an area of his chest where stains splattered his shirt. "Fine enough. There is something vital I must share with Miss Dell that is... private." Angel looked too stunned to frown. Daisy understood – she imagined there was little that Mr Swarz was unwilling to speak about with his dear old friend that he would share with Daisy. There was only one topic that came to mind.

She took Mr Swarz by the left arm. "Let's sit you down in your office, and you can explain." He nodded dumbly and allowed her to guide him there, his cane clutched in his right hand and thunking along with each step. From the way his body tilted, he appeared to be in desperate need of it that morning. She feared what had happened to him, and the careful, limping procession to his office was almost longer than she could bear to wait before receiving an answer.

When Miss Dell had him settled at his desk, she hurried to grab him a glass of water before he began. Andre flexed his right hand while he waited for her to return, wincing along with the creak of his leather glove as he was unable to clutch his fingers tighter than the barest curl. He ripped off the glove and examined the pale, bony appendage underneath.

The white, streaking scars were faint now. The accident had happened in his childhood, when his mother took him to the factory where she worked in the summer because there was no one to watch over him at home. He had somehow gotten his arm caught in a piece of running machinery, and its gears and belts tore at his body, sucking him in to the shoulder and grating his hip and leg before anyone managed to turn it off. He was lucky to have survived, but it left him nearly immobile for several years. Even after he had learned magic, it had never mended entirely – healing was not his forte, no matter that he had first gotten into magic for that exact purpose. His hand would never be able to close all the way again, and the scars would never fully fade, but at least he was now mostly free from the pain of his injuries.

If only he were not so foolish enough to earn himself more.

Miss Dell returned, shutting the door behind her and setting the glass of water on his desk. He reached for it with his good hand and drained it as he considered where to begin.

"This is about my magic?" she asked.

He set the glass aside with a nod. Miss Dell was an intelligent woman, and it was hardly surprising that she could guess what this was about. That made him all the more embarrassed to admit what had happened – the dim-witted error he had committed – and if her safety were not at stake, he might not have told her anything for the shame of it.

"I returned to the faerie ring last night."

Miss Dell's spine stiffened, and they both glanced toward the windows. She hurried over to close the blinds, and Andre took a moment to cast a silencing ward around the room. It wasn't as safe as having this conversation in the speakeasy, but Andre was certain he would never make it down the stairs. Once the spell was in place, he felt the hollow, dizzying sensation that came with the loss of energy, and he fished a small vial of mana from his desk. Draining that as well, he continued before Miss Dell could ask questions or fire accusations.

He felt defensive, regardless. "I'm not fully sure what drew me back there. Curiosity, I suppose." This was true, in a sense, but from the way Miss Dell furrowed her brow at him, he knew he would need to offer more explanation than that. "I wished to see the faerie again."

His typist's expression fell, her mouth dropping in

something akin to horror. "You didn't go to have him—"

"No, nothing to do with artifacts. I swear." He swallowed, trying to ignore the splitting pain in his head. Mana eased the strain of magic, but it did nothing for the abuse he had suffered the night before. "As I said, I was merely curious."

It was as polite a euphemism as he could muster at the moment. In truth, when he first traveled with Daisy to the faerie ring, he had been entranced by her otherworldly friend – Cyan, she had called him. He had a healthy caution toward the creature, perhaps even bordering on fear, but Cyan's sniffing and prodding of him had its own degree of curiosity to it. Andre didn't know what could have been so appealing about him to such a being, especially considering that he hadn't carried any of the faerie's precious chocolate or shiny objects, but Cyan himself had been quite the sight. His vaguely-human features, appearing as some mix of insect or bird, had been... Andre hated to think "exotic," but he could not conjure another word for it. Underneath all the otherworldliness was still an intelligence, a cognitive awareness, and it gave Cyan's beauty something more than a merely aesthetic appeal. There had been something enticingly intimate about the way Cyan had examined Andre, too, and the brief experience with the creature had haunted him. Of course, he had said nothing to Miss Dell of this matter at the time – a wholly inappropriate conversation to have with his employee.

And he felt now that it had been wholly inappropriate to go back, considering the consequences.

"I don't know how, but I was trailed. Someone else found the faerie ring."

Her expression fell again, not to horror this time, but wide-eyed, defeated despair. "No." She shook her head, unblinking. "*No*. How could...? What happened?"

Andre shifted in his seat, trying to shake out some of the

jitters and physical pain before he began explaining. It did little to help, but he willed himself onward.

He told Miss Dell everything, feeling he owed her at least that much.

The evening prior, he had returned to the faerie ring alone. During the drive, he had seen no indication that he was being followed, though he admitted he had not thought to pay much attention to the possibility. Arriving at the farmhouse, he sat down in the faerie ring and laid out his offering – a few glittering knickknacks from his house and the same kind of chocolate that Miss Dell had brought the first time – and he cast a spell of light, summoning a tiny, magical glowing sphere to draw the faerie out. In a matter of moments, the split in reality appeared and expanded, allowing Cyan to crawl forth. Andre had not been sure, at the time, that the same faerie would necessarily appear in the spot, but he surprised himself with a sigh of relief when he recognized the blue-tinted skin.

At first, Cyan was only interested in the offering, marveling at the ball of light for a moment before shuffling through the spoons and glass doorknobs, and then turning to the chocolate. He didn't look directly at Andre until after he had wolfed down one full bar's worth and was halfway through another. The fading daylight seeping through the bare canopy of the dry forest shined off his wide, black eyes as he examined the human man. There was a gleam in that gaze that indicated a sentience equal to that of humans, maybe even surpassing it.

Cyan was a beautiful creature, but Andre's curiosity toward him was as much intellectual as it was sexual. He had no interest in replicating the sacrifices that Miss Dell spoke of, but that such a thing was possible suggested that these faeries had an innate magic far beyond the scope of humans. There was something worthwhile in that, if only from a theoretical perspective. Andre wasn't sure how much he would be able to discover, though – Cyan had not said a word during their previous visit, nor had he reacted in any meaningful way to anything that either Andre or Miss Dell said. It seemed it would not be possible to simply ask Cyan about his abilities with magic.

It felt strange not to speak, though, and Andre gestured with a hand to his chest. "My name is Andre," he said, trying to speak slowly without sounding patronizing. "You are Cyan?"

The faerie blinked and parted his lips, making a soft, "*Ahh.*" Andre didn't think that Cyan understood any of what he said, but the faerie seemed delighted to have his attention. Quickly shoving a few more pieces of chocolate into his mouth and swallowing, Cyan scooted closer to Andre. He opened his mouth again, and a babbling of vowels and soft, almost whispered consonants poured forth. It was not so much that Cyan couldn't speak, it appeared, but that the faeries merely had a language of their own. At a loss for how to respond, Andre only smiled. Much to his surprise, Cyan returned the expression, exposing two rows of teeth that were both smaller and sharper than any human's. He then ignored what remained of the chocolate to begin fiddling with the buttons on Andre's coat, muttering in his lyrical language as he took in the sight of their glinting surfaces. Andre sat still and allowed the faerie to heap his attention onto him. It wasn't often that anyone took such personal interest in Andre, and while that never bothered him, it was pleasant on the few occasions that it did happen.

He wasn't sure how long he sat there, lathered in the faerie's curious attention. Being in Cyan's ethereal presence was at once thrilling and calming, and his sense of time out in those lonely woods was skewed by what he was feeling. When he heard the rumbling of an engine, he looked up to find the sky nearly dark. Cyan heard the car, too, and fluidly pulled himself into a stand, snarling out into the forest. Andre staggered to his feet, as well, spying the glow of headlights some way down the dusty road that lead to the farmhouse. He had his cane with him and several vials of mana tucked into his inner coat pocket, but his revolver rested in the glove compartment of his car. The crashing he could hear through the woods neared at a speed that suggested he would not be able to reach the gun in time. He turned his mind, instead, to hiding the faerie.

"Back inside the portal," Andre said, waving toward the crack in existence. It glowed with a faint white light in the evening dimness, and anyone approaching might be able to see it. Cyan had to get back through and allow it to close completely. The faerie ignored his command and snarled in the direction of the oncoming intruders. At a loss for what else to do, Andre grabbed Cyan by the arm and shoved him toward the portal. "Take your things – go!" Cyan only gave him a few bewildered – possibly offended – blinks, tilting his head and muttering in his mystic language. Andre was ready to push him again when he lunged forward.

A flash of panic froze Andre as he feared the faerie intended to meet his physical roughness with violence of his own, but Cyan darted past Andre and out of the ring. Andre watched as Cyan charged at an oncoming stranger wearing a dark coat. A matching hat shielded their face from any recognition, but their garb was close enough to the description of the attackers at the Gin Fountain.

Someone *was* after the secrets of Miss Dell's magic.

Andre only barely caught sight of Cyan swiping at the intruder, scraping claws against their arm just as they tried to lift a gun. Another figure burst from the wood brush closer to Andre and was upon him before he had the chance to ready a spell. Grabbed by the side of the coat, his attacker tackled him into the dirt, landing on and crushing several mushrooms of the ring.

Incantations filled his mind as he scrambled to produce a spell, but in his panic, he could only think up random spell roots without stringing them together in any productive manner. His attacker produced a knife in their free hand, ready to slash down at him, and his mind cleared of all magic. Instead, instinct took over, and he thrashed under the person's hold. They were smaller than he – something of a miracle, slender as he was – and he managed to successfully buck them off. The person rolled away without releasing his coat, tearing a hole in the side seam. That was enough for Andre to get free, though, and he scrambled to his feet as he tried to focus on a fire spell.

With a specific function in mind, it was easier to build the spell correctly. *Ai – veth – netr*. The language of methodical magic was not one of any spoken tongue, invented by magicians themselves to convey their powers. The correct roots in the correct combinations could have wondrous effects, and what Andre needed now was a pillar of fire that would sear his attacker without damaging any more of the faerie ring. *Meq – oure–*

His incantation was cut short as a hand reached out and grabbed him by the front of his coat, jerking him to the side. A third attacker with an iron club swung at where he had just stood, but Cyan had saved his neck by tossing him out of harm's way and nearly into the side wall of the farmhouse. Andre stumbled halfway to the ground but managed to keep a hold on his cane. With a screech that was dissonant from his earlier gentle muttering, Cyan flung himself at the club-wielding assailant, claws at the ready. Andre tried to steady his feet under himself and return his attention to the one with the knife, but they were up and upon him before he could begin his incantation again. He tried to lift his cane to block, but the hilt of the knife collided into the side of his head, and things went black for him.

The smell of smoke brought him back to reality. The sky glowed with the dull grey of a cloudy morning. Pushing himself up from where he had collapsed near the farmhouse, he spied a bonfire built not far in front of him. After a few moments of hazy disorientation, he realized that it was where the faerie ring had stood. Now, covered in a layer of twigs and crisp branches collected from the forest around them, the circle was ablaze, little mushrooms already wilted or charred. Andre scanned the area for Cyan or their attackers, finding no bodies but scuffed footprints scattering every which way around the farmhouse and into the forest, some appearing to have clawed toes. Andre staggered up, peering about for any flash of brilliant green-blue. When he saw no sign of assailants, he tried to call out to Cyan, but smoke scratched at his throat and it came out as a raspy, wispy bark.

Andre looked back at the bonfire. If the offering he had left for Cyan was still there, it was buried under the bonfire kindling, and the crack in reality was gone. Although the fire itself was low and gentle in its crackling and fizzing, Andre didn't care to think of what might happen if a spark leapt from the pile to a nearby tree of the dry, wooded foothills. He conjured an enclosed but invisible dome around the bonfire, cutting off its access to oxygen. The flame was smothered quickly, and Andre removed and drank one of the vials of mana tucked into his coat pocket. The only one, in fact – the others must have tumbled out during the scuffle, and he didn't pause long enough to search for them. It would be dangerous to try another spell without a supply of mana, and as he hurried back to his car, he hoped he wouldn't have need.

Luck was with him when he found that his assailants

hadn't bothered to slash his tires before abandoning him next to that fire hazard, though he worried about Cyan. Had the faerie returned back through his portal? The tracks around the property suggested he had chased some of those attackers into the woods. Had he found a chance to come back and return to his own plane? Andre could only hope so as he pulled away from the farmhouse and returned to the city to speak to Miss Dell about the matter.

Now there – his tale complete – unmoving where he sat at his desk, he ached from the roughness of his previous night and awaited Miss Dell's lash of fury. He could not blame her; he would have done the same to anyone who so foolishly endangered him.

But Miss Dell's face was awash with concern. "They destroyed the ring?"

"I suppose there's some comfort in that. They won't be able to use it for their own ends, now. Though that seems counterintuitive if that's what they were after the whole time." That in mind, had he perhaps been wrong about them being after Miss Dell's magic?

But that was a question for later. What he had told her was driving Miss Dell into a panic, or so it seemed from the way she began pacing in hurried, tiny steps in front of his desk. "And Cyan disappeared, but you don't know to where?"

"It's possible that he escaped back into his realm, if he returned to the ring before those attackers destroyed it. But he had defended me, earlier – I can't imagine he would leave me there like that if he thought they would come back." It was a whimsical thought, but Andre was too exhausted and worn to worry about keeping such notions to himself.

"Could they have chased *him* into the forest? That would give anyone remaining a chance to destroy the ring. Or could he have destroyed it on his own?" Miss Dell paused and shook her head before whirling on him. He could finally see the heat in her deep eyes that he had been awaiting the whole time. "What were you thinking, going out there on your own like that? And while the rest of us are on lockdown, too! If we can't go out to the clubs, what gives you the right to pursue your 'curiosities' while we're being hunted?"

Andre hung his head, at once humiliated by her accurate judgment of his foolishness and outraged that he was being told off by his own employee. "It was a mistake – a grave one, I know. I apologize." As Miss Dell had pointed out to him not long ago, he had been making too much use of that phrase in recent weeks. Never insincerely, though, and his young typist relaxed her shoulders upon receiving the apology.

"What's done is done – there's no helping that now. But what do we do? Cyan may be somewhere out in our realm, and these hunters know enough of us to follow us about. Do you think they're aware of the office? Or the warehouse?"

Andre appreciated that she was careful enough to keep her language ambiguous while they spoke in the office, regardless of the wards he had put up. Especially now, as he had no answers to her question. It was possible that mage-hunters were already scouting the front office or Pinstripes.

"I'm not sure what to do. We should prioritize our own safety first. I will speak to Angel and Grey about this matter, to ensure that the company can protect you or anyone else here from the consequences of my foolishness. From there–" he shrugged, not caring about the cuts and bruises that ached under his shirt as he did so, "–I don't know what happened to Cyan or how I might even begin going about finding anything on his whereabouts. Unless you know something that might give us a clue?"

Miss Dell shook her head. "I imagine Cyan will not be

able to open the portal back to his realm if the faerie ring is destroyed. Unless he can find another one, he's trapped in our dimension. And I don't know what will happen to him, in that case. I think, at best, he may struggle to find food and shelter and will probably end up hurting himself. And I don't know if there are any other complications to his existing in this plane without a way to return home."

Andre sighed. There was no room to worry about Cyan when he had his own people to look after, and especially not if they had no way to help the faerie. Guilt jabbed at his heart, but he couldn't linger on it. "Very well. Miss Dell, will you please send Angel my way. And–" he winced as he pulled a key from his pocket to hand to her, the key that opened the back way into Pinstripes, "–after that, would you fetch Jonas for me? I fear I'm in no condition to go find him on my own."

"Of course." She took the key and turned to leave.

"And…" Miss Dell paused, glancing over her shoulder at him. Fury had drained completely from her eyes, replaced only with weary concern, sorrow, and something bitter and cold – possibly fear. Andre opened his mouth to apologize again, but he just as quickly closed it and shook his head. He had expressed his regret already, and their time was better spent focusing on doing what they could to safeguard against his wrongs. Miss Dell left when he said nothing, and Andre waited there for Angel and the berating that she would certainly give him.

CHAPTER 11

Grey closed the office and the speakeasy the next day, after hearing Mr Swarz's account of what had happened. Daisy had permitted him to share some of the details with Grey, but as she was not privileged to accompany him to that meeting, she never learned which details, specifically, he had needed to bring up in order to fully explain the situation. All Daisy knew was that, upon his return to the office lobby, Mr Swarz insisted on visiting her at home during the day off.

"To secure your... trinkets," he had said. "It is still unclear what happened at the faerie ring or what these hunters are after in particular. You and your belongings may still be at the most risk." Daisy agreed, but she wasn't keen on the idea of her boss visiting her at home. She wasn't really much keen on Mr Swarz at all, lately.

She did her best to clean her apartment, stowing away unwashed clothes so they were at least tucked into drawers rather than sprawling all over furniture, and making a token effort at cleaning the dishes in her sink until she gave up and threw a towel over what remained. What did it matter if Mr Swarz saw that her place was a mess? He already thought of her as an underachieving layabout.

He arrived midmorning, and the expression on his face when she let him inside was as wrinkled-nosed and offended as she expected. What she didn't expect was the mystified question that followed the snooty expression. "Don't I pay you enough for better accommodation than this?" He hung up his coat on one of the hooks by the door and limped further inside, still battered from the attack at the faerie ring. His eyes were hollow and ringed with dark violet, appearing sleepless since that night.

His inquiry, which didn't sound as facetious as she might have anticipated from him, confused her. "No, not really." He glanced between her tiny kitchenette and the cracked window above her bed before casting her a baffled look. She shrugged. "It's expensive to live in the city. I have more time after working hours because my commute is short, and I can get to the grocery store easily, but convenience is costly."

"I pay you a living wage – enough to support a family, if you needed to." He made a general sweeping gesture at her apartment. It was humiliating. "You could never fit a family into this."

"I've seen families fit into smaller. And it takes more than a few weeks at a job paying a living wage to afford relocating to a completely different residence." Mr Swarz only looked more confused and horrified as the conversation went on, so she changed the subject. "So, what do you intend to do to protect my trinkets?" She nodded toward the box sitting on her dresser, and Mr Swarz approached to begin fingering through them delicately.

"I can cast a ward over this – a field that will harm anyone who gets within a certain radius of the spell's center point, with the special exception of yourself. I will not be able to ward each item individually, so the box itself will have to serve as the spell's focal point. You should not store your trinkets elsewhere. I will need a sampling of your genetic code for the spell to recognize you." He spoke with typical cold professionalism, though he nearly whispered everything he said to keep any neighbors from hearing. The walls here were much thinner than they were at the office, and he probably refrained from casting a silencing ward over her apartment to reserve his energy.

"Genetic code? Like blood?"

"That's... a tad dramatic. A single hair follicle will do." Daisy plucked a curling thread out by the root and handed it over. Taking it by the root, Mr Swarz rolled it in his good hand between a finger and his thumb, his eyes half closing as he focused. Daisy wasn't all that familiar with the inner workings of methodical magic, so she wasn't sure what was happening until a faint blue shimmer appeared as a dome around her box of trinkets. While she stepped closer to examine it, Mr Swarz dropped the hair and reached into the pocket of his pants for a vial of mana.

"I'm afraid I couldn't make it invisible – too much energy," he said after taking a swig, panting softly around his words. "Could you please test it? If anything went wrong with the spell, it's better to know now while I'm here to fix it."

Daisy didn't care to think about what would happen if the spell "went wrong," but she reached out and tapped the shimmering field. Her fingertip passed through without an issue. "Well, the exception worked. Should you test it, to make sure it successfully zaps away intruders?" Mr Swarz's face paled, and she wondered how, exactly, the spell warded others away. "I'm kidding. I'll trust that you're capable enough to get it right."

"Well, it's a relief to have your trust, certainly." He tucked his now-empty vial away and took another glance around her apartment. "I think you are due a raise."

Not that again. Normally she wouldn't balk at the possibility of more money, but she would have sacrificed any amount to get him to leave now that his work was done. "I still don't intend to move any time soon, no matter how much you pay me. You don't need to trouble yourself."

"I do, though." He looked right at her, holding her gaze with a gleam in his eyes that almost dared her to turn away. She wondered about this man as she stared back. He couldn't have been much older than her, not by many years, and his social background had been even worse off than hers if he grew up alone with a mother who worked in a factory. But he was more like Angel than Daisy or any of the working class people in the warehouse – academic-minded and posh and a little stuck-up. How had he climbed up so far in the social hierarchy, and why was he such a tit now that he was there?

"Sir, you don't. Just pay me what I earn."

"That's what I mean." His gaze drifted toward the box of trinkets before locking back on her. "I've made a mess of things. I misled you about the nature of our company, I strongarmed you into sharing your secrets with me, and then I failed to safeguard those secrets, putting you in danger. You deserve so much more than money as compensation for all my blunders."

"Then give me more than money." Anger flared up, rising in her throat like a sickness. Mr Swarz was too philosophically-minded, too detached from people and their emotions as anything other than theoretical data points. All of the methodology of his magic came out in everything else about him. And Daisy nearly choked on her anger, because it felt so pointless to feel it toward a man who had a heart like a machine. Just as well to be furious at a light bulb.

She thought her words would confuse him again, but this time his shoulders slumped. "I understand. I'm sorry, Miss Dell; I never meant to disrespect you in any manner. I will–" His head swung toward the window over her bed as his sentence cut off. "What was that?" Daisy turned to look, as well. She couldn't see anything out there at first, but she heard a staccato of clicks against glass. Leaning over her bed, she peered out and managed to catch sight of a movement beyond the grimy lower edge of the window. A blur of... *something* tapped on her window. She crawled over the bed to get a better angle, thinking that it was a confused or injured bird, until she saw...

"Oh, shit!" Daisy jerked open the window and leaned out to grab her visitor, hauling him up and through. Mr Swarz took a startled step toward the bed as she tumbled back onto it with a blue, feathered being, both sprawling over each other.

Mr Swarz gawked uselessly from where he stood. "Cyan!" The faerie lifted his head and peered up at Mr Swarz with a pleased hum. Daisy interrupted their moment, shoving Cyan off of her and scrambling up onto her knees so she could shut the window and jerk the curtains closed.

"You foolish creature! It's full daylight! What if someone saw you?" Cyan titled his head like a puzzled dog. He probably understood her tone, if not the words themselves. Daisy ran a hand over her face. "The pair of you are going to destroy my life. How did you even find me?"

She got off the bed and hurried to the window in the kitchenette, peering out for sign of any followers before closing the curtains there, too. "He might have been in the area and felt the spell I was casting," Mr Swarz said. "I imagine his innate abilities with magic must make him particularly sensitive to such." That still begged the question of how he managed to get so close, but the faerie knew her and her scent. It wasn't impossible that he had tracked her – or Mr Swarz – to that location.

Daisy returned to where Cyan knelt on her bed and examined him. He had dark blue bruises over his vibrant body, and his feathers were ruffled, and there was even a patch near one elbow where several appeared to have been torn out. A few loose ones drifted off his arm to land on her bed, and she picked them out of the way and absently shoved them in her pocket. His clawed fingers had blood caked around the cuticles, and there was a cut running down one cheek. She reached out to touch him gingerly, and he didn't pull away or even flinch. "Poor bastard, just look at you. The human world is no place for a beast like you." Cyan mumbled in his lyrical faerie language in what sounded like agreement. "Mr Swarz, can you tend to him? I'll see what I have by way of food for this ridiculous ass."

"Of course, Miss Dell." While he settled at the edge of the bed and began looking over Cyan's injuries, Daisy went to her kitchenette and dug up the best imitation of a faerie offering she could find. A jar of jam and a stale heel of bread were the best she could do – having already given up all of her chocolate to Cyan the week before – and she brought it over while Mr Swarz ran a hand over the faerie's face, his eyes half-closed. The cut on Cyan's face began to shrink, though it did not fade completely. If Jonas were there, he likely could have rid Cyan of every bump and scratch in half a minute. All in all, Daisy was quite tired of having *any* of her coworkers applying healing magic to injured patients on her bed.

Cyan happily accepted the pieces of bread dipped in jam that Daisy offered him. "We need to find a way to get him home."

Mr Swarz glanced sideways at her, almost like he didn't care for the suggestion. "Can we take him back to what's left of his faerie ring? Is it the location itself?"

Daisy shook her head. "I can't imagine so. He would have just gone back if that were the case, don't you suppose? Like I said before, I think the mushrooms themselves are part of it, although admittedly my grandmother never really explained that in great detail. I don't understand much of..." She recalled when she had taken Mr Swarz to the faerie ring, asking him what he knew of faeries. "Vinnie is Boltivician, right?"

"What?"

"You told me that you thought faeries had only been seen in Boltivic since the volcanic eruptions here. It might not necessarily be true, but faeries may be more common there. Do you think a Boltivician might know more about their lore – about how to get one back to its realm?"

Mr Swarz shook his head. The movement drew Cyan's attention, and the faerie reached out to pluck the bowler from Mr Swarz's head, shoving his angular face inside to explore it. "It's possible, though that might be a bit presumptuous. Vinnie and his family are from Boltivic, though, yes."

"You told me that Vinnie practices aural magic, not methodical. That's traditional to Boltivic, right? If he knows something of auras, he might know something of other types of magic." It *was* presumptuous, but something had to be done about Cyan.

"We can ask him, certainly. Or, rather, you can. I suspect he's more partial to you." Considering that Daisy had only spoken to Vinnie on a few occasions, he must have had an impressive dislike of Mr Swarz. "What do we do with Cyan in the meantime?"

Daisy didn't dare take him back outside where someone might see him. It would be too easy for that to get back to the mage-hunters after them, if they hadn't already followed him there. "We have to keep him in here."

"By himself?" Mr Swarz cast a wary glance toward the now-warded box. Cyan hadn't expressed much interest in her trinkets when she had summoned him at the faerie ring, but that wasn't to say that he wouldn't grow overly curious without someone there to supervise him.

"No. And I don't intend to leave my home unattended when it's possible that someone traced him here. Can you housesit while I go talk to Vinnie? If it's not too offensive to your delicate senses to linger in my slum-shack, of course."

Open anger lined the crease of his brow. "I just want what's best for–" He broke off with a sigh, and his scowl somehow seemed abruptly turned inward. "Yes, I will watch over Cyan and your home. Do try to be safe. Keep an eye out to see that you are not followed."

She went to locate a scrap of paper and a pen while Mr Swarz gave her the address to Vinnie's residence. Considering her boss' warning, she decided before heading out the door to arm herself with her smokescreen headband trinket and a gaudy, onyx ring that could conjure fire. When she stepped out the door, Mr Swarz had returned to tending to Cyan's injuries as best his highly-specialized healing magic could manage. The faerie kept his eyes locked on Mr Swarz, hardly seeming to notice that Daisy left at all.

Back at her house, Ming pored over documents and photographs procured by her various informants around Soot City while the others licked their wounds. Jase was refreshing the linen bandage wrapped around one forearm, and two other local toughs – Kelsie and Arnold – cleaned off blades and clubs that had not yet been tended to since following that man out to the farmhouse.

The venture had been ill-advised, Ming knew. She and her companions had visited the locations offered to her by Johnston. They had gone to stake out activity when they found the dark-haired man in the bowler hat. He had pulled his car up to a four-way stop near where they sat in their own jalopy down a narrow, connecting street with the engine off. There were no other vehicles or any pedestrians present.

When his car stalled at the stop, he got out, carrying a cane, and went to lift the hood and tinker around a bit inside before closing it. Ming wouldn't have thought anything of it until she watched him get back in the driver's seat, glance around, and pull a small glass bottle from a coat pocket. He appeared not to notice the other car or its occupants at all as he downed the liquid within.

It was enough to make Ming curious, and they had decided to trail him to wherever his destination was, keeping enough distance that he wouldn't grow suspicious of them. When he had reached the limits of Soot City and began to head out into the wild countryside, they had to fall back even further, relying on the tire tracks in the ash to continue tracing him. Stopping the car a little ways down the road from the farmhouse the man had led them to, Ming, Jase, and Kelsie had continued on foot while Arnold waited at the wheel. The sight of the rift cracking reality open and the colorful bird-beast was enough to spook them into rash action, and they had paid for their panic and unpreparedness. In the end, they destroyed the mushroom ring surrounding the rift, hoping it would send its ethereal beast back to his plane, but the creature had already scurried off into the ashen woods. There was no way to tell if their frantic gambit had worked.

Safe at home, Ming focused on piecing together what little solid information she had on the local magicians while she and her companions healed. "How's your arm?" she asked Jase while examining photographs taken from blurry distances of ordinary-looking townspeople.

Jase's ugly features pulled into a grimace. "Birdy bastard got me good. The gashes are still deep, but at least they're clean. A bit of red meat in my belly, and I should heal up fine."

"If any of us could afford red meat," Kelsie said with a

wistful lilt, and she nodded toward the pictures. "But you're burning cash on a few extra eyes." Ming wasn't going to apologize for investing in her own success, but she wasn't sure the extra eyes were enough to get a lead.

She knew about the group from Walter's that had dropped the charm – four women, one a bit older and larger than her waifish friends, and a well-groomed man. And now she knew of this bowler-hat man, as well. She had been in contact with one of her old collaborators earlier that morning, too, which had resulted in the procurement of some enlightening news. Elicia had stopped taking jobs from Ming about two years back, but she had called Ming at Jase's house to tell her about an encounter with two "clean-pressed eggs" who had been asking around about mage-hunters. Apparently, their questions had not been softly phrased.

"Why didn't you tell me this sooner?" Ming asked when Elicia revealed that this had happened over a week ago.

"I was in the hospital." Ming's heart sagged. She understood why Elicia had tried to get out of the business and make a less risky living for herself. It appeared her dark past had followed her, though, and her safer job now in a hotel laundry room did not pay as well. Those medical bills would probably follow the woman to her grave.

But Elicia described what she could of her interrogators. Both had been wearing plain white coats, well-tailored but otherwise unadorned, and hats shaded most of their faces. Elicia had still been able to see that both were white with short, wavy blond hair. The man was fairly average in stature, if a little delicate in the shoulders, and the woman was tall and rotund. And, according to Elicia, the burns on the bottoms of her feet given to her by the tall woman had not come from a match.

Elicia told Ming how those beasts had treated her. She

couldn't say how these brilliant white fiends had found her, but they had come at her at home – a little shack on the north edge of Soot City, near the bleak, wet farmlands. The man, the whimpering beau, had held a pistol that he reportedly never aimed nor fired, and his fearsome miss had been unarmed entirely.

"That's how I knew these people were there to waste me," Elicia reported. Her words sunk Ming's gut. This was the first time she and her people had dealt intimately with magicians, but even a fool knew to be wary of a predator so certain that it didn't even bare its teeth.

Elicia recounted how the pair had cornered her in her own dining room, and the second she went to grab a chair to swing at the young fellow's head, tendrils of light had erupted from the tall woman. The snaking wisps of glowing white had gripped Elicia by the wrists and waist, knocking her into the very seat she had attempted to weaponize.

"It didn't hurt," Elicia said, but that was no comfort to Ming if these beasts had tortured the poor woman, anyway. The tendrils had only pinned and tied her to the chair, it seemed, leaving Elicia prone to the woman's interrogations.

Ming didn't want to know the bloody details, but she had to know what she was up against. Elicia, to her credit, never wavered while she recounted the ordeal.

The white woman had fired questions regarding their assault at the Gin Fountain, Elicia told Ming. There had been no violence at first, only urgent curiosity. Who had ordered the attack? Who had been hired to carry it out; how many accomplices did they bring? What or who were they after? And poor Elicia, who was just trying to clean up her act and move on with her life, couldn't provide satisfactory answers. And the magician woman either didn't believe Elicia's ignorance, or she thought a bit of pain might bring up some tangentially relevant facts. If the latter, she hadn't been wrong.

Elicia retold her experience with the white woman's more aggressive magic, from flames licking the soles of her feet to an invisible garrote that had wrapped around her neck, applying pressure to her throat until she could only breathe enough to give a hoarse shout. Her interrogator would break in this assault if her victim came too close to passing out, giving Elicia a chance to breathe and answer. If the magician didn't like her answers, she would redouble her efforts with a new tortuous spell. Her beau, supposedly, only stood by shifting nervously while his partner plied her skills with a quiet smile. In about an hour of this exchange, Elicia said, the interrogator managed to ask a question about Ming that resulted in information that satisfied her. Elicia was released from the tendrils, left there alone and suffering, unable to even hobble to her phone to call for help, her poor feet burned as they were. It wasn't until her teenage daughter came home and found her there that she was able to be escorted to the hospital, some several hours after the incident.

"She's something that crawled out of hell," Elicia added once she finished her recounting. There was a scratch of static over the phone line as her voice finally began to crack. "That man at least looked back once when they left, with something akin to emotion in his eyes. That she-devil, though, she was all storm and bluster until she found an excuse to whip out the mean magic. Then she just went cold." There was a long pause as Elicia gathered her courage back up. "They're out for your blood, Roxy. You watch out for yourself."

"Thank you, Elicia. Let's hope these fiends are done with you, and you can make a recovery." It was a bland sentiment, but Ming had gone too icy inside to manage much better. She hung up the phone.

When Ming passed the story on to Jase, he nodded along with the descriptions. "There was a big magician woman at the Gin Fountain. She was pale and blonde and well-dressed, too, with a pretty, matching boyfriend tailing her. You remember?" Ming wasn't sure, but she remembered two people like that at Walter's.

The photographs now in front of Ming had been taken a few days after that magician's interrogation of Elicia. Most were just of random people who resided in the general neighborhood that Johnston had pointed Ming to, and a few so blurry that it was difficult to discern if there were people in the image at all. This was the first chance that Ming had to look them over, though, and it wasn't as though she had much better to do at present.

"I don't think Johnston will care for us harassing every possible magician here," she muttered to herself.

"We need to leave enough alive to vote for him," Arnold said.

"I've a thought," Jase said, smoothing the bandage over his arm. "You said you found these magicians to begin with because of a magic charm. But most magicians don't use those, do they?"

"No. It's a different kind of magic, from the Yen nations. It's different from what most everyone else here practices, is all I know."

Jase rolled his shoulders. "Seems to me like it would work best in Johnston's interest to target this magician dabbling in foreign arts."

Ming shook her head. "I need a martyr. I'm already banking on people sparing sympathy for a magician – going after one that's too 'foreign' is going to push it with the moderates."

"Moderates aren't smart enough to know the difference between one type of magic and another," Jase said. "And if you go after this one who's different, there might be less retaliation against us from the other magicians. They aren't like the easily spooked upper crust that Linden is courting – they're like us. Underhanded because they have to be. We don't want to ruffle too many feathers with these people. They have their own networks and their own bullies, and they'll come after us if we keep going after their own. They might not consider some folk mage a part of them or worth getting into blood feuds over."

He had a point. Keeping connections was important, and Ming wouldn't have minded having a few magicians in her corner. If she kept shooting up speakeasies, she might well burn every possible bridge she had there. It wouldn't matter for this job, but Johnston wasn't paying her enough that she'd be able to retire once this was done, especially if every nickel went toward saving her house. She needed to keep avenues open.

"Fair. In that case, I need to find whoever dropped the charm – one of those in that group at Walter's."

"The girl we tried to snipe?"

It kept coming back to her, didn't it? Aside from that girl, the woman that Jase had accidentally shot, and the older magician and her beau, there had been two other young women at Walter's. Ming glanced down at the photos beneath her hands. Several depicted young women traveling along the sidewalks, dressed for either labor or office work. She began browsing through, looking for any shots of any members of the group see had seen at Walter's. What she found, instead, was no less interesting.

"Here's our bowler-hat friend, again." One photograph, taken from behind the corner of a building that crowded a third of the image, depicted the man standing outside a café holding a paper bag and speaking to a young woman while looking mildly annoyed. Probably on his lunch break.

Jase stood and circled around the table to peer over her shoulder at the spread of images before taking the one she examined from her hand. "Do we know her?" He tapped the likeness, a scrawny lass with pale skin and bushy hair. That was one of the women at Walter's, wasn't it? Or was Ming just desperate to find connections between these folks? No, no, Ming had seen her at the Gin Fountain, too, hiding behind the woman in white when the chaos broke out.

"Yes, she was there that night at the clubs. Maybe the charm is hers?"

"She's got the look of an addict," Jase said.

"That mutually exclusive with being a magician?" Ming asked, but Jase shrugged with an "I dunno"-sounding grunt. "Well, we can be fairly certain that she's part of the group that lost the charm – and she's chummy with our bowler-hat man." He had summoned some kind of otherworld beast – was that Yen magic, too? He had looked much too pale to have ancestors from that continent. But even if he wasn't connected to the charm, maybe he would make a good enough martyr himself.

Jase shook the picture in his hand, nearly fanning himself with it as Ming could see the gears cranking and turning in his head. "Well, we know where we can find this miss around lunch hour. I say we have a little chat with the young lady."

CHAPTER 12

Vinnie didn't live far from the industrial district where their office and speakeasy were located. Daisy arrived shortly after noon on the front steps of a clean but aging townhouse between a nearly identical house to the left and an empty gravel lot on the right. There was a mailbox nailed to the wall near the door with "Bartos" painted in neat, fading white letters on its front. That was Vinnie's last name, right? She knocked, and there was little wait before the door pulled open and a boy of about twelve years peered out at her.

"Oh, I…" Daisy nearly thought she had the wrong location until she remembered Jonas mentioning that Vinnie had a younger brother. He had the same muted brown skin and hard eyes as Vinnie, though Daisy did wonder if the Stripes' bartender had ever been quite so scrawny in the arms as his little brother. "Hello. Is Vinnie home? I'm a friend of his from work."

The boy regarded her with the sort of bored disinterest that children his age tended to have for unknown adults before turning his head to shout aimlessly into the house, "Vinnie! Your girlfriend is here!" Daisy could hear Vinnie's stomping footfalls racing down from the upper floor of the little house, and he appeared at the door behind his brother in a rushed blur.

"Marisa, hel... Oh." Vinnie wore the same plain white shirt and practical brown pants she had seen him wear at work, but he had been nearly unrecognizable to her for a moment there with a shy smile on his lips. It melted the instant he realized who his visitor was, though the expression that took its place was not unfriendly. "Miss Dell, hello. What brings you here?" He waved his little brother along, and the child seemed satisfied enough to wander off.

Daisy couldn't quite bring herself to get right to business. "Marisa, hm? Who's that?"

Vinnie's lips pulled downward – *now* his expression was unfriendly. "Nothing – no one. What do you want?"

"I've a... bit of a crisis I need help with. Can we speak inside?"

His ire disappeared, understanding her implications. Glancing past her and into the street, he quickly scanned the area before gesturing her inside. "Please, come in." A cracked voice from a room beyond the tiny foyer called out in a language Daisy didn't know as Vinnie closed the door, and he shouted back in similar fashion. He turned then to Daisy. "Sorry, my grandmother does not speak much of the trade language. We can talk in my room." He led her upstairs to a plainly adorned little space with a window facing the street, situated right next to a similar room where Vinnie's brother had already settled on his bed to read.

Although Vinnie gestured for her to sit on his bed, she shook her head. He didn't make a fuss about it, but he crossed his arms over his chest. "What is this crisis of yours?"

"Well, this may sound a bit lopsided, but I've got a faerie hiding away in my apartment right now."

Vinnie squinted behind his dusty glasses. "Is that... some kind of code?"

"It's a long story, but I have come into the care of a literal, *actual* faerie. Mr Swarz is watching over him now. But I need to get him back to his realm."

The bartender shook his head, making no effort to hide how lost he was. "And how do I help with this?"

"I was hoping you might know something about faeries. I know Boltivic folklore has a lot of knowledge about their kind, and since you were born in Boltivic..."

Vinnie arched an eyebrow, his typically stony face betraying what looked like aghast offense.

"I'm sorry, I know how it sounds! But his faerie ring was destroyed, and I need to know how else I can get him home. He's frightened and injured and I'm desperate! I have to find someone who knows more about faeries."

"Not me. I have lived in Ashland since I was Colin's age. I know as little about faeries as any native." He frowned at her. "Or less. How did you come across this creature?"

Daisy slumped. She didn't see much point in telling him, since he appeared to have nothing to offer by way of assistance. "I don't have time to explain. I just need to get rid of this faerie, before he puts us in danger."

Vinnie took a step closer, his eyes narrowing. "Danger? And which 'us'? You and Swarz, or–?"

"Grandmamma knows about faeries." Daisy and Vinnie swung their heads at the same moment to find his little brother peering through the open doorway. He had a battered comic book clutched in a roll in one fist, and his dark eyes locked onto Daisy with an intense curiosity.

"Colin, get out. This is adult business." Vinnie's admonishment didn't chase the boy off, and Daisy tried to pull Vinnie's attention back before he got too distracted by Colin.

"Vinnie, please. If your grandmother can help me in any way, I need it. It has to do with the, uh..." She glanced toward Colin, who still watched her. "All the big stuff that's been going on with the company lately. Please, I know this is such a strange request, but–"

Vinnie waved a hand. "Yes, yes. OK. You need my grandmamma to tell you… what, how to send the faerie home?" Daisy nodded. "Very well. As I said, she really only speaks her mother tongue, so I will need to translate. And you." He jabbed a finger in Colin's direction. "Do not stick your nose into this. Go back to your room." Colin ducked away, but he didn't scurry at Vinnie's harsh tone. It seemed he was used to his brother's stern manner. Once he was out of sight, Vinnie shook his head and sighed. "And here I hoped having a day off would mean *having a day off*."

"I'm so sorry. If it helps any, you can blame Mr Swarz."

"I will do just that." With that, he led her back downstairs to the living room, where a short, stout woman sat in an overstuffed chair with floral upholstery. A small table was set out before her, covered in the colorful pieces of a landscape puzzle she worked on. Vinnie pulled over two wooden chairs from a larger dining table on the far side of the room and greeted his grandmother as he and Daisy settled next to her.

The old woman bobbed her head as her grandson went off in Boltivician, speaking slow and a bit more loudly than his normal voice. She didn't look up from her puzzle as she responded to him. When Vinnie began asking her questions, he would pause after her answers to translate for Daisy.

"She says she knows many stories about the faeries in Boltivic. They used to visit only Ashland, before the volcanoes. When the big one, Onaol, erupted and fell into the sea, destroying the land of the fauns and the human nations once on this continent, they began coming to our realm through the faerie rings in Boltivic." He shrugged, indicating that he was now giving his own opinion. "Maybe they were drawn back here when the humans returned to this land."

Vinnie's grandmother gave a gravelly sigh and shook her head as she rambled on, her voice pitching lower. Vinnie grimaced when he began to translate. "It cost the faerie folk to find new portal locations. They used to come to our world more often, and it took so much energy that they took to, uh… devouring humans for theirs." Daisy didn't comment – considering what she knew faeries could do with human life-force, this detail of the story was hardly surprising. It might have even been true.

"The faeries used to get along with our kind, and they did not like that they had become our predators, so they came to the human realm less and less, until they forgot our language. But the humans were not ready to see them go. Some were desperate enough that they sacrificed their own kin to fuel the visits of the faeries, and when the faeries answered the summons, they granted these people with gifts of power. In Boltivic, these summoners are called…" He frowned. "They are called *faeya laskvets*, which is like… 'faerie lover,' I suppose." He looked at Daisy with the same kind of watchfulness that Colin had earlier heaped upon her. He didn't know much about her magic, she was sure, but Vinnie was probably clever enough to make the connection between that, her current situation, and his grandmother's folklore.

"This is a very pretty and grim story, Vinnie, but I need to know how to get rid of the faerie I have, not summon more." Vinnie turned to his grandmamma with a string of Boltivician, and he returned his attention to Daisy after her reply, his eyes seeming wider.

"She knows a *faeya laskvets*."

Daisy leaned forward. "What?"

"Or knew. He is dead, now. He was a first-generation Ashlander. Others from our homeland learned of him…" He glanced down into his lap. "Ashlanders are not the only ones who hate magic. Many Boltivicians will kill any *laskvets* they find."

"If there was such a man, though, he must have had a faerie ring to commune with them. Where did he used to live?"

Vinnie relayed the question, and then his grandmother's answer. "Out of town to the north, off the highway to the coast."

That was in the opposite end of town from Cyan's faerie ring. Was there another so close? Or had the man traveled through Soot City to reach Cyan's? "If there was another ring, I need to find it. That may be the only way to send my faerie back to his realm."

Vinnie scowled at her, ignoring his grandmother completely. "And what will happen if you do not? If you let this creature fend for itself?"

"Those hunters found Mr Swarz, Vinnie – the ones from the Gin Fountain. They followed him to the faerie ring and destroyed it. If the faerie remains in our realm, just running about on his own, he might lead the hunters directly to the Stripes. And I don't know for sure what happens when a faerie is loose in the human world for too long, but I imagine it's quite tiring for them, and I don't care for your grandmother's notion that they'll start eating people to replenish their energies." Vinnie flinched at the prospect. "Please, Vinnie. I know this entire ordeal is absurd, but our whole company could be in danger because of this. You must ask her if she knows anything about another faerie ring."

He grumbled something unintelligible beneath his breath – or maybe he just growled – but he turned to his grandmother and asked a question. His Boltivician was now more halting and hesitant than previously. His grandmamma shook her head and snapped back at him, and he began pleading with her until she sighed, muttering her response with obvious reluctance. She cast a knowing glare toward Daisy.

"The man was killed and buried on Hillfarm Road, some ways down from the lumber mill up there, where he was found communing with the faerie. She says our countryfolk will kill faerie summoners on sight, but they fear to tamper with the faerie rings themselves. If there was another ring out there, it may still be whole."

Daisy heaved a relieved breath, slumping to rest her face in her hands. "Oh, Vinnie, thank you. And thank your grandmother! Mr Swarz and I will take him out there right away." She looked up when she heard Vinnie's chair scoot back. He stood over her and held out a hand.

"That is too risky. We will scout the area out first before you bring your mystical friend."

She took his hand and allowed him to pull her to her feet. "You and I?"

"No. If those Boltivicians who killed this summoner are still around, it will be too dangerous for…" He glanced over his shoulder at his grandmother, who was fully intent on her puzzle now, ignoring the young folks standing in her living room. "You will need more protection than just I can offer."

A tightness that had been wrapped around her gut since Cyan crawled through her window finally began to loosen at Vinnie's readiness to help. "Jonas?"

"No, Jonas is a gentle lamb. At least one of the Pasternacks has the teeth we need." He rolled a shoulder, glancing away bashfully. "Besides, they have a car." Daisy agreed with Vinnie that that was something of an important detail.

Andre found himself out of sorts left alone in Miss Dell's apartment. Once he had done his best to tend to Cyan's wounds – several scratches and scars still remaining after all his efforts – Andre perched on the edge of her bed, feeling nervous about touching anything. Clothes lay draped over furniture around the space, apparently clean, but disorderly all the same. There were several stacks of books towered on the floor in the far corner of the room and by the foot of Miss Dell's bed, and he could see scraps of paper peeking out from some of them. The bathroom and pantry doors had both been left open. With nothing else to do, Andre longed to tidy up a bit, but he didn't want to affront Miss Dell again. He thought it would be a decent use of his time otherwise gone to waste trapped in there and a polite gesture besides, but she might regard it as him fussing over how she lived her life again.

Cyan didn't seem pleased to be locked in, either, as he curled on the bed and whined. After a while of sitting in still silence with Andre, the faerie began chewing at the raw skin around his elbow, where feathers appeared to have been torn out. It looked as though he had fought with some animal on his flight from the woods. Andre reached over and tried to swat Cyan's arm away from his mouth. "Stop that." Cyan recoiled and snarled at him. "Oh, hush. You're worse than an alley cat." Although he was certain – mostly certain – that Cyan couldn't understand human words, the faerie sat up at his tone, wrinkling his flat nose. Andre could tell he was growing restless.

"Daisy will be back shortly," Andre said, in a weak attempt to sooth the creature. "We must wait patiently." His tone wasn't enough that time, though, and Cyan crawled off the bed, wandering the room and glancing about. Andre hoped he wouldn't make for the door, as he wasn't certain he could physically stop the faerie if it came to it. He stood, all the same, and paced a few steps behind Cyan. Cyan didn't appear to mind, and he shuffled to the kitchen, poking his head into the open pantry.

"Do you need more to eat?" Cyan began rifling through the contents of the pantry before Andre could step in to handle the food for him, but he ultimately turned away empty-handed. He drifted instead toward the bathroom. "Just exploring, then?"

Andre waited at the doorway, watching Cyan poke about the items in the bathroom, peering into the wastebasket by the sink and plucking an empty jar of pomade from the floor to examine. Cyan was distracted from this when he noticed the mirror hanging over the sink, and he leaned forward to look at his reflection. Miss Dell had said that faeries had a different appreciation of the world, and Andre was not sure how this translated into a human understanding of intelligence. Did Cyan recognize that the faerie he was seeing was merely his own reflection?

"A handsome fellow." Cyan glanced toward Andre at the comment before turning back to the mirror, tapping its glass with a single claw. Andre almost warned the faerie against scratching it, but he knew his words would go unheeded. Cyan lost interest before he could do any damage and returned to examining the jar of pomade still in his hand, peering in and whimpering when he found it empty.

He was in need of something, Andre could tell, but if not food, then he wasn't sure what. Stepping into the cramped bathroom, he reached out to take Cyan lightly by the arm. "Come back to the bed, and we'll figure out what you need." The faerie jerked his head up at the touch, his nostrils flaring, but there was no anger or fright on his face. Instead, he stepped close to Andre – too close – and tilted his head down to sniff the human man as he had that first night at the farmhouse. Andre fidgeted under the heat of Cyan's breath, embarrassed to be so affected by the creature's attention.

With a huff, Cyan lifted his head and pushed past Andre,

hurrying back into the studio. He worried that Cyan might go after the box of trinkets – and be hit by the spell infused into the ward – but instead he went to Andre's coat hanging by the door. Andre had one empty vial of mana in his pants' pocket, but there were full ones still in the coat. He had brought a decent supply, in case something should go wrong with casting the ward. Cyan fished one out and held it up. It still shimmered with a faint glow in the dim light of the studio. Cyan tapped on the glass of the vial as he had the mirror, whimpering before turning to Andre. He held the vial out and murmured in his lyrical language.

"Is that what you seek?" The vial had a tin twist-top that enclosed it, and that seemed too much for Cyan to puzzle out. It was curious, then, if the faerie wanted the contents so badly, that he did not just try to shatter the glass. He must have been at least smart enough to understand that it would do him no good.

Andre took the vial from Cyan's hand but did not open it. "What could you possibly want with this?" Mana was a mortal creation, a mixture of gemstone dust and raw honey and hallucinogenic fungi. Surely the faeries didn't have such a thing in their own realm. Andre worried that the concoction might even be poisonous to Cyan. Mana was sweet, though – a painful, smothering sweetness, the kind that coated the throat and blanched the tongue – and Cyan did have a taste for sweet things.

Cyan hunched his shoulders and whimpered again. He was a strange creature, but the academic in Andre wanted to understand him and his odd mannerisms and abilities. More than that, Cyan was a lovely thing, and he had saved Andre when those mage-hunters attacked, although it was Andre he had to thank for their assault and the destruction of the faerie ring. Miss Dell wasn't the only one to whom Andre owed recompense, and he hoped that Cyan was at least clever enough not to drink something that would poison him.

Andre untwisted the top and handed the vial over.

Cyan, still holding the jar of pomade in one hand, took the glass bottle in the other, gingerly pinching it between a finger and thumb as he sniffed the opening. His dark, reflective eyes flickered up to Andre as he muttered something full of fluid consonants that sounded almost like an utterance of thanks, and his long tongue slid from between thin lips to lap at the vial's contents. Andre only watched as Cyan's eyes closed into pleased lines, and a delicate groan escaped the faerie as his shoulders shook slightly. It was a pretty, intimate sound.

Cyan had licked the vial halfway empty before he pulled away. When he opened his eyes, the sheen to them seemed brighter, and he pulled back his shoulders – no longer shaking – to stand up straighter. The scratches and cuts that Andre had not been able to heal completely were fading before his eyes, the raw skin by his elbow smoothing and returning to a healthy bright blue that matched the rest of the faerie's skin, although the missing feathers did not grow back. Cyan shook his head and licked his lips, his mouth pulling into a more vivacious expression than any he had worn since crawling through Miss Dell's window. There was an alertness to that grin, and Andre knew the feeling. Enough mana to replenish lost energies was a relief, but it was sometimes difficult to judge how much was needed after any given spell and not go overboard just a bit. Andre knew he had a tendency to look down upon mana addicts, but he – as every magician did at some time or another – had felt the rush of even a slight overdose of mana on occasion. A heady surge of energy that battered around in one's brain, struggling to compel one's body to utilize its full power.

But Cyan appeared to be experiencing it somewhat

differently. All the energy was there in his eyes, but it was clear that he had control over it. He handed the vial, still half-full, back to Andre. While Andre screwed the top back on, Cyan returned his attention to the round little jar he held. Cupping it now with both hands, he held it up to his face, his dark eyes shifting to an iridescent white as his mouth dropped agape.

"Cyan?" Andre hesitated, unsure if he should take a step forward – as though there were anything he could do for the faerie if he were in danger – or several steps away.

Cyan's loose lips began mouthing the liquid syllables of his language, but no sound came forward. Instead, a light appeared in the center of the jar. Just a speck at first, a round flicker glowing through the stained brown glass, but it grew until the light was intense enough to cast defined shadows of Cyan's hands and arms on the dusty floor. The faerie's silent incantation stopped then, and he blinked until his eyes returned to their normal, onyx-like state. He peered at the item clutched in his hands, tilting his head as if just now realizing it was there. The glow faded.

"What... What did you do?" Cyan lifted his eyes to meet Andre's and answered in faerie-language, which was, of course, just as useless as Andre's question. Before Andre could do or say anything more to try to puzzle out what Cyan had just accomplished, Cyan held out the jar toward him. After a faint ripple in the fibers of reality lifted the hairs on the back of Andre's neck, the jar began to glow again.

Cyan glanced meaningfully at the box on Miss Dell's dresser, then back to Andre.

Miss Dell had told Andre that creating trinkets required more power than faeries would willingly offer to the task. That was why the energy of a full human life was needed, to supply that power to the faerie crafters.

It seemed that there were alternatives.

"How did you know the mana would work?" Andre asked, more to himself as he took the jar in his hands. It glowed like a little lantern – pretty, but limited in its utility, as there was not even enough light to read by. To think that Cyan might have had to sacrifice a human life to otherwise create such a thing. Glancing toward the box, Andre realized with hollow dread – fully, cognitively aware of this thought for the first time – that Cyan had already committed such atrocities.

The terrified thought flitted off as Cyan's knees buckled, and Andre dropped to kneel beside him, setting the pomade jar-lamp on the floor. It seemed the mana was still not enough. Andre unscrewed the vial of mana again and held it up to Cyan's lips, cupping the back of the faerie's head and tilting the bottle to dribble the liquid in. "There, now. Let's hope this helps."

Clutching Andre's upper arms to brace himself, Cyan lapped at the mana as it trickled into his mouth, smearing it across his thin lips. The same contented moan that had escaped from him before reemerged, and with the faerie now cradled in his grasp, Andre couldn't deny the decidedly erotic shiver that raced down his spine and all the way to the soles of his feet when he heard it. His fingers tightened in Cyan's feathery hair.

When the vial was drained, Andre set it aside and coaxed Cyan back up to his feet before retrieving the jar-lamp. "What a curious thing," he said, again mostly to himself, "that you could use a tool of methodical magic to create a tool of ritual magic." He tilted the lamp to peer directly at the light. It was nothing more than a tiny, floating spark in the center of the jar. "I do wonder if a human magician could accomplish anything of that nature." Cyan watched him intently as he spoke, eyes again alert. "Ah, but our innate power is probably not enough to match yours. Still, this is a marvelous thing. When Miss Dell told me of the sacrifice used in ritual magic, I was crushed to realize that the entire practice might be too dangerous to even bother studying. The implications of this, though..."

Andre didn't realize the rising excitement in his voice until Cyan leaned closer, unblinking as he examined Andre's face. The faerie's enraptured scrutiny only compelled him to allow the thrill of the discovery to take ahold of him.

"These artifacts – these trinkets – they can be created. With a combination of methodical and ritual magic, they can be created without the need for human sacrifice. An exchange of energies that does not destroy human lives!" Cyan nodded along, as though in vapid agreement. Andre hardly noticed. "And these trinkets, they fall outside the regulation of fearmongering politicians and their legislations, at least for now. If there were some way for my people to secure a partnership with a faerie, or multiple faeries, we could–"

He cut off as Cyan stepped right up to him, still unblinking, though his gaze shifted rapidly between the man's eyes and his lips. Regardless of language barrier, Cyan seemed quite swept away by the passion of Andre's revelations. And Andre, as he had upon their first meeting, when Cyan had taken to sniffing him all over, became overly aware of the faerie's lean form, uncanny in its human-like masculinity. Any traces of exhaustion from enchanting the jar were gone, and Cyan was again confident and upright after that second dose of mana. The heat of his even breaths brushed tenderly against Andre's skin.

"Oh, my."

Intellectual inquiries flushed from his head as fresh memories of the feel of Cyan's peculiarly textured hair and the sound of his pleased little moans overtook Andre. Leaning closer, Cyan reached up to run a finger across Andre's jaw, his cheekbone, his lips. His action startled

Andre into dropping the jar, and in an effort to grab it before it hit the ground, Andre nearly lost his balance. He could typically manage standing without the cane, but he was jittery from his excitement over the jar and, truth be told, Cyan's affectionate touch.

Still, he had not entirely meant to stabilize his balance by grabbing Cyan by the hips.

That alarm returned for a fleeting moment, but Cyan responded with a soft trilling noise that sounded almost amused. "So sorry," Andre muttered, and Cyan seemed to accept the apology as he went back to caressing Andre's face. Andre kept his hands where they were, pressing firmly against Cyan's soft skin. The gesture strained on his weaker hand, but Cyan's wandering gaze pleaded for a connection with the man. With a shudder, Cyan slipped both hands to cup Andre by the back of his neck as he kissed him. He was no gentleman who wasted time with flirtation, either, slipping his tongue between lips and teeth to caress Andre's own. Andre could taste the lingering sweetness of mana, but it otherwise felt no different than kissing any mortal man. As he wondered how else Cyan might feel like a mortal man, it occurred to Andre that he had not felt the pleasure of another's carnal company in more months than he cared to dwell upon. He did not think of himself as a romantic sort, like Angel, but he had an inclination toward the occasional fuck, as many did, and it was pleasant to be the focus of another's affection every now and again. Having made such of an ass of himself with Miss Dell, he was ashamed to admit his own wounded desire for another living being's positive attention at the moment.

Wrapping his arms around Cyan's waist, Andre pulled him closer, and, despite how little room there was for momentum, the shift of Cyan's body to press up against

Andre's own was enough to send him stumbling back onto the bed.

No matter how beautiful Cyan was, Andre had thought his allure toward the faerie could be nothing more than standard-variety lust, and yet he found himself unable to resist the impulse to run his hands down Cyan's thighs as the mystic being crawled over him and tried to gently wrestle him out of his clothes.

Even as Cyan's touch distracted him, his shirt half-open and the faerie tracing his fingertips down Andre's bare breast to his ribs, Andre's mind wandered to thoughts of the faerie ring, of the magic Miss Dell had told him of. Of Cyan's claws and teeth tearing into a human sacrifice. That probably wasn't how the process to power the artifacts worked, necessarily, but the imagery had manifested in Andre's head all the same.

But as Cyan leaned close, sniffing and kissing along Andre's neck and jawline, Andre's frightening thoughts gave way to a deep warmth and gratitude toward the faerie.

Cyan did not have the prejudices of Andre's fellow humans. He did not despise or fetishize Andre for his practice with magic or even for his disabilities. Although Cyan had his own magic of a sort, he was unburdened by the realities and politics of Andre's world and too alien in his communications to be complicated. Cyan did not understand Andre's place in Ashland society, how hard he had worked to survive and recover, and how his culture had branded him a deviant for daring to use magic when no other resources had ever been available to him. And that lack of understanding was liberating, as Cyan didn't *need* to understand.

There was something pure in that, and Andre longed for it as much as he did for the heat of Cyan's touch.

Andre dared to half-sit up and slide what remained of his

shirt off his shoulders while Cyan continued to nip at the skin just below his jaw. When he tried to remove his glasses, Cyan plucked them from his grasp, peering curiously into his own reflection in their lenses.

"You should put them on the dresser." Andre pointed, knowing that his words would not be enough, but Cyan understood his intent easily, standing to approach the dresser and set the glasses gently upon its surface. Given their limited ability to communicate with each other, that certainly eased any worry Andre might have had about any potential misunderstandings in their current interaction.

Cyan returned to the bed as a blur of vibrant blue in Andre's now-limited sight, a shapeless and incorporeal phantom of turquoise until he was close enough again for Andre to read the details of his feathers and the lines of his lean muscles. Cyan began climbing back up on the bed, but he paused before touching Andre's cheek again, watching him with watery black eyes. Andre reached out to take ahold of Cyan's other hand, and he accepted the invitation gleefully, encircling Andre into a tight embrace before pulling them both to fall flat upon the bed.

Any lingering fear ebbed as Cyan's gentle strokes brushed questions from Andre's mind, until he was so consumed with want that not a thought remained.

CHAPTER 13

"Sure about this?"

Daisy watched dry evergreens whirring by through the passenger seat window of the Pasternacks' car – the same vehicle she had dented up on her frantic drive from the Gin Fountain to her apartment. It was a relief that it still ran, as she had never really bothered to ask what had become of the car after her night of abusing it.

She ignored Vicks' question, instead glancing over at him and examining the heavy faux-gold bangles clanking from his wrists and bumping against the steering wheel. He had a matching choker necklace, too, but otherwise wore his plain, ratty bachelor's clothes. The wig was absent, but he had thick, smudged black liner around his eyes. "Are you a woman today, or a man?" Daisy only asked to change the subject, as she wasn't sure about their outing at all, but damned if she would admit it.

Vicks shrugged. "Meh. Can't decide."

"Do you want me to use 'she' or 'he,' though?"

"*Meh.*" Vicks glanced at Vinnie in the backseat. "How's it goin', big fella? Car sick?" The rural roads heading out toward the coast were indeed winding, but Vinnie hadn't complained once, nor did he look particularly green when Daisy examined him in the rearview mirror. He just looked stern, as usual, but Vicks could apparently see something there that Daisy couldn't.

"I worry about what happened to the last *laskvets*, the one my grandmother knew." Vinnie tried to meet Daisy's gaze through the mirror. "Likely the folks who killed him live at this lumber mill my grandmother mentioned, or somewhere else nearby. If they find you trying to commune with a faerie, they will give you much the same."

"They'll try." She wished she felt the confidence she laced into those words.

They drove in silence after that until they reached Hillfarm Road. "Now, how are we gonna find this faerie ring?" Vicks asked as he turned down the road.

"Faeries use magic to move between realms, yes?" Vinnie asked Daisy, but she could only shrug. She assumed so, but it was hard to tell what was "magic" to faeries, considering some of their innate abilities. She glanced back at him, only to find him staring out the window. There was an iridescent gleam in his eyes, shifting and multicolored like an oil spill. "If so, I can seek out the aura of the spot. I will tell you when we are near."

"Vicks, you have mana in here, right?" Daisy asked, realizing that Vinnie would be taking a great risk to his health activating his magic without any.

"Always."

Hillfarm Road was longer than Daisy expected, winding up onto a steep hill covered in evergreens and sagebrush. They drove for probably another half mile before Vinnie said, "Here – the left side of the road."

Vicks pulled over onto an empty dirt patch in the area that Vinnie had indicated. They all stepped out of the car and rounded back to the trunk, and Vicks opened it up to reveal a shotgun, a rifle, and a sheathed machete.

"I would have expected more," Vinnie said, grabbing the

rifle. "Don't you use this car to make deliveries?"

"Yeah, but since all the trouble started, Frisk and I been keeping more of our weapons at home." Vicks picked up the machete and handed it to Daisy. "Here you go, Daze. In case any rubes jump us." Daisy took the blade, even though she was certain that her magic would protect her better.

"All right, Vinnie. Where to, now?" He pointed them uphill, and Daisy led the way, hacking through the sagebrush with the machete. The other two followed behind her, firearms at the ready.

With Vinnie directing her, they soon came across a clearing out of sight from the road. There were a few stumps and uprooted saplings, a conspicuous mound of dirt, and a faerie ring made up of deep violet and pale magenta fungi. The little mushrooms were brighter and taller than those of Cyan's ring, but it otherwise looked the same, even about the same circumference.

Vinnie swung his head around, examining the edges of the clearing with his eyes still shining full of magic that swirled iridescently. "I will be able to see if anyone approaches, but mundane human auras are not as bright as magic ones. I may not find them until they are upon us."

"I should test the ring, shouldn't I? To make sure it works before I try bringing Cyan here."

Vinnie nodded. "Be quick."

Daisy set down the machete and approached the ring. "I didn't bring anything to offer, though."

"How's that, now?" Vicks asked, coming up beside her. She caught a glint of gold off his bangles in the dim woodland daylight.

"A faerie will only appear if lured here by magic and an offering. Cyan could be summoned with shiny objects and sweet foods. I hope that the faerie at this ring will respond the same way, but I don't have anything with me." She glanced meaningfully down at Vicks' bangles. He caught the look and sighed.

"All right, all right." He slipped them off one at a time, handing them both over. "You owe me, though."

"I will replace them, I promise."

Vicks shook his head. "Nah, don't bother. They're trashy, anyway. Just make it up to me with a dinner date. Nothin' fresh, though – I only do platonic relations." Daisy smiled at him in thanks and stepped into the ring, laying down the bangles.

She settled into the bare earth, crossing her legs as she adjusted the onyx ring so the stone faced upward from her palm. She only owned two pairs of breeches, and she had been lucky enough to have donned one of them that morning, perhaps unconsciously in her efforts to spite Mr Swarz and his damned expectations. Not that she looked anything short of a stylish if gently masculine Modern Girl in those high-waisted pants.

Comfortable on the ground and with the ring adjusted, she activated it to send a small, wisping flame shooting up from the stone. She allowed the magic flame – more liquid in its appearance than that of regular fire – to dance over her palm for a few minutes, until lines of blinding white cracked across the surface of reality in front of her.

"Daze, what is–?"

Daisy didn't bother to turn to Vicks. "Shh! Never mind it, and just stay outside of the ring. I'll let you know if I need help. Keep an eye out for anyone else until then."

The crack expanded, exposing a glimpse into that rainbow-colored otherworld beyond, and a clawed hand stretched from the bright abyss into the human realm. As the rift grew into a portal large enough for a human to pass through, the rest of the faerie's body followed.

Cyan was the only faerie Daisy had ever seen, and she

wasn't sure what she expected from another of his species. The one that appeared before her looked like an uncanny imitation of a human crossed with an insect or bird, just as Cyan did, and she stood tall with breasts that seemed too heavy for her frame. Her face was nearly identical to Cyan's, with the same black eyes and flat nose, but her skin and feathers came in shades of pastel purple.

Lavender.

When the faerie stood fully in the human dimension, she glanced down at the gold bangles before shifting her gaze to Daisy, and she snarled.

Daisy's heart constricted. She knew how to deal with Cyan from those visits with her grandmother. It had never occurred to her that another faerie might not be as keen on strangers. To her shock, Lavender ignored the offering entirely, instead gazing around the clearing. She looked directly at Vinnie and Vicks, and although she didn't react to either of their presences, that acknowledgement was more than Cyan had done when Mr Swarz stood outside the encirclement of his faerie ring. Her snarl faded when her eyes landed on the dirt mound on the far side of the clearing.

She made a noise like a hungry kitten and stepped toward it, passing by Daisy without another thought. Daisy turned to watch, and when she expected Lavender would halt at the edge of the ring, the faerie stepped over it and strode to the mound. The portal to the faerie realm shimmered and disappeared once she was outside the ring.

"What do we do?" Vicks asked in a whisper.

Daisy stood, watching Lavender kneel over the mound, picking absently at clods of dirt there. "I don't know. I thought she would take the offering, but..." She trailed off, at a complete loss as to what this faerie was doing.

But Vinnie shook his head. "The *laskvets* – he was buried

there." Lavender dug her fingers into the soil and moaned, hunched over in misery. "Perhaps she thought he would be the one calling for her. She seems to be… mourning."

"Why?" Daisy could hardly imagine Cyan reacting that way if something should happen to her.

"To call *laskvets* 'faerie lovers' is not to say that there are merely enthusiastic about the creatures. And, if my grandmamma's story is to be believed, these faeries visit the human realm at great cost to themselves. It may be more than shiny objects that compel them to come here."

"She loved this man?" Daisy asked. Vinnie only shrugged, and Daisy joined him and Vicks outside of the ring to watch Lavender whimper and paw at the dirt.

"What now?" Vicks asked.

"I came here to see if sending Cyan back through her portal would work," Daisy said. "If I could just communicate what I need, I might be able to ask her to help me."

Vicks' brow wrinkled. "You gonna fuck her?"

She returned the question with a flat stare. "I don't think *all* faerie lovers have to take the name so literally. But she won't understand me if I try to talk to her, and I'm not sure how else…" She paused, remembering something from Cyan's visit to her apartment. Tufts of feathers had fallen off of his injured elbow fringe, and she had stuffed some in her pocket. She reached in and pulled out a delicate green-blue feather. It might be enough. With luck, Lavender and Cyan might even know each other on the other side of those portals, and she would recognize it as his.

Creeping around the makeshift grave to approach Lavender from the front, Daisy held the feather out as she tiptoed up to the faerie. "Hello, lovely creature." Lavender looked up at her with loss and hunger painted on her alien features. Daisy didn't know if faeries could shed tears, but the corners of her mouth twisted into the mask of someone consumed with weeping. "Lovely creature, your brother needs your help. This is his – do you know it?"

Lavender stared blankly at her until she pushed the feather closer, and recognition ebbed away the misery from the faerie's expression. She crawled forward on hands and knees to sniff at the feather before carefully taking it from Daisy's hands, turning it around to examine its bright color.

"He needs help," Daisy repeated. "He needs to go back home." She pointed toward the faerie ring and the space where the portal had earlier appeared. "Home."

Lavender's jaw twitched as she sniffed, ruffling her own feathers, and her dark eyes followed Daisy's gesture. She stood and wandered over to the ring, her back unusually straight as she took delicate steps. Returning to the center, she turned to Daisy and tilted her head.

Daisy nodded, putting so much emphasis into the gesture that it hurt her neck, hoping that this faerie understood. "Yes! The portal. Can you take him through the portal? Take him home?" She came closer, pointing at the feather still gripped in Lavender's hand and then at the empty space where the portal had opened.

Lavender's gaze wandered – first to the feather, to the spot where Daisy had pointed, to Daisy herself, and finally to the grave of her fallen lover. When her eyes returned to Daisy, she nodded once, slowly. There was clarity in her black eyes, and underneath that an unshakable unhappiness. Daisy pitied her for her loss, but she heaved a sigh of relief all the same.

"Thank you." Lavender's hand closed over the feather, crushing it. "I will return with him, soon." Her words would be meaningless, but Lavender must have heard the dismissal in them, as she knelt to gather up the bangles and the portal to the faerie realm opened again. Daisy stood still, watching her leave without a glance back. When Lavender was gone and the portal closed, Daisy and her companions were left silent in the woods, with only the distant chirping of a finch in the background.

"That it?" Vicks asked once Daisy picked up the machete and began toward the trail they had cut through to the clearing.

"That's it." She didn't say anything more until they returned to the car.

When they were back on the road, returning to Soot City, she was able to shake the haunting sorrow she had seen in Lavender and was able to speak again. "I think she understood. She'll help Cyan back home."

"And then what?" Vicks asked. Of course, she had only told him the same that she had said to Vinnie – that she had a faerie in her possession and needed to be rid of him.

"What do you mean? Getting Cyan back home is the whole point. There's no 'and then' to follow it."

Vicks' eyes flickered away from the road just long enough to glare sideways at her. It was the first time she had ever seen an emotion other than flippant joviality or hungry curiosity on his face. "Don't bullshit me. This has to do with the Gin Fountain and your little do-dads. Nobody was sending hits after any of us before you showed up, and Swarz never needed to babysit no faeries before then, neither. I'm not stupid, Daze."

He was right, but the accusations in his words put her on the defensive. "Look, I don't understand everything that's going on, but my first priority now is to deal with Cyan, so that's what I'm going to focus on."

Vicks' hands tightened on the steering wheel, highlighting all the cracks and scars on the skin of his knuckles. "My sister got shot. She could've died." Daisy was about to snap back at him, refusing to take responsibility for that, until he added, "*You* could've died. Daze, if there are people hunting us, you gotta think of the bigger picture. This faerie, he landed in your lap because of these mage-hunters, didn't he?"

"They followed Mr Swarz to Cyan's faerie ring and destroyed it, yes," she admitted.

"And don't you think they might try to follow you to *this* one, too?" Daisy's heart sunk. She had been careful in seeking out Vinnie's – and now Vicks' – help, but there was still a chance that someone had followed Cyan to her apartment and was waiting to track him further. She already blamed herself for what happened to Cyan, for showing Mr Swarz the faerie ring at all, and she couldn't bear to be responsible for the destruction of another ring. Especially not after seeing how much Lavender already suffered from the humans' distrust of magic.

But acknowledging the risk didn't do much to change her options. "I can't keep Cyan in my apartment forever!" She jumped when she felt Vinnie's heavy, warm hand rest on her shoulder.

"Mr Swarz is a clever man, and I trust he knows more about your situation than either of us. Perhaps you should consult with him before you act."

Daisy nodded, relaxing under Vinnie's reassuring touch. She might have been at her wits' end with Mr Swarz and his nonsense, but she still trusted him to be an intelligent man, and he did know as much about the situation as she did. She closed her eyes and kept them shut for most of the ride back into town, trying not to dwell on the misery she had seen in Lavender or her own fear that she might end up inflicting more.

"Ouch! Hell!" Ming heard a smack on the other side of the partition. She and her group – still Jase, Kelsie, and Arnold – had taken their quarry to an abandoned shack

in the industrial district that she sometimes used for such purposes. It was the closest of her spaces to where she had found the woman, and she wasn't keen on taking this lady up to her main base. The last thing Ming wanted was for these magicians to figure out where she lived. Ignoring the struggle she could hear, she finished sharpening the blade she was working on. It was just a small jackknife with a heavy hilt – useful for these sorts of interrogations.

Stepping around the partition, she entered a space occupied only by a single wooden chair, a dull electric light hanging from above, her three minions, and their target.

Regina Sadowski – this scrawny, vacant-eyed mana addict found and taken just a few blocks from an ordinary deli where she had gotten lunch, where Ming and the others heard the counter boy call out her name when her order was ready. The woman that Ming's spies had photographed with the bowler-hat mage at that same deli a week back, and who had been with the group that dropped the bird charm. She sat tied to the chair, a pink mark on her face where Kelsie had slapped her. Kelsie now stood the furthest from the captive, clutching her wrist.

"She *bit* me." Ming didn't respond. She wouldn't have done any differently in Regina's position.

Ming stood before Regina, absently spinning the knife in her hand. "Hello, Miss Sadowski. I have a few questions for you."

Regina ignored the knife and instead tried to peer into Ming's face. The room was ill-lit, and Ming and all her companions were dressed in their dark coats and hats. Ming also had a black scarf wrapped loosely around her, and it concealed most of her face. She didn't intend to kill Regina to keep their identities secret – it was so much easier just to cover up. When the young woman didn't speak, still squinting and trying to catch even a glimpse of her kidnapper's features, Ming continued.

"I do hope you will cooperate. We only want information. This can be a simple, straight-forward interaction, if you're willing to make it so. We already know that you keep company with a few magicians – that you haunt Walter's and the Gin Fountain. Tell me: do any of your magician friends do an unusual sort of magic? Something different than what the other magicians do? Maybe some kind of magic with foreign roots?"

Regina stared up at her, and when Ming began to fear that Regina wouldn't readily speak, she stopped twirling the jackknife and stepped closer. Her threats were already clear, but with the knife held at the ready, hopefully it would stir up Regina's survival instincts and get her talking.

The young woman sounded calm – *bored*, even – when she answered. "Yes, I know magicians."

Ming tried to recall the terminology Johnston had shared with her about different types of magic. "Ones that do methodical magic? Or others?"

Regina rolled her head, and her black curls bounced on her shoulders. "Both."

Ming relaxed the arm that held the knife and gestured toward Jase with her free hand. He stepped up and dropped the bird charm in her palm, which Ming then held out in front of Regina. "Do you recognize this?"

The young lady squinted again, seeming to seriously consider the question. "No." Ming believed her.

"It's a charm with magical properties. Do you know who might own such a thing?" Regina's expression remained still as stone, but her cheeks pinkened. The length of her hesitation was telling.

"I don't... I don't know for sure."

Ming closed her hand over the charm and began twirling the knife again. "No guesses?"

"I don't know."

That wasn't good enough for Ming, and she halted the knife and shoved it forward, edge perpendicular to Regina's neck. Ming stopped and held the blade a hair's width from Regina's throat. "I don't have any particular desire for blood," Ming said, and she meant it. "But I need this information. Cooperate."

Regina swallowed, now quaking a bit in her chair. Her eyes were bloodshot, and Ming wondered if it was fear or addiction that shook her. She didn't have any mana with which to bribe the woman, she realized with a pang of embarrassment. That probably would have been more convincing than the knife. But threats, it seemed, were not completely useless.

"Wh– Why?" It wasn't an answer, but it was better than silence. That she spoke at all told Ming that Regina was scoping out her possibilities, trying to see how little she could get away with tattling. Which meant she was willing to tattle, at least a little.

"Just doing my job."

"You gonna hurt her?"

She'd slipped, but that told Ming little except that she probably wasn't looking for the blond man. "Probably." Regina choked back a whimper and set her jaw. Ming didn't have time for that. "I get you want to protect your friend, but here's the thing: we know some of your other friends, too. If you help us out, we won't have to go pestering them." Regina tilted her chin down until it nearly rested against the knife, staring at the floor – a gesture Ming couldn't interpret, so she pushed onward. "Your friend who wears the bowler hat, perhaps? The busty lady in white?"

Regina kept staring at her toes, but she spoke in a whisper. "They will destroy you." Ming frowned, but she refrained from interrupting. "You know what magicians can do?

Everybody – all those politicians and concerned mothers' groups and people who listen to Franklin Blaine – they all think it's a morality thing. 'Unnatural,' or whatever." She glanced up, her pupils seeming too small for the dim lighting. "But they're dangerous. I think people forget that, but a magician can fry your guts from the inside out. They can flay you with their minds, melt your bones, make you bleed out the eyes. So go a-fucking-head. Try questioning them. See what happens."

Ming waited a moment longer, hoping Regina might have more to say. She did, but nothing that helped Ming. In a quiet, wicked voice, Regina whispered, "I dare you."

Ming snarled and pulled the knife back to strike Regina across the face with the hilt. Regina yelped as her head whipped aside, but Ming could only hear her own breathing ringing in her ears as she panted and thought. There were still too many uncertainties, and she needed to narrow it down. She had to be sure. She couldn't afford more mistakes like at the Gin Fountain, kill the wrong the kind of target, and turn every magician in the city against her. Especially not if those magicians were as dangerous as Regina's portents suggested.

Ming dropped the knife and took a fistful of Regina's dark curls, jerking the young woman's bruised face up to look her in the eye. "Just tell me who the little bird belongs to! That long-haired woman?" Regina stared back with vacant eyes, expressing no pain, fear, or even anger. Ming wasn't even sure Regina understood to whom she was trying to refer. Ming tried to remember the others she had seen playing cards, the ones Regina had left with. "The pale one that's all angles? The dark woman in the gold dress? It has to be one of them!"

Unless she had been mistaken. What if someone else dropped that charm there, maybe hours before Regina's friends arrived?

But she noticed that Regina's small pupils had expanded. Which of Ming's descriptions was that reaction to? The last one? Or was Ming imagining it in her desperation? If her suspicion was correct, this would be the same woman that she had tried to capture that night at the Gin Fountain. Perhaps some part of Ming only wanted it to be this woman who she had already once set her sights on.

She decided to bluff, figuring it had to have been one of the last two she had mentioned. "The one in the gold, huh? What's her name?" Regina's eyes widened further. Ming was on the right track, but she didn't want to alienate this woman worse than she already had. She had to be gentler. "Just her name. Then, you can go."

"You don't even know if she's the right one." Not for certain, no, but that was the risk with interrogations. Regina's little tells were enough, Ming hoped. "And what will you do with just a name?"

Ming had used as little to track a target before, but of course she wouldn't tell Regina that. "Exactly. So, you shouldn't be too worried about handing that information out, right?" Ming tucked the jackknife in her belt behind her back as a sign that she meant it when she said that she would let Regina loose.

Regina bit her lip. Ming had struck her with the knife hilt right where Kelsie had earlier slapped the woman, and the bruise on her cheekbone was starting to swell. She had to have been in pain, and Ming was beginning to see that Regina's earlier confidence was waning.

"Daisy."

Ming crossed her arms. She had to admit, she admired Regina's gumption, as much as it wasted her time. Again, she would have done no differently in the young woman's position. "You can't meet me halfway here?"

Regina winced. "Daisy Dell."

Ming nodded to Jase, who came up to Regina with a burlap sack to drop over her head before he began untying her from the chair. She didn't yell or thrash – a smart girl, and Ming was glad that she had not been given reason to hurt Regina any more than she had. She had gone in prepared to do as bad to Regina as the lady in white had done to Elicia, but Ming truly didn't want unnecessary bloodshed. It was all just business.

"We'll take her back to where we found her," Ming said to Jase. Regina would tattle about this exchange the instant she reunited with her friends, Ming was sure, but she hoped at worst that would only scare Daisy into flight or hiding, which wasn't as much trouble as hanging on to Regina and risking her magician friends coming to hunt Ming down in some rescue attempt. For all the hassle of dealing with Regina already, she hadn't offered much, but it might be enough. Ming's main concern, now, was the small window of opportunity she had to find this Daisy Dell.

Ashfall began drifting down in a thick shroud about the time Vicks pulled the car up to Daisy's apartment building. She still had the machete clutched in her hand when she got out, and Vicks failed to ask for it back, even as her fist tightened over its hilt.

"Thanks for the ride," she said as she stepped out.

"Sure thing, Daze. Take care." His farewell was unexpectedly soft-spoken. In the backseat, Vinnie only offered a solemn nod. It was an uncomfortable parting, and she felt ashamed for getting either of them swept up in her mess. She had told Vinnie he could blame Mr Swarz, but she felt more and more like all this was her fault.

She should have never trusted Mr Swarz.

Daisy didn't bother to hurry through the ashfall, indifferent if it clung to her hair and clothes. Night had already come, and she might have a chance for a shower before bed if she could talk her employer into sticking around for a few minutes more to keep an eye on Cyan. Vicks drove off once she was inside the foyer, and she tried to push him and Vinnie out of her mind as she climbed the creaking, narrow staircase of her building.

When she reached her door and began to unlock it, an aching headache throbbed behind her eyes. She wished she could do something for Lavender or something more for Cyan, and she wished that these mage-hunters would just mind their own business. Not even clear still on who was chasing her or why, the stress of it all was finally began to catch up to her, accumulating as a thunderstorm in the center of her skull. She couldn't hold back a weary but relieved groan as she shoved the door open.

"Mr Swarz, I'm back. I think I got a lead."

Stepping inside and shutting the door behind her, she realized she still held the machete and leaned it against the wall. Turning into the studio, she paused at the sight of something unfamiliar. She almost didn't recognize it at first, that pale mass covering her bed, but after a second of mental delay, her mind registered it as a human body, naked and stretched out facing away from her. Mr Swarz turned his head to glance over his shoulder at her voice, and even across the room she could see his pupils widen.

Daisy yelped and backed into the door at the same instant that Mr Swarz tried to thrash his way off the bed, scrambling to grab a knitted blanket that lay crumpled on the floor. At his movement, another shape on the bed stirred, and Cyan pushed himself into a sitting position, looking straight at Daisy as he rose.

Daisy ignored the faerie for the moment.

"What the hell!?"

Her boss was in the process of wrapping the blanket

around his waist as he stood. Not a single piece of clothing adorned his body, not even his spectacles. Even with the blanket draped over him, there was enough exposed to see him blushing down nearly to his stomach. "I'm so sorry, Miss Dell! I can–"

"No!" Daisy held out a hand as though to push him away, and used the other to cover her eyes. "No more of this 'Miss Dell' nonsense. I just saw your bare ass – we are on a first name basis from now on!"

Mr Swarz – Andre – gave a shaky sigh. "All right. Fair enough… Daisy."

"What are you doing?"

"We were–"

"Don't answer! That was rhetorical." She let the hand slip from her eyes, having given herself a moment to recover from what she had seen. Andre had shuffled over to her dresser to retrieve his glasses and slip them on, and Cyan was still on the bed, watching her patiently with the occasional glance toward Andre.

"I apologize. Profusely. Things got… out of hand while you were gone. I swear, I will replace your bed sheets. And burn these ones."

"Oh, blazing embers! Just… just put your pants on." Daisy averted her eyes from him as she stepped further into the room, meeting Cyan's gaze. She was never sure about faerie expressions, but he looked perfectly shameless and quite content, though he did follow her every step with his eyes. He understood that she had been out looking for a solution to his predicament and now waited for her report. Under normal circumstances, she would have envied him for how carefree he was. That he and Andre had been fooling around while she fixed their mess was infuriating. They were both lucky she had set that machete down by the door.

"I'm decent," Andre announced, and she dared to look

back at him. He had slipped into his pants and white shirt, but the garments were crumpled, and his waistcoat and hat were still strewn on the floor. His long hair was mussed, with several wild strands sticking out in tangled loops and arches. It was the least decent she had ever seen him. "Did you manage to speak with Vinnie? You were gone a long while."

"Long enough to have a honeymoon with our otherworldly charge?" The red already splotched across Andre's face darkened, and he ducked his head.

"Yes, we rather lost ourselves in the heat of the moment."

Daisy crossed her arms, digging her nails into her skin until it began to burn, but she was too annoyed to care. She should have made Andre go out and pester Vinnie, and she could have stayed home and relaxed. "Heat of what moment? Weren't you just sitting around in here?"

He looked up, and a puzzled or maybe hesitant expression flitted across his face. "No, the most phenomenal thing... here, I must show you." He stepped closer to the bed and knelt, picking up something she hadn't noticed before on the floor, half rolled under the bed. When he held it out, she saw that it was just a stout glass jar.

"Please tell me that isn't lube." It was going to be too long before she could get the unsightly vision of her boss' bare, flat ass out of her head as it was.

Andre flinched. "Ah, no. Cyan picked it up in your bathroom. Just an empty jar of your pomade. But look." There was only a half-second pause before a light began to grow in the center of the jar, shining through the stained glass so that it glowed warmly.

Daisy sucked in a breath and stepped up to snatch the jar from him. Peering inside, she could see a suspended little ball of light. No electricity, no wires, no oil or wick. It was magic, but none of her trinkets took the form of a jar.

Gripping down on it, she glared at her employer. She

dropped her voice low enough that she wasn't even sure he would be able to hear. It was a question she didn't want to have to ask, and she wasn't sure she wanted the answer. "Did Cyan make this?"

"It's not what you think. There was no sacrifice. He got into my mana, and it made him... energetic. He was able to use that power to create this little lamp." As Andre explained, Cyan crawled off the bed and came to stand beside them, peering over Daisy's shoulder at the item. "I don't know exactly how the mana affected him, but I gave him more when he wavered after enchanting the item. I was marveling over it while he recovered, and that's when..." He shrugged absently, as though she should know what came next. She did, and for once in many days she felt gratitude toward Andre for the small mercy of not saying it out loud.

She shook her head, turning the object over in her hands. "I can't imagine that a bit of mana is anywhere comparable to the complete life energies of a full-grown human."

"That's what I thought. Perhaps he cannot do any more complicated enchantment than this without more power, but he was able to accomplish at least this much with only half a vial of mana. It certainly has wide-reaching implications for everything that's known about methodical magic, and I imagine for ritual magic, as well."

Daisy shoved the magic lamp back to Andre. "It doesn't matter. We're getting rid of him." He frowned, and not his usual disapproving frown. "I *did* speak with Vinnie. His grandmother was able to point us to another faerie ring outside the northern edge of town, down the highway to the coast. I communed with the faerie there, and I think I got her to understand that I need to bring Cyan to her."

"How is it that everyone's grandmothers know so much about folk magic?" If the joke was meant to hide the disappointment in his expression, it didn't work.

"Don't tell me you want to keep him."

Andre flinched and set the jar back on the dresser. "No, no. I understand that he needs to return to where he belongs. But there is so much to learn from his kind and their abilities, and..." He trailed off before he could make any mention of the sex.

"Andre, listen to me. We've already caused enough mess with this. These faeries are connected to their rings, and I don't know what more might happen to Cyan now that his is destroyed, even if we can get him back home. So if I let you come along for this, you have to promise me that you will never go back to this faerie ring without my accompaniment."

"But–"

"There are bigger things than intellectual inquiry! You may be curious about their magic, but we're the ones who keep summoning them to our realm, and they might be in danger because of it, to say nothing of the risk to other people. I can't stand to be responsible for more harm coming to them. Please, promise me that you'll just let it drop."

Andre flinched again, and Daisy choked down an urge to whack him in the face. He was hesitating? As though it was such a difficult decision between curiosity and the lives of others.

"I... Yes. Yes, you're right. I promise, I will assist you in returning Cyan to his realm and... and I won't pursue the matter any further." He cast a forlorn look in the faerie's direction. Daisy was beginning to see that Andre was much more of a fool than he first seemed with his pressed white shirts and tight-laced attitude, but even he couldn't have been airheaded enough to become so infatuated over a creature that reaped human lives. "Should we leave immediately, then?"

Daisy glanced toward the window facing the back street. She hadn't yet seen any sign that Cyan had been followed, but that didn't mean much. "I don't know. I'm worried about those mage-hunters tracking us to another ring."

The sorrow faded from Andre's expression, returning to his typical steely mask, and it was more of a relief to Daisy than she would have expected. "They are rather a bother, aren't they?"

"That's one way to put it."

"It makes it much more difficult to go about our business without having to worry about drawing their attention. And regardless of how we handle Cyan, they will remain a menace even afterward."

Daisy tilted her head. He wasn't wrong, irritating as it was to recognize. They had been pulling the attention of this Ming Wei and her mage-hunters ever since Daisy carelessly dropped one of her trinkets at Walter's, and if it continued to cause them trouble...

"We should draw them to us."

"What?"

Daisy was still piecing the idea together as she blurted it out, and she kept going as the concept solidified in her brain, remembering the conversation with Vicks on the way home. "They're already hunting us, and so long as they've got their eyes turned our way, we'll never be sure we can get Cyan to the other faerie ring without risking its destruction. We need to be rid of them before we try to take him home. And Angel and Rudolph said Wei was an independent contractor, so these hunters won't have a bigger organization behind them to offer protection or seek revenge if someone went after them. So, let's jump them!"

"You want to lay an ambush?" His tone was flat, and she couldn't tell if he was impressed or thought she was out of her mind.

"Whatever it takes to keep them from hounding us. And then they'll be out of our hair for good." Cyan, who had been standing patiently beside Daisy this whole time, finally began shifting his weight and ruffling the feathers fringing his jaw. She couldn't tell if he was reacting to her aggressive energy or merely tired of waiting to be taken home. Andre noticed the faerie's discomfort and nodded to him.

"It may take some time to plan. Will Cyan be safe until then?"

"I don't know. I worry that he and Lavender – the faerie who resides at the other ring – will be in danger for as long as the mage-hunters keep trailing us. How soon do you think we could lay a trap like this?"

"I will have to speak to Angel, certainly... and Grey. That cannot be accomplished until tomorrow, in all likelihood. From there, it will depend on what we can devise and what resources we will need, but..." He shrugged. "As soon as the day following, I suppose."

Daisy glanced to Cyan. Being in the human world did not appear to drain him in any malign way, as he appeared alert and calm. She expected she would soon run out of bread and jam if she kept him around too much longer, but no worse than that. "I think he'll be fine for at least that long." When her gaze drifted back to her boss, his dark eyes were already locked on her. "What is it?"

"I'm not surprised that you're taking the initiative with this matter, but what you're proposing could mean the deaths of these mage-hunters. That could be anywhere between a few to over a dozen people."

Daisy shrugged, but her effort at playing nonchalant couldn't hide the gentle, nervous quiver in her voice. "It's self-defense. I wasn't hurting anyone before with my magic – why should I put up with being harassed and hunted?"

"I don't disagree, it's just..." Andre pushed his glasses up his nose in the brief moment of silence. "I truly only needed a typist. I know I said part of the reason I hired you was my suspicion that you were a magician like myself, but I never intended for you to get directly involved in the 'organized crime' aspect of our criminal organization. Not so soon, at least."

Daisy cocked her head. "Then I suppose you shouldn't have hired me."

Andre cracked a smile, and despite a voice in the back of her mind shouting at her to remain furious at this man for everything he had mucked up in her life and all the disrespect he had heaped upon her, she grinned back.

CHAPTER 14

After putting out a call to Angel to update her on Daisy's plan, Andre ended up staying the night, curling up next to Cyan on Daisy's bed – which she refused to touch until those promised new sheets were presented to her. Daisy made herself comfortable on the floor. The next morning, they swaddled Cyan in Daisy's largest clothes – her second pair of breeches, a baggy cream cardigan, and a wide-brimmed brunch hat. From a distance, one might not notice the blue skin. Daisy quietly hoped for a heavy and hazy ashfall that day, all the same.

They arrived at Pinstripes through the street-side entrance around midmorning. Daisy hadn't expected anyone else to be there yet, but Andre knocked at the door and waited for Jonas to permit them inside.

"Thank goodness," Jonas said through the eye-slot before opening the heavy portal. "Thought you'd never get here." He winced as Cyan stepped into the speakeasy after Andre and Daisy. "This, uh, your friend?"

The emphasis on the final word told Daisy that Vinnie had already mentioned something to Jonas about their outing the day before. She didn't respond, though, because Andre cut in. "You were waiting for us?"

"Huh? Oh, yeah!" Jonas pointed inside, where what

appeared to be the entire damn company huddled around a single table – most standing and speaking softly but anxiously to one another, and only Regina and Amelia sitting, the latter patting the former on the knee. "Something went down with Gina. I haven't got the whole story yet, but..." He shook his head.

Andre huffed before rushing over to the scene, the butt of his cane smacking the hardwood floor with each hurried step. "*Gracious.*" Daisy followed, and Cyan, gripping the back of her dress, scuttled after her.

Angel looked up as they approached and intercepted them. "Andre, Daisy, are you both all right?" Her eyes flickered toward Cyan but she otherwise didn't acknowledge his presence.

"What happened with Miss Sadowski?"

Daisy jammed an elbow into Andre's ribs. "We're fine, Angel. What's going on?"

Angel's usually rosy cheeks were drained, and her eyes were nearly shadowed under her brow in the dim light of the speakeasy. "Regina was picked up by bounty hunters. They dragged her out to some shack, interrogated her, then brought her back."

"Is she hurt?" Andre asked.

"Not as bad as one might expect, but she was bludgeoned in the face a bit. Jonas already saw to her wounds." She took a step nearer to Andre. "They were questioning her about you, and all of us who were at Walter's and the Gin Fountain that night. It was the same people."

"Wei and her ilk?"

"A happy coincidence," Daisy muttered, and Angel flashed a glare at her for the poor phrasing. Before Daisy could apologize or explain, there was a wail from the table, and Regina stood and pushed her way past Rudolph to rush up to Daisy, grabbing her by the forearms.

"Daisy, Daisy! I'm so sorry! I didn't want to tell, but I was afraid!" Regina wasn't crying, but her eyes – normally addled into a vapid and vacant state by mana – were alight with panic.

"Tell what?"

Andre grabbed Regina by the shoulder and gently shoved her off of Daisy. Behind them, Cyan pawed nervously at Daisy's dress, even whimpering once. He might have been friendly with Daisy and even charmed by Andre, but it seemed too many humans in one place railed at his nerves. Considering what had happened the last time he had been surrounded by a gang of humans, Daisy didn't blame him.

Once Regina was detached from Daisy, Andre glowered at her. "Miss Sadowski, what did you do?"

"Andre!" Angel wrapped an arm around Regina, pulling her close against her side, but it did nothing to tame the frantic expression on Regina's face.

"They asked for your name – just a name, and just yours. That's all I told them, and they let me go. But they knew about the rest of us – most of the rest of us. They threatened to do something. I tried to pretend that I didn't know who they were talking about, but after what happened at the Gin Fountain, I was so worried what they'd do to Pinstripes if–"

"Hush, dear," Angel said, petting Regina's hair. "It's all right. You did what you had to, and you came right here to tell Grey, just like you should have. It's all right."

Andre shook his head. "It doesn't matter. Angel, we need to speak to Grey. Now."

Angel glanced between him and Regina, clearly torn on her duties as a Stripes' employee and Regina's friend. She released the younger woman – not that Regina appeared to notice, her eyes locked on Daisy and searching for forgiveness or reassurance – and went with Andre as he headed toward the door to Grey's office on the far side of the open room.

Daisy was left standing stiffly between panicked Regina and nervous Cyan.

Frisk sauntered over in time to relieve her, taking Angel's place on Regina's other side as moral support. "If these bounty hunters are hounding you, Dell," she said, wrapping an arm around Regina and leaning against her, "we should fuck 'em up."

"It would appear that they are, and I intend to do just that." Frisk tilted her head, trying to peer around Daisy to get a glimpse of the faerie hunkered behind her. "Oh. This is Cyan. He's become entangled in all this thanks to mine and Andre's combined boneheadedness. These hunters have been harassing him, too."

Frisk titled her head to the faerie. "Hey, bud." Daisy felt the cloth from her dress drag against her skin as Cyan tightened his grip.

Rudolph crowded in closer to Daisy, and the others — Amelia, Vinnie, and Vicks — inched in behind him. Even Jonas moved from his place by the door to hover nearby. "This all has to do with Ming Wei, doesn't it?"

Frisk whirled on Rudolph. "Yeah, you ass. If you and Angel hadn't gone and fucked up one of her goons, they might not have returned the favor to poor Gina here."

"I'm fine. I'm fine." Regina sounded more her usual dreamy self, but her eyes were still wide as the moon, and she quaked a bit where she stood.

"This person *is* hunting Daisy, then?" Jonas asked. "For sure? Why?"

Daisy scowled. She was tired, annoyed at Andre and Cyan, and furious about what she had seen with Lavender and now what had happened to Regina. There was a growl to her voice that she couldn't hold back, nor did she want to. "I don't know, but I'm damn sick of it."

"Let's fuck 'em up!" Vicks said, punching the air as she

echoed her twin.

"Is that what Swarz and Miss Agatha are meeting with Grey about?" Vinnie asked, his arms crossed over his broad chest and his expression flat and watchful. At his question, Daisy realized for the first time that she didn't know if Grey was a first name or last name, though all of the warehouse workers used it exclusively. She shook off the fleeting observation.

"Yes, so let's…" She glanced toward Regina and reached out to pat her on the shoulder. "Angel is right. You didn't do anything wrong, and it doesn't matter now. Let's just all settle in and have a drink while we wait to get orders from the bosses." She had meant tea, but Vinnie went straight to the liquor shelves behind the bar with Vicks trailing hopefully after him. Everyone else shuffled over to the nearest table, but when Daisy tried to follow, Cyan's grip held her in place.

She turned to him to find his dark eyes shifting and rolling like a wild horse's. Maybe it was all the people, or maybe prolonged exposure to the human realm *did* affect him after a while. Pulling the brim of the hat down over his eyes, she whispered, "We'll get you home, soon. And no one will be left to bother you or Lavender."

His hold on her dress eased, just a bit. Her tone seemed to be enough to soothe him, even if what she uttered was a death threat.

Andre sat with the rest of the gang in the speakeasy while Angel stood on the stage and explained their plan. Grey, as usual, elected not to the leave the office. Although their leader, she preferred to keep an arm's distance from her employees – aside from Andre and Angel – when possible, and she didn't care to be seen on-site except in her office. The industry was too risky, and she came from a family of wealthy land barons with too much to lose. If she were any old face in the crowd, she might get away with being seen in Pinstripes, but she was too recognizable, given her short stature and the telltale streaks of dark silver in her hair. And while Andre trusted Daisy to exercise discretion, Grey did not, or not yet. She would not even risk stepping out to face her employees so long as a relatively untested newcomer was there, and given the chaos that had arisen shortly after Daisy's onboarding to the company, Andre didn't blame Grey for her precaution.

So, Andre and Angel brought the plan out to everyone else.

"We're to set an ambush for Ming Wei and any of her comrades. The location we've decided upon is the Gin Fountain – they're still closed while they recover from the riot, so bystanders are not going to be put in undue danger. Plus, the fact that they discovered us there before may help lure them back.

"Regina told us they found a magic charm dropped by Daisy the night of that attack. Daisy, if we can set it up to make it appear as though you're returning to find some other lost trinket, we think there's a high probability that Wei will follow or send someone after you."

Daisy nodded. Between her and Andre sat Cyan, who nervously pawed at Andre's knee throughout the entirety of Angel's speech. He tried to ignore it. Cyan was uncomfortable there, and he would be happier once Wei's people were dealt with and he could be delivered safely to the second faerie ring, and that was not something of which Andre wanted to be reminded.

"Now, these toughs picked up Regina at Market Deli, so we can guess that they've been scouting this neighborhood and will keep an eye on that eatery in particular. If we can drop hints there to indicate that Daisy will return to the Gin

Fountain, hopefully that will be enough to lure them to her. The rest of us, of course, will wait in ambush before she draws them there."

"And Cyan?" Daisy asked, though she turned to Andre with the question.

"He will stay by my side. Our goal is to keep him out of sight if we can. That way, if our ambush fails, Wei and her kind might take his absence to mean that we already successfully delivered him home, if they are even aware of his continued presence in this realm. If he is spotted, I only hope that he is willing to defend you as he did with me." Cyan mewled and turned to Daisy to reach up and touch her cheek with two fingertips, as though he understood what was being said.

"Daisy can't wander about alone, though, not even with us all watching from the shadows," Jonas said. "It's too dangerous."

Angel nodded. She, Andre, and Grey had already laid out quite the battle plan already. "I agree, and we have a few precautions in mind." With that, Andre settled in to listen to her lay out the entire choreography to their scheme, while Cyan continued to clutch at his leg. Andre wanted to place a hand over the faerie's to comfort him, but he did not.

Their curious and bizarre companionship was about to come to its end, and Andre should never had pursued it to begin with. He could not now risk becoming more attached to the lovely creature. It had already cost them both – as well as Daisy – enough as it was.

CHAPTER 15

"Cute dress. Don't think I've seen it before."

In Frisk's car, Daisy was in her bright yellow, waistless gown, the one she had worn the night she went out celebrating her new job alone. If she had known what that job would lead to, she might not have bothered. She absently twisted the onyx ring on her finger, remembering all the times her mom had warned her that being grown-up meant doing tiresome and dull work. She had never quite believed those warnings, but neither did she think they would have been *that* off.

Frisk didn't press for a response when Daisy didn't reply. She had also been kind enough not to mention anything about the dents in the car that she drove. Daisy hadn't seen much of Frisk at her full-speed since that night, in fact, and she was surprised that Frisk didn't say a thing about it. Not the car, not being dragged onto Daisy's bed, and not the gunshot wound, even after Vicks had taken Daisy to task over that. Now, they were returning to the scene of the disaster, and Frisk didn't flinch once.

"I don't get why we have to be dressed up, though." Frisk was in a cream-colored dress, and if it weren't for the bright blue beading that decorated the collar and hem, she would look naked from a distance.

"To draw attention."

"I thought that was what the handgun was for."

"That's for defense." Frisk rolled her eyes. She was being a good sport, all things considered.

"I'd rather get blood on one of Vicks' old shirts than this little number."

Daisy was about to joke, "We all have to make sacrifices," until she remembered that Frisk wouldn't have been dragged into this mess at all if Daisy hadn't allowed Andre to bully her into revealing the secret of ritual magic and the trinkets. What she said instead was, "I'm sorry."

Frisk's eyes flickered toward her, opened wide but with pupils narrowed from the effect of mana. Aside from that, she displayed no other manic symptoms. "What? Why?"

"These hunters are hounding us – not just me, but also Cyan and our entire company – all because of my magic."

Frisk snorted, the kind of unladylike sound that gave people like Franklin Blaine an ulcer. "Dell, you think this is all 'bout *you?* Hun, we're a gang. An organized criminal family. You think we don't get into this kinda shit from time to time?"

That only made the guilt dig deeper into her, realizing that she still didn't know all that much about her new criminal family. "How long have you been working for the Stripes, anyway?"

"Six years. Vicks and I been on the blue stuff for eight, and we lost so many jobs and so much money that we were on the verge of starving in the streets when Swarz found us. We saw his fancy coat and hat and tried panhandling him as he walked by the alley we holed up in. He could probably tell that we were on mana, and he decided to hire us for a quick job. I know it was just 'cause he pitied us and knew he could control us with promises of mana, but Vicks and I kinda owe him our lives for it. We ran one delivery for him, somehow impressed him, and he talked to Grey for us after that. He hooked us up with solid jobs."

"Did he?" It always seemed to Daisy like Andre could barely tolerate the Pasternack twins, especially from how Frisk and Vicks talked about their relationship with him. And he was responsible for them being in the company at all?

"I know he's a hard-ass, and he ain't no friend to me – *way* too boring – but he's not a bad sort, you know?" Frisk's fingers drummed against the steering wheel as the car began to slow. They were almost to the right neighborhood, where they would park the car a few blocks away from their destination. "I know I've said it before, but he really likes you. He's not the affectionate type, but he does. He doesn't talk shit behind your back or nothing." When Daisy gave her a startled stare, Frisk was quick to add, "Oh, he talks shit to people's faces, too, so I guess you would already know if he hated you."

"He doesn't respect me." Daisy didn't really mean to say it, but she was exhausted and relieved enough to see Frisk back to herself that it got her defenses down.

Frisk pulled up along a curb and parked. "If he didn't respect you, he wouldn't be doing all this. You think if me or Vicks got into this kind of mess that he'd be staying up late and getting in hot water with the Big Boss to save our asses?"

Frisk unbuckled and stepped out of the car before Daisy could respond, and when Daisy scurried out after her, Frisk was already sauntering in the direction of the Gin Fountain. "Hot water? Is he in trouble with Grey?"

"Uh, *yeah*. I don't know all the details, but Angel told me he took responsibility for your faerie friend. I guess the Big Boss was pretty mad about that business." Frisk gave Daisy a wolfish grin as she caught up. Frisk was considerably more athletic in high heels than Daisy. "I think it's all really my fault, though. If I hadn't knocked off your charm playing cards, none of this might ever have gotten started!" She sounded almost proud of herself.

Her words, though, did remind Daisy that they were out in the open and "on stage" for their scheme. She paused and glanced in the direction they had come. In the shadows beyond the streetlights, she couldn't see much except for a few parked cars and one large dumpster rolled up to the side of a building. Wei and her minions could have been lurking there and, against all natural instinct, Daisy hoped that they were. All that really mattered at the moment was that she made a show of looking around for them, assuming someone was, in fact, watching them.

"So, what are we looking for?" Frisk asked, also falling into their act. They both spoke a little too loudly, in hopes that someone might overhear.

"A nickel charm. Just a round coin with a hole punched in it." Daisy wasn't wearing her charm bracelet or any of its remaining components. Instead, she was equipped with her bronze levitation pendant, the onyx fire ring, and her smokescreen headband. The pendant was a bit obvious – it clashed horribly with her dress – but she hoped that these mage-hunters wouldn't be able to spot the other ones for what they were. Her trinkets had limited use as weapons, and she would need the advantage of surprise as much as she could get it.

Frisk had a pistol tucked into a holster hidden on her left thigh under the dress. The gown was just sheer enough that one could spot the dark outline of it, but it was barely noticeable in the city nightscape, especially on an evening so overtaken with swirling ash clouds blotting out the lights of buildings even just two blocks away.

"Right, right. Let's hope someone didn't grab it first."

"They would mistake it for trash, I'm sure," Daisy said as they resumed their walk, trying to appear natural. It was hard, especially knowing what Rudolph and Regina had been up to for their part of the plan.

Earlier that afternoon, Rudolph had gone to the Market Deli and lingered there for nearly an hour, making a show of being a fussy and unsatisfied customer to draw attention to himself. After ordering and sending back three perfectly decent salads, he loudly declared that the Market Deli would never again see his patronage before storming off. Several blocks away, after having enough time to "cool down," he encountered Regina at her predetermined point, a believable distance from the scene where she had been captured. There, they made casual conversation about their coworkers, including references to the incident at the Gin Fountain and Daisy Dell and her grandmother's curious Old Ways, before amicably departing to return to their own business.

If anyone had been watching the Market Deli, they might have followed Rudolph after noticing his great tantrum, and from there they would have certainly overheard him and Regina laying clues that led directly to the Gin Fountain.

They had no way to verify if they had been – or were currently being – followed. They had been too obvious as it was, and could not risk being more blatant in trying to lure Wei to that location. Daisy hoped the trap that they had set was subtle enough to keep from scaring the woman and her goons off. Even more than that, she hoped they had guessed right in assuming that Wei had the neighborhood around their office under surveillance.

She and Frisk continued to the Gin Fountain, the front door of which was boarded off. "We just gotta slip in, find the bauble, and be on our way?" Frisk asked, examining the boards. Of course, the others should have been positioned inside, so the boards would be pried loose already, but Daisy used her pendent to nudge the nails until Frisk was able to jerk the lumber off piece by piece with ease.

"If we can find it, yes." Frisk rolled her eyes as she started removing boards. It felt beyond foolish to have a pretend conversation about a lost item that was, in all actuality, tucked safely in the warded box in Daisy's apartment, especially when they weren't yet sure that anyone followed them at all.

With the boards set aside, Frisk pushed the door open and gestured Daisy through. "Let's get." Daisy took one more half-pretend glance around to scout the area. She saw nothing but shifting clouds of ash in the night, and she stepped inside.

Ming squatted in an alley down the street from the Gin Fountain, Jase right behind her. She had already sent Kelsie off to alert her other hired muscle that skulked a couple neighborhoods away.

Two of her scouts had reported finding the blond man and Regina Sadowski that afternoon, having followed the man after an outburst at the Market Deli, and that they had spoken of the Gin Fountain and plans with a "Daisy" to go out dancing that night. Ming had already tried digging up information on the Daisy Dell that Regina had mentioned in her interrogation, but all she could find were records of her graduation from the Catherine Eleanor Ruthell Women's College. Her scouts' report that Regina had mentioned Daisy again did her little good, and it all kept coming back to the Gin Fountain, which raised some flags given that the establishment was closed after the riot she and Jase had accidentally started. Ming had set up in the neighborhood – between the Gin Fountain and Walter's, just in case – even as her gut told her it might be better to back off.

She still didn't know how bowler-hat man and that... *thing* he summoned fit into all of this. More weird magic she should have asked Johnston about, she supposed. Maybe she should have been going after him this whole time, instead. At this point, she was half ready to abandon her current hunt and deliver Johnston any random corpse and just tell him it was a magician – but he had the right connections and would be able to dig up the truth about that. By the time a car rolled into the empty neighborhood, it was too late for Ming to back out, anyway. Daisy Dell and the woman that Jase had shot stepped out and began making their way on foot toward the Gin Fountain.

Ming didn't even turn to look when she heard gravel kicked across the pavement from somewhere behind her, accompanied by a light panting. "I got ahold of Bruno. The others will be here, soon."

"How many? When?" She didn't tear her eyes away from Daisy and her friend. Kelsie crept closer to peer around the corner of the building before answering.

"Eight, and they'll be bringing arms. Half an hour, at most. I told him to meet us on the corner of Hazel and Winter."

"You and Jase meet them and bring them back here. I will keep watch." The gravel crunched as Kelsie turned and went back down the alley. Ming heard a half-uttered grunt from Jase, but he never said anything before following the other woman. Ming remained crouched as she was. She had pulled a lot of strings to get support in this hunt, would owe a fair sum to Bruno's crew and all those scouts, and she had lost enough resources wasting time with the bowler-hat man and his faerie. Her money from Johnston was nearly dried up. She'd be deep in the red if she didn't bag the martyr for whom Johnston was so hungry.

Ming intended to see the ritual mage's corpse that night.

Smoke-laced dust drifted in the front hall as Daisy and Frisk disturbed the peace. The Gin Fountain had been closed since the riot, and Daisy could now see that its staff had left it largely untouched in that time, too. In the dim shadows of the lifeless club, Daisy could see chairs overturned and tables smashed, but beyond that, the far walls of the dance hall were lost in black void.

"Well, it will take nothing short of forever to find it in this," Frisk grumbled. Her complaining sounded sincere enough that Daisy almost asked what she was hoping to find, not realizing for a moment that it was part of their act.

"I can get the lights." Daisy remembered from their first visit that the Gin Fountain had some old-fashioned lighting for aesthetic effect. There had been oil lamps on the walls and a few candles set out on tables, so she wandered over to the nearest upright table and used the power of her onyx ring to summon a small wisp of fire and light the wick. A small, orange glow spread from that little table in the center of the hall, casting dramatic shadows across the stage backed by a heavy curtain, the scuffed bar, and the grandiose geometric embossments on the walls, pillars, and molding of the architecture. She used that scarce light to hunt down a few more candles and light them, until it was bright enough to see the rubble and debris scattering the floor.

Daisy turned around, remembering a night of music and laughter in this grand, desolate room, now weighed down under a heavy cloak of darkness and dust and hollow silence. "Did they just abandon this place after the riot?"

Frisk shrugged, making a token effort at pretending to dig around in a pile of splintered chair remains for the supposedly lost nickel charm. "Maybe. If the cops came sniffing 'round here, they'd be outta here in no time." She glanced over toward the bar. Daisy followed her gaze, just then noticing that there had been no faint, blue glow of thaumaturcite cutting through the dark when they entered. Even the few liquor bottles that remained on the shelves were mostly empty, not worth saving. "All the mana's gone. They probably figured it was safer to cut their losses and lay low for a while."

"Gracious…" As if it wasn't bad enough knowing that Frisk had been shot over Daisy's lost bird charm.

She was about to kneel in the debris and join Frisk in the phony hunt for her other charm, but Frisk stood straight and stepped up to her, taking her by the arm and pitching her voice to a sandpaper whisper. "Listen – you ever been in a toss-up before?"

"Been in a what?" The firm press of Frisk's bony fingertips into her arm was startling and verging on painful, but she didn't try to pull away.

"Fisticuffs, or a shoot-'em-up – a brawl. Not counting when we were here last, of course. One where you fight back."

In the dim light of the cavernous dance hall, there was almost no reflection off Frisk's eyes as they focused with fierce precision on Daisy. "Uh, well, one time in college I got into a hair-pulling match with another girl at a bar. I shoved her into a wall and she landed weird, breaking a nail. She went home crying."

Frisk's brow dropped to a flat line over her eyes. "Fucking hell, Dell. I mean a real fight. You ever hear the crunch of someone else's bones under your boots or the swing of a crowbar?" Daisy shook her head. She understood the risk she and the rest of the Stripes were undertaking, but it chilled her that Frisk was so flippant with the more violent aspects of their line of work.

It wasn't like Daisy was surprised by any of this, either. Moonshining and bootlegging weren't exactly low-risk business ventures. But that knowledge did nothing to tamper her jitters.

She shook off Frisk's grip. "I'm part of this organization, too, Frisk. If it comes to a fight, then I'll fight."

"Not trying to be condescending. It's just more important that you not get killed than that you be a killer. Otherwise, all this was for nothing." She had a point there, and just as Daisy was about to let the topic drop and get to rooting around for an imaginary lost item, Frisk patted her on the arm in the same place where her fingers had just gripped. "I know you can handle yourself. And knowing when to quit is part of that. You got the rest of us at your back. Which reminds me…"

She glanced toward the door. There was no indication of Wei trailing them yet, but it was possible that she or someone working with her was listening from outside, and Frisk and Daisy's whispered conversation had gone on for long enough. Anyone eavesdropping would start to get suspicious at this point, but Frisk continued.

"Watch out for Angel. She's a sweet lady until she feels threatened, and then she becomes like a devil from the magma. Like, me and Vicks, we get pretty rough-and-tough in a scrape, but Angel is a sick, sadistic fucker when she wants to be. Might see her pulling some stuff, and I'm telling you now, *do not* get in the way of that."

Daisy recalled Angel's ambiguous comments about questioning one of Wei's former lackeys. She had already known that Angel could do – and had done – bad, bad things, and in the same way, she had always known that her trinkets were powered by the lost lives of humans dead by Cyan's hands. Something about Frisk's firm gaze nailed the point home, and Daisy's lungs felt as though they rattled in her chest.

Everything Daisy had – her magic, her job, the protection

of these people she was beginning to see as friends – came at the risk of other people's lives. But without all that was gained by those unwilling sacrifices, what would she have? An arbitrary degree from a mediocre school, a couple of surviving relatives who couldn't afford to take care of her anymore, a life of wistfully gazing at magazine covers and never becoming a rival to the beautiful and determined Modern Girls posing there? What the hell did any of that matter, anyway? What good was being modern beyond conforming to beauty standards and possessing a modicum of financial independence? Were those meager gains worth asking Frisk and Angel and all the rest to put their necks on the line?

But everyone did what they had to in order to get an upper-hand in life. Her current alternative to modest finances was no finances at all, and she had knowingly tangled herself in this line of work when Andre came forward to her about the truth of the Stripes. Daisy wasn't proud of some of her choices, but a girl had to eat. No point in feeling down about it.

Frisk was making things a little too real at the moment, though.

"Right, I got it. Let's just... We need to find that charm and get out of here." She said that last part loud enough to be heard across the room. Frisk got the clue and, without another word on anyone's ruthlessness, returned to shifting through the debris with her foot.

After Daisy crouched and rooted around for several minutes through broken shards of furniture and items abandoned by club patrons, she caught a movement at the edge of her vision, somewhere above. She looked up to the several half-circle balconies peering down at the dance floor. She caught a flicker of movement again between the railing on one, and she sucked in a breath and jumped to her feet.

Frisk spun at the abrupt motion. "What is it?"

"Up–!" She pointed, but snapped her mouth closed when she got a better look. Through the shadows, she caught a glint off of two small, glass ovals, and when she squinted, she could make out Vinnie's blocky features behind the spectacles. He crouched in the balcony with a weapon – maybe Vicks' rifle again – cradled in his arms. Of course, she had known that the other Stripes were supposed to already be positioned around the club, but she had nearly forgotten in the midst of their fake search.

She lowered her hand, pretending to swat away a gnat. "Oh, never mind. It was just a bug, I think." Frisk had already glanced where Daisy had pointed, but she turned away from Vinnie without any acknowledgement before returning to her task. Daisy was finding that the other woman was much smoother at improvising than she.

They busied themselves in their search for nearly half an hour more, checking the stage, behind the bar, in the pockets of strangers' dropped coats. They were nearly out of places to pretend to look, and still there had been no sign that Wei had followed them. Daisy was feeling the deflating sensation of defeat when Frisk asked, "So, how much longer do we look before we give in and go catch up with the others?"

Daisy took a casual look around the Gin Fountain. Silent, empty. She dared to glance up at Vinnie without moving her head, and even he had melded back into shadows. Everyone else must have been watching her and Frisk's little show from hiding places, too, but it seemed Wei was not.

"Maybe a little–" There was a screech of abrupt sound, of scraping metal followed by the whine of an accordion laced with wavering scratches. Daisy spun toward the stage. There were several large, abandoned instruments, but of course the sound had come from none of them. At the back of the stage was a gramophone that Daisy hadn't noticed when she had been "searching" underneath the nearby piano. A black record spun on its table, delivering an upbeat but snide song through the needle and out the brass horn. The stage was otherwise empty. "What in the hell?"

"Someone's here." Frisk hiked up her skirt to grab the pistol strapped to her thigh.

Daisy whirled back to face the archway to the front foyer, though she still didn't see anyone. "Are you sure?"

"I told you Angel liked her sick games, didn't I?"

"But–" A gunshot went off, followed by a scream, but the echoes through the open hall made it impossible to discern the direction it came from. Daisy turned her onyx ring on her finger so the stone faced out from the palm. Before she could get into a defensive stance – very well a pointless effort, considering her narrow heels – Frisk grabbed her by the arm and pulled her over toward the bar.

"Come on! We're just the bait – let the others handle this."

Andre had not attempted to lean out from his hiding spot in the kitchen. He knew the cue, and would emerge only when Wei or her minions appeared. Until then, he leaned against the wall of the dark room, one hand on his cane and the other on Cyan's back as the faerie squatted beside him.

They had abandoned Daisy's hand-me-downs in favor of one of Andre's older coats to disguise the faerie, though the blue skin and inhumanly large eyes were a giveaway still. Lucky for them, there was little need for Cyan to blend in as a human at the moment. They wanted to keep him out of sight altogether, and if he were spotted in the ambush it would hardly make a difference.

While Daisy and Frisk puttered around in the main hall, Cyan occasionally whimpered and pawed at Andre's leg.

Something unsettled him, but Andre did not know nor had any way to determine what it was. There were several vials of mana tucked into the inner pockets of his coat, but Cyan had stopped sniffing at those a while ago, after Andre had swatted him for it. He wondered, once, if it was that Cyan was trying to express concern over his or Daisy's safety, but he pushed the wistful thought aside.

"What in the hell?"

Andre turned his head toward the ajar door leading into the main hall. Daisy and Frisk had been speaking softly enough before then that he hadn't been able to catch their exact words even when he could hear their voices, but now Daisy raised hers.

"Someone's here." Andre could hear, at that point, the aggressive whine of a record on a gramophone in the background.

The cue.

Andre pushed away from the wall just as a gunshot rang out. Cyan stood and clutched Andre's arm as he stepped without hesitation to the door, but Andre shook him off. "Stay close behind me," Andre said, pointing toward his heel in a feeble attempt to communicate. Cyan's eyes only drifted down toward his feet at the gesture. He didn't understand. Andre tried taking him by the wrist, pulling him closer until their hips touched. "Close," he repeated, and let go of the faerie to swing his arm in a short, chopping motion. "No fighting. Stay close. I will protect you."

On "protect," he settled his hand on Cyan's chest. Cyan whined again and clutched at it, pulling it up to his lips to kiss. Andre tried to ignore the weight that settled in his heart. Cyan was a beautiful being, and there was so much of magic to learn from him and his kind, but Andre had promised Daisy. To pass up all the opportunities within Cyan left him feeling hollow, but his debt to his employee and friend was beyond mountainous now, and it was his curiosity that caused all this disaster to begin with.

He had no choice but to part ways with the affectionate faerie.

But the sounds of shouts and gunfire in the main hall reminded him that there were steps to be taken before Cyan could be delivered home. Gently pulling his hand from Cyan's, Andre turned and rushed out of the dark kitchen.

CHAPTER 16

Frisk nearly threw Daisy behind the bar as invaders in long coats began rushing the dance hall. Daisy's gut clenched at the sight as she caught herself on the bar top, steadying her wobbling legs as they threatened to collapse over her high heels. Unlike last time, when Daisy and Frisk had been able to disappear within the crowd to hobble to safety, the Gin Fountain was an empty cavern now, and any attackers would have to face them head to head. Daisy wasn't sure if that made her more or less anxious, but if someone didn't interfere soon, these attackers would corner her and Frisk behind that bar.

Frisk grabbed Daisy by the shoulder and shoved her down before ducking beside her. The mage-hunters appeared not to notice them, which Daisy only realized as she peeked up to watch the three that had rushed in turn toward a specter pursuing them.

Angel stalked with slow and deliberate footfalls after the three, a pistol in her hand and spatters of blood on the fluffed collar of her white fur coat. Daisy could hear muffled shouting, and it must have come from behind Angel, as the hunters before her did not move their mouths. Two held handguns while the third had what appeared to be some kind of small cannon cradled in his arms.

"What is that, even?" No one looked Daisy's way at her whispered question. The hunters were too preoccupied shaking in their boots as Angel approached them without a flinch or pause. "Does it shoot some kind of explosive?"

"Not quite," Frisk said. "It's called a reverb cannon. Probably made from scrapped riot gear pawned off by some dirty cop. Their blast makes a shaky, whiney screech that messes up magicians – methodical magicians, at least. Screws their focus, and makes a lot of smoke besides. Oh, and it'll kill you if you get hit with the bullet. 'Cause, you know, it's still a cannon."

The man holding the reverb cannon leveled it to aim at Angel, but on the stage behind him, the heavy velvet curtain lining the back wall whipped aside, and Amelia came charging out with a wooden bat in hand. Underneath the music and the howling from the foyer, none of the hunters heard the light footfalls of Amelia's satin flats, and the man with the cannon had no warning as she hopped from the stage and came up behind to swing the bat right into the base of his skull.

Daisy bit down on her lip as she watched the man crumple, but neither Amelia nor Angel flinched at the violence. The former, instead, had barely finished the follow-through of her swing before turning on the woman to her right, aiming for her kneecaps. The third hunter spun to see his companion laying in a limp heap, and he was rewarded for his distraction with a shot in the shoulder from Angel's pistol.

Two more hunters entered behind Angel, but they were pursued by Regina, Vicks, and Jonas. Regina was wielding a fire axe half her own height, Vicks had his shotgun, and the ogre appeared to be unarmed. His long legs made it easy to catch the closest hunter, and he snatched the man up by the wrist, hauling him up to dangle in the air. Regina came in so smooth that Daisy would have thought they had practiced this, and she rammed the butt of her axe into the man's crotch. The man wheezed and dropped whatever weapon he held – some kind of knife – and Jonas released him. He dropped to the floor and curled into a helpless ball.

Vicks, meanwhile, chased after a nearly middle-aged woman holding a gun who was heading right toward Angel. He hesitated to shoot, probably because of Angel standing just beyond his target, so he instead called out, "Six o'clock, Angel!" Angel whirled, indifferent toward the man she had just shot in the back, and pistol-whipped the woman charging her. She hadn't time to aim, so her attack only punched the woman high on the chest. Painful, but not enough to stop her.

As the older woman straightened herself from recoil, she leveled her gun and fired point-blank at Angel.

Daisy couldn't see what happened, but there was a blast from the center of the conflict, and smoke and the smell of soot and sulfur dusted the air.

"What was–?"

"Stay down!" Frisk shoved Daisy in the chest as she tried to stand up straight, knocking her onto her backside. "I dunno – I think Angel used magic to cause a misfire." She stretched her narrow neck to peer over the top of the bar at the conflict beyond. "I hope."

There was another blast – louder and tinged with a metallic echo, probably from the reverb cannon – and the smoke in the center of the hall thickened. Someone cried out from within it, and Daisy thought it might have been Angel.

"Shit!"

"Don't worry," Frisk said, steadying a hand on Daisy's shoulder. "Those reverbs will throw off the methodical magicians, but we got a secret weapon."

A storm of butterflies flurried in her gut. "Me?"

There was another gunshot and scream from across the room. Daisy could see Regina charge out from the smoke, rushing to the corner of the room to the left of the bar, where Andre had appeared without Daisy noticing. He knelt against the wall, clutching his head with one hand while Cyan pawed at him with motherly concern. The gun – or another one – fired again.

"No, Dell, I didn't mean you," Frisk said, nodding across the room. In the balcony where Daisy had earlier seen Vinnie crouched, she could now see through the smoke and darkness two shimmering, iridescent points of light. A hazy silhouette was attached to those glowing eyes, and it shifted. When a third shot fired, the blast of light illuminated Vinnie's snarling face for a sliver of a moment.

"He can see their auras through the smoke?"

"Spot on. Reverbs don't mess up aural magic, neither."

"Daisy!" Andre hobbled over with the help of Regina. Cyan trailed behind them, glancing back and forth between his human companions and the chaos in the center of the room. There was still a faint echo from the cannon, and although it didn't bother Daisy, Andre clutched one side of his head as he spoke. "There's no reason for you to still be down here. Please, find a way to safety, and we'll take care of this."

"These guys are gonna have bodies posted at the back exit," Frisk warned, "just waiting for us to hightail it."

"There's a fire exit on the second floor," Regina said. "Down one of the back hallways. I'll bet these people haven't paid it any notice, so it should be safer than the front or back doors."

Daisy was embarrassed to find herself bristling. It wasn't like anyone else in Stripes was exactly a heavyweight boxer, so why was Daisy the one being babied? She climbed to her feet, saying, "No. I can fight alongside the rest of you. I have my trinkets, I can–"

Andre held up a hand. "I don't doubt your capability, Daisy, but you are the one they are after. Whatever else happens here, let's see their goal unfulfilled."

There was that. "I suppose if I just vanished from the scene, it could divide their attention long enough to give you all a better advantage." She said that to convince herself as much as anything. It still felt like cowardice, though.

Andre seemed happy enough to accept her reasoning. "The goal is to keep as much of our team alive as possible, yes. Now, go quickly – the smoke will start dissipating soon, if they don't fire another of those bombs."

Daisy nodded and rounded the bar, sprinting off through the thinning smoke toward the stairway to the balcony level and activating her own smokescreen from the headband. Whether they fired that cannon again or not, they would never see her escape.

Ming had held back while her bigger minions tried to deal with the magicians and their friends. Bruno and his team were local to this part of town, and it hadn't taken long for them to catch up and join Ming as she advanced on the Gin Fountain, following the trail of those Modern Girls. While Bruno took a few the back ways, the rest went with Ming through the front.

Ming and her crew had been lurking in the foyer – where they had gathered and paused to examine the scene of Daisy Dell and her friend shifting around the dance hall – when they were found by the lady in white and a few others with her. The woman had snuck up on one of Ming's people, executing him with a shot to the base of the skull, and several more of Ming's helpers fled into the main hall. The white lady, Regina Sadowski, an unknown human and an ogre followed them out there without noticing Ming huddled in a shadowy corner. The blond beau was with them, delicately tip-toeing around the man his lover had shot dead and lagging behind in his effort to keep blood off his suede shoes.

Ming took the opportunity to lunge out at him with her knife in hand, hoping to catch him with the hilt for a debilitating but non-fatal strike. She wasn't quick enough, and he noticed her approach and spun to block with a crowbar he carried. It was slow and unwieldy in his refined hands, but it was enough to crack against her knuckles and knock the blade away from her. Ming leaned back and powered a kick into one of his kneecaps before he could swing again.

He toppled back into a pillar framing the entry into the main hall. "Ah! Angel!" But Ming rushed in and delivered a pound with her fist to the side of his jaw, knocking him limp. She might have gotten away with killing this one, but that would antagonize his lover in particular, and Ming still wanted to cling to whatever fragile hold she had on the possibility of future partnership with the magicians of this city. She doubted this Angel person would ever be interested in working with her, but if she killed the woman's boyfriend it was entirely possible Angel would turn the hunt on her.

Ming grabbed her knife off the floor and left him there, alive but unmoving.

Slipping into the main hall, she found it already overrun with chaos and smoke. She pressed against the wall as she tried to make out movements in the haze and listened for her allies' voices to discern their locations, but the smoke was too heavy and the room too wide and echoing. She followed along the edge of the wall, passing under the nearest half-circle balcony. There was a blast from above, and although she was not at an angle to be hit, she ducked.

She heard a shout and saw a silhouette collapse to the ground. It wouldn't serve her to pause and try to determine who fell or if they were dead, so she kept inching along.

"*Gah!* Fucker!"

"Vicks? Where are you?"

Ming would have been happy scurrying along the wall, apparently out of sight from the vague shadows she could see struggling within the silvery cloud filling the center of the room, but she reached the stage in the back corner. Dropping to hands and knees, she crawled along before its front ledge. The smoke was beginning to thin, especially near the ground, and she hoped that everyone else would be too preoccupied with each other to notice her until she was in a less vulnerable position.

A flash of yellow streaked ahead of her.

Ming squinted to see through the smoke, which was somehow thicker ahead, away from where her team struggled with the magicians and their people. She scrambled after the movement until she reached the back wall and an opening leading to the upward staircase. It was filled with smoke, but she had not heard any reverb cannons being fired since she joined everyone else in the dance hall. It had come from some other source.

One of the magicians – and one who could use magic in the wake of the reverberation.

Ming pulled herself up and staggered blindly upward into the haze.

The ringing in Andre's head began to fade, but he still could not quite focus well enough to cast. Many people unfamiliar with reverb bombs liked to say that it was only the echo their blasts created that unsettled magicians and distracted them from casting, but if that were the case, they would have a similarly debilitating effect upon non-magicians.

Andre knew others could hear the ringing, but not feel the jarring pain in their inner ears that he was experiencing now. Something about the bombs – perhaps something about their smoke – could find the lingering presence of magic within magicians and react viciously to it. Apparently, the magic practiced by Daisy and Vinnie did not elicit the same side-effects. Those bombs had to involve some kind of artifice – some other obscure form of magic that Andre would have liked to study – which would suggest that somewhere in the city were other magicians willing to produce such weapons used to hunt their cousins and sell them to mercenaries like Ming Wei.

An alarming thought, but one he did not have time to consider.

With Daisy fleeing to safety, Andre stumbled away from the bar, needing to lean on his cane as disorientating shocks continued to echo in waves through his body, starting at the inner ears and washing down through his torso and limbs. All his old injuries on his right side flared, and even his left hand spasmed until he lost grip on the cane.

A hand caught him before he fell, and he was surprised to find it wasn't Cyan.

"Lia's still in that scramble," Frisk said as she steadied him. "I gotta make sure she's all right. We–" She broke off and raised her gun to fire at a man with a long, jagged-edged knife who rushed toward them from the thinning cloud. The bullet hit, but it must have only grazed his arm or passed through the loose cloth of his coat sleeve, as he continued without pause. Andre clambered in his mind for the root phrases for electricity spells, the syllables slipping easily from his thoughts amidst the buzzing, but Cyan darted past him before he or Frisk could attack again.

Andre instinctively reached out to grab Cyan and pull him back, but Cyan shed Andre's old coat as he pounced and had no clothes to clutch. His strange, feathery hair danced out of Andre's grasp as his fluid steps brought him upon the attacker. Andre couldn't stop Cyan as he lunged at the approaching man, claws out, aimed for his throat.

Andre had never thought of himself as squeamish – he had seen Angel perform interrogations or "teach lessons" to clients in debt to Grey, which was far from a sanitized experience – but he looked away as shimmering claws shredded through cracked human flesh, exposing bright muscle and blood beneath. The man dropped limp on the floor, and a flicker of mercy left Andre hoping that he was already dead.

Frisk's concerns about her girlfriend vanished long enough for her to let out a low whistle. "Ash and embers, Swarz, your birdman is a piece of work."

He ignored her commentary. "Do we know how many are here?"

"Angel's the one who sounded the alarm – you'd have to ask her." As Cyan returned to lurk protectively beside Andre, the two Stripes peered into the chaos at the center of the room.

In the fading smoke, Andre could see Jonas wrestling barehanded against one of the taller mercenaries, and there was a smaller shape flitting around him, though Andre couldn't tell if that was Amelia or another of Wei's people. Angel's magnificent white getup shimmered through the haze as she knelt on the ground, and there were several unidentified, unmoving masses strewn about her. There were more bodies within the cloud than Andre remembered seeing entering the dance hall – which stood to reason, considering multiple diversions, but it made him tense. They had no way to tell how many people Wei might have brought along, no way to track them or count heads.

Andre glanced over his shoulder to find Regina hovering

close behind them. "Check the kitchens, make sure no one snuck in there behind us. Frisk, can you help me reach Angel? I need to make sure she's not hurt – and Amelia, too, of course." Frisk nodded, and Andre reached out to grab Cyan by the forearm, staring him dead in the eye. "Stay close. No fighting. Control yourself." Cyan's jaw fringe fluffed out as creased lines formed around his enormous eyes. Tone, again. Andre hated to upset his ethereal friend, but Cyan was still unfamiliar with much of anyone except him and Daisy, and Andre did not want him accidentally hurting any of the Stripes in his frenzy. Especially not if his frenzies resulted in the bloody mess that lay just before them.

Frisk knelt to grab Andre's cane before she helped him hobble to the center of the chaos. Closer, and with the smoke fading, Andre could see Angel squatting next to Vicks, who was bleeding from an injury in his side. Four strangers lay in heaps around them, dead or too wounded to move, Andre wasn't sure. Angel looked up at Andre and Frisk as they approached, her eyes cold. Frisk didn't appear as grim about Vicks' injury.

"Get off your ass, layabout."

Vicks winced and writhed with a hand clamped over the wound, but he managed a lopsided smirk. "Like you got room to talk. Weren't you out cold the last time there was a skirmish here?"

Neither Andre nor Angel addressed their familial teasing. "Daisy?" Angel asked.

"I told her to flee."

Angel nodded curtly. "There's another reverb cannon. Jonas and Amelia are struggling to contain him, but..." Frisk released Andre's arm and ran over to help them before Angel finished, darting off with Andre's cane in hand. When Andre wobbled without any support on his right,

Cyan slipped to his other side and allowed Andre to lean upon him.

"Do we have any idea how many are left?"

"No. I killed one in the foyer and the one with the gun–" She nodded toward a slightly older woman lying in a gunpowder-smudged heap, and it was then that Andre noticed Angel's own pale face and clothes were coated with dark dust and blood already dried and blackened. Her chest heaved unevenly as she breathed – she was hurt, shaken by the reverberation, and needed mana. "Amelia took out the first reverb cannon, and Vinnie sniped two other gunners."

"Are there any alive, except for the second reverb cannon?"

Angel nodded and pointed to a man with a knife struggling to his feet and trying to charge Jonas while the ogre attempted to wrest the reverb cannon from a tall, lanky man. The tall fellow's hat had been knocked off in the scuffle, and Andre recognized his rugged features from the attack on Cyan's faerie ring. When Jonas swatted the man with the knife away with a careless backswing – like shooing a fly – Andre returned his gaze to the crumpled bodies surrounding Angel. He had seen three people at the farmhouse that night, and he suspected one of them was Ming Wei herself. There had been that short, square-shouldered woman with a knife who had gone after him in that attack, but he saw no one here matching that body type.

"Any sign of Wei?"

"I don't know," Angel answered. Vicks winced again and coughed, and Angel glanced at him before lifting her head with ice in the gleam of her eyes. "Wait... Where is Rudolph?" She tried to push herself up but wavered on her heels and slumped back down beside Vicks. "Andre, you have to help take out that second reverb cannon. I need

Jonas free to help Vicks so I can..." She clutched a hand over her heart and winced, her eyes not quite opening fully again when the moment passed. The reverb had to have still been affecting her, too, on top of everything else. Andre wondered how well Jonas was faring, struggling with the same condition while wrestling with Wei's minions.

He hobbled with Cyan's help closer to the struggle with Jonas and the tall man. If the ogre could keep him from firing the reverb cannon again, Andre might be able to recover enough to contribute to the fight. Amelia and Frisk had likely been hounding the mercenary as well, but something in the scuffle had tossed Amelia to the ground. Frisk crouched uncertainly next to her, one hand holding Andre's cane and the other checking Amelia's ankle. Frisk kept glancing rapidly between Amelia prone on the floor and Jonas struggling to catch the mercenary in a bear-hug to disarm or disable him. As Andre neared, though, the mercenary swung his weight hard enough to ram an elbow into Jonas' gut, sending him staggering back and giving the mercenary an opening to ready the cannon.

Andre would not be able to reach him before he fired it.

Frisk jumped to her feet and unscrewed the head of Andre's cane. She had seen him use it before in skirmishes not unlike this one, and Andre realized that she had walked off with it on purpose. Sliding around to the cannon-bearer's backside and pulling the blade from its deceptive sheath, Frisk slashed across the back of his neck.

He cried out and released the cannon with one hand to clutch at the wound. The cannon was too heavy for him to hold upright without both hands, and his aim drooped to point at Jonas' feet. It didn't matter, Andre supposed – Frisk readied the blade straight and horizontal before her, throwing her weight into a lunge toward the man. The steel slid between two back ribs, impaling him right in the kidney.

Andre couldn't see from the angle he was at, but judging from how far the blade sank into the man and Jonas' wide-eyed stare, he guessed that the tip of the blade poked out from the front of the man's torso.

Frisk jerked the sword out, splattering her dress and snarling, bone-white face with splotches of blood. The reverb cannon fell and clattered as the man toppled over in a motionless heap. Jonas was still just staring at the man – he was a decent bouncer, but the boy was used to tossing out rambunctious drunks on their own territory, not the messier sort of violence to which others in their gang had to attend more regularly.

The man with the knife who had been inching toward Jonas and the cannon-bearer a moment ago now hung back, clearly questioning the wisdom in trying to pounce Jonas again, so Andre ignored him and tugged Cyan over to where Amelia was pushing herself up.

"Ah, dammit!" She sat, but one of her legs writhed when she tried to clamber to her feet, sending her back down on her butt again. She scowled at her own foot. "I passed on heels tonight to avoid this very thing! Landed all wrong, anyway…"

The ache in Andre's head was beginning to fade to nothing but a weak throb, and although his old injuries were still stiff from the stress, he could move well enough to offer his good hand to Amelia and pull her up. She was able to stand steadily if she put all her weight on her uninjured ankle.

Frisk spun on them, eyes like a wild animal and face masked by blood. "Babe, you OK?"

"Fine enough, thanks to my hero swooping in to save the day." Andre was almost flattered until he realized she was referring to Frisk's actions, not his own. He tried to brush aside his embarrassment by turning to Jonas.

"Angel needs you to see to Vicks. Take Amelia with you

and tend to her ankle. Frisk, go find Regina, and the three us of can begin digging around to see if there are any more of Wei's people tucked away in here." The man with the knife had already taken off toward the foyer. Andre let him go, figuring that either he would leave for good or, if he tried to sneak up on any of them, Vinnie would shoot him down. He was more concerned about Ming Wei's whereabouts, at the moment.

"We got them scattered, now," Frisk said. "I'll beat down anyone else I find, but I'm gonna keep my eyes peeled first and foremost for Gina and Rudolph and get them to safety. Anything else you need afore I get to that?"

Andre held out his hand. "Yes. Please give me my cane back."

Daisy reached the second floor disoriented from the acrid taste left by all the smoke and gunpowder in the air, from the commotion below and the adrenaline that felt like lead in her veins. She tried to shake this all off and focus on getting to safety, even as a voice in her head said it wasn't right, that this whole mess was her fault and the others shouldn't be left to answer for it alone. Instead, she tried to remember the layout of the second floor from the last time she was here.

The entrances to the balconies were along the hall to her left. To her right was a narrower hallway that connected perpendicular to her current one and contained three doors: one to the right, one to the left, and the last at the end of the hall, likely leading out to the fire escape she was supposed to take. She dreaded the thought of climbing down such a thing in heels – the stairs had been hard enough. In her weariness, or perhaps worry for the others, she glanced to her left to the nearest half-circle balcony. As before, plush chairs were set up around it, creating a cozy but open alcove where patrons could drink and chat in peace while admiring the dance and music from above. Devoid of patrons, it was almost unfamiliar to her.

Daisy deactivated her headband's magic and crept out onto the balcony at a crouch, peering between the railings to get one last look at her allies before she took off.

Through the dissipating smoke, Daisy could see Angel and Vicks huddled together on the floor near several toppled forms, Jonas and Amelia wrestling with two of Wei's people, and Frisk and Cyan carrying Andre over to the scene. Regina and Rudolph were nowhere in sight, and when she looked to the furthest balcony on the perpendicular wall, neither was Vinnie.

She didn't think to be startled by his absence until she heard his deep voice call out from behind her. "Daisy!"

She spun just in time to see a woman in a long coat appear in the opening to the balcony, but this stranger ducked as gunfire cracked through the hallway. She wasn't hit, but someone behind her cried out, and there was another gunshot. Daisy didn't understand what was happening in the hallway as the other woman hurried to join her on the balcony, knife in hand.

Daisy stood as the woman charged, and she held out her hand bearing the onyx ring.

Fire erupted from the black stone and spiraled toward her attacker in a whip of flame. Her assailant leaned away from the heat, tilting her upper body so far back that she lost balance, collapsing on the floor as another gunshot rang out in the hall. Daisy heard Vinnie grunt, although she couldn't see him past the brightness of her trinket's flame.

"Roxana!" A low voice shouted the name, and the woman on the ground half-turned her head toward it in response. Her hat had toppled off during her tumble, revealing jaw-length black hair and a round, golden face. Daisy thought she looked familiar, although perhaps it was just the name that gave her that impression.

Ming Wei – the hitwoman known on the streets as Roxana. If Angel and Rudolph's intel was correct, the woman responsible for all the disasters that had befallen Daisy since that first night there at the Gin Fountain, weeks ago.

Daisy released her hold on the trinket's magic, and the flame disappeared. Through the opening into the hallway, she could see Vinnie grappling on the floor with another man about his same height and breadth, both of their guns apparently knocked away or abandoned. Vinnie's eyes still glowed from his aura-detection – he must have seen through the smoke as Wei and the other man followed Daisy upstairs.

She was distracted long enough to allow Wei a chance to get to her feet, readying her knife again. There was a gleam to her eyes that Daisy didn't recognize, but it frightened her. Maybe Frisk was right – she had never been in a life-or-death fight before. She didn't know what it felt like to kill, or to have someone try to kill her face to face.

Considering the snarl on Wei's lips and the wild flicker in her eyes, Daisy suspected she was going to gain the experience that night.

Wei rushed in, and Daisy was ready with the onyx ring again.

A pillar about three feet long shot out this time, but Wei ducked low and slashed just below Daisy's knees, right at the bottom hem of her dress. Daisy couldn't dodge in her heels, and a burning line seared across the fronts of her legs. Acting on instinct, she shifted her hand to redirect the fire pillar into Wei, but the other woman rolled aside, and the flame collided with the plush chair behind where she had just been crouched. Fire licked its velour upholstery, and before Daisy could deactivate the ring's power, a small patch of flame caught on the fabric.

"Daisy!" There was a flash and another thunderous gunshot. Daisy tried to swerve aside, unsure of where the bullet was firing from or if it was aimed anywhere near her, and she lunged back into the balcony railing, nearly tipping backward over it. Clutching the top of the railing, gripping until it hurt the bones of her fingertips, she managed to keep herself up on the balcony.

She heard someone shout her name again – not Vinnie, but someone below.

Her position left Wei with another advantage, and she charged in again, knife held up and pointed down.

Daisy's instincts failed her, or rather, went a more primitive route. Instead of activating the onyx ring again, she reached out to grab Wei's knife-wielding wrist before she could bring the weapon down. With her other hand, Daisy shoved into Wei's face, trying to push her back. When Wei tried to wriggle her head away, Daisy clutched down on the woman's jaw, but Wei thrashed and bit down on the base of her thumb. Drawing her hand back, Daisy yelped and kicked out, striking Wei on the outside of her upper thigh. It appeared to do no damage. Daisy was doing about as well as she had in that one bar fight during her college days. But her opponent then hadn't had a knife.

Wei ripped her blade-wielding hand away, spinning the knife in her grip to hold it as if to slash at Daisy's throat, and Daisy imitated Wei's roll from earlier to escape it. Her dodge spun her along the curve of the balcony's edge, ending with her nearly crashing into the chair she had set ablaze.

Her head whipped toward the opening to the hallway when she heard another loud grunt. Vinnie collapsed on the floor under the force of his opponent's fist, and the other man scrambled to retrieve his fallen gun. Daisy was trapped between him and Wei.

She was back on her feet and had her fingers to the bronze pendant as the man aimed his barrel at her. She didn't need to touch the trinkets to activate them, but she just felt like she needed something to hold on to. Just as the man was about to fire, she channeled the trinket's magic into the gun in his hands, tilting it up and aiming its trajectory harmlessly over her head as he pulled the trigger.

How many bullets were even left in that thing?

"Daisy!" Whoever called out to her again from below was too late – Daisy heard her name just as Wei grabbed her by the back of the neck and flung her against the railing again.

"This is more effort than it's worth," Wei said, her voice wheezing with exhaustion as she brandished the knife.

"Then leave me alone, if it's such a damn hassle!"

Wei scowled at the response, but Daisy's attention was pulled by a cry from below.

"Daisy! Jump! Just jump – I'll catch you!" She didn't dare pull her eyes away from Wei to look down at Angel, shouting at her from below. Instead, she held Wei's gaze. The hitwoman was hesitating, just standing there with the knife as the man behind her held back in uncertainty. Apparently, Wei really was debating whether there was any point to putting forth any more effort in attacking Daisy and the Stripes.

But Daisy wasn't going to wait for her to make a decision.

Slipping her cumbersome shoes off, Daisy gripped the top of the railing and climbed backward up it, indifferent to how far up her skirt Wei or anyone below could see, settling her bare feet to perch between her hands.

"You're going to do it?" Wei asked. She arched an eyebrow – impressed or incredulous. Daisy sort of felt the same about her own actions right about then. "You're going to jump?"

"It's two dozen feet at most. It won't kill me." Daisy's

eyes flickered toward the knife, and Wei actually grinned in response to her banter.

"True enough. Jump, then."

"*Daisy!*"

She released the railing and pushed her feet against it, launching herself back into the open. Gut dropping as she felt abrupt weightlessness, her fingers instinctively clutched at the bronze pendant again. Its power was not enough to levitate something of her body's weight, though, and she winced in preparation for impact. The awkward looseness in her stomach tightened back up when something got ahold of her.

Wei had jumped after her and grabbed her by the leg.

What happened next dizzied and disoriented her enough that it took several seconds for her mind to piece together what was going on. Gravity seemed to settle, but without the painful crash of landing on the polished dance floor. Light burst all around her – not the candles she had lit, but something pale with a glowing blue undertone that swirled around her, wisping about her waist and legs and hair, a cloud of semisolid light that slowed her fall. She could feel those tendrils not just as they supported her – their gentle brush against her skin left her feeling jittery and alert. They were made of pure magic. She had never actually consumed mana before, but the sensation matched the symptoms that all those concerned mothers' groups described in their scare campaigns. Not that Daisy was afraid of the ribbons wrapping around her and slowing her fall, or at least not as much as she feared the armed woman who was cradled in their embrace with her.

Wei didn't try to swipe at Daisy with the knife again as they loftily descended, but her eyes still gleamed with determination. Daisy had seen that look on athletes at sporting events in her college days – a runner with the finish line in sight. She could see that Wei was only waiting for them to be on steady ground again before she tried to take a killing blow.

Daisy decided to beat her to it.

They couldn't have been more than four feet off the ground when Daisy lifted her hand with the onyx ring and shot another lash of fire directly at Wei. The hitwoman screamed and tried to thrash away without releasing her grip on Daisy's calf. She mostly succeeded, as the flame only singed a bit of her hair without catching anything ablaze, but the whip of fire tore through Angel's magic ribbons. Daisy hadn't expected that, and as she watched the blue become engulfed by orange heat and felt the cradling support weaken, she braced herself.

Angel's ribbons unraveled, and Daisy and Wei were dropped full weight the rest of the distance.

Daisy was able to curl forward when she hit so as not to smack her head against the hardwood floor, instead taking all the impact on her shoulder blades and ass in a singular, fierce jolt. She heard footsteps scramble, but Wei was on top of her before any of the Stripes could rush up to retrieve her. Daisy saw the knife, and alarm drove her into throwing a punch at Wei. Much to Daisy's astonishment, it hit. As Wei's head whipped to the side under the impact, the momentum carried her body halfway off of Daisy and loosened her grip on the knife. It dropped, and rather than scramble after it, Wei just righted herself and punched Daisy back.

The pain that blossomed in Daisy's left cheek hurt, but not enough to stop her from kicking one leg hard enough to knock Wei off and rolling to pin her to the floor. Wei responded by reaching up to try to claw at Daisy's throat and face, and from there, the battle between the determined, blood-stained hitwoman and clever, educated young magician devolved into a frantic scramble of violence and pained grunting that was below even common alley cats. As Daisy tried to keep Wei wrestled to the ground while enduring scratches from her nails and kicks from her knees, it occurred to her that either these sorts of shoot-outs were not as glamorous as the cinema made them seem, or she was very awkward as far as gangsters went.

Eventually, a pair of hands hooked under Daisy's arms and lifted her into the air. Wei began to scramble after her, trying to catch her again by the leg, but Frisk appeared with a gun pointed directly at her.

Wei shrunk back, lifting both hands in surrender.

Daisy was settled on her bare feet by her interloper, and she turned to see that it was Jonas. "Are you OK?" he asked. She nodded, even though her shins were bleeding, her left cheek was swollen, and her shoulder blades and hips blazed in furious misery.

"Boss, what you want me to do with this?" Daisy's attention was pulled back to Frisk, who kept her gun trained on Wei as she shouted over at Andre or Angel a few yards off.

"Not now, Frisk." Daisy looked over to see Angel kneeling on the ground, hand pressed over her heart again. Her eyelids fluttered, and Andre crouched next to her with a vial of mana in hand. Cyan hovered just behind him, his dark eyes shifting rapidly between Andre and Daisy. Even through her concern for Angel, Daisy was glad to see Cyan had come through all that unharmed.

"Where's Vinnie?" Jonas asked. Daisy pulled her eyes away to catch him examining the balconies, and she remembered seeing another of Wei's toughs knocking him out. That man was still conscious and armed.

"Oh, shit. He's in the hallway up there, and one of Wei's people is with him." Without thought – maybe her reasoning had been knocked loose by Wei's strike to her face – she turned to go charging back upstairs to defend her friend, but Jonas caught her by the arm as she spun.

"Whoa, whoa! You stay put! If Vinnie's in danger, someone else can–"

"Don't think so, big fella," Frisk interrupted. "I think we're the only ones still standing, and I'm not letting this one scamper off. Lia and Vicks can't walk, Swarz can but only *barely*, Gina went to go find Rudolph, and Angel's damn near having a heart attack right now."

"Jonas, go help Vinnie," Andre's voice called out. "Daisy, will you please come here?" Jonas released Daisy's arm with a nod and took off through the last fading wisps of smoke to charge upstairs, having to duck and turn himself sideways to navigate the stairwell. Daisy, meanwhile, jogged over to Andre and Angel. The latter was gulping down the vial that Andre offered her like it was water in a desert, and Daisy noticed another vial lying empty nearby.

"How much of that do you have?" Daisy asked, and Andre shook his head.

"Not enough. She really spent herself slowing your fall, and she was drained already by that point." Andre's dark eyes were locked on Angel even as he responded to Daisy.

Daisy wished with all her might that she could just run out to a payphone and call for an ambulance to help Angel and everyone else who had been hurt. For all that Wei had done to her – in the past few weeks and even the past ten minutes – Daisy felt a pulse of anger only toward Ashland's laws that now put her friends in a position where they had to choose between medical attention and imprisonment. And that thought only reminded her of the ruckus they had made – if any neighbors or passersby had overheard it, they could expect the police to show up soon. The same situation as the first assault on the Gin Fountain. She really did pity the owners of the establishment, wherever they were now.

"What do you need?"

"You didn't happen to see any mana left behind the bar, did you?" Daisy shook her head. Scoffing to himself, Andre placed a hand reassuringly on Angel's leg as she panted and winced. She didn't seem to notice the gesture.

"We need to get her somewhere that she can replenish. Daisy, will you take over Frisk's position? Pasternack! I need you to drive Angel somewhere that has mana."

Frisk cocked an eyebrow. "Where?"

"Anywhere! Just make sure you are not followed." Andre glanced over where Amelia and Vicks sat slumped against each other. Amelia had one leg awkwardly stretched out in front of her but otherwise appeared fine; Vicks, on the other hand, was conscious but slack-faced and vacant-eyed. A makeshift bandage wrapped around his abdomen outside of his clothes was stained with one, large dark red circle. "Take them with you. Rudolph, too, if Regina has located him." Frisk grunted and waved Daisy over, handing her the gun as she approached. Wei remained as she was, all the predatory drive gone from her eyes. She almost looked like she was about to fall asleep there on the floor, except for her hands still raised in submission.

"What about you, Andre?" Angel wheezed as Frisk came over to help her to her feet.

The man's eyes flickered between her and Daisy, the indecision plain on his face. He was worried about both, and not particularly fit to help either. Frisk provided an observation that settled the matter for him. "I can't carry everyone out to the car on my own, 'specially not if there are still mercs crawling around."

Andre blinked, looking lost. Daisy guessed he was also in need of mana replenishment. "How many are left?"

"Fuck, I don't know! Ask her." Frisk tilted her jaw toward Wei.

Daisy nudged Wei in the shoulder with her foot to urge the woman to sit up. She did so, staring at the bodies of her comrades strewn around her. Although Rudolph and Vinnie's fates were still unknown, all of the other Stripes were alive for certain. Wei's people had not fared as well.

"One of your goons charged out of here a short while ago," Andre said to her, each word clipped with a sharp bite. He seemed to find clarity in his anger. "Our faerie clawed another to death across the room, and one is shot dead in the foyer. How many does that leave?"

Wei's gaze rolled up to the balcony from which she and Daisy had leapt. There had been no further sounds of gunshots from above since Jonas charged up there, Daisy realized. "Bruno followed me up there – he was still alive when we jumped." Her attention returned to the five sprawled around the center of the dance floor. Her stare lingered longest on a lanky man with a bloodied neck lying next to a reverb cannon. "That's it. The rest are dead here."

"This Bruno might have fled," Daisy said to Andre, "going through the fire exit that Regina told me about. I think we would have heard him try to shoot Jonas, otherwise."

Andre nodded and turned back to Frisk. "I'll help you carry them to the car and do what I can to watch your back for the two who escaped. Cyan can come with us." As if hearing the exhaustion in his voice, the faerie crouched down to grab Andre's cane where he had settled it on the floor, handing it to the magician as he helped him up. "Daisy, I'll return soon for the rest of you. If anything happens, shout out for Jonas. Until then, please just hold this woman here." Daisy wondered if he had already puzzled out that the woman in question was Ming Wei herself.

Daisy nodded, and everyone left whole in the center of the hall began working to help the rest to their feet and shamble collectively toward the foyer. Once they were gone, Daisy couldn't hear anything from Jonas, Vinnie, or the man Wei had called Bruno. She was alone with Wei in the silence.

Wei just kept staring at the dead lanky man slopped in his own blood.

"I know this might seem a silly thing to ask," Daisy said, keeping the gun trained on Wei, "but why in the blazing embers did you try to kill me?"

Wei's expression was unwavering. Without the drive to complete her kill, she just looked haggard – as worn as Daisy had been feeling ever since Wei's pursuit of her and the Stripes began. "Some sleazy politician paid me for it."

Daisy flexed her fingers on the handle of the pistol. "Care to name them, so I know who not to vote for next election cycle?"

The other woman only shrugged. "I'm paid for my silence. It's part of my service." She closed her eyes and sighed. "Not that I'm likely to get paid at all if I don't bring your head back."

"Why *my* head?"

"It didn't have to be yours – I just needed one magician to make an example of. I thought that because your magic isn't the mainstream sort, the other magicians wouldn't have your back if I went after you." She huffed, seeming to try to blow loose strands of hair out of her eyes, but sweat on her forehead kept it plastered in place. "And what a brilliant thought that turned out to be."

"That's really what this was all about? You were just taking a politician's money in exchange for some random person's life? Why?"

The glare Wei fired at her burned into her skin. "Why do people always ask that? What do you think I intend to do with that kind of money? Buy fancy watches and imported silverware? I need to keep a roof over my head and put food on the table, same as anyone else. I have a grandmother alone and sick up north, plus a shit-brained brother who keeps getting his ass kicked by other hooligans and cops alike. And I have my own bones and guts to worry about, or do you not know what the price tag of a hospital visit looks like? A factory job's not going to set me up for when age and illness sets in.

"I'm not doing this because I'm greedy, and I'm sure as shit not doing it for fun. I am *good* at this work, and I don't have the luxury of an upper crust education or important family friends to get me better. What I have instead is politicians grabbing at my lease and threatening to sell my house off to developers if I don't do their dirty business. So if you're not going to spare me your judgments, then just fucking shoot me. It would be more tolerable, I'm sure."

Daisy lowered the gun – not so much that she couldn't pull it back up to fire if she needed to, but no longer aimed directly at Wei's forehead. Wei scowled in nervous uncertainty and disbelief.

Frisk and Vicks might have been howling to destroy these mage-hunters, and Angel apparently had a sadistic streak a mile wide, and even Andre was ready to eliminate any threats at all cost with little thought to them as fellow human beings, but Daisy supposed she wasn't like that. Maybe she wasn't yet hardened enough, as Frisk had insinuated, or maybe she just didn't have it in her soul to begin with. Regardless, whatever Wei's intentions for her, Daisy had no desire to kill this woman or to hold her in place until Andre came back to do it for her.

She glanced toward the stairs leading up, where Jonas was. Daisy knew there was an exit on the ground floor somewhere, and Jonas would never be able to get down those stairs in time to block it.

"Look, just get out of here. Before my friends come back."

Wei didn't move. "Why?"

Daisy huffed out a breath, the gun tilting further toward the floor as her shoulders sagged. "I had a grandma, too. She also did what she had to in order to get by in this world, even though it hurt some people. I know what it's like to have unpaid bills and costs that keep piling up. We aren't so different, are we?"

Wei looked Daisy up and down. "You think so? 'Cause from where I'm at, you look like you're sitting pretty cushy."

Daisy rolled her eyes. Wei must have never discovered the location of her trash heap of an apartment, after all, if she thought that. "Oh, please. I found this dress in a bargain bin." She gestured with the gun toward the back corner of the building. "If you don't want to run into my boss again, you'd better go now. You can stay if you want, but it'll be easier to keep all your blood inside your body if you get out of here."

Staring at Daisy with a flat, disbelieving brow, Wei pushed herself up to her feet. They both knew that if Daisy wanted Wei dead, she would have pulled the trigger several minutes ago. Without looking away from Daisy, Wei took off in quick, backward steps to the kitchen. Once she had disappeared into the dark opening, Daisy groaned and lowered herself to the ground, dropping too heavy on her already-bruised behind and stretching her legs in such a way that the cuts on her shins opened wider, trickling thin trails of blood that circled around the girth of her calves.

"Ah, damn."

Without the immediate threat of Wei's knife, the pain that covered Daisy's body in flaring patches was no longer muffled by the presence of crushing fear.

She heard heavy footfalls not long after she settled on the floor, and although she knew it had to be Jonas coming back down the stairs, she tightened her grip on Frisk's pistol all the same. The ogre ducked and sidestepped through the opening to the stairwell while awkwardly herding a limping Vinnie behind him. Vinnie carried his rifle in one arm while Jonas steadied him by the other, and the glow to his eyes was gone. In its place, he had a purple shiner on his left cheekbone (Daisy probably had a similar one to match, she realized, as she noticed her vision blurred in her left eye) which his eyeglasses sat askew over. He otherwise appeared sound, and Jonas' attention shifted from him to Daisy when he saw her sitting alone on the floor.

"Daisy, are you hurt?" As Jonas jogged over to her, she noticed black bruises along his grey-toned arms and neck. Like Daisy, Jonas didn't seem to have the teeth that some of the other Stripes did, but he had endured quite the battle for his gang. A defender more than a warrior, Daisy thought.

"Bit battered, but nothing major."

"Where is the woman?"

"She escaped." Jonas frowned, probably aware that she was lying. She didn't care. "Can you do anything about my legs?"

He winced and wiped a few budding droplets of sweat from his forehead. "I don't know. I've been... been working it pretty hard, with Vicks and Vinnie. I gave some of the mana I brought to Angel and used all the rest already, so..."

Daisy shook her head. "Don't worry about it. Nothing I won't survive." But Jonas approached the cleanest corpse and removed its coat to begin tearing into strips, returning to kneel beside Daisy and bandage her leg. Vinnie hovered over them while Jonas worked, scanning the perimeter in case Wei or any of her few surviving people returned. As Jonas finished tending one of Daisy's legs and began on the other, Andre returned, trailed by Cyan and Regina.

"Daisy! Where is she?" Daisy could hear a fleck of accusation in Andre's question, but Jonas covered for her.

"Got away. So did the guy who gave Vinnie that attractive black eye."

"Did you find Rudolph?" Daisy asked, more to change the subject than from actual concern, although it did occur to her with a heart-sinking jolt that it was entirely possible that the worst had become of him.

Regina nodded, looking half-asleep where she stood. "Yes. He was knocked out, but I think he'll be fine."

"Frisk took off with all of them," Andre added. "I trust she'll get them the help they need."

"And the rest of us?" Vinnie asked.

Andre glanced toward Cyan, whose elegant claws were still stained with human blood. "We should vacate the premises before anyone comes to investigate the noise and smoke. Though if Ming Wei is still about–"

"She won't be a bother." Andre glared at Daisy's declaration. She felt small and silly under his stare, but she pressed on. "She won't. I'll make sure of it."

She expected Andre to push back, to insist that she explain what she intended if not reject her outright without hearing a thing in her own defense. But he only closed his eyes and let out a long breath through his nose. "Very well. Then it is time for us to leave." He opened his eyes and looked straight at Cyan. Andre said nothing, but the faerie appeared to understand that silence better than any human words. He ducked his head and whined, reaching out for Andre's hand.

CHAPTER 17

Andre's car was much too small for what remained of their group. Jonas was placed in the passenger seat with his legs pulled halfway up his chest, and Cyan was tucked away in the seat behind him. Vinnie sat directly behind Andre, his shoulders too wide for a backseat overfilled with passengers, and Daisy and Regina doubled up in the middle, the latter half-sitting on both the other young woman and Vinnie. Andre was too tired to be annoyed or uncomfortable with the arrangement.

"Just drop us off at my place," Jonas said. "I know it's a little out of the way, but Regina and Vinnie can stay the night, and I can get you a bit of mana before you go on your way."

Jonas' consideration warmed Andre in a way he hadn't expected. He didn't often get down to Pinstripes when it was open, and so he rarely got to see his own speakeasy's bouncer. Andre had always preferred it that way, assuming that the ogre would be as airheaded and obnoxious as the Pasternacks, or at least comparably unpleasant. Perhaps Andre had been too cold with him, though – Jonas had certainly proved himself not only capable, but loyal and compassionate through all this mess that Andre had caused.

"Thank you, Mister Bauer. I appreciate that."

"Thanks, Joney," Regina echoed from the back seat. Beside (and slightly under) her, Daisy sat with her chin tilted toward her chest, on the verge of sleep. Andre wished he could leave her to rest with Jonas, too, though of course he wouldn't be able to locate the faerie ring without either her or Vinnie.

Andre drove them across town to Jonas' neighborhood – a dingy, ramshackle area within walking distance of the office. Like many city-dwelling ogres, Jonas had to make do with a home that was too small for his frame, some little one-storied cottage with thin strips of greying lawn between it and neighboring houses of a similar build. Andre parked on the curb before the house and went to unbuckle himself, but Jonas held up a hand.

"You can stay here. I'll be back in a moment with the blue stuff." He, Vinnie, and Regina all piled out, and Andre gestured to Daisy to move up to Jonas' spot. She was about to slide out after Regina, but she paused in the seat with a grunt.

"I left my shoes there." Instead of stepping out barefoot onto the curb, she closed the car door and just clambered up to the front between the driver and passenger seats. Jonas was back shortly with a small bottle of mana wrapped inside a stained washrag to hide its contents.

Andre rolled down his window to accept the bottle. "My thanks. I will compensate you for your trouble as soon as I am able." Jonas waved dismissively, though it was telling he didn't verbally reject Andre's offer. Mana was expensive, even for those within their company, and Jonas clearly didn't have much by way of disposable income. Andre knew he had to find some better way to give the young ogre his due – to give all of them the comfort and security they deserved. Daisy was not the only one who did not deserve to live in squalor, and Andre's hope in his work had always been to build a better world for his fellow magicians. Years now into his work with the Stripes, it was becoming clear that the logistics of how to accomplish such a thing continued to elude him.

As Jonas went back inside, Andre drained the bottle, wincing at the suffocating sweetness even while every cell in his brain flexed and sighed in ease as the liquid rushed down his throat and hit his stomach. Normally, he would have tried to be more measured in his mana intake – Jonas' bottle was rationed for a man of his size, not Andre's – but he had spent himself so thoroughly at the Gin Fountain, and the night was not yet over. It was likely that drinking the whole bottle in a single sitting would result in some effects of overdose, but he would rather suffer that than be left as exhausted and feeble as he was. When he was finished with it, he set the emptied bottle on the floor behind him. Cyan scooted to the middle seat and leaned over to sniff at it, but he showed little more interest than that. His wide eyes were drooped in an expression that, on a human, would have appeared melancholy. Andre wondered if he understood what was coming next.

"Daisy, are you well enough to direct me to where I need to go?"

"Well enough."

From Jonas' house, it took nearly two hours to drive through and out of the northern edge of town, taking the highway that led toward Ashland's coast. Andre sometimes found need to come out in this direction for work – meeting with clients living in the countryside or shutting down bumpkins running independent moonshining operations that interfered with the Stripes' own. He had not been to the coast itself, though, since he was an adolescent boy going on the occasional trip with his mother. He wondered how she had been faring the past few months, and he promised himself that once everything calmed down, he would give her a call.

Daisy's directions eventually lead them down an unkempt road, and from there, her instructions grew hazier. "We parked somewhere on the side of the road and followed Vinnie's aural sight to the spot. I'm not sure I could find it again just looking for the trail we left the first time."

"We'll do our best. Just tell me when you see something familiar."

But in the early morning dark, Daisy couldn't make out much of anything, and eventually she was left with only guesswork. She pointed to a spot along the road that she referred to as, "Good enough."

It took nearly half an hour of scouting the forest underbrush on the edge of the road before they found a fresh trail cut by a blade, some dozen yards from where they had parked. Daisy led the way down it, with Cyan behind her and Andre at the rear. It led them far out of sight from the road, to a clearing spotted with drastic shadows from the surrounding flora contrasted by the moon's shine. There was a curious mound of dirt near the edge of the clearing, but closer to the center was a faerie ring. Andre's gut tightened as Daisy stepped into it, but she hesitated and turned to him.

"I didn't bring anything to offer." Her face was slack, but her warm eyes began to water. Andre wasn't sure if it was from exhaustion or sorrow. "With everything else happening… I forgot to bring anything."

He thought of the bottle he had drained and placed in the back seat, but what few droplets still clung to its interior would probably not be enough to tempt a faerie to the human realm, if they were interested in offerings of mana at all. Daisy was still wearing three trinkets, but the faerie might object to have such things returned, and he could not ask Daisy to give them up. He himself had his cane or his glasses, either of which might be shiny enough to attract a faerie's attention, though without them he would be nearly unable to function, incapable of even driving them back home without the glasses.

His hand tightened on the head of the cane. Walking was easier again, now that the effects of the reverb had worn off completely, and he could always get a new one. It would be expensive, getting the custom hidden blade installed, but the loss was not unthinkable.

Just as he began to lift it to hand over to Daisy, Cyan plucked the hat from his head. "What are you doing?" Andre asked gently, and the faerie stuck his face inside it.

Cyan was so like a mere animal at times, but Andre had taken Daisy's early warnings about faerie sensibilities to heart. Cyan was far from unintelligent – more cognizant than most humans Andre knew, he guessed – and he understood that he and Andre could not communicate through spoken language. The magician was beginning to understand that these almost childlike gestures were meant to convey Cyan's intentions in place of words, though he rarely could make sense of them.

He waited for Cyan to give another clue in his odd imitation of charades, and the faerie peeked out from the inner curve of the bowler before shuffling over to join Daisy inside the ring. His graceless steps, so unlike his usual fluid movement, fretted at Andre even though Cyan did not appear injured. Cyan handed the hat over to Daisy, who took it with enough surprise that she lifted her eyebrows.

"This? Really?" Cyan murmured something in response, stepping back and bobbing his head. Daisy glanced at Andre, who could only shrug, and she shrugged back before setting it down between herself and Cyan. With that, she lifted her fingers to the bronze amulet, absently tracing its edge as she activated its levitation power. The hat lifted up, wobbling a bit, and she held it in place until a sliver of white appeared in midair, brightening the nighttime clearing.

Cyan watched as the crack expanded, although with his head turned away from Andre, the man could not read his face. Soon, the shimmering opening was wide enough for a feminine creature to step through and forward. She was taller than Cyan, and wider too, with broad shoulders and long legs. Her hair was the same texture and length as his, though it and all of her skin and feathery fringe were a pastel shade of violet. She snatched the hat out of the air with her long fingers and locked eyes with Cyan.

"Hello, again, Lavender," Daisy said, but both faeries ignored her. Lavender stepped closer to Cyan, leaning in and sniffing him. Andre felt an unexpected pang of jealousy, remembering how Cyan had tasted his scent the first time that Daisy had shown Andre the faerie ring by the farmhouse. Lavender would be taking lovely Cyan and all the secrets of magic he held for their kind back home, and all Andre would be left with was his own shame over causing everyone so much strife.

The violet faerie pulled away, and Cyan turned to look at Andre. His black eyes shone like oil in the haze of night, and he curled his long, clawed fingers toward himself to beckon Andre over. The magician glanced toward Daisy, seeking any warning in her expression, but she only watched Cyan carefully, as did Lavender.

Andre stepped forward, joining them all inside the ring, and stood before Cyan. He started when Cyan lifted a hand to his face and caressed along the right side of his jaw, staring at his eyes and nose and lips while muttering in that lilting faerie language. Andre stood still, almost afraid of what Cyan was doing, until the faerie laced his fingers in Andre's hair and leaned in for a kiss. Even as he feared how the other faerie might react to this tender interaction,

Andre dared to rest his left hand on Cyan's hip as he kissed him back.

Such a lovely being. Andre's own attraction to the faerie didn't make sense to him, but he accepted it for what it was, as much pain as that brought him now that they were saying their farewells.

When Cyan drew away, Lavender spoke to him in their language, and although she sounded annoyed, it seemed more from impatience than at the display of affection. She gestured with one hand at the portal, shoving the hat toward him with the other. Cyan took the hat with a gentle touch, and Lavender turned to re-enter the portal without any further acknowledgement of the humans. Cyan glanced once toward Daisy and then to Andre before turning his back to both and following Lavender back to their realm. The portal shrank once they were both on the other side, withering into a thin line and, soon after, complete nothingness.

Perhaps if Andre hadn't been so exhausted – sleepless and physically battered and still in need of replenishment from the magic he did earlier – he might have been able to choke down the sob that rose in his throat. But it escaped him in a shaking hiss, and he had to place his other hand over the one already clutching his cane to keep himself standing upright. He closed his eyes to allow himself a moment to gather his nerves.

He jumped at the soft warmth of Daisy's arm wrapping around his shoulder, but rather than begin escorting him away, she permitted him that moment. When he lifted his head, she patted his upper arm. "Come on. We set it right. Time to go home and rest."

He wanted to argue – Cyan might be returned to where he belonged, but Ming Wei had escaped, and Daisy's life could still be in danger. He was in no state to properly protect her now, though, so he nodded along to her conclusion. She sounded confident in her assertion, and he respected her enough to trust her judgment that things were settled for the time being.

Andre did not think of himself as a person who relied on others, but in that moment, he was glad for the strength her presence shared.

More days-off were provided for Daisy following their ambush of Wei and her goons. At first when Andre offered it, as he dropped her off at home that night, she had tried to refuse, but he shook his head.

"I'll be calling Grey later and asking about shutting the whole company down for a few days. We all could use the rest." If the office was closed entirely, Daisy had no choice but to accept. She had sounded begrudging when she agreed to Andre's idea, but secretly she was relieved. She went to bed that night planning to sleep away half of the next day, which was exactly what she did.

Around nightfall, she had other plans.

She headed to the Gin Fountain on foot. The police had apparently arrived at the scene sometime after the Stripes had cleared out. Their bright yellow tape was left behind, roping off the sidewalk in front of the building and blocking the opening where the front door had once been beyond that. She ducked under both rows of tape and stepped into the dark dance hall, even more battered and ruined than it had been when she and Frisk had arrived the night before.

Daisy didn't know how she had been so sure, but as she expected, Ming Wei was already there. Ming stood above a dark stain on the hardwood floor, staring at it. All the bodies of her fallen comrades had been removed by the police.

Daisy approached her. Under her coat and tucked into the sash around her dress was the machete she had borrowed from Vicks, and the onyx ring embraced the middle finger of her right hand, but she had nothing else by way of armaments. She didn't expect this encounter to result in violence, but better to be safe. Ming didn't even lift her head as Daisy neared.

"What do you want?"

Daisy stopped just out of arm's reach. "I left my shoes here." She glanced down at the bloody stain on the floor. "I'm sorry–"

"No, you're not. You let your trigger-happy friends trap us here. For all I know, you orchestrated the whole thing." Ming looked up just as Daisy opened her mouth to argue. "I'm not saying I blame you. We did try to kill you first, after all. I should have been more careful. This is going to ruin my reputation, my whole career. I'm going to lose my house. And..." Her eyes drifted back to the bloodstain, and she closed them with a faint sigh. "I lost some good people last night. You don't make a lot of friends in this line of work, but Jase..."

Daisy reached into her coat and pulled something out. Not the machete – she had brought something else in hopes of seeing Ming that night.

"Here, to help you out. Maybe enough to get you out of here to start a new life." Ming stared at the offering before reaching out to take it tenderly between her fingers. "I know it's not much – I just started this job, so I don't have a lot in savings, but I thought..." Ming looked up at her with such open bafflement that it bordered on horror. Daisy only shrugged. "A girl's got to eat, right?"

Ming held the check so delicately that it seemed she was repulsed by the thing, but she didn't return it to Daisy. "This is twice my monthly cost of living, including the money I send to my grandmother. You would just... give this to me?" Daisy shrugged again, like it was no small thing, though it was more than two months of living for her, too.

There was wariness in her expression, but Ming folded the check and pocketed it. When she looked back up at Daisy, she said in a clear voice, "Jacobus Johnston." Daisy tilted her head. "A candidate for city council, running against Daphne Linden. They both hired me to kill one of your people. Linden played me dirty, so I turned to her opponent and talked him into hiring my services. He wanted a martyr to rally voters around. All things considered, he could probably still spin this in his favor." There was a flicker of amusement to her tone, but it was tarnished by her weariness and loss. She patted the check in her pocket. "Linden warned me that her friends at the bank were going to buy out my lease – I won't be able to pay it off before they get around to it. You're right, you know – I need a new start. I suppose if I get out of town, it might be worth my time to expose Johnston and Linden's dealings."

Daisy smiled. "That'd be something to see. If you pull that off, I'd be willing to forgive this whole matter of going after my blood." Ming smiled back. It was a strange moment of sympathy and camaraderie that Daisy hadn't been expecting, no matter what she had figured might be the best-case scenario for this interaction.

Ming turned away from Daisy, then, heading toward the back exit of the building. "I should go, before any of your friends get the same foolish idea to wander around here as you did. Thank you for the gift, and I'm sorry that it all came down to this." She stepped into the pitch black kitchen before Daisy could reply. It didn't matter. She had already said everything she had wanted to say.

That out of the way, she went upstairs to retrieve her lost shoes.

Although she had been with the Stripes for weeks, it was the first time she had gone down to Pinstripes while it was open to the public, in full swing and brimming with life. She went through the front door, following behind a well-dressed couple who were examined and allowed inside by Jonas.

"Evening, Daisy. Rest well?" The office had been closed all week, but Grey had reopened Pinstripes that night to keep the clientele appeased. That still gave all the "warehouse" workers a few days to recover, and Jonas looked his normal self that night – pleasant and calm.

"I did, Jonas. And you?"

"Just fine." He let her inside, and she gazed around at the clusters of magicians, mana addicts, and their friends chatting in groups, playing billiards, or drinking near the stage while listening to Regina's mystic and charming but almost mournful piano songs. Vinnie was behind the bar, making drinks for patrons already half-drunk and swarming about, while Amelia rushed in and out of the kitchen with dishes loaded with salty snacks. At one table near the stage sat Angel, Rudolph, and Andre – like Daisy, all off that day while the employees who tended the speakeasy were put back to work and given an extra night of pay. Frisk and Vicks were at another table nearby, chatting with some people that Daisy thought she recognized from that first night at the Gin Fountain.

Andre was the one who had invited her down, and he waved her over when he spotted her across the room.

Although the man hardly looked any different than usual – only lacking his coat and, of course, his hat – Daisy gawked at him as she neared the table. She had thought that he'd sooner be caught dead than out in a club, enjoying himself with friends. He even smiled, although it was crooked and self-deprecating. No doubt he saw Daisy's amused incredulity painted on her face.

"Good evening, Daisy. Enjoying your week off?"

"Yes. And I'm surprised to see that you apparently are, too. Pleasantly so, of course." She took a spare seat between him and Angel, who patted her arm as she settled in.

"This is the first you've gotten to see Pinstripes when it's awake, isn't it?" she asked.

"Yes. It's lovely." Daisy remembered Angel telling her that Pinstripes catered to a more intellectual nightlife, and she saw a nearby table crowded with young university men in well-ironed waistcoats drinking and waxing philosophical a little too loudly. Beyond them, a pair of older women in fur coats spoke with their heads close together, glancing occasionally toward the door leading to the mana cellar in between pleasant remarks about Regina's talent with the piano. A different sort of crowd from the Gin Fountain or Walter's, but warm and vibrant all the same. She could see how Andre might feel at ease enough here to visit from time to time.

"Things are set to return to normal once we're all back at work, though, right?" she asked, thinking she was only making pleasant chitchat, but Andre's smile melted.

"There's still much to handle. Grey is not particularly pleased with how these events have unfolded, though I doubt any of that ire is directed at you, Daisy. Our operations have been enormously disrupted by all this time off, and the Gin Fountain was one of our most prominent partners. Other establishments are on edge in light of everything, but I expect that will blow over soon. It will take time for our business to stabilize again, however." He waved a hand as Daisy opened her mouth to respond. He wasn't wearing gloves that night, and she could see faint, white scars running in overlapping streaks over the back and palm of his injured hand. "But I will ensure that as little of this trickles down to you as possible. You've already put forth admirable effort in helping me fix this mess, and I would not ask more of you. A brief break and a return to normalcy is what you deserve."

Daisy smiled, but it felt crooked on her face. She wasn't sure how she felt about Andre's protectiveness anymore. On one hand, he was right – she had busted her ass fixing disasters that had not been entirely her fault. But his constant fretting over her well-being was beginning to feel personal, and she was unsettled to find that she worried about him, too.

She had never had many close friends growing up. This new sensation was warming, but left her feeling off-balance.

Regina shifted into a new song, and Angel reached out for Rudolph's hand resting on the table. "Oh, I love this song! Darling, would you?"

Rudolph smiled, looking more at-ease than Daisy could ever remember seeing him. He appeared fully recovered from being clonked out by Ming's people. "Of course, love." They rose together and moved to the small dance floor between the tables and the stage where Regina performed on her lonesome. The sound from the piano was at once tinkling and heavy, laced with Regina's reedy voice singing out lyrics of pure love for some hypothetical individual of great inner beauty. Angel and Rudolph waltzed close to the steady, flowing tempo.

On impulse, Daisy stood and held out her hand to Andre. "Care for a dance?"

Open surprise flickered across his face, but he quickly masked it under another self-conscious grin. "My thanks for waiting for a slower song," he said, taking her hand and allowing her to pull him to his feet. "My poor muscles are still recovering, and they were never fit for much dancing to begin with."

Leaving his cane at the table, Daisy led him to the dance floor and swept him into position for a waltz. Of course, they kept to a more professional distance from each other than Angel and Rudolph, but with a hand each on the other's hip, it was more physical intimacy than they were used to. The only other time Daisy could remember sharing such closeness with him was at Lavender's faerie ring, when she held him while he cried after his goodbye with Cyan. It was apparent that Andre's feelings about Cyan weren't romantic in a traditional sense – and the other Stripes had made it clear that Andre's heart didn't patter in that way, regardless – but being apart from the faerie still impacted him as much as the loss of a true lover might have. He had been so distraught that night, and she wondered how he was feeling now.

Their waltz was kept at about half-pace of Angel and Rudolph's, who stepped along with the beat of the heavier notes of the song. Andre's movements were a little stiff, but he was otherwise mobile, and that eased a worry that Daisy had not consciously recognized she held.

"When you have a moment," Andre said as they danced, "I have something for you. It's upstairs, in my office."

"A gift?"

Andre's lips pulled into an anxious line. "A debt repaid." He winced, and Daisy almost pulled to a stop, fearing his old injuries were beginning to bother him, but he shook his head. "I owe you so much. And after everything that happened, Wei still managed to escape us."

Daisy had her own guilt there, but she didn't say anything about it. If Andre suspected that she had intentionally let Ming go, he never raised an accusation. "Don't worry about it. I don't think she will bother us again."

Andre arched an eyebrow, and just when Daisy expected he would scold her or demand answers, he only said, "Very well. I'll trust you on that."

Thinking on Ming's disappearance reminded Daisy of the

sacrifice she had made to get her out of town and away from the Stripes' wrath. "I don't suppose that offer for a raise is still on the table?" she asked.

"Of course. May I ask why the change of heart?"

Daisy smirked at him. "No, you may not."

He nodded, apparently deciding to trust her with that, as well. "As you wish." As Regina's song trailed off, Andre pulled their dance to a stop and took Daisy's hand. "Come – I'll show you what I brought, before either of us forgets. We can return to the festivities shortly."

Daisy followed him upstairs to the front office, dark and lonely in the nighttime. He clicked the light switch as he stepped inside, illuminating the single overhead lamp hanging above his desk, but there was already a faint glow in the room even before that. The jar of pomade that Cyan had enchanted sat beside Andre's chicken phoenix trinket, giving off a faint, orange light. Andre ignored that and went to the middle drawer of his desk, pulling it open and removing a square parcel wrapped in brown paper.

Daisy took the package and unwrapped it over his desk, exposing beneath the brown paper a pastel yellow cloth. She pouted, tearing away at more of the wrapping. "What on earth is...?" But she broke off, nearly laughing as she realized.

"Bed sheets," Andre said, "as promised."

"Thank goodness. I washed my old ones, but I've just been too nervous to try sleeping in them. I've been crashing on my floor since that night." Andre chuckled as he slipped into the chair behind his desk, but any joy that he might have been faking slid away when his eyes fell on the jar lamp.

"You miss him, don't you?"

Andre winced, folding his hands upon the desk. "Of course not." The chicken phoenix began wobbling, as it did when it detected a lie. Andre snarled at the trinket, picked it up, and slapped it on its side. "You know, I've always hated that thing."

Daisy clutched her bundle of bed sheets against her chest. "You were that sweet on him, huh?" But her boss shook his head.

"It wasn't that... not just that. What he could do with magic, especially with mana, might have changed things for every magician in Ashland. We might have been able to move toward a world where people like us didn't live in fear of people like Ming Wei and her clients. And perhaps our magic could have served some use to his kind." He shrugged. "He was beautiful, though, and rather tender. I would have liked to have shared more with him, is all."

Daisy wasn't sure what to say. She didn't know how to comfort people over those kinds of disappointments.

Perhaps it was better for them to simply move on.

"I'll be happy to have things quieter around here," Daisy said.

"Yes. It occurs to me that you've hardly spent any time doing the primary task I hired you on to do, running around as you have been trying to clear away my messes." He tore his gaze from the glowing jar, meeting her eyes. "I am sorry, truly."

"You need to stop saying that."

Andre frowned. "I won't have you think that I'm not."

"No, I mean, you need to stop *creating reasons* to need to say it." Andre looked stricken by the admonishment until she smiled. "But apology accepted."

He nodded, though he made no move to stand again. Instead, he pulled the key to the stairway door from his pocket and slid it across the desk to her. "I'd like a moment to gather up some work to take home until Grey officially opens up the office again. I imagine you'd prefer to return to the party, if you'd care to go on ahead of me."

"Yes, it's important I get in as much fun as I can before I return to my dull day job, as a Modern Girl should. You'll come down again, though?"

"Yes. I'll even share another dance with you, if you'd like."

"I would. I'll see you shortly." Daisy returned with her bundle to Pinstripes, where she was roped over to the bar by Vicks and Frisk almost the instant she arrived back downstairs. The rest of the night passed without raids by mage-hunters or mysterious malfunctions of magic. Just Daisy dancing and drinking and playing cards with these people she worked alongside. It felt comfortable. She was right where she belonged.

ACKNOWLEDGMENTS

A huge thanks, of course, to the amazing team at Angry Robot for all the hard work they've put into making this book a reality. Mike Underwood was my first point of contact with Angry Robot, and I would be nowhere without his guidance and patience. Marc Gascoigne has been an absolute delight to work with and has made me feel so welcome in the Angry Robot family. Penny Reeve has been so wonderful to work with, too; any day when I get an email from Penny is a good day, because she always has such marvelous news for me. Phil Jourdan is such a fantastic editor, and I'm so grateful to have had him for *Moonshine*, as he knew exactly what it needed to make this the best book it could be. A thanks to Paul Simpson, as well, for his keen copyedits.

Thank you to my agent Laura Zats at Red Sofa Literary, who uses her passion and industry knowledge to do so much to advocate on my behalf. It has been an absolute honor and privilege to be represented by Laura. Thanks also to Dawn Frederick at Red Sofa for filling in when Laura's on vacation.

Thank you to John Coulthart for his amazing work on the cover art and for considering my input during its creation. I cannot imagine a more beautiful cover for my book.

I owe an enormous debt of gratitude to the wonderful Beth Phelan for organizing the #DVPit event that allowed me to connect with Angry Robot to begin with. Thank you, Beth, for all the hard work you do to champion for underrepresented authors. Thank you also to Nita Tyndall for helping workshop my query letter, and especially to Idris Grey, who provided invaluable feedback on Daisy's portrayal and the worldbuilding of Ashland.

Abbey Gaterud and my fellow Oolies at Portland State University's Ooligan Press also deserve a big thanks for all of their support and for sharing in my joy. I can think of no better graduate program to be a part of during this exciting time.

I owe my biggest thanks, of course, to my family for all of their support. Without my dad getting me hooked on fantasy books when I was a kid or my mom's unwavering support in my endeavor to make a livelihood from my writing, this book would not have been possible. I would also be nowhere without the support of my found family, Stacie, Audry, Flynn, and Eli, and from my other friends, Nita, Roya, Sierra, and Rachel. I love you all.

Finally, thanks to you, the reader. *Moonshine* was a project that I began in earnest during a particularly brutal depressive episode, and there were many uphill battles for me in putting it down onto page. I am so glad to see all of that hard work paid off and to see my book speak to so many people. My experience working with Angry Robot has been nothing but delightful, and I hope the book that they've helped me create can bring as much joy to its readers as it has brought to me.

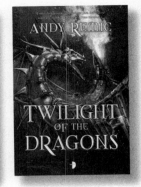

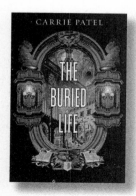
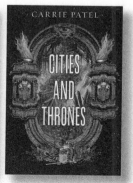

SIGN UP FOR MORE MAGIC

angryrobotbooks.com

twitter.com/angryrobotbooks